MAYBE WE'LL REMEMBER

Among These Bones — Book 3

AMANDA LUZZADER

KNOWLEDGE FOREST
PRESS

For Lilly (spelled like Billy),
An intelligent, charming, and beautiful
young woman.

I write for readers like you.

CHAPTER 1

It wasn't a cane, Ruby insisted. It was a walking stick.

"Canes're for old ladies," she said, "an' I might be old, but I ain't no lady."

The walking stick helped Ruby negotiate the uneven terrain and sometimes rocky mountain trails between camps, but it was mostly for her "bum knee," she said. It hadn't improved, of course, and the stick took just enough weight off the leg to make the pain tolerable. It still hurt, though. You could tell. It showed when she slowly lowered herself to sit and when she winced and strained to stand. She'd rub the muscles around the knee absently while she sat talking, debating.

It was a nice piece of maple, the stick was. Ruby had inscribed intricate patterns along its length. The knob at the top was carved into the head of a grizzly bear. A crude countenance but nevertheless fierce-looking, not unlike the stick's owner, I thought.

And the stick certainly did not make her seem like a weak old lady. Instead, she brandished it like a field marshal, pointing at a distant ridge line where she wanted a new observation post, or thumping it into the ground to drive home a point. She was even known to use it to administer the occasional rap upon the head of some underling who'd screwed up or failed to follow orders.

Ruby stood by the executive fire pit, where a few officers were still seated in a ragged circle after their breakfast and the first of the day's coordination meetings. Ruby had one hand on the walking stick. The other was balled into a fist and planted on her hip. She stared at the dying fire. Her long coat was hiked back behind her fist to reveal the old pistol she wore on her hip. One might mistake her for a stout, immovable military commander standing for a battlefield portrait.

Someone offered to fetch her a chair. Ruby didn't answer. The offer was repeated a minute later.

"Don't want one," she said without taking her eyes from the fire. "If I sit down, I'll just hafta stand back up again. But thanks, Dan. For the offer."

In a strangely direct contrast, Arie was tall and rangy and remained in a sort of constant, youthful motion. He stood across the fire pit from Ruby, staring at her and shifting his weight fluidly from foot to foot. He'd crossed his arms high across his chest, fingers tucked tightly into his armpits, thumbs sticking up. It was a statement of body language I understood to mean he was annoyed, anxious.

"Well?" Arie said after remaining there, fidgety but silent, for several minutes.

Ruby shot me a look as if to say, "Would you please do something about him?"

I only shrugged.

When she didn't answer Arie said, "Rube?"

"Jeeze, kid," said Ruby, "y'ever consider givin' it a rest?"

"You said you'd have a decision this morning," said Arie, yanking his hands out of his armpits and holding them out imploringly. "Then you said wait 'till you had your coffee, then you said wait 'till after breakfast. Well, it's morning, it's after breakfast and—" here he stepped up to the fire pit and lifted the lid of the blackened coffee pot that sat on the fender "—and the coffee is gone."

"Fine," said Ruby, looking up at him and jabbing her stick into the dirt. "The answer's no. Not this month."

"What? Again? When then?"

"Sorry, kid. We're just too busy providing for and protecting ourselves. I got a thousand people strewn across these mountains." She flourished the stick vaguely at the surrounding hillsides.

"We aren't the only people who matter," Arie replied. "What are we gonna do about the people still in the system? You think just because they can't remember anything that they're not suffering?"

Ruby's jaw muscles flexed.

"We're free," Arie continued. "We have a responsibility to them. We should at least be making plans, gathering intel. That's all I wanna do. I'm not proposing some full-on frontal assault, but we can't just forget about them."

"We got plenty of people here who need looking after, kid. I can't forget about them, neither."

"They won't need looking after if we bring down the Agency once and for all. The best defense is a good offense."

"We been over this, kid."

Ruby was right about that. It was an old debate. How to move forward? Were we to risk our own safety for those still held captive and ignorant by the Agency, and possibly become captive again ourselves, or should we stand off a bit and build our resources and capabilities? I couldn't begin to count how many times we'd been over it. I could recite Ruby's retort almost word for word before she made it.

"Every time we go down there, even just t'look around or do some reconning, we put ourselves at risk 'a bein' found, and every time we go up against Agency troops, we just make them stronger—our people get killed or captured, and to be honest I'm not sure which one 'a them two options is worst, cuz it's terrible when someone dies, but at least when they're dead, those Agency thugs can't wipe their minds and put 'em back to work against us."

"Yeah but so if we—"

Ruby held up her hand and pressed her mouth into a straight line. "Kid, you're smart. You got a good head and a good heart. You wanna help them people. I do, too."

"Yeah but that's not what it sounds—"

She snatched up her stick and pointed it at Arie, as though it might shoot out some dreadful magic spell. Arie shut his mouth.

"We're just not in a position to take them kinda risks right now. You wanna talk about helpin' people? Let's talk about last time we got found and how many people got taken and killed when we got attacked. You wanna help people? There's mushrooms to be foraged ever' time it rains and we need a bigger pottery kiln and hell you know you can go bring up water from the crick any damn time y'like. Felix's peas are comin' on an' he's got bushels of 'em that need shelled. You wanna help? Then help. You asked me for an answer. Answer's no. Least for now."

Arie looked at me as if to say, "Would you please jump in here and help me out?"

I only shrugged.

Ruby leaned on her stick again and looked at Arie. "Now. You're gonna stop houndin' me about this, or I'm gonna put you on latrine duty for the next year."

Arie pursed his lips and tried to make his face impassive. "Fine," he said, his voice flat. He stormed off.

"Dan!" Ruby barked. "Were you gettin' me a chair here 'er what?"

Dan sprang up and placed his own chair behind Ruby, then stood without appearing to know what to do with himself as Ruby eased herself down into it. She sighed and ran a hand through her hair before turning to me.

"Quite the revolutionary ya got there," she said testily.

"I don't know where he gets it," I answered.

She scoffed loudly and rubbed at her bum knee. "Like he ain't the spittin' image 'a you."

The fire had dwindled to white-flaked coals. Ruby leaned forward in the chair and stabbed at them with her stick, sending a plume of ash into the air. A few flames were rekindled.

"Not many kids his age care s'much about other people that way," she added.

4

I smiled and nodded.

"Thing is, I wish we could do more. I really do." She sighed. "This world—" She closed her mouth, then opened it again, then shook her head, as though she really couldn't find words to complete the thought.

"I know what you mean," I offered.

"Will you talk to him, Al? Make him understand I ain't tryna be the bad guy here?"

"Sure," I said, rising from my chair. "But right now I'm on dish detail."

Ruby kneaded her knee and thigh. "I'm gettin' too old for this."

"For which part?" I asked.

"All of it. Everything. Don't ever get old, Al. It's the pits."

CHAPTER 2

I appreciated the communal nature of Ruby's camps if only because I was a lousy cook. Everyone pitched in to help on nearly every kind of task at one time or another, but we were more often given duties that matched our capabilities, which allowed me to enjoy the delicious meals the others produced—venison and squirrel and wild greens and even garden produce like carrots and squash and garlic—before going to work on guard duty or hauling water or, like today, dish detail. The camp fostered a lifestyle that I would have considered entirely wholesome and healthy and even enjoyable, if it weren't for the constant threat of being found by Agency troops or roving raiders.

A pile of tin cook pots and cast-iron pans was waiting for me at the wash station by the kitchen fires. The cooking crew was finishing up, and we exchanged waves and smiles as I approached with the other members of the dish detail.

I began by placing the cast-iron pans face-down over the coals of a cook fire to scorch away the oil and food residue, then I put on a large pan of water to boil while the others took the bushel baskets of scraps and leavings to the composting area.

After my first couple times on the cooking crew, I wasn't invited back. I could hardly peel a potato properly. But apparently, I had a knack for doing dishes, and I rotated onto that crew more often than almost any other. I didn't mind. Not at all. It was simple work that allowed me to think and let my mind wander. And lately, my thoughts turned to what I'd began to think of as "the Arie Problem."

When the water reached its boiling point, I filled a washbasin with hot and cool water until it was hot enough to wash but not too hot to tolerate, and then I set to work. The others chatted quietly around me as we worked. Telicia, busy with her own wash basin, had been trying to get the attention of a young man she'd met on a foraging trip, and now she was being pressed pointedly for any romantic updates.

"What'd you guys do?"

"Just went down to the big tree by the stream. Put our feet in the water."

"Anything happen?"

"We talked."

"About what?"

"Just whatever. Nothing. Everything."

The others groaned with disappointment.

I had developed a dish-washing sequence. First tin mugs and flatware—they dirtied the wash water the least, so they came first, followed by the plates, which everyone was asked to scrape clean before placing them in the dirty-dish bin. Next was the crockery, which was liable to break if washed with lots of other pots and plates. Last in line were the big pots and pans, which were blackened and crusted with cooked-on food. If I cleaned the dishes out of order, I had to refill the basin more often. Oddly, the dirty pans and pots were my favorite. We used sand from the riverbed and a little crude, camp-made, lye soap to scrub them clean. There was a meditative aspect to polishing away the soot and food.

Arie acknowledged that I was his mother, and so did everyone else in camp. Ruby and others had uninterrupted memories which confirmed our relationship, but things nevertheless could be odd between Arie and me. After all, I didn't know him. Not truly. And he didn't know me. And we got along well enough. I felt an unmistakable kinship toward him, but I felt continually that I should be doing something "motherly" for him without knowing what exactly that might be or how to go about it. He was too old to take orders or discipline from me, and he was too smart for me even to provide much useful guidance. He was practically an adult, but still he seemed lost.

And while I was happy with the quiet, rustic tranquility of Ruby's camp, it was clear Arie was deeply dissatisfied. Even without my memories of our previous lives together, it was obvious to me that Arie was smoldering inside. He wanted challenges, and he wanted change. Most of all, the injustice of our world goaded and galled Arie. I sensed that the heat inside him was likely to consume him completely if he wasn't able to put it to some good purpose. It had occurred to me more than once that if Ruby and the other officers kept turning down his proposals to undermine the Agency, Arie might go off and do something on his own, something that could easily go wrong and make things worse, maybe much worse. This is where I felt I should step in as a parent, to provide comfort or advice or just an understanding ear. But what could I say? What could I do?

I placed the last of the cook pans on the drying rack. Their burnished metal sides shone dully in the morning light.

Surely it was my responsibility to encourage and nurture Arie's ambitions and opinions. No one knew exactly what the future held for us, but everyone agreed that Arie would make an excellent leader in the years to come—if we could keep him from turning resentful or reckless.

The Arie Problem.

The dish detail was finishing up and going their separate ways.

"See ya after lunch."

"Kay. See ya."

"We want more details, Telicia."

"Yeah, yeah."

I had no idea what I should say or do for Arie, but as I untied my washing apron and hung it on a tree branch, I knew it was time to talk to him.

I went to find him. It took a while, but I finally spotted him sitting beneath a stand of aspens at the far edge of the grassy, hillside meadow up above the camp. It was almost like he was hiding there. One of his long legs was stretched out before him, and the other was bent and gathered in almost to his chest. He sat there shelling peas. He worked mechanically, his hands dropping into the bucket for a handful of pods, splitting them open with a practiced motion, and spilling the peas into a small basket. He repeated the process without ever seeming to pay attention to the peas themselves. Instead, he stared across the meadow at something happening at the lower edge. I followed his line of sight. Just down the hill was an open, sunny area where lines had been strung between the trees for clotheslines. A group of people was there hanging laundry. That's when I understood why he'd come all the way out here to process the pea pods, and I felt a twinge of sadness. Sandy, the woman who had cared for Arie when they'd been part of the Lotus project, was there hanging laundry with the others. I continued crossing the meadow.

When I came near, Arie smiled faintly and waved.

"You all right?" I asked.

"Yeah. It's just frustrating." He grabbed a handful of pea pods and let them drop a few at a time into the bucket. "Shucking peas and doing laundry are bigger priorities than helping people who are where we used to be just a year ago."

"You gotta remember that Ruby has a lot on her plate," I said.

He shrugged.

"She knows it's important to go after the Agency. She agrees with you. But she's also looking out for all of us, too. She's trying for a balance between making progress and managing risks. You know the argument better than anyone."

Arie shrugged again and took up another handful of pea pods. He was no longer looking down at where Sandy was, but I knew she was on his mind. I looked down the hill. The blankets and sleeping bags they'd hung to dry waved sluggishly in the breeze like wet, heavy flags.

I picked up some pods and worked on them. Arie and I sat there awhile that way, silent except for the muted plinks of the peas dropping into the bowl. He stole a quick look at Sandy as they gathered up their empty baskets and left the meadow in the direction of the camp.

"Have you talked to her?" I asked.

Arie looked up at me, maybe a little embarrassed that I'd read his thoughts. But then he shook his head. "A little. Not really."

"Why not?"

"What am I supposed to say to her?" he replied. "'Hello, my name is Arie. You don't know me, but I feel like you are my mother, even though you aren't really. Please accept me into your life'?"

It stung to hear Arie say that he still considered Sandy to be his mother. He and I had a good relationship, and I would do anything for him, but my heart nearly burst with longing for him to see me in that way—to think of me as his mother, someone he desperately wanted in his life.

But I would never tell him that.

"Honestly?" I said, "I don't see a problem with some form of that conversation. None of us here remember everything. I think she'd really appreciate someone who knew her before, someone who could fill in some gaps. She's very nice, you know. I'm sure she'd be understanding."

"That's just it," said Arie. "I know she has no memory of me, but part of me keeps thinking that if I just hang around her and interact with her, there would be some, you know, like a glimmer of recognition. I don't expect her to just alla sudden remember me, but just maybe see that I'm someone more in her life than some annoying kid that always seems to show up where she is. But there's nothing. She doesn't know me, doesn't care. I dunno. It's stupid. Doesn't matter. It's just that—"

"It's just that you remember."

"Exactly," he said with a heavy sigh, voice cracking. I thought I saw tears start in his eyes. "I remember all of our time together and our routines and all the stupid little in-jokes and I can't make those memories go away and so from my point of view it's like she's just stopped caring. I just want her to, you know, like see me. Just notice me."

"If she could remember, she would still feel the same way. You know that, don't you? Intellectually, academically, you know that?"

"Well, yeah, sure, of course."

"So?"

Arie scoffed and with the heel of his hand he roughly rubbed his eyes. "Maybe one day we'll remember," he said, a sardonic edge to his tone.

"Don't be that way, Arie. Really things aren't that bad."

Sometimes I went too far in thinking that I could know what was in Arie's mind. I felt a genuine connection with him, and I knew I could read him in a way others could not, but I often had to caution myself that I didn't know everything about him. And sometimes I almost acknowledged that it might not be a motherly connection at all and instead was the simple result of paying him so much attention and thinking about him.

Whatever the reasons, the Arie Problem had come into sharper focus, and I saw a reason he might be so restless and petulant lately. It was his way of dealing with the crushing confusion and frustration of our lost memories and connections, our long days in limbo, resisting the Agency but not confronting it as the source of our misery. If Arie couldn't have the relationships and connections that the Agency took away, he would pull the Agency down brick by brick. I knew this was how he felt.

And as much as I wanted to be Arie's mother, his one and only true mother, it wounded me to see him so upset. It wasn't enough to escape the Agency serum and to keep our memories—we had still been robbed. I wished then that Sandy could remember Arie. I wished that she too would feel that she was Arie's mother and would regard him the way I did—with pride and love and the terrible and constant worry that is in some ways the actual foundation of parental joy. How could something like that detract from the way I felt about Arie? How could five or ten additional mothers ever do that? I didn't own Arie, I loved him.

I wished Sandy would remember because Arie was my son and he was hurting over her, and a mother will do anything to keep her child from pain.

And with that I felt a smolder begin to awaken in me, too.

All the peas were shelled. Arie sat looking at the tree line where the laundry party had gone.

"Hey, I know it's hard and things aren't perfect," I said.

Arie shot me a look of unvarnished skepticism. He was probably right to do so.

"But things are going to get better," I went on. I wasn't sure what else to do. "Look at us here. Out from under the Agency's thumb. Living free, keeping our memories."

Arie nodded in a passive, almost impatient way, as if only waiting for me to stop talking.

"Just try to be patient, Arie. We'll figure it out." The words felt weak and awkward even to me.

Arie gathered up his peas and the bucket of empty pods and then without answering he stood.

Just then we saw Chase hurrying toward us from the lower end of the meadow.

Life in the mountain camps agreed with Chase. He was leaner through the middle and broader in the shoulders. He wore a faded, plaid flannel work shirt, which was repaired with his own coarse mending and patched at the elbows with buckskin. The knees of his pants were similarly mended and reinforced. His face and arms were as brown as a nut, and his gray and black beard was wild and bristling. He'd let it grow out for weeks until it was impossibly thick and aggravating, then he'd chop it down to stubble like it was some troublesome hedge of brambles. And then it'd grow out again.

"Ah. There you are," he called, half walking and half jogging up toward us. "What are you guys up to?"

"Shucking peas," I said as he approached.

He stood over us and examined the bucket of empty pea pods. Then he looked around.

"Came all the way up here for that?" he asked, squinting.

"Chase. What's up?" I asked.

Chase shoved his hands into the front pockets of his pants, tried to act nonchalant. He failed. "Well, I don't want to interrupt. I mean, I love peas as much as the next guy."

"Chase?"

"Well, I just need to talk with you for a second, Al."

"I'll see you later," said Arie.

"You don't have to go, Ars," Chase was quick to add. "Stick around. It involves you."

"Nah, I got some stuff to do." He was already striding away.

I caught his arm as he passed by me and gave it a squeeze. He smiled his faint smile again as he continued toward the camp, letting the down-slope pull him along. I watched him go, shielding my eyes against the sun with my hand at my brow. When Arie had passed into the trees, I turned to Chase.

"What is it?" I asked.

"It's a surprise," he said, raising his eyebrows. "Can we go somewhere?"

"Okay, but I got dish duty today after lunch."

"This won't take long," said Chase.

"What's this surprise?" I asked.

"Just hold on," said Chase. "I want the moment to be just right."

We walked down a game trail, off the hillside, and into a shady hollow. The morning breeze gently shook the leaves of the aspens, and the shushing noise they made seemed to heighten my anticipation. We came to the old gray trunk of a fallen tree, and Chase spun me around and pulled me close to him, tucking his hands into my back pockets as I wrapped my arms around him.

"Tell me you love me," he said as we embraced, swaying together.

I smiled. "You know I love you."

"Come on," he said. "Tell me."

"Chase, I love you."

"I love you too, bunny."

We kissed and for a moment, all my thoughts and worries vanished as I felt the security of Chase's arms and the warmth of his body. When we finally parted, my lips tingled.

"I'll never get tired of that," Chase said.

I smiled.

"But are you ready for the surprise?" Chase asked.

"Yes! I've been ready this whole time. You really have a surprise?"

"Yep. A big one."

"Okay, already. What is it?"

"Guess," he said.

I chuckled, bit my lip, and blurted, "A book."

Chase frowned.

"What?" I said.

"You're no fun. You always guess everything on the first try."

I laughed. "It really is a book?"

He frowned and nodded.

"Well," I said, "I don't know which one."

Chase reached behind him and pulled the book from the waistband of his pants.

"You had it with you this whole time?" I said, still laughing.

He handed it to me.

The cover was a deep bluish-purple with a lady's face superimposed over a view of an amusement park and a Ferris wheel. Goosebumps formed on my arms.

"It's—"

"*The Great Gatsby*," said Chase, tapping the cover with his finger. "I thought you'd like it."

"Where'd you find it?"

"Oh, I've been asking around here and there since back before you can remember."

"Arie's notebook."

"Yeah, it'll help with that, too, but I know you're just as curious to find out what happens with Daisy and Gatsby."

I held the book close to my chest. "Oh, I am."

Chase grinned.

"Thank you," I said. "I can't think of a better surprise."

"You sure about that?"

"Well, I can't think of many that'd be better right now." I looked at the book again, it was worn with yellowed pages and water damage, but to me it was priceless.

I was thinking about the Arie Problem. The real surprise was still to come.

CHAPTER 3

Ruby's big cabin tent was festooned with a crazy assortment of tools and tchotchkes and needful things. Bundles of dried herbs, little bleached mammal skulls strung together on a length of jute, a hunk of flint with a steel striker on a key chain. Tattered maps with curled edges covered the back wall like faded wallpaper. One shelf of her small bookcase was set aside for wooden animals and figurines she'd whittled—she gave them to kids who'd "done a good turn." On the upturned, sawed-off log she used for a nightstand there lay an obsidian knife someone had knapped for her. I had once made the mistake of idly testing its edge with my thumb, and there was still a small white line through my thumbprint to remind me of how amazingly sharp it was. There was a dream catcher the size of a hubcap suspended from the roof. Woven with cream-colored deer sinew and complete with raven and eagle feathers, it turned slowly in the air over Ruby's cot. She had a basket of woven willow branches that held scavenged magnifying lenses and reading glasses in various states of wholeness and repair.

The place reminded me of a shaman's laboratory.

Ruby sat at a desk that served as her headquarters, her workstation. It was constructed of rough-sawn planks of knotty pine or fir, held together with rusty nails salvaged from who knows where. Along with the big central command tent and the main fire-pit, Ruby's desk was one of the camp's primary nerve centers.

Arie, Woolly, Chase, and I had gathered one by one in Ruby's tent and we stood almost shoulder to shoulder just inside the front door flap. Ruby sat at the desk with a camp-fired clay mug of steaming coffee.

"All right, one 'a you lay it out for me," said Ruby between sips of the coffee. "I never did get the whole jist of it." She gestured in Arie's direction with the mug. "You, kid. Go. What's this here book 'a codes all about?"

The spiral notebook in question lay on the desk. It was now battered and water-warped and beginning to fall apart, but the skull-clock symbol scratched whitely into its red front cover was still distinct, and the page upon page of number-code were all still very legible.

"Would you believe I don't remember?" Arie said with a diffident laugh. He ran a nervous hand through his hair. "But I have been informed by those who do remember that the notebook contains coded information that I wrote down before my last memory scrub, or maybe the year before that, and in any case, we need to find out what's in it."

I held my breath. Arie wasn't exactly making a strong case. Chase tightened his hold around my waist. Woolly looked on with a sort of clinical curiosity, stroking at the now-thick fringe of whiskers that lined his jaw.

"Al? Chase?" Ruby waved the coffee mug in our direction, as though she didn't care one way or another if any of us had a better argument to make.

"I just want to know what's in it," I said, with a jittery exhale.

Chase pointed a finger at me and nodded his head in assent. We weren't making the case, either.

"Guess I shoulda started with you in the first place," Ruby said to Woolly. She took a slurping sip of coffee and then let out a loud, "Aaah." Then she nodded at Woolly and said, "Well? Can ya figure it out, Wool?"

Woolly picked up the paperback edition of *The Great Gatsby* Chase had given me. The book was also battered and appeared strangely small in Woolly's big hands. He thumbed the frowsy pages. Then he opened the notebook and examined it as if it were the last remaining documentation of some passed-away culture. He blinked, turned the pages, blinked.

"Yes," he said at last.

We waited for him to go on. Ruby had just lifted the mug to take a sip, but had stopped with the mug just shy of her lips, as though she couldn't drink until Woolly continued. Woolly laid the books on the desk again. No one said anything for a while. The mug hovered at Ruby's lips.

"That's it?" she said after a few moments more. "Yes?" She plopped the mug down.

"Yes," Woolly repeated. "I can figure it out. It's a cypher. To decode the cypher, I'll need the key. I have what is purported to be the key—" here he held up *The Great Gatsby* "—and I have the person who created the cypher." Here he gestured at Arie.

"Yeah, but I don't remember this," said Arie, pointing at the red notebook.

"Doesn't matter," said Woolly. "I think I could sort it out without you. But if we look at it together and talk about it, maybe it'll shake loose faster."

"Well," said Ruby, "what're ya waiting for? Grab a pencil. Piece a' paper. Tell us what's in it."

Woolly chuckled softly. Then he tented his fingers beneath his nose again and said, "No. No, it's not that simple. It's not like a crossword puzzle or the Daily Jumble."

"What's it like then?" I asked.

"Right off the bat?" His finger traced a line of the numbers in the notebook. "I'm thinking maybe these numbers represent page numbers, line numbers, and then words or letters. First number: page. Second number: line on that page, counting down from the top. Third: letter in that line counting in from the margin. Something like that. You go through the code number by number, and then consult the book page by page, and you end up with a string of letters that form words and sentences."

"That doesn't sound so bad," said Arie.

"No," replied Woolly, "unless I'm wrong, which I probably am. Maybe the numbers are in the reverse order of what I said. Or some other order, or maybe the entire notebook was encoded from the last page to the first. Or upside-down. Or maybe the code is something entirely different or has more layers to it. Maybe Arie translated the entire matter into Latin before he encoded it with *The Great Gatsby*. Arie, do you know Latin?"

Arie thought about this for a moment, looking as if he thought it would be good if he did. But then he answered, "No."

"Point being," Woolly continued, "there are any number of permutations, but I'll never know which one it is without trying a few lines in a few different ways and seeing if they pencil out as words and sentences."

"Why in tarnation would someone go to all 'at trouble, though?" Ruby asked.

"I wish we could ask him," said Woolly, aiming an arch grin at Arie.

Chase spoke up. "I think it's safe to say Arie had a secret, and this was his way of keeping it, preserving it through a potential memory wipe. Something he wouldn't want just anyone to find. Like if his house was searched or if someone stole the notebook—there's obviously a secret here, and if it was worth the trouble of all this coding, it's probably information that will be valuable to us."

Woolly nodded emphatically.

"Yeah," said Ruby, "okay, but how would he remember what he did after he had his memory scrubbed? How would he remember he even had a secret? Or a notebook fer that matter?"

I looked at Arie. He'd furrowed his brow and one of his eyebrows stood about two finger-widths higher than the other. How odd, I thought, for him to be a party to a conversation about an earlier version of himself, a person he knew but had never met, a person he was but wasn't.

"I'm not sure," said Woolly in answer to Ruby, "but if I had to guess, I would say he left himself clues or reminders that would lead him back to the notebook and the code after his memories were confiscated. Clues explicit enough for him to investigate, but meaningless to others."

"That's exactly what he did do," I said excitedly. I turned to Chase. "Right? I've lost those memories, but you remember—right, Chase?"

"Yeah," Chase confirmed. "We figured it out that night we slipped on the ice in the tunnel at the park. Things got pretty wild after that, you remember, but we figured out that the kid left symbols and quotes from the book in places that he knew he'd be drawn to. He used graffiti at Thrill Harbor, at the Ferris wheel. The book has a Ferris wheel on the cover, see? A clue, a coincidence too coincidental to be a coincidence. He kept the book at their house, knowing he'd notice that kind of thing. And who knows what else there was that we didn't notice? Because he knew he was smart and would keep being smart even if they scrubbed him."

Arie's awkwardly pained expression told me that while he was impressed with this person everyone was talking about, he felt weird about admitting his own forgotten plan was impressive.

"It's brilliant, really." I spoke up for him. "And this was years ago, when he really was a kid."

Arie smiled at me as his face reddened.

"Doesn't matter, though," said Woolly, spreading his hands and then tenting them beneath his nose again. "We have the encrypted material and the key. I think we owe it to ourselves to decode this. Doesn't matter how it fell into our hands."

We all nodded. Ruby did, too, though she was chewing the inside of her cheek as she did so. Arie and Woolly leaned in to peer at the books. They pointed to the lines of numbers and turned the pages of *The Great Gatsby*. Ruby put her chin in one hand and drummed the fingers of her other hand on the desk.

Chase put his mouth to my ear. "You doing okay?" he whispered.

I nodded. "I just want to know what's in there. It's killing me."

He nodded, kissed me on the ear.

Ruby stopped her drumming. "Here's what's bothering me, though," she announced, taking up her walking stick and thumping the floor with it. "What if there's like a hunnerd of these per— perm—"

"Permutations," offered Woolly.

"Yeah, those," Ruby continued. "What if there's a hunnerd of 'em? Won'tcha hafta work on this for a whole day to find the right one?"

"No," said Woolly.

"No?" echoed Ruby.

"No, much longer than that, I would think," said Woolly. "Several days. A week, maybe. Or even longer."

"Yeah," replied Ruby. "That's what I thought. And then ya still might come up empty, and even if ya do come up with the right per"—

—"mutation," said Woolly—

—"you'll have to spend time un-coding it, and that all by itself is a whole other big job."

Woolly stuck out his lower lip and gave a nod.

"See? Now follow along what I'm tellin' ya. Back when Al and Arie and all of us lived in Zone 1891, back when we were holed up in the terror ride at the park, we thought we needed the Agency serum to live, right?"

Nods.

"Everyone did, didn't we?" said Ruby. "Oh, we thought the serum was legit but maybe the memory effects was bogus, and we was runnin' around trying to find a serum without the memory effects, but we also was tryna figure out just what was true and false about everything, and course we know it was all a bunch of horse-hockey now, but back then we was obsessed with finding it all out."

"Right."

21

"Sure."

"Now," Ruby drawled, holding up her hands leading us further into her argument, "'parently, sometime back then, Arie found out something that he figured was important enough to put down into a code. Great. But what was it? Hell, I wanna know as bad as you all do. Sure I do. But it's gonna take manpower to find that out, which is something I ain't got a lot of. So, best thing for me to do is narrow down what it could be. Yah? Narrow it down before we waste that manpower, see. And when I start narrowin' it on down, I betcha that was it—Arie found out that the serum was a fake. Or that the memory effects was fake. Or something related to that. Follow? That's the most likely thing it could be, and we already know alla that."

Arie objected. "Yeah, but we don't know—"

"Bup bup bup," Ruby held up her stick. "You're right. We don't know, do we? We don't know nothin'. But follow my logic. That's the most likely thing ya found out, kid. And so not only could this notebook un-coding burn up a whole lotta valuable manpower and not amount to nothin', it might amount to somethin' we already been knowin' for a while, and in fact I think it's most likely that that's the big secret! No offense, kid, but what else could you of found out back in the 1891 that we haven't already learned for ourself since we got outta there? We pretty much know everything now, and nowadays it's not s'much about finding out more about the Agency as it is about stayin' outta their way so they can't make us forget all of what we done learnt."

She was right. I had forgotten what had happened to Arie and me when we lived in the Zones, but I spent an entire year living within the Agency. What was there left to discover?

Several seconds passed without an answer from any of us.

Then Woolly held up an index finger and opened his mouth to speak.

Ruby cut him off. "An' don't you go tellin' me you'll work on this in your spare time just outta your own personal curiosity, ya' big lummox. Y'ain't got no spare time 'less I give it to ya, and even if I did, you'd burn up alla yer candles stayin' up nights working on this without any sleep."

Woolly shrugged his guilt and nodded again.

"See? I can't afford that," said Ruby.

I somehow caught Ruby's gaze and in the span of a second or two, a complicated exchange took place. In that short glance, I managed to remind Ruby that Arie needed this. This or something like it. He'd been told "no" too many times. Even if the notebook were a wild goose chase, and I was beginning to agree that this was probably the case, Arie needed something to occupy his mind, something besides hanging laundry and shucking peas. Sometimes I thought it would almost be better for Arie if he were back at Lotus or even out in the Zones somewhere, because from what I could tell, that was where he thrived—building a resistance, making plans, working under pressure. All this peace and quiet was driving him nuts.

Ruby was disappointingly right. The notebook almost certainly contained information that we'd already discovered, but here at least was a solution to the Arie Problem, I told her, pleading with my eyes.

And Ruby understood.

When the moment passed, I saw the twinkle of covert understanding in her eyes, though it was shadowed by a certain dark reluctance. She sighed loudly and stared at the notebook for a few seconds.

"All right," she said. She thunked her walking stick on the floor and then passed a heavy-lidded gaze over each of us in turn. "Maybe there's something here. Maybe there ain't. Personally, I think there ain't. But I think you's have got a point about valuable info. We eat peas and garlic and them little funny wild strawberries, but we live on information, don't we?"

"Indeed," murmured Woolly.

"So, tell ya what I'm gonna do," said Ruby, her voice low and a little apologetic. "You got three days. Woolly? Just you and the kid. Not you, Chase. Or you, Alison. Just them two." She wagged her finger at Arie and Woolly.

They traded a look and nodded with no little eagerness.

"I'll relieve ya both from yer camp duties, but if this ends up being another one of them diaries about what kinda soup you ate or howta fix bicycles for your neighbors, so help me I ain't gonna be real pleased. Three days, and after that it's back to business as per usual. Got me?"

There was a collective sigh of relief and repeated assurances from all of us that the notebook would not be a distraction. I gave Chase a squeeze.

"We won't let you down, Boss," said Woolly.

"There's no way you can," Ruby replied gruffly. "Now go on. Git."

CHAPTER 4

All throughout the first day, I popped into the big command tent every couple hours to see if Arie and Woolly were making progress, trying each time to avoid being caught by Ruby—even when I wasn't supposed to be busy at some camp duty or assignment.

It didn't seem to be going well.

When I peeked through the front door flap just after breakfast, the notebook lay open between them on the table, and they sat writing lines of letters and passing *The Great Gatsby* back and forth. It seemed like the most tedious thing in the world two people could do together. Woolly consulted a page in the novel, ran his finger along the lines of text, wrote down one letter, then passed the book to Arie. Arie ran a finger along a line from the notebook, consulted the novel, and then passed it over to Woolly. This happened over and over. I slipped inside the tent as quietly as I could manage.

Neither of them looked up at me.

"Arie," I hissed, looking behind me through the gap in the tent door to see if Ruby might be watching.

Arie looked up and met my gaze, but he only gave me a curt, almost dismissive head-shake and then went back to his work. I stepped out of the tent and hoped for a better result next time.

When I came just after lunch, I could see the guys had been served hash and coffee and water and camp cakes. This time Woolly read numbers aloud from the notebook while Arie looked up letters in the paperback and wrote them down. There were balled-up wads of paper and more dirty dishes scattered on the table top.

That time I didn't even try to get their attention.

Lamps and a few candles were lit when I came around just before my post-dinner shift on dish patrol. This time when I saw them, I thought they were sleeping with their chins in their palms, but then I realized they were staring at long lines of letters they'd been writing down all day, presumably looking for words or maybe even just patterns. They were beginning to look a little weary. Rumor had it they'd downed a full week's ration of coffee between them.

"I knew it!" barked Ruby from outside the tent.

I considered diving under the table.

"An' don't go and try hidin' in there, Al," she said. "I saw ya go in. I knew you'd come sniffing around." She swept the heavy canvas door of the tent aside.

"You said you wouldn't hang around 'em," said Ruby, shaking a finger at me. "Said you'd stay busy and not bother 'em."

"I'm not bothering them," I told her. "They barely know I'm here."

"Not entirely true," said Woolly dryly. "We've just been ignoring you."

Arie nodded without looking up from the decoded lines. Then he paused, rubbed his eye with a fist, the way a little boy would, and went back to his work.

"G'won," Ruby said to me in a loud whisper. She jabbed a thumb at the tent door. "Git. You think they're not gonna tell us if they find somethin'?"

"It seems like this might be a bigger challenge than I led you to believe," said Woolly. His mouth gaped in a great, lionesque yawn, and then he pinched the bridge of his nose.

"Yeah?" drawled Ruby. I could tell she wanted them to give up. "Well, fellas, that's all right. Ya did your best. Maybe you can try again when things settle down."

The pair looked at each other and nodded slowly, their eyelids puffy. Then they stood. Arie put his hands in the small of his back and arched his spine backwards. Woolly gathered up *The Great Gatsby* and the notebook and handed them to Arie, who nodded wearily. Then the four of us shuffled out of the tent and off in different directions. I wanted to say something. I kept quiet and went off to work the dinner shift.

That night, as I got ready for bed, I saw a glimmer of lamplight on the other side of camp, where the admin tents and structures stood. I put on my sandals and crossed the camp in the dark. My feet knew the way without any light.

Lights burned brightly in the command tent. I crept up to the nearest window, and there they were in the light of two oil lamps and three or four candles, reading numbers and letters to each other again. I smiled. Then I looked more closely at the table, and I saw sheets of paper with writing on them. Not just strings of random letters or numbers, but words, fashioned into sentences, with spaces, punctuation. I couldn't read any of the writing, but I knew what it meant, and I gasped, surely loud enough for them to hear me.

If they did hear, they made no signal to indicate it. I turned to leave, but as I turned away, Woolly did look up, craned his head around, and saw my face in the window. There were circles under his eyes and his face was drawn.

But he smiled at me and gave me a thumbs-up.

I was aching to know what they'd decoded, but I felt strongly that I'd break the spell they'd finally conjured if I interrupted for even a few moments. And so I stepped away and spirited back to my tent.

I did not sleep, and just before first light, I got up and peeked out of my tent. Light still shone from the command tent. I got dressed.

CHAPTER 5

I was never really sure about how Ruby felt about me after I'd gotten my memory scrubbed, after the time I spent with Gary Gosford in the Agency housing block. It was nothing she said to me directly. She never had a truly unkind word, and she often told me how much she loved me and how highly she thought of me. She treated me like I was her daughter or niece—she gave me advice and asked me for advice sometimes, too. I'd never heard from anyone else that she'd said anything negative about me, either. But I got a certain feeling from Ruby, like she no longer fully trusted me, no longer thought of me like she did before. Maybe, I sometimes thought, Ruby suspected that my time with Gosford and Rachel had endowed me with some kind of hidden loyalty or a Manchurian-style plan to betray everyone.

In fact, in the back of my mind I thought Ruby might have excluded me from her leadership team had it not been for the fact that Chase and I were together and had grown quite close. Ruby seemed to realize that wherever Chase went, I went, too. We were partners, and even if we hadn't been a couple, we often thought alike.

"I think Alison's right."

"I like Chase's idea."

In planning or strategy meetings, that was sometimes all we had to say.

I'm sure we annoyed others with this closeness, but there was something that drew Chase and I together. I never wanted to be very far away from him, nor for very long. I knew I could take care of myself—I knew that Arie and I had lived for at least a year and probably longer out in the Zones on our own—but there in the mountain camp, Chase had a way of stepping in to help me out at just the right times, whether I asked him for help or not. Sometimes it was something as simple as bringing a bowl of stew to my tent after a long day, so that I didn't have to walk across camp for dinner. Other times he'd take a shift of my duty when I wasn't feeling well, or when I wanted to spend an afternoon with Arie.

Memory erasure and the conditions the Agency forced us to live in caused all kinds of conflicts and in-fighting, so I tried not to return Ruby's supposed mistrust in-kind, but I wasn't about to object that it might be Chase's influence that kept me close to Ruby's decision-making, especially now that Woolly and Arie might have wrested something important from the mysterious red notebook.

As I came out of my tent, I saw Chase approaching in the half-light.

"We're meeting at the firepit," he said. Then, turning about-face he headed in that direction, waving his hand and beckoning me.

When we got there, someone had started a small fire that snapped and clicked quietly, sending a plume of grayish smoke into the still air. The chickadees and mourning doves were busy singing the morning into life, but it still felt like the middle of the night to me. My head buzzed with a lack of sleep.

Arie sat in a camp chair with his elbows on his thighs and his head hanging practically between his knees. Woolly was pitched back in his chair, fingers laced across his big chest. His eyes were closed, his mouth was open, and he was beginning to snore.

"Guys?" I asked. "You all right?"

Woolly stopped his snoring and nodded slightly but did not open his eyes; Arie nodded without lifting his head.

"Where's Ruby?" asked Chase.

"She'll be along," croaked Woolly.

"I'm here, I'm here," said Ruby, limping up from behind us, her cane thudding in the duff. There was a weary edge in her voice.

We all came to a sort of collective alert, as we often did when Ruby appeared among us. She shuffled into our midst and stood in front of Woolly and Arie. They'd sat up in their chairs and were yawning and stretching and blinking.

"So?" she grunted.

"We've only decoded the first ten pages," said Arie. His voice was thick with fatigue.

Ruby took off her glasses and rubbed her eyes. "And?"

"And the first part explains the purpose of the journal," said Woolly. There was the same sleepy, baritone rattle in his voice. "It's like we all figured—he coded the information because he thought it was important, and then he left himself little hints and puzzles to point him back to the notebook on the far side of a memory scrub. So, we were right about that."

"Yah, yah," said Ruby. "So, what's the big secret?"

"Well, summarizing a little here," said Woolly, "but it was close to the end of the year, and Arie came across a man named Eudrich on the side of the road."

"Yoo-jrick?" said Ruby.

"Close enough," said Woolly.

"How'd the kid find 'im? He was just laying there in the road?"

"Arie was out searching some old buildings outside Zone boundaries, as was his habit at the time, and he found this guy, who'd apparently been left for dead. Basic Agency goon, young Arie thought, but this guy had been ambushed by thieves and for whatever reason, Arie decided to help him. Pretty bad shape. So, Arie helped the guy make it to a friendly house where some friends treated his injuries and fed him."

"Why didn't you tell me any of this?" I asked Arie.

"Maybe he did," said Woolly. "Or, maybe it was to protect you."

"Right," continued Arie. "To keep the information compartmentalized. But then I found out he wasn't just some goon. He was a scientist, a researcher. He told me that a lot of what the Agency had told us was true. For example, they really were working on a cure for the memory loss, at least back then. Eudrich was one of their main researchers and, according to the coded journal, he told me that at that time they could successfully and reliably restore memories almost back to the most recent previous dosing incident—they could bring back a year or so worth of lost memories. And they were working on reaching further back."

I almost didn't believe that I'd heard Arie correctly. I guess it was because he'd said just what I wanted to hear—that there was a way to reclaim our memories, if only some of them. Our memories before Year One—surely those were out of reach, but even one year of lost memories would mean so much. We would remember each other. Sandy could remember Arie. Arie could remember me.

I couldn't read Ruby's expression.

"Keep going," I said, but my breath was so shallow it came out in a whisper.

Woolly and Arie looked at each other as if deciding who should go ahead.

"Well, that's kind of it," said Woolly, "at least so far. The journal documents the details of the Agency's research on restoring the lost memories, as told to Arie by Eudrich before he died," said Woolly.

"He died?" asked Chase.

"Yep," said Woolly.

"We were recording everything in our journals at the time," said Arie, "and the Agency didn't approve, but we were apparently getting away with writing down mundane details like where to find firewood and how to stretch our rations and who had what to trade. But Gosford was breathing down our necks at the time, gently discouraging us from using journals and looking into the past. If I wrote down what happened with Eudrich, I could have been disciplined or taken prisoner or who-knows-what. End of the year was coming up, and Eudrich said the virus was real. So, it's like we guessed—I put it all in code."

"So, nothin' new," said Ruby. "Like I said."

"What are you talking about? This means there really is a cure," I said, "for the memory loss. This changes everything."

"Now hold on, Al," said Ruby. "Simmer down. These fellas ain't got but to page ten yet. What if on page eleven they find out this You-jerk guy was lying, or delirious, or just plain wrong?"

Woolly nodded. "There's a lot more to this notebook—there's obviously more to it than this first revelation. And it's slow-going. We'll probably need four or five more days to finish the rest of it."

"I still say this changes everything," I blurted. "How could it just be wrong? Or a lie?"

"Well," said Ruby before I could go on, "maybe it ain't wrong or a lie but it's just a red herring, something we chase and chase and never get nowhere. We're doing all right just as we are."

I scoffed. "You're telling me that if there's a solution to our memory loss we're not going to do anything about it?"

"I'm not sayin' yay or nay, Al," she replied, a defensive darkness in her tone. "Course I want my memories back, but it's a matter of risk and benefit."

"Sure, but the benefit in this case is everything!" I said.

"It would give us a huge advantage," said Chase to no one in particular, "depending on what we knew before. It really could change everything."

We'd taken shelter and established our camps in mountainous wilderness areas that were remote and had been difficult to reach even before society collapsed. Still, detection by the Agency was a constant threat, something we had to be constantly vigilant against. I imagined Rachel relentlessly sparing no expense or resources to find us, leading the charge even, ordering all the camps to be wiped out until every person submitted or lay dead. I even had the occasional nightmare that it would be her who swept open the door to my tent and shined her blinding white LED flashlight into my face.

"I've got her," said Rachel in my dream, staring down at me from behind her light. "Get in here and secure her."

And Ruby was fiercely protective of the camp network—preached vigilance constantly. She considered the camps her own—every path, every guard post, every patch of wild strawberries. And it was all hers and we were all under her protection—she was the mastermind of the sanctuary. I understood why she was so protective.

"There was another name in the book," said Woolly. He turned to Arie. "What was it? Bellingson?"

"Bellington."

"Bellingson?" Ruby perked up.

"Bellington," said Woolly. "Ton. With a 't'."

"That's what I said." She was snapping her fingers, trying to recall something. "Hey, don't we know a Bellington? From the old days?"

Chase was already nodding. "David, I think. David Bellington. Did a bunch of surveillance on him for a few months before we met Alison and Arie. I mean, it's been a while, but yeah, we know him. What's the notebook got to say about him?"

"Nothing, really," said Woolly. "Eudrich mentioned him to Arie, and so he's in Arie's narrative, but we're not sure yet why he's important or if he is. We were hoping the next few pages would say more."

"Rube," said Chase, "we have been talking for a while about grabbing a prisoner or two to see if we can short-circuit the whole cat-and-mouse game, find out how they keep finding us up here in the woods. If this Bellington guy is more or less where we left him, he wouldn't be hard to nab, and we might squeeze him for answers we were already looking for and maybe get something about the info in this notebook, too. It'd take a week or so to pull off, but it could pay off big."

Ruby was chewing the inside of her cheek again, as if she had been thinking the same thing already. Lately she'd been moving against the Agency in safe, conservative maneuvers, trying to protect what we'd gained, trying to keep moving forward, even if it was slowly. But the Bellington issue had gotten her attention. It was one thing to nab an Agency goon and pump him for random bits of information, but it was another to interrogate a prisoner with pre-determined objectives in mind. Those moves had leverage, potential. Even I knew that.

"Rube?" said Chase. We were all looking in her direction.

"Sounds like we should pick him up," I nudged.

Ruby rubbed her chin, trying to downplay her interest, but her eyes had narrowed. She still knew a good move when she saw one. "I guess it wouldn't hurt just ta' ask him a few questions. Chase, go ahead and put together a team. Bring me a plan."

Again, there was a collective sigh of relief. Chase made a fist and smacked the palm of his other hand with it. A calculating grin spread across Woolly's face, and he nodded slowly.

I tried to stay quiet and still, not wanting to jinx Ruby into backing out. But Arie reacted the way I would have if I could have—he leaped from his chair and pumped his fist in the air. He'd wanted to go prisoner hunting for a while. He'd been told no so many times he could practically answer on behalf of Ruby. But it was more than that. It seemed we had all been feeling like Arie—the restlessness of sitting around and playing it safe for too long. It seemed we were all growing impatient to take it to the Agency again, like the old days, waging war in the shadows. We felt stuck. I know I did, anyway, and I'd forgotten almost all the skullduggery I'd ever played a role in.

"Meanwhile," Ruby hastened to add, "Wool, you and the kid keep working on that damn notebook. I don't care how long ya stay up. If we're picking someone up, we gotta know what it says in there."

"We're on it," said Arie, barely concealing his excitement.

Woolly made a half-bow to likewise consent.

I thought they might head in the direction of their tents to grab a few hours of rest before starting again, but they were going in the direction of the command tent. I didn't object. Let them sleep when they want to, I thought.

"Everybody else," said Ruby, turning to me, "which pretty much just means you, Al—you'd best be on your best behavior and go about your business like normal, which in your case probably means doing some breakfast duties."

"I'm on it," I said. I mimicked Woolly's half-bow and then I turned on my heel and almost sprinted to the kitchen area. I no longer felt tired, I no longer felt worried. For the past few days I'd been feeling that I could only take about half a breath, that I could only half-relax. Now it was as though I could fill my lungs all the way up.

Of course none of us knew what this Bellington character would have to say, or if he could even be found, but my reckless optimism had kicked in again and it seemed like almost anything could result from this coded notebook information and the impending prisoner grab.

We could end up with a year's worth of restored memories.

Or more.

I almost tripped on the trail to the kitchen as I fantasized about it, and I actually did trip when my thoughts turned to the possibility of having all our memories restored. As I got up and clapped the dirt from my palms and knees, I laughed. That was the entirety of all my wishes for the future—that we would find ourselves again. Cost-benefit analysis goes out the window when something like that is at stake.

And so there was an energy in the camp, a crackle or current that I'd felt before, but not for a long while. I felt it in my head and my chest and I'd seen it in Arie's face before he'd turned to go back to the command tent. I knew what it was, but I didn't want to name it for fear that it would vanish or burst like a bubble of soap.

It was hope.

CHAPTER 6

For days, I begged Chase to tell me their plan to take Bellington prisoner.

"How long will you be gone?"

"Al, you know I can't say."

"Where is he at? Main Zone complex? Where I was? Is he farther north? Is he out in the new settlements?"

"Al. Quit. Please."

"Well, do you even know where he's at? How are you gonna find him?"

"Al."

"Just tell me who's out looking for him, then? Is this thing even happening? Just tell me something!"

For days, he wouldn't budge.

I knew he wasn't supposed to say anything. It was for my safety, of course, and Chase's, too—the less I knew about where he was or what he was doing, the less I could say about it if everything went to hell and we were captured. It's not like they wouldn't torture me either way, but it'd be better if I had nothing to divulge.

I knew this; I just wasn't happy about it.

Just about everything in our existence was supposed to be on the QT, need-to-know, etc. Who were the leaders of the other camps? We didn't know exactly, didn't even know precisely how many camps there were, unless we needed to know, and we were supposed to keep everything to ourselves. Compartmentalization was our motto, our mission. And it wasn't just to prevent getting information tortured out of us. The Agency had on several occasions tried to infiltrate our camps with outsiders posing as wanderers or Agency defectors, and so we were not supposed to gossip or share information or ask each other about our roles in camp. In fact, Ruby had implemented a policy that forbade us from even talking about or asking each other what jobs we did in camp from day to day— picking berries, cutting wood, boiling water—not because it would endanger anyone to know that I did dishes all the time, but because it helped to develop good, tight-lipped habits, so that we weren't blabbing about everything we knew or thought we knew.

But Chase also knew that I couldn't not ask.

Whenever there was any kind of operation, I was consumed with knowing all the details. For a week I obsessed about knowing when the prisoner grab would happen, extrapolating what would happen next, and from there predicting how long it might take before we made any progress on the whole getting-our-memories-back thing. It was a light at the end of the endless tunnel.

I'm sure I drove Chase absolutely insane. And it made me angry, but he finally told me that we needed to stay apart for a few days while he worked on the plan.

"Babe, I can't say no to you forever," he said, "so I'm gonna have to ask you that you stay on that side of the camp and I'll stay on this one."

I harrumphed at him, shot him my most withering glare, but he held his ground.

"It's for the best. You know it is."

"So, you're just going to ignore me until it's time for you to go?"

"I'll come by and tell you good night," he said, "but we gotta do this by the book if we're gonna realize any benefit from it."

The rest of the day crept by with a glacial deliberateness. I watched the shadows on the ground outside my tent slowly slant with the changing angle of the sun. I barely ate, I did my dishes in a half-trance, skipped dinner, and crawled into my bed as soon as the crickets began to sing.

How long could something like this possibly take? A week to catch this Bellington guy, a week to interrogate him, and a week to get back? Add a week for unforeseen happenstances—that was a month. Add another full month for making the plan to get the memory cure, or synthesize it, then a full month after that to execute that plan—so, we'd be getting our memories by early winter? Let's say something goes really bad wrong, I thought. Something always does seem to go sideways, so let's add two months to recover— could we maybe get back on track over the winter, and maybe get the memory-restoration up and running by next summer? Could this take a year? Could it take longer than that?

Chase came to my tent as he said he would. He ran his finger along my temple, tucked my hair behind my ear, and kissed me on the forehead. I pretended to be asleep already.

"Sleep tight, bunny," he whispered. "I love you."

I lay still, kept my eyes closed.

As he blew out my candle and turned to go, I snagged his arm and pulled him back.

"Ah," he said, laughing. "Not sleeping after all, eh?"

"Please!" I blurted. I thought I might wake up the whole camp. "Just tell me something. So I can sleep? Please?"

It was almost dark, and there was only a faint light remaining inside my tent, a hint of the dusk that was still draining from the sky, but in that half-light I thought I detected a smile stealing across Chase's bearded face. The crickets had fallen into a synchronous rhythm and thrummed softly outside. Chase shook his head slowly.

"Okay," he said, smoothing my hair with his hand. "If I tell you one thing, you'll go to sleep?"

"Mm-hm."

"You promise you'll go to sleep and shut the hell up?"

"I promise."

"Okay," said Chase, with a sigh of relief. "They found him. Bellington. I won't say where, but a runner came into camp tonight with the news. We know where he is. It's on. We're gonna go grab him."

"When?" I said, sitting up in the bed and tugging on Chase's arm. "How long will it take? When will you go? When will you be back?"

He laughed and ran his hand over his face. He was exasperated at me again—I didn't need any light to know that. But I couldn't help it.

"Go to sleep, bunny," he said. "I gotta go. Lots to be done. Sleep now."

"I can't," I cried. "Not now that I know it's really happening. Chase, can you imagine? Getting it all back? Getting yourself back?"

"Yeah, babe. I do get it. And I'm excited, too. Haven't felt this way since back in the early days, back at Thrill Harbor, back when we met. It's all very exciting, for sure. But you gotta learn some patience."

"You're right," I confessed, shaking my head emphatically. "I'll work on that. Right after you tell me how it's all going down."

"Dammit," he breathed. "How can I say no to you? Okay. I'll tell you a bit. But if you breathe even a word to this to, well, anyone, at any time, even after it's all over and even if it all works out fine—if anyone anywhere ever finds out I told you anything—you know Ruby will have me skinned alive, right?"

"I promise I won't tell anyone. I swear it. Cross my heart." In the darkness I drew an X over my heart. "It's just—I'm going crazy, Chase. Just tell me when, how long, and when you'll be back. Tell me that and then I swear I can lay down and go to sleep."

"It's tonight, babe," he said, cupping my face. "Me and Bostwick and Thompson."

"You were just gonna leave me without saying good bye?"

"That's why I came over here, babe. I'm saying good bye."

"Yeah, but I didn't know that!" I insisted.

"Babe, all of this is supposed to be classified."

"Yeah," I said, trying to keep myself from crying. "I know. I'm sorry. Where will you hold him? The Bellington guy. How long will you question him? How long will you be gone?"

Chase sighed deeply, and I saw him shake his head. "We're bringing him here, Al. Ruby's plan. Ruby's orders."

"Here? My god," I said. "Isn't that kinda crazy?"

"Definitely. A huge risk. But Ruby wants to question this guy himself, and she just can't travel very well anymore. She's been wanting a prisoner for a while, of course, we all have—to try to get some distance on the cat-and-mouse. Now that the boys are making headway on that crazy notebook, who knows what else we might find out? But remember, no one knows we're even grabbing a prisoner, and even if they do, they don't know why. So keep a lid on it, for god's sake."

"Okay, so when? How long will this take? When will you grab him? When will you be back?"

"Grab him probably on Thursday, Friday at the outside. We're hoping to be back here within nine or ten days. If the weather is good, we could be back within a week, I guess."

I threw my arms around his neck and pulled him down on top of me. The cot squeaked in rickety protest. We lay that way for a while, noses touching.

"I want to know who I am, Chase," I said. "I want to know who you are."

"Ya know, babe," he replied, "we know quite a bit about each other already. For example, I know that I love you."

"I love you, too, Chase," I whispered.

We shared a long kiss.

"You happy now?" he asked, getting to his feet again.

"Yes, very."

He sighed. "You're my weakness, Al, you know that? Back when we were in the 1891, before Gosford got to us, I told Woolly that you would be the end of me. He doesn't remember, of course, but I did. Fact, I'm not sure how I've survived this long."

"Well, give me a little more time," I said.

"Get some sleep," he said.

"How can I sleep knowing it's happening tonight?"

"Al!"

"Just joking."

He bent over, drew the top of my sleeping bag up, and tucked it under my chin. Tucked it tightly, just the way I like it. Then he straightened, but I took his hand in mine.

"Be careful, Chase." I squeezed his hand.

"I will." He squeezed back.

"Come back."

"I will. I told you I will."

"Getting my memories back won't mean much if you're not here to make new ones."

He went out without another word, and the only sound then was the slow thrumming of the crickets in the darkness.

I didn't think I would be able to sleep, but I felt sure now that we'd have the antidote, soon, or at least eventually.

Antidote.

I didn't even really know what it was. Was it a drug? Some kind of brain-stimulus treatment? Maybe a psychological technique. The details didn't seem important. What mattered was that this was not just another plan to survive better or to find a new and safer place to subsist. This was an actual antidote for everything that was wrong with our lives, our world. I didn't think I would be able to sleep that night with all of this running through my brain, but I'm almost sure that before five minutes had passed, I was fast asleep.

CHAPTER 7

I woke up early. The air was crisp and cool and even though it was still late summer, there in the mountains the mornings were getting cold enough so that you could see your breath. I sighed and a tiny cloud billowed up into my tent.

Most of the camp was still sleeping, but the birds in the trees were awakening. I lay on my cot staring at the roof of my tent, sleeping bag pulled up to my chin. Had it been five days now, or six?

Soon I heard cook pots clanking and a few distant voices. The breakfast crew was up and working. I heard their laughter, muted and muffled by the distance. I got up, rinsed my face, and got dressed.

I wasn't on kitchen duty or any other duty that day, but I joined the others and found the coffee and filled the scorched, blue-enamel percolator and set it on the fender of the main fire-pit. I don't know why, but it felt better just to be near other people, even if I didn't speak with them or interact.

After a few minutes, the deep-brown coffee was bubbling up into the glass button at the top of the pot, and a steady stream of water vapor issued from the spout. I filled my cup and cradled it in my hands, the warmth radiating up my wrists and into my arms.

Chase wasn't back yet. Every day when I got up, I checked his tent first and then looked around down at the vehicle yard. Two vehicles were missing—an F-150 we'd recently acquired and the old Taurus that seemed to have been around forever. Chase didn't tell me those were the vehicles he and his small team had taken, but I assumed, and I ached to see them parked there again.

The kitchen staff was making grits with eggs, and it would have smelled wonderful if I'd been hungry. I pulled up a chair and sat in front of the fireplace. I'd brought my unzipped sleeping bag with me and I sat there with it wrapped around my shoulders.

The steam from my coffee mug curled up. I took a sip, and just then I heard a soft commotion from the tents. I turned to see Ruby stumbling out of her tent with apparent difficulty. Another charlie-horse, by the look of it. She limped back and forth in front of her tent, kneading the back of her thigh, punching it with her balled-up fist.

It was no secret that Ruby was in frequent pain. She would sometimes mention her bum knee or the effects of getting old, but more than that, it was most evident in the way she'd plant herself somewhere and have everyone come to her. Once she got comfortable, the other officers and anyone needing to speak to her would have to line up and wait.

Even with her new walking stick, she struggled to get up and down, and there were certain areas there on the mountain that she simply could not access. Although there were nicely worn paths, most of which were easy to walk, in most ways the camps were still very much wilderness and there were many paths that were steep, rocky, uneven, or strewn with cobbles. And when it was dark, Ruby required an escort just to go down to the latrine or cross from the command tent to her own.

I worried all the time that one misstep could put Ruby out of commission for good, but then again in other ways she seemed indestructible, like she could stand up against a tank. God knows she would almost surely try if it ever came to that. And when her physical body sometimes failed her, her unflagging mental toughness compensated.

Like when she contracted walking pneumonia the previous spring. She had horrendous coughing fits—I heard once that you could hear her at the remote guard posts—but in some ways she was more productive than ever because she didn't have to take a break from working to walk across camp for meals or do anything for herself.

But there were other times she surprised everyone—she was often the first one up and about in the morning, especially when the weather was dry and warm. And if there was a major operation to complete, she'd stay up long after everyone had gone to bed. She had some bad days with her health and her knee and all the rest, but she had good days, too.

I sometimes thought about what Ruby might have been like when she was my age. At first I pictured a younger and sexier version of herself—kicking ass and taking names and never backing down from an adventure. Had she been in the military? A rough woman-warrior who'd seen combat? Or a merchant sailor? Or maybe she'd been part of some criminal element before Year One, too. Maybe she had always been a ringleader like the one we all knew—boosting warehouses and running rackets.

In the end I thought maybe the opposite were true. What if Ruby was a UPS driver back before, or a waitress, or something completely innocuous, and she'd only taken on the persona we knew after the world had gone to hell?

I loved Ruby, we all did, but mingled with that love was more than a little fear. I'm not sure what we were so afraid of—even the slowest of us could easily outrun her on her best day. I think it was more about wanting to please her and impress her and the fear of letting her down.

I was painfully unlike Ruby. I wasn't a natural-born leader, nor was I particularly adventurous. But I hoped that she saw some value in me, and I took pride in knowing I was much more like her than I had been when we'd first met.

And so I was careful about what I did and said around Ruby, and I often felt like I was faking it until I made it—

pretending to be like her until someday I would be. I wanted her respect, but more and more I felt that my efforts fell short of that aim. It seemed like I either wanted too much or too little. I was too complacent or naively ambitious.

All of this was in sharp contrast to people in the camp like Chase, who had many skills and abilities that were valuable in a place and time like this. If it came down to choosing one or the other of us, Ruby would pick Chase in a heartbeat. Still, I tried. Even as it seemed like we might be nearing some new and better chapter of our life outside the Zones, I still wanted to win Ruby over.

Ruby labored up the path in my direction, still clutching at the back of her thigh where I knew a muscle cramp was knotting up and spasming. She winced and muttered as she came along. When she came near, she nodded at me but didn't say more, and when I realized she was joining me at the fire pit, I hopped up and got a chair ready for her. She limped past me and collapsed into the camp chair, then nodded at me again by way of thanks. Then she sat there panting.

The kitchen staff must have detected her presence because one of them, a girl of about Arie's age, almost immediately brought her a coffee. She hadn't caught her breath and so she nodded at the young lady to thank her. Then she scowled into the fire pit, her expression one of deep annoyance and exhaustion.

Today would be one of her bad days.

She looked somewhat like a cat might look after being doused with a garden hose. I could tell that she was in no mood to talk, but the silence was just too much for me.

"Sleep okay?" I said. I don't know why. I don't know what I was thinking.

Ruby looked in my over at me without turning her head. Then she looked at the fire pit again.

"I haven't been sleeping well, either," I went on. "Can't seem to get warm these days. I'm thinking I need some new wool socks, but I can't think of what I might trade for some."

Ruby nodded her head almost imperceptibly, but said nothing.

"Smells like grits and eggs for breakfast," I rambled. "I wonder if there's any bacon this morning. We haven't had any in so long. And I hear we're running low on coffee."

"Al," she said.

This time it was my turn to nod and say nothing.

Then, there came a sound from the upper half of the camp. A low rumbling and a high, keening sound. The sound of an old truck engine and of tired old brakes squealing to a halt.

We both sat up straight in our chairs and looked in the direction of the vehicle yard. The sound of another approaching engine drifted up from that direction. I stood up and threw off my sleeping bag.

"Where ya goin'?" Ruby drawled.

"It's Chase!" I chirped. "They're back! Finally!"

"Yah," she returned. "I know that. But you ain't sposed'ta."

I sat back down.

"Chase was s'posed to've told you he was going on some routine business to the lower camps. But I guess you got the real story out of him, huh?"

Ruby rocked herself back and forth and then rocked up out of the seat and onto her feet. I stared into my coffee mug like there was something amazing inside it.

"Now you listen here," said Ruby. "You stay away from them this morning. I know you and Chase're tight and all, but I get the sense you already know much more than your sposed'ta. And there's nothing you can do right now to help anyway, so stay out of it."

I didn't dare say anything back to Ruby, especially not on one of her bad days, but I watched as she hobbled toward the vehicles.

I followed a little ways behind, hoping Ruby wouldn't look back. I had to see. Through the trees and underbrush, I glimpsed Chase, and a man with a pillowcase over his head and his hands tied behind him.

We had kidnapped the man, and I couldn't say that fact sat very comfortably with me. In fact, I felt awful about it—kidnapping and interrogating seemed beneath us. We were trying to avoid being forced into doing things against our will, and yet here was a man who was almost certainly minding his own business a few days before and now here he was a prisoner and his fate a complete mystery to him. We were supposed to be the good guys.

Still, there was no doubt in my mind that this was something that had to be done. We needed that information. Ruby had pointed out many times in the past week that, even if there was some kind of medicine or technique that could bring our memories back, all we'd really gain was more to lose if we were captured again by the Agency.

And she had a point—it didn't matter if you woke up in the Agency infirmary after having lost one year's worth of memories or thirty-six years—you were still a walking shell of your former self.

But I was hoping she was wrong. Something inside me said that if just some small portion of us could regain all of our memories from back before, something would change. The world would somehow change back.

And after that, perhaps we could work on making it up to each other—to Bellington and all the other Bellingtons who'd been punched in the head and tied up and thrown into a truck.

I saw Chase gesture to Bostwick and Thompson, and they led Bellington to the command tent. A couple guards were posted as Chase and Ruby spoke outside for a moment. Chase nodded at something Ruby said, and then they both went in the tent.

Woolly walked up beside me.

"What's all the excitement?" I asked. "Do you know?"

He gave me a sideways glance. "Don't even try it," he said. "I know you know way more than me about what's going on over there."

I shrugged. "Thought you might know something I don't."

He stuck out his bottom lip and shook his head slowly. "I know what I know and that's all I need to know."

Sometimes I wished I could be more like Woolly, too.

"What about the notebook? Anything new you can tell me?" I looked up at him and gave him a sheepish grin. "All this knowing about stuff just makes me want to know more."

Woolly took Ruby's chair and looked at the fire.

"Arie wrote a lot about the memory effects and his theories about why the memory loss was occurring," said Woolly. "Pretty technical for a kid that age, but not particularly revealing or useful or even interesting. Plus, Arie apparently started using an entirely different encoding system about halfway through the notebook. That set us back a day or two. We don't know if it was extreme paranoia, or if the notebook might have been written through not one but two memory scrubs. But we're still working on it. We're kind of into a rhythm now. Won't be long before we've got the rest of it decoded."

I nodded. Arie was busy and Chase was back in camp. It might not be a great day for Ruby, but things were looking up for me.

"They got the guy in there, huh?" Woolly gestured with his chin at Ruby's tent. "What's his name again? Bellingham?"

"Bellington."

"Right. They got him, huh?"

I nodded. "Yep."

"Ruby told me they'd canceled that trip, and that Chase was heading to the lower camps to trade for coffee and bacon."

"And you believed her?"

49

"No. Especially after I realized Thompson was gone, too—our best driver—and Bostwick; our best grab-and-bag guy."

"I'm just glad they're back," I said.

"Yeah," Woolly nodded. "Think this Bellingson will help us?"

"Bellington," I said. "ton. And yeah, I hope so."

"Think he'll want to?"

"I dunno. Our best grab-and-bag guy just bashed him on the head a few days ago."

"True. But Ruby has a way of getting people to talk."

"That's true, too," I said.

Woolly tipped his head back and closed his eyes. "Not like the Agency does though," he said.

"No," I said. "Not like the Agency. I mean she has a way of showing people how things could be better. I don't know how to say it."

"According to the journal," Woolly said, "the memory cure they were working on could at the time restore a test-subject's memories to the point just prior to the last time they were dosed with the serum. It differed from subject to subject, apparently. Wanna know something funny, though?"

I nodded.

"I think I remember some things. Things you don't remember. Like you and Chase debating about if the serum was really necessary and deciding that it wasn't. I think I remember that."

"How can that be?"

"I don't know."

"Even just that," I said, "I'd be so thankful to remember. Chase has memories of me, of us, that I don't have. It makes me feel like I'm missing something. Like he knows me better than I know him. Or something like that."

"Well," said Woolly, "maybe someday we'll remember."

CHAPTER 8

I did my chores that day. I carried water from the stream to camp several times. I helped harvest garlic and asparagus. But I was in a haze the entire time. My mind was on the man held captive in the command tent. We brought water up from the river in five-gallon jerry cans mounted to backpack frames. They were terrifically heavy, and it was one chore I didn't like very much. Usually, it wore me out completely, and I could only make two trips. This time I made three, and all I can remember was getting to the top of the hill and to the place on the trail where I could see the command tent. I don't know what I thought I'd see-it's not like they'd bring him out or something. I never saw anyone come in or go out at any point. Not even to use the latrine, apparently.

I was sure that few people in camp even knew about the new prisoner, and if they didn't know, I didn't want to tip them off and get in hot water with Ruby, so I found Woolly. He was in the wood pen splitting logs.

Woolly was large, his arms like great slabs of meat, and he was known throughout the camp as one of the best at chopping wood. The big maul we used for splitting was nearly too heavy for me to swing, but Woolly wielded it like a flyswatter, and when it came down on an up-ended log, the two resulting halves flew around the pen like bowling pins hit by a speeding ball.

"You again?" he said with a chuckle. He brought down the maul and a stout log burst asunder. "I suppose you're here to gossip."

"Is that okay?" I winced.

"Sure. I was just starting to get bored."

He leaned down and picked up one of the split hunks of wood. I picked up the other.

"How about, you crack 'em, I stack 'em?" I said.

"Sounds good to me. The cracking is my favorite part. The stacking, not so much."

"I can barely lift that thing."

Woolly set up another chuck of pine, stepped back, and swung the maul. It was less like the cord-wood was being split open and more like it was detonating. The flying pieces even sounded like scattering bowling pieces. I picked up the pieces, stacked them.

"What do you think is happening?" I asked, craning my neck to see the command tent.

He shrugged and set up another chunk on the block. "I would theorize that they're trying to establish whether the information in the journal is accurate, but without letting Bellington know that they don't know. You know? It's very important in these situations to manage what the prisoner knows about what you know. If he detects that he knows something that they have no way of knowing he knows, things get difficult. If I said that right."

I shrugged.

The maul came down in another detonating blow. The wood flew apart and tumbled across the pen. I thought for a moment about how I would not want to be on the receiving end of Woolly swinging that maul, or anything else for that matter.

I stacked the resulting firewood and said, "So, you don't think they've discovered anything yet? They're just, what? Probing?"

"Most likely, yeah. You know. It's a dance. It's all about finesse. Speaking of which, watch this," said Woolly. He set one small log on top of a large one and swung the maul again. When he brought it down, it split both logs, wood flew in all directions.

"Now you're just showing off," I said.

"Just a little trick I've been working on."

And he split another half dozen pieces of cord-wood, but I'd fallen into musing about what Ruby or Chase or whoever else was questioning Bellington.

"Al?" said Woolly.

"Hm?" I replied.

He gestured at the wood pieces that lay scattered all around him. "I stack, you crack? My shift's almost over, and I wanna finish up this pile."

"Oh, right. Sorry." I collected up the shivered hunks of firewood.

"Listen, Al, we'll find out soon enough, okay? You got somewhere else to be? Got other plans? Why're you so impatient? When they're finished with him, I'm sure we'll find out what they've learned."

Woolly was right, of course. But that didn't stop me from sneaking up behind Ruby's tent and establishing my own personal listening post. I brought a book with me, and I held it up to my face at first, so that if anyone saw me, I could semi-plausibly claim to be just taking a break to read. And so I sat there straining to hear something, anything.

The voices were muffled. Bellington was apparently in the far corner of the tent, but I couldn't go to that side without being spotted by the guard they'd posted out front.

"Just seems odd, see." Ruby's voice. "I mean I understand why you'd never invent something like this for the poor schmucks in the Zones or out in Lotus, but I happen to know a lot of you in management have been scrubbed at one point or other, too, an' something like this could come in handy for you all almost more'n us."

"Sorry." A man's voice. Had to be Bellington. "I keep saying this, but I have no idea what you're talking about."

"Really. Nothing? Never heard anything about nothing like this. Here we got hunnerds 'a thousands 'a people with huge memory losses cuz of a treatment for a disease that really can't do us no harm anymore, and you're saying you never heard about someone working on getting those memories back, even just for you mucky-mucks in the upper esh-ee-lons?"

"No," said Bellington calmly. "Never. But, look—I'm in project management. There're dozens of project managers in my region alone. Comms aren't what they used to be. Maybe this fantasy memory antidote is out there under someone else's department."

"Chase?" said Ruby.

"Doesn't smell right," said Chase. "Seems odd."

"Yah," said Ruby.

"The complete denial," said Chase.

"Uh huh," said Ruby.

"You'd think he'd throw out a red herring. You know?"

"Right."

"The cave?" Chase asked.

"Yah," replied Ruby. "A week."

"Bit harsh," said Chase.

"Yah? What were you gonna say?"

"Couple days."

"Couple days? Hell, Becky's two kids stay in there overnight fer fun."

"Yeah, but they have candles. And food. And sleeping bags. And they can come out whenever they want."

"Oh, come on," sneered Bellington. "A cave?"

"What?" said Ruby. "You okay with a week?"

"I'm telling you," he replied, and I thought maybe his smugness was waning a little, "I don't know where you're getting these ideas."

"And when was the last time you took the serum? When was the last time you got scrubbed?" Ruby asked, her voice raised.

"I don't know. It's been years. Five, I guess. Yeah, five. They diagnosed me virus-free and classified me for no serum. Lots of people are that way. You should know. Here, tell you what—go back and pick up a couple of my co-workers. They'll tell you the same thing. I'm in project management. I know nothing about medical matters."

"Okay," said Chase. "That's what we'll do. It'll take us some time, though. Let's get you to the cave and we'll catch up with you when we get back."

"I don't know anything about this!" he growled, but there was fear in his anger.

"Right," said Ruby. "It's just, see, that ain't what Eudrich told us."

The man paused. "Eudrich? Benjamin Eudrich?"

"Yeah."

"Did you take him, too? Is he alive? What did you do to him? Where is he?"

There was a pause in the tent.

"He's dead," Ruby said. "But we had nothing to do with that. How'd you know him?"

There was another, longer pause. "We worked together. We were friends."

I couldn't hear anything clearly after that. Just movement within the tent, but no talking. I thought I heard Ruby whispering, then Chase. I moved closer to the tent, almost placing my ear on the canvas.

"Al!" shouted Chase. He was behind me. I startled so hard I practically threw the book across the camp.

I stood up.

"What are you doing? You really can't stop yourself can you?"

I shook my head.

"Well, Ruby says to tell you that if she catches you out here again you're going on permanent latrine duty," Chase said.

I frowned. "I'll go," I said. "I'm just wanting to know what's going on. You guys really should issue some updates or something. The waiting is killing me, Chase. I feel like I've won the lottery but then finding out that before you can pick up your prize, you have to jump through ten more hoops and fill out paperwork and do a bunch more requirements and then when you do those you go back and they say, 'not yet,' and add even more red tape."

"I know, I know."

I wrapped my arms around Chase's neck. "I just want to remember."

"You gotta be patient, Al. We're doing the best we can. I'll tell you everything that happened when we're finished."

"Promise?"

"Promise," he said.

There was nothing to do but wait.

CHAPTER 9

Chase found me late that night. I hadn't gone to bed, but I was lying on my cot dozing. There was a chill in the air, and I was thinking of making myself some tea when he poked his head through the tent fly.

"Come in, come in," I said.

He stepped inside, hands in his pockets. I could tell before he spoke that he didn't have any good news for me.

"We questioned him all day, all evening, and he maintains he doesn't know anything. Says he's just a middle-management goon. We did pick up some good intel about how the Agency squads conduct searching, but he's adamant that he doesn't know about this memory treatment."

"So, nothing? Nothing at all?"

Chase shook his head slowly. "Even me and Ruby are beginning to believe him. For all we know there might not really be an antidote."

"He's lying," I said.

"Maybe," said Chase, "but what can we do?"

"Put him in the cave. Beat him up. I don't know. This is what you guys do. Get the info. Make him talk."

"Al, we don't torture. You know that. Feels wrong even to grab prisoners, sometimes. I don't know. We are gonna stick him in the cave for a few days. We're giving him forty-eight hours to change his story, tell us something we can verify, but, I'm thinking, hell, we did our best. If he knows something, he's not going to tell. We'll just have to live with that. I mean, think about it—this whole thing was kind of a longshot to begin with."

I sighed. For every one step we took forward, it felt like two steps back.

"So, what are you going to do with him?"

"Ruby offered to let him stay in the camp, if he could tell us about the treatment, but he didn't seem to be very enticed by that."

"So now what?"

Here Chase frowned. "Well, we'll hold him. Work on him. See if we can't bring him around to our way of thinking. I don't know. We can't just let him go, obviously, because he might be able to lead someone back here, even if he was drugged for the trip in."

"Well, when you kidnap a person and keep them under guard, it shouldn't be that surprising that they wouldn't find the place all that appealing."

"Hey," snapped Chase, "this isn't easy. It's a fine line. We want to better ourselves, but we can't do that by kicking the shit out of people who have information we need. I suppose you got a better idea?"

I wasn't angry at Chase. I could tell he really was doing his best, but it was infuriating—the better life we wanted was always dangling just out of reach. And all of this frustration seemed to aim itself right at Chase, with no help from me.

"So," I said, "that's it?"

"Like I said, we're keeping him here for a while. We'll sweat him out in the cave. After that? Not sure. He hasn't been mistreated—other than being detained. Maybe he'll change his mind."

"He's just sitting in the command tent?" I asked.

"He'll be under twenty-four-hour guard for a while, yeah. I'm gonna take another shift with him later tonight.

"And if he doesn't change his mind and join the camp? What then?" I asked.

Chase didn't answer.

"What do we do then? Kill him?" I asked.

"What? No! You know better than that." He looked horrified.

"Then what?"

Chase rubbed his forehead. "We'll figure it out. Maybe we'll take him east. Drop him off and let him fend for himself. I'm not sure. But I gotta go grab a couple hours of sleep before my shift. I'm exhausted. Gonna be a long night."

"Fine," I said, my voice low and buzzy. Of course I didn't mean fine. "Fine" was the word I always used when I felt that nothing was fine. And Chase knew it. He'd been around me long enough to have figured that out.

But he left anyway.

I tried to sleep that night, but my mind roiled. I felt certain Bellington knew something that he wasn't saying. I could almost hear it in his voice just in the short time I listened. He was hiding what he knew, and we were losing what could be our only chance to get our real lives back. Something made me certain of all of this.

And so the fire inside me was stacked and stocked and grew hotter. It was the flames that had first started during my conversation with Arie on the hillside about Sandy and his frustration with the camp's inaction. The flames had grown with the news of the notebook and the antidote. Now it felt blinding and unquenchable and ready to break out and burn wild. I had to do something.

CHAPTER 10

"Hey," I said.

Chase was sitting on an up-ended log with his back leaning against the tree, watching the command tent. There was a lantern burning with a low flame, hanging by its bail from a nearby branch, and Chase was listlessly polishing a pair of army boots.

"Oh, hey, Al," he said. "What are you up to? Thought you were mad at me."

"Yeah," I said. "Sorry about that. I'm not mad at you. Just frustrated with the situation. You're right. I need to be more patient. Give it time."

"So, what are you doing up?" he asked.

"Couldn't sleep, so I brewed some tea. Then I got to thinking about you staying up out here all night."

"Ah, bless your heart, bun," he said, setting down his boot and polishing brush. "C'mere. It's freezing out here and you don't even have a jacket on."

He unzipped his coat, and I slipped my arms underneath it and leaned into the warm pocket of air around him. He wrapped his arms around me and kissed me on top of my head.

"How's your prisoner?" I asked.

"Sleeping, I hope," said Chase.

"And how much longer are you here for?" I asked Chase.

"Couple more hours. Larson should be coming around three or four to take his shift."

"You said you were exhausted, and that was a couple hours ago," I said. "How you doing now?"

"Actually, I'm glad you came along when you did. I keep dozing off. Don't tell Ruby. It's been kind of a long few days. I think I'll be fine. I mean I'm really knackered, but I'll crash later.

I don't know when I came up with the plan. It may have started stirring in my mind as I lay in my tent, before I got up out of my sleeping bag and sat on the edge of the cot, and it may have begun to take shape as I tied my boots and crossed the dark camp for the command tent. I don't know when it became an actual plan. I wasn't sure if it even was a plan. I just started talking.

"That tea is in my tent. Still hot. And it's warm in there. Got a couple coals burning. Go have some tea and take ten minutes. Take twenty. Take a nap, for all I care. You know what, in fact? I think I still have a shot or two of that homemade hooch that Lorenzo and Chester cooked up. Have a drink. I'll sit here." I hoped that the moonshine would seal the deal.

Chase pursed his lips and squinted at the command tent, as though weighing the risks. I looked, too. Everything was still in the soft light of the lantern. There was no light or sound issuing from the tent. Chase unwrapped my arms from his middle and put his finger to his lips. Then he crept to the front flap of the command tent and quietly opened it. He stood there, listening. After what felt like a full minute, he walked softly back to me.

"He's asleep, pretty sure," said Chase. "I can tell by his breathing. And if he's not, he's doing an outstanding job of faking it, so, respect to him. And if he's planning to make a run for it or something, he's gonna have to get out of a pair of handcuffs and those leg manacles hitched to a twenty-two-pound boat anchor."

I nodded. "So, go ahead."

"Okay. If he comes out, just scream like hell, okay?"

"Sounds like a pretty easy job. Maybe you don't really deserve a break."

"You really don't mind?" said Chase. "You said everything was 'fine' just a few hours ago. We all know what that means."

"Yeah, yeah," I said. "I don't mind. I said I was sorry about that."

"All right," he replied. "If I'm not back in like, a half-hour, jog over and get me." He kissed my cheek. "Thanks, hon. I appreciate it."

As I watched Chase disappear into the shadows between the command tent and mine, I felt a sudden twinge of guilt form in the pit of my stomach. It dropped there and rolled around a few times. I'd never tried anything like this before, but there was no way Chase would go along with it if I told him what I planned to do, girlfriend or not. And there was no way I could lie in bed and watch the one thing I wanted just evaporate.

He'd forgive me.

If I could even pull it off, that is.

Would he forgive me?

Would Ruby?

Of course they would. Because I was certain that the ultimate, eventual pay-off was finding ourselves again, meeting ourselves, and starting again. I wanted to remember. I had to. I wanted Arie to remember. And Chase and Ruby and Woolly and everyone else. It was the first and last thing that been taken from us. It was what we were owed. What we deserved. I had to try. I don't know if I realized it fully at that time, but the fire inside me had gone wild and tumbled from the andirons and spilled out over the fender and flagstones and into the room and the walls were now ablaze.

And so I stared at the kerosene lantern Chase had left hanging from the tree branch. Reaching through the darkness I turned the wheel that raised the wick and the flame grew. I had to squint my eyes, accustomed as they were to the dark of the night. I lifted the lantern and went quietly into the command tent.

Bellington lay on his back on a low, aluminum-framed cot. His wrists were encircled by a pair of Chase's nickel-plated police cuffs, and his hands and fingers were sort of spraddled across his chest in a way that to me looked very uncomfortable. His feet were likewise cuffed in a set of prison manacles which looked positively indestructible and were, as Chase had said, threaded through a big steel boat anchor. What that particular piece of equipment was doing in this mountainous place was anybody's guess.

I set the lantern down and looked at Bellington for a few long moments. He looked to be very peacefully sleeping in spite of his situation.

"Tell me what you know," I said in a voice almost too quiet even for me to hear. Bellington didn't stir.

I slid my hand into my pocket and wrapped my fingers around a folding Buck knife. This was Chase's, too, but he told me I could have it. It had a dark wood and brass handle, and the locking blade was perhaps five inches long. It wasn't much of a weapon, and I wasn't much of a fighter, but the blade itself was terribly sharp, and I supposed I hoped that my appearance in the middle of the night and the blade in the dark and Bellington's hapless state as a prisoner far from home would give me an advantage in the early going.

I took the Buck knife from my pocket. The care-polished blade glowed dully in the flame light. When I opened the blade, it locked open with a sharp click that seemed like it might be as a rifle shot in the stillness.

Then I came closer and crouched at Bellington's cot, near his head. I took a deep breath to steady myself, but in that moment, I felt panic rising in me. What am I doing here? What am I hoping to accomplish?

Chase would be so angry. Would he leave me? And Ruby. Ruby would lose her mind completely. Would she banish me? Maybe she'd turn me over to the Agency to have me out of her hair. Did I really think I could get him to talk when no one else could? The seriousness of the situation, along with its absurdity hit me like Woolly's maul impacting a hunk of firewood. It was all so stupid. My little plan.

I stood up slowly, moving as quietly as I could manage. My heart thudded like some broken machine. I began backing away from the cot, backing slowly and gingerly toward the tent flap. What if Chase came back? Or Chase's relief? Or anyone? Or what if Bellington woke—

He opened his eyes.

CHAPTER 12

Maybe, I thought, he wouldn't see me? Maybe he'd think it was just a dream and roll over and forget the whole thing? Or would he spring up and stick my own knife into my heart.

A look of terror was on Bellington's face. I could only imagine the expression on mine. His eyes darted from my face to the knife in my hand and back again. Mine darted from his face to his handcuffs and manacles.

Running on pure instinct, I lunged, crouched at his side again, and put the knife to his throat. He flinched a little but said nothing.

"Listen here, you little goon," I hissed at him, "it's time for you to start talking. I know you're lying. Tell me what you know about an Agency memory cure or I'll make you pay."

Even as the words left my mouth, I knew nothing like that would ever happen. I didn't believe it myself—how could he? Me? Cut a person? Chase once told me a story of a night back before they wiped my memories—we'd broken into an Agency building together, and I apparently didn't have the heart even to bonk some Agency goon on the head with a baseball bat.

Still, I gritted my teeth and pressed the Buck knife closer to Bellington's throat.

He stared at me, the light of the lantern reflecting in his eyes. He blinked a few times, and his terror seemed to transform into confusion, then irritation.

And then—he laughed. With a knife to his throat, he laughed. Then he shoved me away with a great heave of his arms and shoulders. I fell back on my ass like a puppy tossed aside. I dropped the knife and it thumped away into the shadows.

"I—I'm sorry," he said, chuckling. "It's just so—" He groped for a word.

"Ridiculous?" I asked, raising an eyebrow.

For his answer he just laughed more and nodded his head.

I sighed hard and sat there on the tent floor with my arms on my knees.

He sat up and rubbed his eyes sleepily. "Whose idea was this? Was it theirs? I guess I should say, what's the plan here? What are you up to?"

He had a faint British accent. I glared at him.

"I mean, really," he said, his voice thick with drowsiness. "I bet there's not even a real cave, is there?"

I sighed again and looked at the floor.

"Oh. Listen. My pardon. It's just—no offense, but you're about as frightening as a three-legged kitten."

"I was that bad?"

He shrugged, nodded.

"What gave it away?"

"Oh, it was everything. Your posture, your tone of voice, your word choice. Even your weapon there. I mean it's a pocket knife."

I frowned.

"I haven't offended you have I?" asked Bellington.

"No," I said. "I guess not."

"Good. That wasn't my intention. But you're all quite desperate, aren't you?"

I nodded. "I don't know when the last time was that you lost your memories, or if you ever have, but it leaves you feeling very unsettled. You're missing parts of yourself, but you don't know what the parts were. It's like you don't know yourself anymore."

"Oh, I know," he said, his gaze drifting to the tent floor. "That I know well." He tilted his head. Then he added, "Uhm, look, this may sound odd, and I assure you I'm not trying to trick you, but, haven't we met?"

I hadn't recognized his name, but now that I looked at him closely, he looked familiar.

He raised his brows and held up a finger. "I know. You're married to Gosford!"

"You—knew him?"

"We worked together on projects sometimes. I went for drinks with him a few times at the canteen, and I saw you once or twice, scurrying off into another room when we'd drop him home."

I hoped he wasn't one of the men I'd tried to blow up at the amusement park.

"So you lived at the Agency dorms?" I asked.

"Building F-9," he replied. "Right across from yours, G-9."

It was almost surreal, catching up and comparing notes with someone who was apparently fond of Gary Gosford.

"Oh, trust me, you're lucky," said Bellington. "In F-9 lives an old retired general who took to karaoke, serenading the entire building every night, singing at the top of his lungs in his bathroom."

Despite myself, I laughed. "Serious?"

"Well, I'm being somewhat overly generous when I use the word 'singing,' of course. Sounded like an alley cat trying to perform an opera."

"Oh, wait!" I cried. "I think I may have heard him! He sang rock anthems, right? Like 'We are the Champions' and 'Don't Stop Believin'?"

"Yes!" said Bellington, laughing. "'Don't Stop Believin' is his favorite!"

I laughed again. "Well, did you have anyone in your building who tried to make liquid rubber by melting their shoes?"

"What? That didn't happen," he said.

"Yes! Mr. Murmont!"

Bellington shook his head. "Maybe you did have it worse. Wasn't there a shooting in your building? Didn't someone gun down an intruder in the hallway near your flat?"

I gasped and covered my mouth.

His mouth gaped. "No, it was you?"

I nodded sheepishly.

He leaned back. "Well, well, well. P'raps I should be more frightened of you."

"I really didn't intend to harm you. I guess I was just so hopeful. So eager."

"No harm, no foul, as they say," Bellington drawled. "But tell me, how does a high-ranking officer's wife end up here?" Bellington asked. "Is Gary—here?"

"No," I said. "Gary's dead."

"Oh," he said. "I'm sorry to hear that. My condolences."

I gave a slight nod.

"I didn't know, hadn't heard," said Bellington softly. "I thought they merely transferred him. Huh. Second bit of bad news I've had today." Then he raised his cuffed hands to point at the tent door. "Did they—?"

"No, no," I said. "It wasn't them."

"Was it the Agency? Is that why you're here, with them?"

"No. I'm here because I've escaped from the Agency and I'll never go back. That bullshit serum and their mind-control techniques. It's inhumane, unjust."

"About that," he said, his tone earnest. "Do you know why your friends think that I of all people know something about a memory cure? A treatment that will restore the memories erased by the Agency serum?"

"It was in a journal we found."

"A journal?"

"Yes, with information about you, and an Agency scientist named Eudrich."

Bellington grew quiet, then contemplative.

"What is it?" I asked.

He looked toward the door and pressed his lips together.

"The thing is," he confessed. "I do know some things."

"About an antidote?" I asked.

He nodded, but lifted his chained hands to place a finger on his lips.

"Why wouldn't you tell us?"

"Would you talk to someone who had abducted you off the streets, placed a bag over your head, and took you to god knows where?"

"Listen," I said, "even they regret having to do that. But the Agency won't leave us alone. They hunt for us constantly. We've lost dozens of people just this year alone in Agency raids. They killed some, they took others back. Chase and Ruby—they're not bad. We just want to remain apart from the Agency and taking the occasional prisoner seems like the only way we can stay a step ahead of you."

"Did you ever hear of just asking nicely?"

"You would have told us?" I asked.

"I don't know," he said. "But I wouldn't have this horrendous crack on my skull and a pounding headache."

We were quiet again. The lamp had burned low. I stood up and adjusted the wheel and it was brighter in the tent.

"It's David, right?"

He looked up and nodded.

"I'm Alison."

"It's nice to finally meet you," he said with a smile.

"Likewise," I said.

I went to him and put out my hand. There was a soft metallic clatter as he raised his hands to take mine. We shook hands.

"Well, David," I continued, "listen to me. If there's any way you could help us out on this, I'm begging you, please, consider it." Tears formed in my eyes and my voice cracked. I was asking him not as an enemy soldier, but as a mother. It was the only thing I could do.

Bellington looked at me for a moment, but then looked away.

"Please? Neighbor to neighbor?"

"It's not a cure," he said. "It doesn't necessarily bring back all your memories."

"But it'll bring back some?"

He nodded. "Some, most for some. It's different for everyone, seems like. They're still working on it. Refining it."

"Oh, gosh, even just that would be a miracle for me, for us. To even just get a glimmer of memories back. You understand that, right?"

He nodded again. "There's a reason I was working with Eudrich. You must remember those of us in the Agency lost our memories, too."

But how many times had the Agency continued wiping the minds of citizens when it was no longer needed? I wanted to ask him, but knew I wouldn't be able to control my anger if I did so.

"So, David, will you help us?"

"My friends call me Davey."

CHAPTER 12

Chase whistled a lot. While he was fishing, while he was walking or working. Chase whistled while he worked. And not just idle, disconnected notes—anything but. He was actually really good, and he'd whistle entire songs, start to finish. He had great pitch, too, a great range, and he could whistle a seemingly endless number of tunes. I could almost always pick them out—the tunes he whistled—and I'd sing or hum along, or, if I didn't know the song, it was nice just to listen. Old rock tunes, opera arias, folk tunes. All very clear and sweet. He was the closest thing I had to a radio.

And so I heard Chase before I saw his headlamp bobbing along through the trees. He was a whistling the refrain from a classical piece I recognized but didn't know.

When he came into the lantern light, I was sitting cross-legged outside the command tent, just where he had been when I approached him. The lantern was on the ground at my side, glowing warmly. His headlamp was turned to a low setting, and he had a mug, which he sipped as he approached. It was probably coffee to help keep him awake or maybe it was tea.

"Sorry, hon," he said.

"What for?"

"Didn't mean to be away that long. Guess Chester's hooch knocked me out for a bit. You all right? You still don't have a coat on. You must be freezing."

I stood up, and he unzipped his coat and I slid my arms inside again.

"I'm okay," I said. "Everything's okay."

71

Chase leaned away from me and looked me in the face. His headlamp made me squint.

"What's going on? What's up with you?"

"I don't know what you mean."

"You seem—different. Not mad. Not worried. Something else, something weird. Satisfied? Content?"

I grinned into his headlamp, my head lolling, eyes lidded. I knew there was trouble ahead, but I'd gotten what I wanted.

"Oh my god. Why are you content? What's happened?"

"Chase," I said. "I know how to get the antidote."

Chase immediately set his mug on the ground, pushed past me, and went to the front flap of the command tent. He ripped it aside and looked into the dark void, shining the beam of his headlamp this way and that. Then he looked back at me.

"Oh, Al," he said. "What did you do?"

CHAPTER 13

"We've got to go get him," said Chase. "Where is he?"

"I gave him the keys to the red car," I said.

"The red car? You mean the Honda? You gave him a vehicle?"

"No, he's just borrowing it. He said he'd leave it for us to pick up outside the Zones."

He was pacing furiously around the command tent. On his face he wore an expression I couldn't exactly describe. He looked like he might be sick.

"Are you angry?"

"Angry?" Chase spluttered. "I'm—I'm—I'm—."

But he didn't say what he was. He just grabbed his hair as though he might pull it out and emitted a high-pitched growl.

"But Chase, Davey told me about the antidote. We're going to get our memories—"

"Davey?" Chase's eyes were wide, wild.

"We kinda got to be friends."

"You set me up, Alison. You used me to get your way!"

"No, I—"

"—used me. You tricked me into leaving and you let our prisoner go without even a thought of talking to me or Ruby or anyone else. Ruby will have your head for this. Shit, she'll have my head for it." He rubbed his forehead.

"I'm sorry," I moaned. "It's just I knew you'd never let me talk to him."

"And there's a reason for that, Al. Did you ever think about that?"

I looked at the ground. "I'm sorry; I am."

Chase groaned. "Ugh, what do we do?"

"We could go after him," I suggested feebly, though I didn't want to. Bellington had only given me the information about the antidote on the condition of his release.

"In the dark? When he's had a head start? In a car? We'd need a whole team for that."

"He won't tell about us," I said. "He promised."

"And you believed him?" The tone of Chase's voice was cutting. My stomach fell.

"Chase, don't be mad."

He looked at me, his jaw muscles bulging.

"I'm hurt, Alison," he said.

"I didn't mean to hurt you," I said. "I was trying to help." I hugged him, but he stiffened and didn't hug back. I dropped my arms from around him and began to cry.

"No," said Chase. "You don't get to do that right now. Not after what you did."

"I can't help it," I said. "I didn't think about how you'd feel about this. I want that memory antidote so bad."

Chase sighed and his face slackened. Then he set his jaw and his eyes narrowed and he gave me a hard look. But then he sighed again. "Come here," he said at last. I went to him and he hugged me. "What am I gonna do with you?"

"Love me," I whimpered.

"No, I'm serious. What am I actually going to do with you—hide you in camp? Take you to another camp? Because you know you can't stay here—Ruby's gonna go ape-shit on you. I wonder if I could drop you off at an Agency depot and just drive away."

I jerked away from him and pounded his breastbone with the heel of my fist, and he hugged me closer. Something in him had shifted at that moment. He was still angry, probably would be for a long time, but in that moment, I could tell, he had decided to forgive me.

I sniffed. "Should we wake Ruby?"

74

Chase took a deep breath and released it slowly. I looked up at him. He was thinking hard. He always got a certain occupied look when he was puzzling over a hard problem.

"Just go to bed, Al," he said finally, a weary edge in his voice. "Just go. I'll take Larson's shift so he won't know, and we'll just have to figure it out in the morning."

He wouldn't say anything more. Every time I tried to speak, he only shook his head and pointed toward my tent.

It's difficult to say if it was my biggest victory or my biggest mistake. It resulted in a lot of suffering—for me, for the others. But it also changed absolutely everything. I'd have to work hard to avoid getting lost in musing about that night and the days that followed, wondering if I should have done things a different way. Was there an easier way? Was there a smarter way? Was that night a fork in the road that led to two entirely different places, or was it one of those forking roads that ended up at the same place?

It was so wrong to set Chase up that way. He trusted me implicitly, and I know he was probably as hurt about that as he was angry about Bellington. But what is a mistake, really? In the middle of a fight, in the middle of a struggle to win back the person you used to be, can there really be what is known as a right and a wrong way?

CHAPTER 15

I awoke to someone shouting. And someone was blowing a whistle. Within a second or two I realized it was lots of people shouting. I heard distant vehicles starting up. I got up from my cot and fumbled for my shoes, and I was too groggy to puzzle out right away what was happening, but there could be no mistaking that it was directly related to what had happened the night before. Or, I should say, what I did the night before.

I opened the tent door and stepped out. People were hustling up and down and across the camp. Tents were being pulled down. People were wearing backpacks. I saw the big cargo truck parked in the middle of camp. An older woman named Maria hurried by, but I stopped her.

"Maria, what's going on?"

"A prisoner escaped," Maria said.

"Oh."

"I didn't know we even had any prisoners," she said, eyes wide.

"Well, so what's going on? We're bugging out?"

"Yeah, Ruby said so. We gotta evacuate."

Maria continued on without saying more. I sprinted for the command tent.

I didn't know how Chase had broken the news or when Ruby found out. I didn't want to know.

Before I ever got near the command tent, I heard Ruby yelling, haranguing. Then I saw Chase. He had his hands on his hips, and his head hung low. Ruby was shouting at him, waving her arms. Woolly and Arie were nearby, too. Her voice carried throughout the camp and echoed off the nearby hills.

"Who was it?" She was practically shrieking. "Who done it? Huh? One 'a you knows somethin' I just know it."

The three men all tried speaking at once, holding out their hands, trying to calm Ruby, trying to quiet her. Her voice rose above theirs, cut them off.

"It was you, wa'nnit?" Ruby jabbed one of her stubby index fingers at Arie. "You let him go so's we'd hafta take action, didn'tcha! Alla your talk about the Zones and alla the people. You're tryna force my hand, aint'cha!"

Arie was protesting, his face splotchy red with rage, but he could only just be heard over Ruby.

I never in a million years thought she'd pin it on Arie.

"You can't just accuse me that way, Ruby! You can't just say, 'Oh, well this guy's got a different opinion, so he must have done something idiotic!'"

Arie was lunging at Ruby, shouting, pointing his finger. Chase was between Ruby and Arie, and Woolly was holding Arie back.

I ran faster, "No, Ruby! Wait!" I cried.

Everyone was screaming. I'm not sure they even knew I'd joined them. Woolly's booming voice called for everyone to "quit acting like a pack of fools."

Ruby was screaming, "Admit it! Just admit it!" Chase was saying something without raising his voice, but I couldn't hear him.

"Ruby! Ruby!" I shouted. "Listen! It was me! I did it!"

Chase was repeating something over and over, and I think I heard it from the first but couldn't believe it, couldn't process it. He said it again and again.

"Ruby, I did it. Ruby, I did it. I did it. Rube, it was me, not him. I did it," said Chase.

One by one, we all went silent.

"Everyone just shut up and listen, okay?" said Chase. His voice was low and even, as though he might announce that he had a blister on his heel, or the kitchen was out of vegetable oil. "It was me. I let him go."

Ruby stood still, her mouth open. She and Chase looked each other in the face. Ruby blinked a few times, closed her mouth, opened it again as if to speak, but then just stood there.

Chase nodded, his face calm, serious.

"Chase," she breathed at last, pushing her glasses up her nose. "Not you."

"Yeah. Me."

She squinted at him, leaned forward, as if there were something she herself had to decode before proceeding. Then she shook her head. "No," she huffed. She trembled with anger. "Don't cover for whoever did this. I know you didn't do it. I won't believe it."

Arie scoffed. "Oh, oh, oh," he stammered, "so, he comes right out and tells you it was him and you don't believe it, but I tell you I didn't, until my head practically explodes, and you don't believe me! Well that's just great!"

He was leaning again, stabbing an accusing finger at Ruby, but Woolly grabbed him and reeled him in.

"Well, yer a kid!" Ruby exclaimed, "an' not only are kids always doin' stupid things, but I've seen you do things that was even stupider'nis!"

"Quiet!" boomed Woolly. "All of you. Seriously. The whole camp can see and hear you. They're panicking. Get a hold of yourselves. You're embarrassing me."

Woolly was right. An entire gallery of onlookers had gathered, an expression of collective mortification in their faces. Ruby sheepishly looked from face to face.

"Yah," she said. "Yah, you're right, Wool. All right, you all go on. Go about your business. We're just havin' a polite disagreement."

"You heard her," said Woolly, not angrily, but loud enough to be heard and obeyed, and the crowd reluctantly dispersed.

"Call off the evacuation," said Chase. "It won't be necessary."

"Waddya mean call it off?" hollered Ruby.

"Ruby!" barked Woolly. "Everyone, let's finish this discussion in the command tent."

Within a few minutes, Ruby had given a tentative order to pause the evacuation, and we were in the command tent. Woolly put on some coffee, and the rest of us took seats. Ruby thudded her walking stick into the tent floor. Arie glared at her. Chase sat with his elbows on his knees, looking down.

"All right," said Ruby through gritted teeth. "We're here. We're calm. We have coffee. So. Now. Chase, start talkin'."

Chase sat up straight in his chair, but as he started to speak, I interrupted.

"He didn't do anything," I said. "It was me."

"Aawww, dammit all!" Ruby growled smacking her forehead with her big, meaty hand. "What inna name of sweet baby Moses is goin' on around here! Who in the mother-slappin' hell is in charge!" She looked from person to person. They flinched as if she might attack if they spoke. "Cuz it sure as shit ain't me!"

"I made a deal with Bellington," I went on. "And he won't betray us. And I know how to get the antidote."

"You? You, Al?" she moaned, her voice hopeless, desperate. "But how did you even know about—and how did you get in here to—" But then she looked at Chase, whose facial expression looked more guilty than it had outside.

"Aw, hell," said Ruby. "I get it." She shook her head, rubbed her face as though trying to wipe away some distasteful, filmy substance. And if her face had been red before, it now took on a purple hue. Her anger was conspicuous, radiating from her like fumes off gasoline, like heat from a radiator.

"Al," she said, with a calm that was actually fairly terrifying. The kind of calm that can only result when someone is seething. "Al, do ya even realize how much danger you put us in?"

"Rube, come on," said Chase, getting to his feet. "Calm down."

She swiveled in her chair, turning savagely on Chase. "And you!" She held the walking stick out as though she might skewer his head on it. "You of all people shoulda known better. You're s'posed ta be my right hand. You're s'posed ta be on my side. I just don't know what ta say anymore. I've never been more betrayed in my entire life." She glared fiercely at Chase, but her eyes were watery. A single tear started from each one, but she wiped them away with the palm of her big hand before they fell.

"Ruby, it wasn't Chase," I said. "I tricked him. I trapped him. I set him up." I described how I sent Chase to take a break and then did what I did without him suspecting anything. "But, I really think we'll be okay. I don't think he has any interest in turning us in."

"Ah, just hush up," Ruby said. "I am so damn turnt around and flustergated I don't even know if I got any more t'say t'any of ya's."

"No, really. He and I, Bellington, Davey, I think we connected. We knew some of the same people and—"

Ruby interrupted me. "Al, I never thought I'd hear myself sayin' this, but sometimes you are really stupid."

I could never explain what it felt like for Ruby to say that to me.

"No, Ruby, let me just tell you what I—"

"Al, not now," said Chase.

Woolly nodded in assent. Even the look on Arie's face told me he agreed with them. I'd gone too far, they seemed to say, and there was no explaining it, no justifying it. And then I knew, too. I hadn't ever been sure what I was up to, I suppose. I'd been looking for a fast way forward. It hadn't been a scheme I cooked up and sat on and nursed and then hatched when the time was right. It was all just kind of thrown together and set aflame when I saw the opening. I couldn't explain or justify it to Ruby because I couldn't explain or justify it for my own sake.

When I looked at Ruby again, her head was bowed and she was digging her fingers into her eye sockets, slowly sobbing. The tears filled the lines in her face around her eyes and they seeped down into the wrinkles and creases on her hand and they drained down her wrist and into her sleeve. She sniffed wetly and sobbed more. No one seemed to know what to do. All I knew was if someone was going to do something, it should definitely not be me.

"Rube," said Woolly at last.

"What!" she bleated. "Whaddya want?"

"I'll walk you back to your tent."

"Thanks, Wool," she said, sniffing again. Her face was wet, and she'd dropped her glasses onto the tent floor. Chase picked them up and handed them to her. Woolly helped her up by the arm and she leaned hard on her walking stick.

As she walked past me, I caught her gaze, and there was no anger in it any longer. Only deep, hopeless hurt.

CHAPTER 15

Things quieted down, eventually, or maybe that is just how it appeared. Ruby ordered extra guards and deeper patrols, but Chase convinced her to cancel the evacuation—based on the way I convinced Chase. The tents that had been taken down were put back up. Everything was put back where it belonged. Everyone tried to go on as before, making breakfast, making lunch, carrying water from the river.

But I saw people looking at me in the chow line and at the nightly campfire. It could have been just anxiety or paranoia but I thought I saw them lean toward one another and whisper. In my sleeping bag at night I could almost hear what they must be saying to each other in their tents, and I didn't like it.

I actually didn't know what was known and what was only guessed at among the camp's population. The shouting match outside the tent the morning after I let the prisoner go was heard by a few and likely misheard by lots more. And like any group of people with limited opportunities for entertainment and distraction, games of Telephone were probably well underway and into multiple rounds of mangled whispers by now, so who knew what they all might think?

There wasn't anything I could do about that, though, and with a few very select exceptions, I didn't care what anyone in the camp thought of me, and so I kept to myself and kept my mouth shut.

Late summer thunderstorms had been rolling through periodically, so I at least had an excuse to stay in. They didn't seem to miss me at kitchen duty, and so on the day after the incident, I sat in my tent all day reading the same page of some stupid book over and over again.

Around sundown, Chase brought dinner to my tent so I didn't have to leave the tent and stand in line. It was like he knew I didn't want to anymore. He brought two bowls of rice and beans, but it was on the watery side, and the flavor was quite bland. We both poked at it with our spoons but didn't eat much.

"I thought I heard we were out of red beans," I said.

"I kinda wish we were," quipped Chase, scooping up a spoonful of the grub and letting splat back into the bowl.

"How is it out there?" I asked.

He shrugged. "Morale is low. Everyone's confused. The kids don't like to see the grown-ups fighting."

I knew what he meant. The evacuation was off and everyone was going about their regular business, but there was a tension in the air that you could feel.

"Did anyone say anything to you?"

"Nah. They just stare. Just like little kids. Just staring, wondering if everything is gonna be okay. Something needs to be done."

Yes, something needs to be done, I thought, we need to move ahead. We need to move into the next phase. The memory cure.

"Do you think Ruby will ever talk to me again?"

Chase shrugged again.

"Really?" I said, putting down my bowl and spoon. "You don't think she will?"

"Well, of course she will, Al. But, you know. It's a little—I don't know. Weird."

"Weird how? What do you mean?"

"Al, come on. It's complicated. She's hurt. Hell, I'm hurt. We're all hurt and confused and no one knows what to do. You're gonna have to give it time."

"Chase, I know I messed everything up, but we have a chance here. We have an opportunity to move into a new phase."

"I understand, Al. I do," he replied. "But do not approach Ruby right now. I am one-hundred percent sure she does not want to hear anything about any new plans right now."

"What does 'right now' mean? How long should I wait?"

"Wait until she comes to you, Alison. Seriously. Don't make a move."

Chase poked at his dinner, pushed it around in the bowl. The evening was cool, and I was completely out of firewood for the small stove in my tent, but I didn't want to go out and find more. I pulled my hands into the sleeves of my sweater and hugged myself against the chill.

"Don't worry," said Chase. "I'll grab you some firewood when I take the dishes back. Might be cold tonight."

I smiled inwardly. Chase was very good to me—not just in the way he accepted my mistakes and shortcomings, but the way he often read what I was thinking, was always a step ahead, anticipating my needs.

"Thanks, hon."

He stood and picked up my bowl and spoon. He went to the tent fly, but before he went out, he said, "Are we on the same page? Do not talk to Ruby. Not until she comes to you. There's no exception here. She's not talking to me, either, and if you two have another big blow-up, you and me might be looking for a new place to live. Wait for her."

"Okay."

He went out.

CHAPTER 16

I didn't have to wait very long.

Four days after I'd released Bellington, Woolly came to my tent. It was a gray, rainy day. The sun had just risen, but clouds obscured it, and the dreary patter of rain sounded on the tents.

"Hey, Al," said Woolly. "You awake in there?"

"Yeah, come on in."

He wore a bucket hat made from waxed canvas, and he was draped in an olive-drab army poncho, which fit him more like a barber's cape, barely covering his wide shoulders, massive chest, and expansive middle.

"Hi, Al," he said in a way that made me think he might apologize for something. A chain of little water droplets were suspended from the brim of his hat. When he moved his head, they fell onto the poncho and drained down to drip from the corners and onto the tent floor.

"Hey," I said.

"How you been doing?"

"Okay, I guess. Ruby wants to see me?"

He held out his hands in a conciliatory way. "Not exactly," he said.

I raised my eyebrows.

He smiled apologetically and continued. "She wants to hear what you think should happen next—not because that's what she wants to do, but I guess, you know, like to understand your thinking, to understand what you thought would happen. If that makes sense."

"Sure," I said.

"So, mind if I sit down? And you can tell me?"

I sighed. "I really think it would be best if we all sat down and discussed it. The whole leadership group. And Ruby."

"Ruby's been talking to the others," he said. "She's got some ideas about what to do next, but she's having some trouble—" he paused and grimaced faintly "—I wanna say she's having trouble getting past this?"

"That doesn't sound like Ruby."

"I know," he answered hastily, dropping his diplomatic facade. "I've rarely seen her this worked up over something."

I didn't like hearing that. "Do you think there's any chance I could have just a quick word with her? We wouldn't have to discuss anything about plans or intentions. I just want to make sure she and I can get past this. Even if it's not right away. I've been thinking of leaving, moving out."

"Al, that might not be the worst idea," said Woolly, his eyes narrowed and a pained expression on his face. "Ruby's talking about a lot of changes, and that's one of them."

My talk of moving out hadn't been a bluff, exactly. I had considered it. But to know that Woolly was ready to call that bet—it felt final and sad. I loved Ruby and even though I couldn't remember all of our adventures, I didn't relish the idea of parting ways with her.

Woolly stood there without saying more. The rain made multitudinous popping sounds on the roof of the tent that blended to sound like very loud radio static. There was thunder in a distant valley and it rolled and echoed against the mountains like a barrage of far-off cannon fire.

"I really burned a bridge, this time, huh?"

"I don't know if that's the best way of putting it," said Woolly, his eyes downcast. "It's just—well, like I said, she's having a hard time wrapping her head around this."

I nodded.

"And it's not just this," Woolly was quick to add. "There are so many problems, so many people relying on her. It's not just you, not just this Bellingson thing."

"—ton," I said quietly.

"Right. Bellington. It's not just him. Ruby's getting, well, tired. You've noticed, I'm sure. She's getting up there in years."

"Yeah," I replied. "I've wondered how long she would keep at this. I guess I just figured she'd last until we won."

"Me, too," said Woolly. "And whether she does or not remains to be seen. But, will you talk to me? Tell me what happened? What you were thinking?"

I thought about this for a while, maybe for as long as a minute. And then I said, "No."

Woolly flinched, blinked, as though the word struck him like a blow.

"I may have royally screwed up here," I said before Woolly could reply, "but I'm owed more than this, Woolly."

He nodded, once, almost too subtly for me to notice.

"She has to talk to me herself," I continued. "She can't just send you. No offense."

Woolly held up his hands again in his diplomatic way and said, "None taken. You have a point."

"Will you tell her?"

"Yeah," he said, nodding so that more droplets fell from his hat brim. "I have a feeling she'll agree, even if it's reluctantly."

The rain seemed to increase as he walked out. I sat on my cot and lit a small fire to warm some water for tea. When I heard Woolly's heavy tread outside my tent just a half-hour later, I knew it could only mean that Ruby had refused my request. And it made sense. Why would she agree to speak with me? What good would it do? Just stir up a bunch of hard feelings. No one wanted that. Maybe not even me.

"Al," said Woolly as he came to the tent flap. "Still in there?"

I went to the front flap of the tent and pushed it aside. Woolly stood there, the bucket hat pulled down low over his eyes.

"She said no?"

He said, "No. She said she wants to talk to you."

It was a long walk across the camp to Ruby's tent. When I got there, I said, "Ruby? It's me."

"Come on in," she said, her voice flat, almost void of expression.

I pushed back the tent fly and ducked inside. The window covers were drawn down and it felt dark inside. Ruby lay on her bed at the far end of the tent. The light was such that I almost could not make out her features.

"Have a seat," she said with the same flatness of expression.

I sat in her desk chair.

"Are you sick?" I asked.

"No," she answered. "Just very tired. Everything makes me very tired nowadays."

"Ruby, I'm so sorry for everything."

"Eh," she said with a wave of her hand. "You don't gotta be. I was only ever in charge because I said I was, because I called the shots and everyone seemed to go along. Weren't no vote made me boss. Truth is there's better people to be in charge than me. Maybe you'd do a better job."

I opened my mouth to speak, but Ruby continued.

"Anyhow. Ya did what ya did and now it's over."

"Okay, so—"

"So, here's what I gotta say. That what you want? Ta' cut t'the chase? Hm?" Her voice drifted in from the shadow where she lay and I noticed that she wasn't looking in my direction. She seemed to be just speaking into the air, to the canvas of the tent above her.

"Well, yeah," I said.

"Okay," she said. Then she took a deep breath and let it slowly out. "Well, it's like this. They's some of these people here in the camp who want me to keep bein' in charge 'a them, and if I'm to do that, I gotta have everyone signed on and stayin' in line. Maybe we do need a vote or a signed paper or something like that, but what I can't have is someone who's gonna make a move like that with no kinda checking in or asking."

"Oh, Ruby I would never—"

"—do something like that again? I guess I believe that's how ya feel. Or that's what ya think. But, see, I can't know that anymore. We been together a long time, Al, longer than you remember, 'a course. But somethin' changed when you let that feller go. It's a trust thing."

My heart sank.

"I can't run things here with that kind of—I don't know what ya call it. Uncertainty? Yeah. That. I'm already plumb ragged just managin' them that do what I tell 'em."

"Ruby, I'm sorry for what I did. I honestly won't ever—"

"No, Al, stop," she said, holding her hand up. "You notice I ain't never said you did anything wrong? I'm not sure it was wrong, what you did."

I tilted my head. "What do you mean?"

"Well, it ain't necessarily that you did something wrong so much as you did what you wanted to do, what you thought was right, but without consulting the rest of us—not even Chase. I just need one less chief around here so I can be the best chief I can be."

"Yes, but I'm telling you—"

"Al, stop a second."

"No, I want to explain what—"

"Al!" she cried rising from her cot, "shush!" Her eyes gazed at the roof of the tent but she wasn't actually looking at it. She was listening. "Hear that?"

I listened for a moment and heard what she had heard. The bell. The big brass bell at the southern approach observation point. The guard on duty had spotted an intruder, and from the way the bell kept clanging, it wasn't just one or two people.

"Your man Bellington brought them back," said Ruby, getting to her feet. "They're coming for us."

CHAPTER 17

The panic which erupted after that could not have been more acute if an actual god reached down from the sky and turned the camp upside-down. My friends and camp mates ran literally in every direction. Some even ran in circles, but none of them had any apparent idea of what to do or where to go.

We had emergency procedures—Ruby and Chase had made sure of that. Everyone had a bug-out pack, which was supposed to contain shelter, clothing, and supplies to last a week or so. In case of attack, each person in camp was supposed to grab their pack and race into the woods along one of a dozen designated routes, faintly marked game trails mostly, or routes that followed ridge lines and other discrete geographical features.

As Ruby put it: "Grab your shit and scatter."

And most of us had executed this plan many times. We'd been attacked by the agency before, and we also held regular emergency drills. Everyone should have known almost exactly what to do, but when Ruby and I emerged from her tent, it was actual pandemonium.

That's because this time was different.

In the past, the Agency troops hadn't been so incredibly close when the alarm was raised. In the past, our own patrols and look-outs had spotted the Agency troops from a distance, giving us time to mount a defense and make a more orderly retreat.

This time, however, the troops were practically on top of us from the start. The sound of gunfire clattered and echoed down from the north ridge. I heard people shouting, "Run! Run! They're here!" as they fled down from the high side of camp.

"Grab yer shit and scatter!" Ruby shouted, her hands cupped around her mouth, "like in the drills!" she added, but there was too much noise for anyone to clearly hear even her shrill voice. "Damn these people!" she shouted to no one particularly. "They never learn! Panic last, you idiots! Not first!"

Now the gunfire was closer and was followed instantly by the sickening zip! of bullets in the forest canopy. I thought I heard the rumble of heavy vehicles out by the motorpool. They really were close.

"Ruby," I said, grabbing the sleeve of her sweater.

I could not stay one instant longer. I had to find Arie, had to find Chase. I had to get away. But there stood Ruby, turning her head one way and then the other, watching her city in the mountain disintegrate. And she looked so tired, so worried.

"Ruby, I—"

"Go!" she cried without turning to me.

I didn't wait. I sprinted away. On the way back to my tent, I saw Woolly hustling in Ruby's direction. As he ran, he was trying to adjust the shoulder-straps of his bug-out pack, which looked absurdly small on his broad back. I slowed and watched him join Ruby. She had evidently ducked into her tent and got her worn bug-out pack, which now dangled from the crook of her elbow like an enormous purse. Woolly took the pack, grabbed Ruby by the arm, and turned to go. I ran on. Everyone else seemed to still be heading in random directions. The gunfire was getting closer and heavier. I smelled the sickly smell of diesel exhaust, and I heard barked commands that I knew had to be from Agency troops. Some massive and dark vehicle was pushing through the trees on the far side of the camp.

They weren't just close. They were in the camp. And surely they were already rounding up everyone they could, and those they couldn't round up, they were shooting.

As I came to the bend in the trail where my tent stood, I saw Chase. He had his pistol in one hand and my bug-out pack in the other. He tossed the pack into my path and I caught and shouldered it without breaking stride as we ran for our escape route. Chase fell in behind me and we ran like hell.

"Have you seen Arie?" I panted.

"He's ahead," he said. "Pick it up, Al. Run like you got somewhere to be."

To my amazement my stride lengthened, and I thundered so hard down the trail that by the time we caught up to Arie I'd put six yards between Chase and I.

"Pick it up, Chay," I hissed over my shoulder at him. "Run like you got somewhere to be."

Arie led the way. I followed him, and Chase followed us, keeping an eye out behind us.

"Know where we're going, kid?" said Chase, his voice calm, raised just enough for Arie to hear.

"Down the ravine and over the river," Arie said. He sounded calm, too. Good. I was the only one panicking.

The three of us pounded down the muddy trail. I couldn't remember the last time I ran so fast. My lungs burned but my pack felt light and I thought maybe I could keep going that way all day.

Because there was no way I was going back. They would never take me.

We went deeper into the forest. The sounds of the chaos in the camp became fainter. The rain fell steadily. When we came to the ravine, we slowed down some. The way down was a rocky staircase, but the rocks were slick with rain. We hopped down from rock to rock with care, but I knew we were making better time than in any practice drill. Soon we came to the river. There was a shallow ford there, a way to cross quickly without leaving any trace, and it wasn't easy to find if you didn't know about it. We stopped at the bank.

Chase crouched behind a big shaggy growth of intertwined bristlecone pine trees.

"You guys go on," he said, his voice very low, "like we practiced. I'll see if anyone's coming up behind. Go, go, go. Get across. Quietly. Quiet like mice. I'll be right behind you."

I clenched my jaw at the thought of leaving him behind, but this really was how we practiced. If we could get to the other side of the river, our chances of getting away clean were better. Arie stood looking at me. Chase nodded, and we turned for the ford.

CHAPTER 18

It was all my fault. I knew it. Everybody knew it.

That's why it was very good, in a very dark way, to be fleeing for my life deeper and deeper into the forest. Yes, I had to get away from the Agency troops, but it also meant getting farther and farther away from everyone whose existence I'd turned upside down, some of whom had almost certainly died. I wouldn't have to face what I'd done. No more pointing at me and whispering as I reported for dish duty. And I wouldn't have to discuss anything with Ruby. They wouldn't have to send me to another camp.

At least not anytime soon.

Because it would be a week or more before we could ever regroup. And how long after that before we could re-organize and begin to re-establish our camp? Winter was on its way and soon these mountains would be covered in fourteen feet of snow. We might be able to wait for spring at some other camp, if we could find one that escaped the Agency's notice in this latest attack, and even if we could, they might refuse us—winter provisions were always scarce. We'd been pushed so far into the wilderness, the nearest un-scavenged towns were now days away by vehicle—who knows how far on foot?

And these speculations were, of course, best-case scenarios, which assumed the camp leadership would not only evade Agency capture or murder, but also survive a stay in the wilderness for long enough to come back out of hiding, and the chances of this were particularly shaky with Ruby, who, when last I saw her, was moving at a velocity more associated with toddlers and tortoises. The more I thought about it, the more I realized just how grave things were for us.

So, I did the only thing I could think to do: I ran harder.

It was only when I felt that my lungs would burst that I finally stopped. Arie was ahead of me and must have noticed that I had stopped, because he did, too. He turned to me, his breath smoking in the damp air. I stood on the tiny game trail bent over, hands on my knees, gasping. A drop of sweat hung from the tip of my nose but would not fall.

"What's up?" Arie panted. "We stopping? You good?"

I couldn't draw a breath deep enough to answer, so I held up my hand and waved him onward.

"What's the matter?" he said, still breathing hard. "You hurt?"

Between breaths I said, "Just need—to rest—for a second."

"I could use a break, too," he said. "I'll circle back a ways. Stay right here."

Arie broke from the trail and stalked through the brush, working back the way we'd come. I stood up and put my hands on my hips and tried to catch my breath. A fit of coughing overtook me and I felt lightheaded. I bent over again and rested my hands on my knees. After two or three minutes, my breath came more slowly, and I felt like I could go on.

And then, from behind me—from only a few feet behind me—a man's voice: "Hands in the air."

I startled violently, and some primitive center in my brain almost triggered me to bolt away at a full gallop, but the voice was Chase's. I turned around to see him walking toward me. Arie was behind him. I gave Chase a hard shove. He chuckled, but I didn't.

"So?" I asked. "Anyone follow us?"

"I don't think so," said Chase.

"You don't think so?" I returned. "What's that mean?"

"It means I don't think they followed us."

"Do you think Ruby got away? And Woolly?"

Chase's face was dark and shadowed. "I don't know. But all we can do is assume they got away and hope to link up with them later."

I sat down on a fallen tree and took some deep breaths. Arie joined me.

"So, what now?" I said.

"Well," said Chase, "we can't just stop. We've only come a few miles. I don't think we have to keep running, but we ought to keep moving west."

"To where?" asked Arie.

"There's a ranger station not too far from here. I've never been there, but I've seen it on a map. And I've talked to someone who's been there."

"How far?"

"Well, only about six or seven miles, if I'm remembering the maps right."

"Oh, that's not bad," said Arie.

"No," said Chase, "but."

"But what?"

"But it's over that pass," said Chase. Squinting into the sun and pointing upward.

We turned our heads to look. Chase pointed to a saddle slung high between two rocky peaks.

"Oh heavens," I moaned quietly. "Can we even get up there?"

"It'll be a climb," he answered. "But I heard once there was a truck at the ranger station. Probably doesn't run. Anyway, probably take us a half day to get over the ridge. We'll need to go slow, cover our tracks as we go. We can try for it tonight and maybe get stuck halfway up in the dark, or we can hike to the base of the ridge, make a cold camp, and then climb over in the morning."

"I gotta get some water," said Arie. "Sounds like there's a creek down that draw. Anyone want a refill? I'm buying."

We got out our plastic bottles, drank the remaining water, and handed them to Arie.

"Thanks, Arie," I said.

"Yeah. Thanks, kid."

"No problem," said Arie.

"Hey, keep your eyes open," said Chase.

Arie gave us a thumbs-up without looking back as he headed toward the stream.

I sighed wearily.

"You okay?" asked Chase.

I nodded, trying hard to keep my composure and probably failing. My chin and bottom lip began to quiver.

"Wrong question," said Chase. "You're not all right, are ya?"

"This is all my fault," I said.

"Well—yeah," he replied, "but you didn't know any better. People who're scared do dangerous things."

"That doesn't help."

"Come here," he said quietly.

Now that I had my breath back and my legs were no longer rubbery with fatigue, all I wanted to do was dig a hole, climb in, and cover myself over. I wanted to be by myself so I could suffer without witnesses, but I knew I couldn't be alone. I wanted to feel the full weight and measure of my guilt, but I also didn't want to think about it.

Chase wrapped me in his arms. I buried my face in his shoulder and cried. I cried deeply and desperately—for what I'd done to Ruby, for what I'd done to everyone else. But there was something in Chase's embrace. I wouldn't say it was absolution, but perhaps a sense of safety, though I hardly deserved it. He blamed me for what happened, and perhaps at some point he would say so, and maybe he'd even hold me responsible, but I knew he was there to help me carry my burden.

CHAPTER 19

That evening we hiked very quietly and very slowly westward, staying on the faintest of the natural game trails left by the elk and deer. Every half hour or so we stopped and hid ourselves in the brush and trees. Then we'd spend ten or fifteen minutes watching and listening for any sign that someone was following us. Chase said we should even sniff the breeze for a stray whiff of cigarette smoke or the smell of a sweaty Agency trooper. Chase scanned the forest behind us with his binoculars. All the caution and paranoia had me feeling like we really were being followed.

We gradually neared the great flanks of the mountain and the approaches to the high pass we'd have to cross to leave the valley. Hopefully, on the other side, we'd find somewhere to hole up. When the sun set and left us within the cool blue shadow of the mountain, we stopped for the day and found a grassy hollow to rest for the night.

Each of our bug-out packs contained a small tarp and some cord. We stretched these between two trees to fashion a ramshackle shelter, then huddled close beneath it, sharing our collective warmth.

We had food, but not much. We each had a supply of dried berries, a little corn meal, and some oily pemmican that was grudgingly ingested only after vigorous chewing. Enough for four or five days, but Chase said we'd probably have to make it last for much longer.

"I can't see us finding any way to resupply for at least a week, probably longer. Might wanna chew real slow."

I'd hoarded away enough tea to last at least two weeks, but Chase wouldn't allow a fire.

"Not even to heat up a little water?" I pleaded. "Just to get warm so we can sleep?"

"No. Sorry, Al. Tonight, as the air cools, this breeze will turn around and head down into the valley. We make a fire and the smoke will lead anyone following us right to our front door."

Chase piled up a floor of dry brown grass that made our nest under the tarps slightly more comfortable and warm, but it wasn't even as comfortable as the cot I had in my tent in camp, which itself was quite rickety.

Still, we'd been on the move all day, and with the nagging shadow of paranoia that we might be followed or found, it felt good to at last lie down. With Arie to my left and Chase to my right, I suppose I got the best bargain in terms of staying warm. I put my head on Chase's chest and he wrapped an arm around me. Even though I was leaner and probably in better condition than I'd ever been in my life, I felt utterly used up for the day, and I dropped off in just a few minutes.

At some point very early in the morning, maybe an hour before dawn, I awoke. At first I thought Chase was still there with me. I thought I smelled him or felt him, but then I realized he was gone, and my head was resting on his coat, which was balled up like a pillow.

I sat up under the tarp. My eyes having been shut all night, they were well adjusted to the night. To my eyes, the little grassy hollow was as bright as midday, but instead of bright white sunlight, everything was awash in bluish and silvery starlight. I looked around. Arie was lying on his side, facing away from me, breathing in a deep and steady cadence. But Chase was not around. I crawled out from under the shelter and stood up.

Probably off taking a pee or getting some water, I thought. I put my hands in the small of my back and arched myself backward. My back made sad little popping sounds. I rolled my neck from side to side and it popped, too.

In the sky, the stars were brilliant and unthinkably numerous, like some whitish liquid flecked with specks of silver. I never tired of the sky in the mountains. But I was missing my little cot and everything lay in ruins. Above me loomed the ridge we'd have to climb in the morning. It seemed to head straight upward like a wall.

A few minutes passed, and I stepped away from the shelter to see if I could spot Chase. Had he left the shelter and was sleeping out here under a bush or something? Maybe I'd been snoring. Had he crept off for a pee and been nabbed by Agency troops?

"Chase?" I hissed. "You out here?"

I walked a circle around the makeshift tent where Arie lay asleep, but there was no sign of Chase. I quietly said his name again but there was no answer. My pulse quickened.

Then I heard something. I couldn't say it if was the snap of a twig or the crunch of grass underfoot—it was quiet enough to register only as a noise. There was another noise, louder now, and I turned in that direction. Was it the sound of a pine branch brushing on someone moving through the woods? Was it the sound of a boot scuffing on stone? I still couldn't tell, but now I saw something moving, too.

It was just a dark form among the other dark forms, but this had to be Chase, I told myself. It had to be him.

"Chase?" I said, almost too quietly for me to hear.

"Al?"

I let out a long breath and the dark form coming through the trees took shape.

"Al, what are you doing out here?" Chase whispered as he took me in his arms.

"What am I doing? What are you doing? Is there someone out there?"

"No, no, no," he said, looking back over his shoulder. "I was just making a little patrol. Doing a little security. Can't be too safe. Come on. Come back and lay down. We got a big day ahead of us."

As we went back to the shelter I looked back over my shoulder, too.

CHAPTER 20

I woke up sore and creaky from sleeping on the ground. It took me a while to get up and start moving around, but I was looking around for danger right away. I sat on a rock with my back to the sun. Arie had gotten up early and brought us all water from the nearby creek, but Chase still wouldn't let us have a fire.

"Chase," I complained, "I just need a little cup of tea. I'm not gonna be the same without it. It'll take like five minutes."

Arie nodded his head. "C'mon," he said, "don't be such a hard-ass."

"I'm telling you guys, it's just not a good idea," Chase said quietly. "One little wisp of smoke like that can be spotted from miles away. And another thing—we should keep quiet if we can. Keep your voices down and talk as little as possible."

"Why are you being so paranoid?" I asked. "We're probably ten miles from the camp and we haven't seen or heard another living soul in almost a day."

"I'm not being paranoid," he answered. "I'm being careful. And the way I'd put it is that we're only ten miles from the camp and it's only been a day since we saw a whole platoon of Agency thugs."

We ate a little breakfast, which was indistinguishable from what we had for dinner the night before. It wasn't particularly satisfying, and without the tea I really was feeling sluggish.

Arie sat with me in the sun, but we didn't say much. Chase went off to re-fill the water bottles and didn't return for something like thirty minutes.

"Where've you been?" I said. "I was getting worried."

"Just checking our backtrack," he said. "Just following SOP."

"For a half-hour?" I said. "Did you see anyone?"

"No," he said. "You guys ready to head out? It's up and over the mountain today. Quicker the better."

Arie and I stood up, scratching and stretching and yawning. We collected our things and took down the shelter and got our packs on.

"Look at this mountain for a minute with me," said Chase.

We looked.

"Okay," he began, pointing, "we will follow this incline up to the ridge, and we'll cross over that low point. See it?"

I nodded a little but I sort of shrugged, too.

"Well, do you see it or don't you? If we get separated, you're gonna have to make it up there without me. There's a low place along the ridge that I think we can get over with a minimum of climbing. Right there. Do ya see it or not? Arie, do you see it?"

"Yeah," I said, "okay, I see it. The little notch up there, by that big triangular rock?"

"Yes, that's it. I think there's gonna be some switchback trails heading up, but there might not be a trail leading all the way up there. From here it looks like there'll be a lot of scree and loose rocks, but I think we can make it. Once we get up there, we'll know more, but the point is we wanna go over the lowest point if possible and then get down the other side fast. Okay?"

Arie and I nodded.

"Good," said Chase. "Now, the other thing is that we're gonna be more and more exposed as we head up these switchbacks. There's not a lot of cover, not a lot of trees. So, we're gonna go fast and we're gonna go quietly. Minimal breaks, minimal rests."

"Fine," I said. "Let's get moving then."

"No, Al," stammered Chase, "listen, maybe I'm not being clear. We really need to get over this ridge quickly, and we need to do it without attracting attention."

"Attention from who?" I said.

"Yeah," said Arie, "attention from who? What's going on?"

Chase sighed and ran his hand roughly over his face. "All right, all right. I should tell you. Someone's following us."

"What?" I cried. "Who? Where?" I didn't know if I'd really been having the impression of being watched, stalked, but now it didn't matter.

Chase held up his hands to quiet me, then he held a finger to his lips. "I don't know who exactly," he said quietly.

"It's them," I hissed. "They've found us. They've followed us from the camp when they attacked. We're screwed."

Chase held his hands up more emphatically. "This is precisely why I didn't tell you. We can't panic. Besides, I don't think it's a full Agency detachment."

"Why not?" I asked.

"Because if it was, they'd've overtaken us by now. Or they'd have just shot us. Whoever it is, they're back there following us very carefully. I get the vibe that it's just one person. Like maybe he's trying to figure out what we're up to, where we're going. And that's why we gotta get over this ridge without being spotted. If we can get up and over, we might leave our stalker in the dust."

"Why don't we wait until dark, then?" asked Arie.

"I've thought about that," Chase replied. "But we've never been up and over that trail. I've seen it on a map, but without light, we could get lost or fall or go up a blind trail and then just have to come back down. Might be a big fiasco."

Arie looked up at the route. "If someone's following us, they're gonna see us before we're even halfway to the top of the ridge."

"Right," said Chase, lowering his voice to a whisper, "but I figured whoever's following us will have to show himself, too, in order to stay behind us. On that last long pitch."

He pointed. We looked.

"When we get to that point, there'll be no hiding for either us or him, or her, or whoever it is," said Chase. "Maybe if we get him up there on that last pitch, we could ambush him, turn the tables, and then we could find out who it is and deal with them accordingly."

"That's what you meant by us getting separated," I whispered.

Chase nodded.

"I don't like this," I said.

"Yeah," said Arie, "what if they don't even follow us? They could easily just watch us from down here, then follow when we get over the top."

"Good thinking, kid," said Chase. "If that happens, then we'll ambush them on the other side."

"They could pick us off with a rifle," Arie added.

"Nah, the closest shot they'd be able to take is at least 500 yards. And if that's what they were interested in, I'm sure they've been much closer than that before."

"I don't like this Chase," I said. "And why didn't you tell us?"

"I didn't want to cause a panic. We needed rest and I know you wouldn't rest with something like this on your mind. Hell, I even thought you'd up and run off and make things worse. You were running like a jackrabbit before—I was worried about even catching up to you."

"Fair point," said Arie, giving me a sideways glance.

I gave him a shove.

"Look, let's focus," said Chase. "We've been going slow and careful, and whoever's back there has been keeping a very respectful distance. I've already laid some false trails out of our camp. We're all well rested, and I think if we haul ass straight up the mountainside, we've got a good chance of getting up and over that ridge without being detected. If we're followed, we'll know it, and we'll deal with that."

Chase looked from my face to Arie's and we nodded.

"We together on this, then?" asked Chase.

"Yeah," said Arie and I together.

"Then let's boogie," said Chase.

CHAPTER 21

The first mile or so of the hike to the ridge was not challenging, and it ran along within the deep cover of forest at the foot of the mountain. The incline was gentle at first and we made our way along the trail as though we might be out on an excursion for wild forage. In fact, just off the trail, in the shady patches of grass, I saw a few scatterings of morel mushrooms that had sprouted after the recent rain. I recognized their tall, withered-looking caps, and I reflexively paused on the trail for a split-second to gather them. Then I remembered what we were up to. They were a real treat up there in the mountains, sometimes hard to find, and none of us in the camps ever passed them by. I laughed inwardly a little when I thought of how Chase might react if he came up behind me to find me picking mushrooms, even though he'd been the one who'd taught me to identify morels.

"You can eat these?" I'd asked.

"Oh, these are gourmet forest forage, Al," he'd told me.

"They look like evil baby aliens."

"Try one," he said.

I refused at first, but I later learned that they were truly delicious—raw or cooked.

When we emerged from the shady cover of the trees, the way became rockier. We jumped from boulder to boulder up a steep staircase of rock.

"Careful, now," said Chase. "We need to make good time through this section, but we can't do that if someone falls and breaks an arm."

With his long legs, Arie made easy work of the hopping and climbing, stopping and turning back to give me a helping hand.

As we progressed higher onto the face of the mountain, the trees and shrubs thinned out until there was no cover at all, and I realized what Chase meant about being exposed. Along this stretch of the trail we could look down into the valley, meaning anyone looking up could see us. We walked up the trail but kept our eyes on the terrain below and behind us. The sun rose higher in the clear sky, shining down hotly like a glaring, searching eye.

We came to a section of the trail where there was a flat place in the rock like a shelf where we could sit and hide ourselves from the view below. Chase signaled us to stop, and Arie and I sat down and took off our packs. Chase joined us as we were uncapping our water bottles.

"Good job, team," said Chase, his voice low. "We're making decent time. Anyone see anything down there? I haven't seen a sign of anyone."

"No, nothing," said Arie. "I've been hauling ass out ahead and stopping to watch while you two catch up. I haven't seen a bit of movement or anything."

"Good scout," said Chase, drinking from his bottle. "How about you, lady?"

"No, I haven't seen anything. Sure feels like we could be spotted easily, though. It feels like we're being hunted," I said. "But I don't know if it's real or if I just know."

"Yeah," said Chase, "I get it. That's the whole reason I stayed behind us and happened to see whoever it is that's following us. I just got this feeling. But I think we're doing good. Here's your reward." With this, he produced two handfuls of morels wrapped in a square of old cotton shirt. They were almost surely the ones I'd seen.

"Ahh," exclaimed Arie, helping himself to several of the mushrooms. "My favorite."

"I think I passed by these mushrooms by on the trail back there because I thought you'd yell at me for slowing down!" I told him.

"Well, yeah, matter of fact I probably woulda, but I'm at least glad your mind was on survival. Here. Have the rest."

Chase said we should wait an hour and then continue if no one came up behind us. Arie and Chase stared down the trail while I laid my head on my backpack and dozed in the shade of the advancing day. When Chase was convinced no one was coming up behind, we went on.

In the early afternoon, the sky clouded over again, and even the patchy shadows they cast made me feel a little better about walking up the barren switchback trails that led us higher and higher on the mountain. When we were a mile or so from the ridgeline, we stopped again and hid among the rocks to check behind us. This time Chase got out his battered old binoculars and glassed the valley below.

"See anything?" I asked.

"No, nothing," he said. He sounded almost disappointed.

"Is that bad?"

"I'm not sure. I was hoping to see something."

Arie chimed in. "If whoever was following us came up to our camp, we should have maybe glimpsed them down there somewhere. Is that what you mean?"

"Yeah," Chase answered. "I was hoping to see him following one of the false trails I laid the other night. Or I was thinking maybe he'd come up here and lose our tracks in the rocks and have to cast about a bit looking for us."

"But we don't want him to follow us," I said.

"Sure," said Arie, "but it'd be nice to get a good look at him. Make sure it's just one guy. Or gal. See how he's armed. See what we're up against."

Without taking his eyes from the binoculars, Chase jabbed his thumb at Arie as though to say, "What he said."

Chase continued to scan the forest floor with the field glasses. Then he handed them to Arie.

"Give it a good look, kid. Your eyes're younger than mine."

But Arie reported no sign of movement. I was happy for another rest, but I took a turn looking, too.

"Nothing," I said. "I see some deer, though. Wanna look?"

Chase sighed and sucked his teeth and put the binoculars away. "Well, I think we have to assume that we've either lost him, or that he doesn't want to follow us." He chewed the inside of his cheek for a few seconds and then said, "Let's keep going. Drink up the rest of your water. This last bit is liable to be kind of a grunt, and going down the other side won't be much fun, either. But there's a stream on the other side where we can fill up."

We put on our packs and took deep breaths and squared our shoulders. But Chase was right. The climb was strenuous and soon we were dripping sweat, despite some cloud cover that had moved in and the breeze that blew across the mountainside.

Arie came to a place where it looked as though we'd have to climb straight up a craggy face of rock. Chase and I caught up to him and we examined the way.

"If we back up and go up there," said Arie, panting and pointing back down the incline, "it might be easier than going up this."

"Yeah," I said, nodding. "Go back to that big slide and then cut up that way. What do you think, Chay? Will that be easier than this way here?"

He was nodding. "Yeah, I think that's where the trail is supposed to be. If there were hikers and hunters up here every summer, there'd be cairns to mark the right way, but those are long gone now. Let's go back. But let's hurry."

Chase led the way now. We scrambled back down the mountainside a couple hundred yards and found the faint line of a trail in what little dirt lay between the boulders and rock faces. It was likewise steep, but now we could see the way to the ridge and over it.

"Everyone feeling okay?" Chase asked. "This is it. We're almost over."

We nodded and flashed thumbs-up, but the final piece of the ascent took us through loose scree, and the footing was precarious.

Ruby came to my mind. She would never be able to make even the simpler parts of this trail, and I wondered with sudden despair if she'd gotten away. Where was she? Was she okay? Was she alive? All at once I wished I could see her, talk to her.

Chase stayed ahead of us and climbed to the crest of the ridge. He drew his pistol and looked over to the other side, as though someone might be waiting there in ambush. Then he beckoned us and we exchanged quiet little high-fives as we climbed over the knife-edge ridge.

On the other side, another valley lay below. It looked tranquil and lush and I could hear the distant roar of a steeply flowing river.

"The cabin's down in that ravine there, I think," said Chase. "Or the next one over. Been a while since I've seen the map, but there's the logging road. See it? All we gotta do is get to that road and it'll lead us to the ranger station. The accommodations will be better, that's for sure. From there we'll decide what to do."

We nodded to each other and smiled. The breeze blew over us. The way down the mountain looked rugged but not severe.

"Shall we go, then?" I chirped.

"Yeah," said Chase. "Hey, listen, you two. Great job today. Proud of you."

"Yes, I agree." It was a voice from behind us.

"You've done quite well," said the voice.

In terrified unison, we spun about.

Standing on a rock a hundred feet away and slightly above us stood a man. He took a few steps and emerged from the shadow of the mountain. His arm was extended, and he trained a pistol down on us. He looked to be on the short side, maybe only a bit taller than me, but very solidly built. He wore a uniform of some sort, but it was faded and worn to the point that it would be difficult to identify its origin. Even though we could see him, he seemed to blend into the backdrop of the mountain. His skin was browned deeply by the sun, and his head and face were cleanly, eerily shaved.

"Hands on your heads, folks," he said. "Right now, please."

We looked at each other. Chase nodded his head with weary reluctance and then laced his finger and put his hands on his head. Arie and I did the same.

"Good," said the man. The tone of his voice was steady, relaxed.

He was older than me and Chase. Perhaps by a decade or more.

"Spread out a bit, please?" he said. "Step away from each other."

He waved the muzzle of the gun as if to disperse us, and we complied.

"Thank you," he said. "Now, if you would, just turn around, face away from me, go to your knees, and then cross one ankle over the other."

We stood there looking up at him, our hands on our heads. Chase breathed hard through his nose.

"Do as I say, please," said the man. "I won't hurt you. If I wanted to do that, I'd've done it last night, while you were asleep."

I looked at Chase. His lips were pressed firmly together, and he had a look in his eyes I knew very well—it was the look he got when he was getting ready to do something sudden, crazy, and violent.

The man took a step in our direction, and he braced the pistol in his free hand, training it on Chase.

"Listen, you three. The weapon is fully loaded. Sixteen in the mag and one in the chamber." His voice was calm, as though he were giving us driving directions. "I am a well-trained and very experienced marksman. I can shoot all three of you before the first of you could make it to me. That is why I am standing up here."

Chase's chest rose and fell conspicuously. I could hear his breath pass in and out of his nostrils.

"Sir," said the man to Chase, as though reading his thoughts, "I have the advantage. Clearly. Please comply."

"What do you want?" said Chase.

"Right now? For you to comply. You don't really have a choice."

Chase let out a loud, heavy sigh. Then turned on his heel and kneeled down. Arie and I did the same.

"Thank you, folks," said the man. "I'm grateful. Now. Just remain still. Remember, I have no desire to hurt any of you. If I wanted that, I would have already done it."

I heard the rasp of his boots on the rock as he came down from his vantage to join us.

"Don't speak to each other, please," said the man, again with an almost aggravatingly relaxed tone of voice.

He came around to stand in front of us. The sun was in our eyes, and I got the impression he'd planned that, too. We squinted and blinked up at him. He maintained a distance I judged to be several long steps. He kept the gun pointed at us in a way that made me believe he could shoot us all before we could to our feet.

"Good afternoon," he said cordially. "My name is Colonel Steele." He spoke as though addressing guests at a luncheon.

Arie scoffed and clucked his tongue. "Seriously?" he said. "That's your name? Colonel Steele? Sure it's not Major Slaughter or General Mayhem?"

I shushed Arie.

The man raised an eyebrow, and by way of answer he tapped the right breast pocket of his uniform with his index finger. We squinted through the glare and sure enough the name *STEELE* was stitched there.

"There's one more thing I didn't tell you guys," said Chase with a heavy sigh.

"What?" said Arie.

"The guy who I said was following us? He's good. He's really good."

CHAPTER 22

Later that day, I finally got to have a cup of tea.

Colonel Steel had bound our hands with zip-ties, tied us together with a length of strong cord, and marched us back down the mountain.

"Who are you?" I asked as we walked down the trail we'd just climbed.

"I believe I introduced myself before," he answered. His reply was not sharp. It was matter-of-fact and almost friendly.

"Yeah, but who are you?" I insisted, turning back to address him.

"He's with the Agency, obviously," said Arie. "You're with the Agency, right?"

Steele didn't answer.

"You went over the ridge to the south," said Chase. "Didn't you? Got ahead of us and then came down to the trail where you reckoned we'd cross over."

"Yes," he said.

"Phew," breathed Chase, raising his eyebrows. "Nice work."

"Tell us why you're holding us," I demanded. "Who are you?"

"Let's just say I'm the one with the gun, and so for now I'll ask the questions," he said, as if patiently addressing an errant teenager. "So let's have no talking for a while, please. If you'll comply with that request, I'll maybe answer a few questions when we're back down off this mountain and settled in for the night."

Steele had sifted through our belongings and he'd patted us down very thoroughly, relieving us of anything that might be used as a weapon, even the string we used to build our tarp-tents, and including a pencil and some pens I had in my pack, but actual weapons, too—he found a small fighting knife Chase had hidden up his pant-leg, something not even I knew Chase carried. Our packs thus neutralized, he returned them to us with our supplies and water and provisions.

And so we walked in front of Steele, strung together like resentful livestock. The cord wasn't thick, but it seemed strong enough to hinder us from running off together, and I knew that Steele could have used it to pull us off balance if we turned on him. But it also got in our way, tripped us up, and we often stalled and pulled at each other awkwardly.

"Arie," I snapped, "slow down. You're gonna pull me off my feet."

"I'm sorry," he hissed back at me. "I'm not even walking fast!"

"Cool it, guys," said Chase wearily.

"Don't tell me what to do."

"All of you," said Steele in a firm voice. "Stay quiet, please."

That suited me. Oddly, I grew even more nervous than I was before, and the feeling that someone was watching or following us had not gone away. As we returned to the valley floor, I swiveled my head around, expecting to see someone following the man who'd been following us. It was a weird form of paranoia within a greater paranoia.

When we finally got off the mountain, not far from where we'd camped the night before, Steele halted our little pack train and, just before sundown, he built a fire that burned hot and with very little smoke.

And he let me brew some tea.

The tensions between Chase and Arie and me eased just a little. Arie and Chase regarded Steele with wary, hostile gazes.

"Ahhh," I sighed. "This is all I've been wanting for two days."

We ate our food in silence as it got darker. Steele would not remove our zip-ties (he said they were "getting regrettably difficult to come by these days"). But he removed the cord that strung us all together so we could move freely. He opened his large military rucksack, the fabric of which was patterned in camouflage but so frowzy and faded you almost couldn't tell what color. From the rucksack he brought out some chocolate-covered oat-bars and shared them with us. They tasted good, and freshly made, and they were packaged how I remembered Agency food was— wrapped in brown waxed-paper with terse, military wording on the labels: *OAT BAR, CHOCOLATE, 300 CALORIES.*

Steele sat with his back to a tree. He'd put a knit beanie over his clean-shaven head and he was reading a battered volume of Meditations by Marcus Aurelius. In a small tin pot he'd warmed up some kind of reconstituted soup. He blew on it to cool it.

"Thank you," I said to him, sipping my tea, "for the fire and the food."

He nodded, and after a while he put the book back into his rucksack and said, "If you're still hungry, please say so. I have some spare rations set aside for you."

"You said we could ask some questions," said Arie.

"You're right," he said quietly. "And you behaved reasonably well, so, yes. Ask your questions."

The three of us began all at once, asking three different questions all in unison, talking over each other. "Where are you taking us?" "Who are you?" "Why'd you take us prisoner?"

Steele laughed, and we stopped, paused for a few moments, then tried all at the same time again.

Steele held up a hand until we were quiet again and then pointed at me. "You go first."

"Well—we want to know all of that. Who you are, why you've taken us hostage, where you're taking us. Et cetera. Obviously."

"Of course," said Steele, nodding and setting his soup aside. "Uncertainty leads to fear, and fear leads to poor judgment. I'm not here to hurt you, least of all kill you, and I don't want any of you to do anything that will lead to any harm, especially to me, so I'll answer your questions to the best of my ability."

Chase and I traded a glance. He was so polite. For some vague reason, this was annoying to me.

"As I said," he began, "my name is Colonel Steele. I've been hired by an individual—I can't say who, of course—to apprehend the three of you and bring you in."

"You're not Agency, then," said Chase.

Steele considered this. "I'm a private contractor."

"Rachel," I said. "She hired you."

Steele didn't respond to this. His expression didn't even change. "As I mentioned, I'm not free to tell you very many details."

"How can you work for them?" sneered Arie. "You have to know what they do to people. It's inhuman. They treat people like animals. Not even as good as animals."

"I respect your opinions. I'm sure we differ on many subjects, but unfortunately, such disputes these days are most often resolved with force. There was a time when it wasn't that way, and I miss those times. I will say I'm glad you three seem reasonable and I haven't had to use much more than the threat of force. In any case, I've been hired to apprehend you, and I have to do my job, and I can't say much more than that. Speculate all you want. I can neither confirm nor deny."

I realized what it was about Steele's politeness that was off-putting. It wasn't that it came off as false or patronizing. It did not. It was very much the opposite—Steele was respectful and even genuinely kind when possible. This almost had me believing that everything would be okay. And that bothered me—I knew that everything would definitely not be okay and I did not want to be put at ease.

"Were you hired to round up anyone else?" I asked. "Anyone we know?"

Chase shot me a glance as though he thought I might give too much away. I returned Chase's gaze but then looked back to Steele and waited for his answer.

Steele pursed his lips. Then he shrugged. "Normally, I wouldn't respond to a question like that. Details, you know—you never know when a piece of information can be used against you. But I've taken a liking to the three of you, and I can't see how this can cause any trouble, so I'll admit I was assigned to take you three. No one else."

"Do you know anything about anyone else who was in our camp?"

"No," he said. I believed him.

"You're military," said Chase.

"Former, yes."

Chase furrowed his brow and said, "So, you came out of the Zones?" asked Chase. "Or you were in the Agency before and left them?"

"Neither. I've been on my own since Year One. I'm not in anything nor do I belong to any group. I serve my own interests."

"That's all we were trying to do," Arie complained, holding up his bound wrists. "We're all just trying to be free. We deserve to be free."

Steele looked at me as he jabbed his thumb at Arie. "Quite the revolutionary you've got here."

I tried not to crack a smile, but it didn't work.

"So, you've never been in the system?" Chase asked. "Never took the serum?"

Steele shook his head, took up his pot of soup, and sipped it.

"Well then you've gotta let us go," Arie cut in. "You don't know what it's like. They wipe your memories, make you into zombies. Slaves."

"I'll remind you that I can't remark on who hired me. You assume it's the Agency, as if that organization is the only one who might take an interest in you. I won't insult your intelligence by acting like I don't know what you're talking about. I know of the Agency. I sometimes take contracts from the Agency. But there are other, similar organizations and individuals. Some of which, I might add, are worse than the Agency."

"We know you're with the Agency," I scoffed. "We know better than anyone who's out to get us and who'd pay to get their hands on us, and we know what they'll do to us when they've got us."

"Well then," he returned with a relaxed shrug. "I suppose you have no further questions." With that, he gulped down the rest of his soup.

"You saw it all happen," said Chase with a tinge of what I thought might be envy. "You saw everything collapse, and you remember it."

Steele admitted this with a small shrug and nod. His admission didn't strike me as proud or superior. Again, his expression didn't change much. He seemed patient, conciliatory, but he didn't say more for a while. He only stared at the campfire. The reflected light of it flickered in his eyes.

After a few minutes, Chase said, "I think I know the answer to this next one. But I'll ask anyhow. Can you tell us about what happened? In Year One? Before and after? We've all been scrubbed, obviously, probably more than once. We don't remember anything. We don't know much of anything beyond the past few years."

Steele nodded some more and looked at Chase. Did I see envy in Steele's expression, too? All at once it seemed likely. Because of course Steele must have lost family and friends and comrades in Year One, just as we all had. But Steele hadn't forgotten a single face or moment from those times. That would be a burden of sorts.

I'd never considered that being free of memories, being free of the past, could be something enviable. I'd always considered it a vile thing to take away someone's memory, someone's true identity. Could it be that the Agency was correct in this one, twisted way? Did I really want to know what had happened to me in the back before? By some astronomical chance, I'd been reunited with Arie, and I'd found (or had been reunited with?) this man Chase. Wasn't that enough? Did I really want or need to know what happened before? Did I want to know what I'd lost?

As Arie and Chase and Steele continued to converse across the campfire, I thought about this, retreated into the questions. Did I want to know who I was or what I'd done before my last memory scrub? Did I want to know who I'd been before the first memory scrub? What regret and loss and irreversible decisions lurked behind those memory wipes? Did I really want to know?

Yes. I did. And, no, the Agency was not right. Not in this one aspect, and not in any other.

Because I wanted to know myself, wanted to know who I really was. If that meant recalling bad and painful things, I would find a way to own them. Had I not suffered pain already? And had I not owned those parts of myself? Indeed, my life since my last memory wipe had been largely pain and hard times and even regret—I thought about Ruby. No, I would have my memories, all of them, and I'd own them.

"The Agency surely told you some version of what happened," Steele was saying. "They had some kind of story they told you, didn't they?"

"It's a bullcrap version of the history," said Arie. "I pieced together a lot of the timeline from old media and snooping around, but even an accurate, detailed newspaper or magazine article is still just a single point of view, a single point of reference. And, of course, the news reports run out. As people died, as everything fell apart, there are no records of the very end. So, we have some information, but it's like there's this black hole in our minds, you know? Wondering how we ended up like this. Maybe not so much wondering what happened, but wondering what it was really like."

Steele was quiet for so long I wasn't sure he was even planning to answer. But then he drew a deep breath, exhaled, and said, "Yes. Yes, I know what you mean. I know many people who don't remember it all, who don't remember all the way back. I know some people who do. Not as many of us remember everything. What I can tell you is this: knowing everything that happened back then won't make you feel any better about how things are now."

I didn't believe that.

"Okay," said Chase, "but what else have we got to talk about?"

Steele stuck out his bottom lip, tilted his head, and raised his eyes to gaze into space above our campsite. Then he looked at us. "I suppose I could tell you a few things," he replied. But then he blinked and shook his head a little.

The sky was rapidly darkening to black and a sharpening chill was in the air. Steele rolled up onto his knees and placed a large, bleached-out log on the fire. It took flame and burned brightly.

"But it's gotten late," said Steele. "So, I'm sorry. Not tonight. On the other hand, we'll be on the trail for a few days, so, perhaps another time."

He stood. We looked up at him. Then he did a singular thing. He drew his pistol. There'd been no disturbance, no apparent reason to do it. And he drew the pistol with such quickness, I didn't even see it happen in the truest sense. There was a blur of motion, and in an instant the barrel of his gun was aimed directly at my forehead. I thew my zip-tied wrists up and turned my head away. Chase scrambled on his knees to place himself between me and the gun.

"What are you doing?" cried Chase.

"Hold still. Everything's fine. However, in situations like this one—multiple-captive situations—I find it prudent to periodically remind everyone of two very important points." He maintained a cool, almost charming demeanor. "First, while I am sympathetic to your situation and your disappointment at being captured, I will use deadly force if I have to. Second, although it's not exactly something to be proud of, I am very skilled at the use of deadly force, and I have a reputation for successful multiple-captive work. I don't mean to boast—if you'd had to work as long as I have in this occupation, you'd be just as good as I am. It's not bragging. It's a warning."

Steele holstered the pistol almost as quickly as he had drawn it, then put his hands on his hips. We stayed still. He calmly picked up a few branches of firewood and set them against the burning log. The fire gave off a pleasant warmth. I felt exhausted.

"I like you three," said Steele after he'd stoked the fire. "I can tell that under other circumstances, we might be friends. I'd like to have this mission over with as quickly as possible, without you coming to any harm. And me, too, of course. I don't want anything to happen to me. Once you're out of my custody, you can work on saving your skins or escaping or whatever else you want to do. Just—please, let me do my job. Okay?"

I nodded.

Then I felt myself getting very drowsy. Not just sleepy, but deeply tired. It had been a long day, but a profound need to lie down suddenly overtook me.

Through a mild stupor, I listened as Steele instructed us to retrieve our coats and tarps and make ourselves comfortable on the ground near a few large trees that stood close together a few paces from the fire. It would provide a little cover in case of rain, he said, and was still close enough to the fire to feel its warmth. Low grass and moss covered the flat area beneath the trees. We stood and shuffled in that direction. I felt as though I might fall asleep in mid-step.

"Hey," said Arie woozily, holding his bound hands up and pointing an accusing finger at Steele, "you drugged us."

"The oat bars," said Chase, nodding.

"Merely a sedative," Steele returned with a smile. "It's for your own good. But mainly for mine." He chuckled.

We went to the flat place among the trees and lowered ourselves groggily to the ground, spreading our tarps and wrapping ourselves in coats and blankets.

Steele collected our packs and set them near his own things. Then he returned and kneeled on one knee at our feet, where he began to tie something to my ankle. I blinked at him sleepily. My eyelids seemed to close and open again at a half-speed. It was the length of cord he used to keep us stitched together on the trail. I began to doze off, my eyes closing now and refusing to open again, but I fought it, trying to see what Steele was doing. He tied the cord around our ankles and then looped it over a tree branch and back to where he'd been sitting at the fire—it was a tripwire.

When he finished, he crouched by the fire and laid on another large log.

"I appreciated our chance to talk this evening," he said arranging the wood and banking the coals. "As you can imagine, this kind of work involves long periods of solitude. Even a short conversation is sometimes welcome, if it's pleasant."

I looked at Arie and Chase. Arie was lying still, apparently asleep already. Chase was scooting around, trying to get comfortable on the mossy ground.

As my eyelids dropped for the last time, I heard Steele say, "Sleep well."

CHAPTER 23

I dreamed of a Ferris wheel. A man at the turnstile of an amusement park put a colorful band of plastic around my wrist and I clunked through the gate and into the park. There were games and food and rides, and there was laughter all around. It was nighttime and the lights of the rides shone festively as they strobed and flashed. I walked through the crowd. There were families and couples and groups of young people. I came to the place where people waited in line for the Ferris wheel. When it was my turn, I sat in a gondola and a young lady in a sun visor secured the restraining bar over my lap, and then she worked a control on an instrument panel and the gondola went backward and up, backward and up. Other people got on the ride in the other gondolas, and then it was turning. I looked out over the amusement park, at the trees and the flashing rows of lights and the bars of neon on the other rides. Then I noticed that Chase was on the ride with me. He looked over at me and put his arm around me. He smiled and laughed. Then Arie was with me. Arie as a boy, Arie as a man. Then it was the three of us together. Soon the Ferris wheel turned very fast, like a bike wheel. I rocked and swayed as it moved faster and faster.

Then I realized it wasn't the movement of the ride I felt. Someone was nudging me. I felt the chill of the damp ground, heard the crackle of my tarp wrapped around me. Nudge, nudge, nudge. Someone's foot was nudging me, gently but rhythmically. Nudge, nudge, nudge, nudge, in the small of my back. Something hard, like an elbow or the toe of a boot. I tried to open my eyes, but my eyelids were heavy, and I felt as though I were emerging from some dark and deep cocoon. I'd been drugged, I recalled. The tarp crackled like a gigantic newspaper. My arms and hands ached from being bound so long. And I was cold.

I opened my eyes and lifted my head.

The sun was shining but, as far as I could tell, it had not risen. Everything lay in a cool purple glow. My breath smoked in the chilly air. I looked around, and as my surroundings came into sharper focus, I saw Chase's face. We were lying on our sides, four or five feet apart and facing each other. Chase had his bound hands up to his chin, and he held a finger to his lips. I blinked at him and nodded.

By way of reply, he parted his hands to show me they were in fact not bound. One of the zip-ties was broken but remained looped around his wrist. It looked like it had been mangled or chewed. He pressed his finger to his lips.

I nodded again and mouthed the word, "How?"

Chase bared his teeth and mimed chewing on the plastic.

How long had that taken? I wondered. I looked around for Steele. At first I couldn't see him, but then I spotted him thirty yards off, squatting in the undergrowth. He was looking idly around the small copse of trees where we were camped. I saw his bare knees, legs, and part of his bottom and I reflexively averted my glance when I realized he was relieving himself.

I turned my head and saw Arie—he was lying farther away, but he was on his back and I saw that his eyes were closed, mouth still gaping open, and he breathed deeply and steadily. My eyes returned to Chase. He was showing me two ends of the cords that Steele had used to make his tripwire. They were shockingly frayed and severed and soggy-looking. Apparently, he'd chewed through these, too.

I heard sounds coming from Steele's direction. He was standing now, pulling up his pants and fastening his belt. Next, he leaned down and picked up an armful of branches

126

he'd evidently collected before his bathroom break. I turned back to Chase with a questioning look.

With small, minimal motions, Chase pointed at himself and then he pointed in Steele's direction. Then he clenched his fists and made an angry face.

I shook my head and mouthed, "No!" but Chase closed his eyes and nodded steadfastly. I could hear Steele returning. Chase pointed at me, put his hands alongside of his cheek, and feigned sleep.

"Lie down," he mouthed.

I shook my head again.

Then Steele was at the campfire again. "Time to wake up," he said.

He dropped his bundle of branches near the campfire. I heard him poking at the fire. He laid some branches on the coals, and they began to crackle and smoke.

"I hope you all slept well," said Steele. "We'll have a hot breakfast this morning, and it's on me. It'll be ready in, oh, say twenty minutes. Just gotta get this fire—"

Chase sprang up and was sailing over the fire and across the space between us and Steele before I could draw another breath. I knew Chase could move fast, but I'd never seen him move like this before. I lifted myself from the brush to see.

Chase collided with Steele like a charging bull. He was larger than Steele, and I thought Steele would crumple under Chase's bulk like a kicked-over lawn chair.

But Steele was quicker.

He absorbed Chase's lunge, twisted, and hurled Chase to one side, flinging him headlong into a clump of scrub-oak as though he were a clumsy child.

With blinding speed, Steele produced a long, savage-looking knife. Again, I didn't see him draw the knife—it was almost as if it materialized in his hand.

Chase was getting to his feet, but Steele was on him in an instant.

I cried Chase's name and fumbled to my feet and ran in their direction but stopped short when I realized that Steele held the point of the knife at Chase's throat. Chase lay tangled in the brushy growth of scrub-oak. Steele was coiled on top of him like a python. He'd pinned one of Chase's arms with his boot, and he'd pinned the other with his free hand. The point of the knife made a small divot in the skin of Chase's neck. As best he could, Chase showed his palms, capitulating.

"Alison," said Steele, coolly, without taking his eyes from Chase. "Go back over to the trees by the fire and sit down, please. I don't know what you're thinking of doing, but the best thing to do right now is to sit down and stay out of this. I'm in control."

I did as he said, quickly. Then I said, "Chase?" I couldn't see him clearly from where I sat. "You all right?"

"Yeah," said Chase from his place in the brush, his voice full of disdain.

"That's right," purred Steele. "I'm going to stand up now. Chase, I'd like you to stay on your back, please. Now that we know who's the better fighter, the choice should be clear."

Chase must have signaled his agreement, because Steele stood up. He drew his pistol and pointed it down at Chase.

"You had a busy night," said Steele. "Gnawed through a zip-tie and my best para-cord. That's a new one. What'd ya do? Spit the oat bar out when I wasn't looking?"

"Yeah."

"Then you faked sleepiness and stayed up all night chewing on my zip-ties. Yes, sir. That's a new one." Steele nodded; the gun still pointed down at Chase.

I watched without moving or even breathing.

"Well, it wasn't a bad effort," said Steele. He shrugged one shoulder and smiled grimly. He hadn't raised his voice throughout the entire incident. He wasn't even breathing hard.

He calmly cocked the pistol.

"You know," he continued, "in the service, we were taught that escaping captivity wasn't just something we ought to try to do if we got a chance. We were obliged to attempt it. It was a standing order. So, I understand that you had to make the attempt."

Chase said nothing. I saw the steam of his breath rising from the scrub-oak.

"And we all knew you would go for it," said Steele. "I knew it, she knew it. Shucks, even the kid knew it, and he's still asleep. Unfortunately, I find it's best to kill captives who attempt escape. It's just a sound policy decision, one that's kept me alive for a long time. Because the prisoner who attempts escape will often try again. Right? That itch to try again is always there."

Chase remained quiet on the ground.

Steele released a heavy sigh. Then he thumbed the hammer of the pistol and let it down gently. "Lucky for you, it's obvious to me that if I kill you, I'll have to kill your friends, and I'm not fond of killing anyone, least of all friends, a family, I guess, is what you are. And, without easy access to conveniences like photography and DNA analysis, the methods of verifying the identity of a deceased captive have become limited and, well, very—" here he paused and sighed "—distasteful." He holstered the pistol.

I exhaled.

"However," added Steele, "if you try it again, you'll force my hand." Steele then looked at me. "You all right?"

"Yeah."

Steele bent and offered his hand to Chase. Chase reached up and Steele pulled him to his feet.

Steele looked up at Chase's bearded face. "How about you, big guy? You all right?"

Chase clapped the dirt and leaves from his clothes. "Yeah," he said, almost too quietly for me to hear.

"Nothing broken?"

"Just my spirit."

"Don't take it too hard," said Steele, giving Chase a friendly slap on the arm. His voice was genuine, kindly. Not arrogant. "You're reasonably quick. And you're definitely a big 'ole boy. But this is what I do. Truthfully, unless I'm confronted by a force of exceptionally overwhelming strength, I'm confident I'll consign the three of you without further incident. Now, could you have a seat over there, please, while I fetch another zip-tie?"

Chase rubbed his wrists and joined me by the trees where we'd slept. He collapsed disgustedly into a seated position.

Arie raised his head. Twigs and leaves were suspended in his long, tousled hair.

"What's up?" he croaked. "S'morning already? When did I even fall asleep?"

CHAPTER 24

I didn't get any tea that morning.

"In light of what happened," said Steele, "I hope you'll understand that we'll skip the hot breakfast this morning." But there was no anger in his voice.

"We were gonna have a hot breakfast?" said Arie as he stretched and brushed the duff from his hair.

"Feel free to snack on whatever rations you have," Steele added, tossing our backpacks to us.

As the sun came up, Steele marched us farther down the valley, and I knew from the ridgelines and mountain peaks which came into view that we were not too far from our camp, and that Steele was heading for the main highway. There was an eroded, crumbling remnant of a jeep trail in the vicinity that had run between our camp and the highway, but my guess was that Steele had sneaked into our valley on foot from the highway and probably had a vehicle stashed there to take us to Rachel. Or perhaps the highway was where he'd deliver us to the Agency and to the oblivion of their memory-erasing treatment.

I heard branches snapping far off to our right, up the hillside. It was a very faint noise, and could have been anything from a dead branch falling from a tree to a deer nibbling fresh shoots of grass from under the deadfall, but my eyes went there almost involuntarily, searching, trying to penetrate the thick undergrowth and trees. Was no one else hearing this? The impression of being watched had never really left me. At first I told myself that it was because we were near our old camp and I was expecting to see some of

131

our old camp mates or perhaps Agency thugs, but the feeling grew as we walked. I began to imagine movement in the spaces between the trunks of the trees.

"Colonel," I said, "do you know anything about the raid on our old camp?"

"Only that it happened," Steele replied.

"You weren't there?"

"No."

"Do you have any partners? Team members?"

"Can't say," he said.

"Where were you?" asked Chase. "When they attacked, I mean."

"Close by," he said. "Close enough to hear all the racket."

"All that 'racket'," I said, "was the sound of our friends being chased down, captured, and probably shot."

"You're right," Steele admitted. "Forgive me for my insensitivity."

Chase said, "There were probably twenty of us that could be called soldiers, combatants. The rest were just regular civilians. A couple hundred. Old people. Kids."

"I had nothing to do with that attack," said Steele, "but it is unfortunate. I'm sorry for your loss."

"But you're still taking us in," said Arie.

"Yes, young man, I am. We've been over this."

"You know," said Chase, "I think you'd fit in with us. I think we'd get along well. Ruby would love you. You'd be her new favorite."

"Thanks, but no thanks," said Steele.

We walked along. I could have sworn I saw movement in my peripheral vision. It wasn't just once. It wasn't just a trick of the light. I was going to try to somehow bring this up with Chase, but he wasn't through goading Steele.

"How long do you think you can keep this up, Colonel Steele?" he said. "I mean, if you think about it, you're really living on the edge here. This job of yours. It's hazardous.

You know? You could give it up and have a good life with us."

"I have a good life now," Steele replied, and I thought I heard something slightly defensive in his tone.

"Do you?" asked Chase, turning and walking backward to address Steele. "What? Sneaking around and 'apprehending' people? Constantly risking your neck to deliver prisoners to an organization like the Agency? And you say there are worse organizations? More murderous? How long until one of your prisoners gets lucky and gets the drop on you? How long till one of your employers turn on you?"

"Turn back around," said Steele.

Chase did, but he talked louder. "You don't know anything about any of us—what if we're innocent? What if we're the good guys? I mean—I got a feeling you know we're good guys."

"We're all good guys," Steele said. "Just depends on who's telling the story. Besides, we've been over this."

He was definitely getting defensive. This was new. I took a quick glance back at him.

He said, "We definitely differ in how we view the various forces and influences of the world as it is today. You fight your battles and I'll fight mine."

"Yeah, I think that's the point," said Arie. "We're fighting for a cause. You have no cause, no purpose, and every time you turn someone over to these 'employers' of yours, you're basically committing murder. You're not doing anyone any good but yourself."

"And just what makes you think you know anything about me?" asked Steele.

"You've said so yourself," Arie continued. "You said you work for whoever pays you."

"That's what we all do," answered Steele. "That's how life works. That's how it worked before, and that's how it works now. You wanted to know about happened in Year

One? Well, aside from a whole lot of people dying, not very much changed. We work. We get paid. We survive."

"No," said Chase. "You might work for a paycheck, but we don't. We're working to improve our lives and the lives of the people around us. We're not just doing jobs, collecting pay. We're trying to build something. At least we were before the Agency attacked us and you ambushed us."

Arie looked back over his shoulder at Steele and shot him a disdainful glare.

"That's just how you view it," said Steele. "You want to view the world and yourself a certain way, so you frame it that way with your words. You tell a story about yourself, and in that story you're the good guy. But you're still just working and picking up a paycheck. Just like me."

Arie scoffed loudly.

"Yeah, how do you figure that?" Chase sneered.

Without hesitating, Steele said, "Your sense of building a better world, and the gratification you receive from helping these people you speak of—that's your payment. You're taking that as your pay. You could have your pay in the form of coin or food or anything else. But you've taken your pay in a certain kind of companionship and camaraderie and the feelings you get from fighting for a cause. But it's still just a transaction."

Chase and Arie gave no answer.

"You have a family," I said. I waited to say it until there was a switchback in the trail so I could look him in the eye without having to turn around. I looked him in the face. "Don't you? You're a family man. You do this for them."

From the moment Steele captured us, the look on his face had been one of utterly cool composure. Even in tense moments, like when he first took us as prisoners, or while he subdued Chase by holding a knife to his throat, Steele's face was a serene mask, as if none of this were any more challenging than making a peanut butter sandwich. Now, however, for the first time, Steele's gait faltered, he slowed his pace for a few steps, and a surprised and uncertain aspect flashed across his face. This lasted only a moment. Had I not been hoping it would happen, I would have missed it completely.

But I saw it.

So, I thought, he's not just a cold-blooded bounty-hunter or hired killer. He has someone in his life. There were so many people in this world we lived in who had no heart, no soul, no feelings. Steele wasn't one of them.

Then the moment passed. Steele's confident stride returned, and his face was the inscrutable mask once more.

"And what makes you say that?" Steele said, trying hard to sound less-than-completely interested.

I couldn't see him now, but I continued. "You're too human for this job. You said yourself—it's something you 'have' to do. You wish you didn't have to. But like you said, it's what you're good at, and you think it's the only way to keep your family safe."

I turned my head quickly to see his face again. He was gazing at the trail, lips pursed. The bill of his cap screened his eyes.

"So is it your family, then?" I asked. "What's left of it? Or is it the people you adopted after Year One? How many are there?"

I looked back at him again. Arie and Chase did the same.

"I'm gonna need you all to keep your eyes forward," said Steele. "Last thing I need is for one of you to stumble and turn an ankle."

"Uh huh," I said. "Whatever you say."

"And let's walk awhile without all the chatter," Steele added.

"Nice job there, babe," whispered Chase with a chuckle.

CHAPTER 25

Hiking through the woods, arms bound and strung together, and with Steele at our backs was much more tedious and fatiguing than all the fleeing we had done after the Agency attack days before. My wrists and arms burned and ached, and the paracord jerked and tripped us, which made it difficult to walk properly, but it was more than that. It doesn't matter what you remember or what you've forgotten, there is something about involuntarily being under someone else's control which is onerous, taxing, exhausting.

And hateful, too.

On the morning of the second day, Chase was feeling it acutely, I could tell. I could see it in the stiffness with which he walked, the way he stole looks behind him, and scanned the trail ahead. I knew he wasn't satisfied, wasn't ready to give in and let Steele hand us over to the Agency like sacks of some commodity. Just as Steele predicted, Chase needed to scratch the itch, needed to try his luck again. I was feeling it, too, the restlessness of the captive, but Steele was too ready, too quick. I couldn't think of any plan that didn't end with somebody dead; maybe all of us.

Steele had done an exceptional job of putting us at ease at first, almost becoming a friend to us, but I knew our time with him was almost at an end. He had told us we'd be on the trail for "a few days," and the terrain we crossed agreed. We'd descended out of the pine and spruce forest and now we saw more aspen and tall grass and I knew we weren't more than a day and a half from the road.

"May I ask a question?" I asked as we hiked.

"You can ask anything," said Steele.

"Do you have a security team?"

"Security team?"

"Yes, is there someone out here with you? Following us?"

He thought about this as we continued down the trail a hundred feet or so. Then he said, "I suppose I'm not opening myself up to any risk if I tell you, no, I don't have a security team. I work alone. Why do you ask?"

I weighed the risks of telling him what I was thinking. "I just feel like we're being followed. I keep hearing things. Or I think I do. And seeing things, I think. Is it just me?"

Steele slowed his pace and looked around at the hillsides to either side of our trail. "No," he said. "It's not just you."

It was around seven in the evening when Steele halted us as we crossed a lush meadow near a small, spring-fed pond.

"We'll stop here for the night," said Steele, "camp up there on that rise." He pointed.

We turned off the trail and climbed the low hill. There were trees for shelter and a small, clear-running stream nearby. We were still strung together, so we all sat down in the shade of the trees, just at the margin of the hilltop, which was covered with waist-high grass. Steele surveyed the area and took a long drink from his water bottle.

Chase had almost gotten a knife in the throat just the day before, but I could see the furtive glint in his eyes again. His gaze roamed restlessly, and I knew what it meant. He was looking for an opening, any bit of leverage. I gave him a stern, prohibitive glare, but he pretended not to see it.

Steele said. "Well, if you three will gather a little firewood, I'll make dinner tonight and give you a break from your seeds and berries. Agreed?"

"Agreed," said Chase abruptly, "but if you'd take this cord off us, it'd be about ten times easier, and it'd happen about a hundred times faster."

"True," answered Steele, "but pardon me if I veto that plan. You chewed up one my best lengths of para-cord just the other night."

"Yeah, and I'm really sorry. But like you said, I had to try. I tried, and I failed. You win. Just take the cord off and I promise you won't have to gather a stick of firewood tonight."

I would have shot Chase the glare again, but Steele had his eye on us and Chase wasn't even looking my way.

"Yeah, come on," Arie joined in. "It's really hard just to walk down the trail all tangled together like this, let alone pick up a bunch of firewood."

Steele looked from one face to another. "All right. Turn around and kneel down. But no funny business."

We did so, and he removed the cord. Then he backed away, and we stood up together to go hunt for fuel.

"Alison," said Steele, "you stay here, please. Stay with me. We'll take a break and let these two gather tonight's firewood."

Chase and Arie shrugged and then went off into the grassy area, bending now and then to pick up branches and twigs and logs.

Steele watched them as he unshouldered his rucksack and leaned it gently against a tree. I took my pack off, too. I sat in the grass while Steele kicked a few fist-size granite stones together to form a small fire ring.

"Chase is right, you know," I said. "About you living on the edge."

"I take risk-management very seriously," he said, arranging the stones with the toe of one boot.

"So, you really don't have any partners or team mates out here? Watching your back?"

Steele shook his head, and I saw the muscles of his jaw pulse. He looked out on the grassy area where Chase and Arie roamed in their search.

"No," he said. "I honestly do work alone."

I believed him.

"But you're right," he added. "We're not alone out here."

A half-hour later or so, Chase and Arie came back out of the grassy meadow with big armloads of branches and logs.

"Wow," said Steele. He was kneeling at the ring of stones he'd made, fashioning a little bird's nest of tinder and kindling. "I'm impressed. Well done."

"Where ya want it?" asked Chase.

Steele jabbed his chin at a clear, flat space across the fire ring and said, "There."

Arie dropped his armload where Steele had indicated. It landed in the dirt with a clatter. Arie sat down by the fire ring. Chase dropped his firewood, too, but when the branches and logs had fallen from his arms, one stout log remained, grasped in his fists like a baseball bat.

Steele had only a split second to realize anything was wrong before Chase was swinging the log in a swift, powerful arc. The log looked dense, heavy, and sound. Steele was only just beginning to react when the log connected with his shoulder and neck. The sound was unpleasant. Something in Steele broke or tore or shattered, and this time it was he who went tumbling onto the ground.

Chase pressed his advantage, moving in quickly and placing his feet for another heavy swing of the log. I thought I heard him growl savagely. Arie and I were scrambling to our feet to assist. Chase had already drawn the log back for a blow that I judged would lay Steele out cold and insensible, but Steele would not be over-matched.

His pistol was in his hand. He was so fast. He leveled it at Chase.

There was only six feet between Steele and Chase, and there was no way someone like Steele would ever miss, even if the distance between them was ten times what it was. Steele fired the pistol.

Not at Chase.

Not at Arie or me.

Steele fired the pistol at the enormous brown shape that had emerged that instant from the tall grass of the meadow twenty yards from our would-be campfire. He fired at the enormous bear that barreled at us like a speeding, runaway train. Chase dropped the log and turned around. Arie turned around. I felt the pounding of the bear's furious gallop in the ground beneath us. I'd never seen such a display of animal speed and power.

The bear was more massive than the four of us combined, a full-grown male grizzly, and he was on us in only a second or two. But even in that flash of nerve-freezing terror, the bear's swift, bounding grace was impressive, beautiful. He crossed from the grassy margin to the firepit in an eye-blink. Steele may have fired his pistol again; I'm not sure. If he did, it had no effect on the bear. There was cursing and screaming and the sound of a huge animal snarling with fury. Dust and dry grass swirled in the air. The bear swung a massive forepaw and Chase was flung out of sight. The bear swung again, and I was airborne, tumbling. I landed roughly in the trees some fifty feet away and when I came up again, I saw the bear looming over Steele. Chase was back on his feet and sprinting in my direction. His eyes were wide and crazed, but he'd apparently had the presence of mind to grab Steele's large military rucksack on his sprint away from the bear.

As I watched him approach, I saw Arie get to his feet and run in my direction, too.

Steele was on his back and the bear was pressing in, snapping with his long fangs at Steele's arms and legs. The man seemed tiny beneath the animal, but he kicked mightily at the bear's snout nevertheless, delivering solid blows with the heels of his boot that certainly would have caved in the skull or ribs of a grown man. To the bear they were nasty swats that made him squint and flinch like a dog smacked with a rolled-up magazine.

The bear reared up as if he would stomp Steele to a pulp with his front legs, but Steele had animal quickness of his own. He rolled backward, out from under the bear.

Chase and Arie reached me, and we cowered like primitive humans by the trees, just fifty or sixty feet away from where Steele faced the bear. All we could do was watch. Steele was on his feet now. His face was streaked with blood and dirt, and he bled freely from a gash in his head, probably from where Chase had struck him with the log. His uniform sleeve was torn and dark with blood, too, perhaps from being clawed or bitten by the bear.

But Steele had put a few paces between himself and the bear, and he held his long knife in his fist. He side-stepped and circled and backed away from the bear, feinting then angling away from the bear like a boxer. The bear lunged repeatedly, swinging his massive paw at Steele, but Steele was quick, dodging the blows by the narrowest of margins, angling out of the bear's path like a toreador facing a bull. And so they circled. Steele held his combat knife at the ready. I remembered how long and murderous the weapon had looked when he held it to Chase's throat. Now it looked tiny. I wondered if he could hurt the bear at all with it.

As we watched, Steele's eyes darted to mine. In that moment I knew that Steele was ready to admit that the "force of exceptionally overwhelming strength" had indeed arrived, and that his mission had failed.

I could not help but feel a terrible pity for him. In this world, which had gone so hopelessly savage, here was a man who had maintained his dignity, humanity, and kindness even as he escorted Chase and Arie and I to what was certain doom. He'd shown us more compassion than he really could afford to. I wondered about his family, or whoever it was he cared for, whoever it was that depended on him. I knew they were somewhere waiting in vain for his return.

With a deft motion, Steele flipped the knife in his hand so that he held the point lightly in his fingers. Then, with a quick sideways snap of his arm, he flicked the knife in our direction. It whirled through the air, end-over-end. I thought it would hit Chase square in the face, but it instead buried its point in the tree we stood next to.

"You three better take off," said Steele without taking his eyes from the bear.

Chase grabbed the knife and tore it from the tree, and then he took two or three steps in Steele's direction. But I grabbed him by the shirt and yanked him back.

"He's finished, Chase," I growled. "He's trying to help us."

"She's right," said Steele. "The jig is up. My time has come."

Chase looked back at me and I knew he felt the same stab of pity.

The three of us traded a quick, soulful look.

And then we ran.

CHAPTER 26

And so we found ourselves running yet again. Chase had cut the zip-ties from our wrists, and we made good time going back up the trail we'd just walked down earlier that day. We stopped to look down the trail periodically, but we said little to each other. We had left our own backpacks behind, but Chase at least wore Steele's large military rucksack on his back.

A few hours later, as the sun got low, we reached a grassy place by a creek where we could camp. We stayed by the trail for a while, watching to see if the bear, or by some miracle Steele himself, would come along. Then we opened Steele's big military rucksack. Inside it we found rations enough to last the three of us at least a few days. There was also a bottle with a water filter and other survival essentials. We found a syringe and the drugs Steele had used to dose us. There was even a very well-used but also well-maintained Swiss Army knife.

"Dibs on that," Arie said.

Chase said, "I suggest we camp here tonight. Then, in the morning, we go back to where the bear attacked."

"Out of the question," I cried.

"Yeah, why would we wanna do that?" said Arie.

"We're gonna need our supplies," he said. "We've got some rations here and a Swiss Army knife and a water filter, but we don't have any for shelter or our rain jackets. Steele's got a rain coat in here, but we can't all three wear it. It's getting colder. Without our shelter stuff, we're gonna freeze our asses off tonight as it is, and if one good snowstorm comes along, we'll be in deep shit."

"I don't know about this," I said.

"I also want to know what happened to him," said Chase.

"Yeah," I replied. "I do, too."

And Chase was right—we spent a very cold night without our tarps and coats and blankets. But it turned out Steele was not kidding about making us hot breakfasts and dinners. He had freeze-dried soup and oatmeal and even some dehydrated fruit. The next morning, we ate a hearty breakfast and then set out.

Being able to walk freely, without the cords and zip-ties to slow us down, we made it back to the site of the bear attack in just a few hours.

I had a surreal sensation as we approached. It was quiet, peaceful. Chase had Steele's knife in his hand, but I only recalled how small it looked as Steele faced the bear.

We walked slowly toward the flat place by the grassy margin where we would have camped. Chase was in the lead and he stopped before we got there. He was looking down, studying the ground. He pointed—my bootprints. We took a few steps. He pointed again—his own bootprints, and some of Arie's. We went a little farther. The firewood Arie and Chase had collected lay scattered, stepped on. More prints. Chase's, Steele's, mine. Then we came to the place where Steele had faced down the bear. We saw the bear's tracks and the prints of Steele's small boot. Chase crouched and pointed. The prints overlapped. There were dark patches in the soil—blood. Smears of blood on the grass.

Chase followed the confusion of prints through the dirt. There was crushed grass and brush and more dark patches. Then Chase stopped and put his hands on his hips.

"Well?" I asked.

Chase shook his head and shrugged. "I don't know. There's no body, obviously. No human body and no grizzly carcass."

"Well, do you think he's dead?"

"The bear or Steele? Either way, I'm not sure. I mean there's blood here. Right there. More back there, and there. But none of these are like a big kill site. There'd be lots of blood if either one of them died. And there'd be drag marks if the grizzly hauled Steele off."

"Look what I found," said Arie, behind us.

We turned. He held up Steele's pistol.

"That doesn't bode well for Steele," I said.

"Any ammo in it?" Chase asked.

Arie removed the magazine, then racked the slide. A bullet was ejected from the pistol, which Arie deftly snatched from the air. He'd become quite an expert in guns and fighting and other brutish arts; my feelings were mixed about that. He examined the magazine, then said, "Fourteen in the mag and one in the chamber."

"Two shots," said Chase. "So he fumbled the piece when the bear hit him, and he never got it back. That does not bode well for him at all. Poor bastard."

Arie joined us. Along with the pistol, he'd found all three of our small backpacks. They appeared to be intact. I looked inside mine.

"Ah, my tea," I said, removing the small cloth bundle and pressing it to my nose.

We spent an hour crisscrossing the grassy hilltop and along the creek looking for Steele or the bear or any additional signs of what might have happened. We even called Steel's name and listened for any response, but both combatants had left the arena.

"Could he really have just gotten away from that bear?" I asked when we regrouped and prepared to go. "It was so huge, so fast."

"Well, I couldn't have gotten away," Chase reasoned, "and you couldn't have, and any other mortal human probably could not have gotten away. But that guy? I guess I wouldn't put it past him. And the signs and tracks definitely do not indicate that he was killed here."

145

"What if he's still around?" asked Arie. "What if he finds us?"

"I don't think we need to worry about that, kid," Chase said. "He's totally unarmed, for one thing, and I know I gave him a good walloping with that tree branch. The bear knocked him flat on his ass, too, which surely didn't do much for his health. He's lost some blood, maybe a lot. If he really is still drawing breath, he's busted up and at least no threat to us."

"And what about the bear?" asked Arie.

"A more serious threat, for sure," said Chase, nodding. "But we know Steele got two shots off before he lost this pistol, and he never struck me as the kind of guy who missed at that range. Those little 9 mm rounds weren't enough to stop the bear in its tracks, obviously, but even a grizzly feels a nine-millimeter bullet when it hits center-mass. My guess is that he's holed up somewhere he feels safe, and he's gonna need a few days to get back on his feet, too."

"So," I said, "they fought to a draw."

Chase nodded.

"Okay," I went on, "then let's head for that ranger station and see if there's a vehicle we can use to get us back to Agency turf."

Chase looked at me. "Agency turf? What are you talking about?"

I looked between Chase and Arie. "So we can get the antidote," I said, "get our memories back."

Chase furrowed his brow. "You still think there's an antidote?"

I nodded. "Yeah, I do."

"But that Bellington guy," said Chase, "he tricked you. Told you what you wanted to hear."

"I know. I know."

"So, why on earth are we going back? To follow-up a ridiculous pack of lies?"

"Chase, I know this may not make much sense, but I have a feeling. A gut feeling. I think what he said was true."

146

Chase's expression was contorted with incredulity. "Huh? You just said—"

"I know, Chase. Just listen. Yes, I think he told me what he knew I wanted to hear. He told me what he had to tell me to get away, but I have this deep-seated feeling that what he told me was the truth. He told me the truth because he knew it would sound truer than anything else, and he told me the truth because he thought I'd never have the chance to take advantage of it."

"That's a lot to bet on a gut feeling."

"How can I convince you?"

"I'm not sure you can," he said. "But that doesn't mean I won't follow you."

"Really?" I said, putting my arms around his neck.

"I don't know. Let's talk about it when we're off the trail."

"If we can get the antidote, and if we can join up again with Ruby and the others, it might help to make up for this disaster I've caused."

Chase seemed to both nod and shake his head. "Let's just get to the ranger station and then we'll figure things out from there later." The way he said it reminded me of a parent placating a child who'd asked for a treat. "Later" was just a soft "no."

I looked at Arie, but he nodded in agreement with Chase. "Sounds like a plan," said Arie.

"Okay," said Chase, "but I want to do something, first."

He unshouldered Steele's rucksack and removed the heavy paracord, the water bottle, the rain jacket.

"What're you doing?" I said.

"Leaving Steele a little care package if he comes back here." Chase opened up his own small backpack and into it he stuffed Steele's water bottle, filter, raincoat, sleeping bag, and the chocolate-covered oat bars. "It's all stuff we don't need," he added, "I'm not eating those oat bars—they're probably dosed."

147

Arie reached into his pocket and produced the Swiss army knife. "Here," he said, holding the knife out. "I should give this back to the poor guy if he's still out here somewhere all tore up by a bear."

Before Chase took it from Arie, he asked, "You sure? I mean he'll probably never even find this."

"Yeah," said Arie. "I'm sure."

"Tell ya what," said Chase. "If we're gonna give him a knife, let's give him a knife." Chase produced the big survival knife Steele had bequeathed us. "You keep that little folder, kid. I've got my own Buck knife back and this big pig-sticker of Steele's doesn't have a sheath."

Chase dropped it into the small backpack with the other articles and closed it up. He then tied the paracord to the backpack and tossed it over a tree branch about twenty feet up. He secured the loose end of the cord to a tree trunk so that the backpack was suspended fifteen feet or so off the ground. The pack was red—anyone coming to the hilltop would notice it eventually.

"I guess it's the least we can do," I said with a shrug.

CHAPTER 27

After all the running, stumbling, consecutive nights of sleeping on the ground, stale rations, inadequate rations, rations with drugs in them, and on top of it all, the specter of being turned over to the Agency once again, we were disheveled and hollow-eyed.

"I feel like I've been dragged by the feet behind a train," muttered Chase.

Even Arie, usually out front and practically jogging up the trail, was trudging more than hiking. I felt especially filthy, as though I were coated in a layer of fine, dark dust. Grime had worked its way into the creases on my hands and fingers, and my elbows were sooty-looking. My clothing stank.

It was early morning when we wearily prepared to again ascend the high ridge and cross into the adjacent valley. I hadn't slept well. I'd drifted in and out of a light doze, hearing twigs snapping in the night and glimpsing the shadows of huge forms stalking through the trees. I'm sure I'd dreamed or imagined it all, though I certainly didn't feel that way at the time. Chase and Arie looked similarly sleep-deprived.

Still, I arose that morning feeling grimly eager to be underway.

"Think we can have a fire this morning?" I asked Chase.

He chewed the inside of his cheek and scanned the woods surrounding us. "Yeah," he said. "I don't think there's anyone out here anymore."

"I'm glad you said that," I said with a yawn.

149

"Why's that?"

"Because I was gonna make some tea no matter what," I said, gathering some tinder.

Chase laughed quietly. "Well, I only said yes because I want some, too."

We cooked up more of Steele's oatmeal, and I shared my tea with Chase and Arie. My supply was running low. How would I get more when it was gone?

After we'd splashed our faces in the creek and refilled our water bottles, we got on the trail. Having already walked this trail once in each direction over the past few days, we made it to the top swiftly, easily, crossing over the ridge before the day had even warmed up. That's another outcome of living rough for long periods—even though you feel grimy and tired, you begin to forget the comforts of indoor life and adapt to your surroundings, becoming a sort of forest creature, only partially civilized.

Once over the ridge, we picked our way down the opposite mountain face, still making good time despite our fatigue. Chase once again pointed out the fold in the terrain where he thought the ranger station stood. It looked to be about a full day's walk from where we were, though it would be faster if we found the logging road. The hope of (at the very least) a roof over our heads seemed to lift all of our spirits. I was feeling a reserve of energy from somewhere. I didn't know where it came from, but I was grateful for it and picked up my pace. In fact, I was beginning to again feel hopeful that we could pursue the plans we'd laid.

We hiked into a long, narrow valley. The stream widened here and cottonwoods and aspens grew to either side of it. The sun was beaming down, and I had one of those rare and welcome moments where the surroundings you've become so familiar with suddenly strike you as stunning. I made a suggestion.

"Hey, you guys," I said. "Hold up for a second."

Arie and Chase stopped on the trail and looked back at me with weariness showing starkly on their faces.

"It's pretty hot out," I said.

They shrugged, nodded.

"Well," I continued, "the stream is right over there. Bet it's got some nice sandy pools in it."

"Yeah? So?" said Chase. "Whaddya wanna do? Go swimming?"

"Yes," I said. "Yes, I do. I haven't had a bath since before the attack. Fact, I can't even remember when my last bath was. I feel like I'm covered in dirt. We're making great time. Let's have a bath, sun ourselves dry, have some lunch, and then hit it hard again."

Chase looked to Arie, as though disbelieving it was me who was being laid back and not one of them. They both chuckled and took off their backpacks.

We stripped to our underwear. The water was freezing, almost glacially cold, but we found a shallow bend in the stream with a large, flat floor of granite, and here the water slowed and the sun warmed it up enough so we could sit in it without shivering too violently.

And so we washed ourselves and our clothing. I became more relaxed than I could remember being in a long time. We even had a water fight. I rinsed my hair again and again, and I scrubbed my hands and feet with sand until they were clean and soft and wrinkled. I brushed my teeth with the pulverized end of a willow twig, as Chase had once showed me. Soap and shampoo and toothpaste would have been nice to have, but it was so lovely to be at least rinsed clean with river water. I began to consider myself an actual human being again, rather than the primitive forest-dweller.

I draped my clothes on the scrub-oak, where they steamed a little in the heat. Then I climbed onto a big rock with a large flat surface tilted toward the sun. There I lay on my belly, sunbathing like some vacationer. The rock was warm against my bare stomach and thighs. I lay my head on my arm and closed my eyes.

Chase and Arie joined me.

"Hey," I protested, "this is my rock. Go find your own."

Arie set my freshly filled water bottle next to me, within arm's reach.

"Thanks, kiddo," I said. "You can stay."

Chase swept my hair from the nape of my neck and rubbed my shoulders with his large, strong hands.

A moan escaped me, almost involuntarily, as he kneaded the stiff, knotted sinews.

"Mmm," I purred. "Okay, you can stay, too."

Arie sat with his bare back to the sun, idly scanning the little valley with the field glasses.

"Any sign of large, murderous animals?" asked Chase, "or bald-headed, lethally skilled little bounty hunters?"

"Nah," said Arie. "Nothin'."

I breathed deeply and began to doze a little as Chase rubbed my back. A light breeze passed through the trees. The aspens shimmered and made long, soft whooshing sounds, their leaves beginning to turn brown and gray here at the close of summer. Mountain ravens clucked and quarreled. The ever-present water-dippers cried and darted up and down the river. The river sang its endless song of white noise.

Chase had massaged a fair amount of the fatigue from my back and neck and shoulders. The warm rock had dried and warmed me. I turned onto my back. Chase lifted one of my calves, cradled it in his lap, and began to massage my foot. I flinched at first, but then my eyes rolled back into my head.

"Oh my gosh," I moaned. "That is heavenly. What did I do to deserve this pampering?"

"Shh. Just rest."

I did exactly as he said. He rubbed one foot and then the other. The pain was exquisite.

"Hey," I said to Chase, "Don't think you can pamper me into taking a day off. We need to get back on the trail."

"Who, me?" said Chase. "Never."

"Hey, Chase," said Arie.

"What's up?"

Arie held out the field glasses. "Here, take these and look—" he pointed "—over there, across the stream, by that tall dead tree."

Chase took the glasses. Arie pointed. Chase peered in that direction.

"See anything?"

"No," said Chase. "Oh, wait." He looked a moment longer, rolling the focus knob on the glasses. "Good eye, kid," he said, lowering the glasses. "We're not alone."

"That's what I thought," said Arie.

"What is it?" I said, sitting up. "The bear?"

"No, no," said Arie. "Look over there. By that big tree."

Chase handed me the field glasses, and I swept them over the valley. I wasn't very good at looking through field glasses, but with a little more direction, I saw what they'd seen.

A tent.

And what looked like a camp chair.

Our clothes were still damp, but we hastily dressed and put on our packs, glancing repeatedly toward where we'd seen the tent. We didn't speak. Chase kept his pistol in his hand as we crossed the stream on a snag of waterlogged fallen trees. Arie had Steele's pistol at the ready. Even though we'd been laughing and splashing around in the stream only a couple hours earlier, we crept like cats to the big dead tree. Behind a brake of cottonwoods and undergrowth, there was a flat, narrow clearing. They kept the pistols ready.

Then we saw the tent. Secluded and well away from the trail, it was a perfectly screened and almost charming little area, perfect for a small campsite. And the tent was erected almost as if the campers wanted to avoid being seen. Only by the faintest random chance, using binoculars, had Arie spotted it.

But it had been standing there for many years, abandoned.

The tent was roomy, the two- or three-person variety, with lightweight aluminum poles arched across one another. A rain-fly was stretched over the outside. But it was just the ghost of a shelter now, sun-faded from its former bright colors to a kind of blue-gray. The fabric was dry-rotted and deteriorating; thready shreds of it moved lightly in the breeze. Around the bottom hem of the tent there grew generations of black lichen and mildew that spoke of multiple seasons of rain and snow and heat.

The camp chair was also of the ultralight, packable type, and it had also sat there for years upon years. Blades of wild grass grew up through where the canvas seat had rotted away. There was an old ring of stones for a fire, too, but its remnant of scorched firewood was now almost obscured by a lush growth of late-summer wildflowers.

I walked around the tent, lifting the sagging rain-fly and looking into the mesh windows.

"Found the campers," I said.

The forms of two people lay wrapped in a two-person sleeping bag inside the tent. They looked to be spooning each other. There was no smell of death, nor even the musty odor of the very long dead. The couple must be have died here long ago, mere bones by now. The way the sleeping bag had been pulled up around their shoulders, their heads and faces were mostly obscured from view, and they appeared to be only sleeping. And they'd cuddled so long in their nap, grass had sprouted in the tent around them.

"Did they freeze to death or what?" said Arie peeking into the tent.

"No," I said. "They've been here for years and years, probably since the back before. I bet they had the virus and got sick out here and died."

"Yeah," Chase agreed, "this has been here for, what, eight years? Ten? Not a bad place to be for the end of the world, I guess," he added.

Arie wandered away, surveying the rest of the camp. I stared into the tent. Shreds of rotted fabric waved in the

154

breeze. I had to admit the couple looked cozy, contented in their eternal mountain sleep.

"Why are we going back?" Chase mumbled, almost as though he'd meant to say it to himself.

"What do you mean?" I asked. "Why are we going where?"

"Back," he repeated, louder. "Why are we going back to the Agency?"

"Because they've got a treatment, Chase. The memory treatment. We have a plan."

"Yeah," he said, "but why? Why are we always on the run here and there and all over hell? Why not stay here? Build a cabin—" he turned and surveyed the valley "—right over there, maybe? Or there, on that hilltop? It's got a southern exposure. We can catch fish, eat wild strawberries, hunt rabbit and deer, maybe grow some potatoes. We might find a dog somewhere. Train him as a watchdog. Why's this such a bad place to spend the end of the world?"

Nothing he said was unreasonable. But that's not what I wanted. "No, Chase," I said. "We've got to keep going. We can't change the plan now, here, in the middle of the forest, with winter coming on."

Arie came over. "We're changing the plan?"

"No," I said, without taking my eyes from Chase.

Arie stood there, questioning.

"No," said Chase, holding my gaze. "We're not changing the plan."

"Well," said Arie, looking from my face to Chase's. "Okay. Then let's keep going."

"Yeah," said Chase. "I just wanna look around before we get going again. Make sure there's nothing here we might could use later."

He and Arie kicked around at the backpacks and gear bags moldering into the ground and at first, he found nothing.

"Well, they packed light," said Chase. "Good for them."

155

Arie picked up a rotted backpack, but it was empty and encrusted with mud and duff. He dropped it again. "Yeah, nothing much here. It's all rotted and ruined."

Then Chase shouted, "A-haaaa!"

"What? What?"

From the grass and brush, Chase unearthed a large metal tube or case.

He clapped the dirt that clung to it. Then he unlatched the closures, opened it, and inside there was a beautiful fly-fishing rod and reel. It had been inside its weatherproof case all these years and looked like it was perfectly ready to go fishing. Chase grinned like a little kid.

"We dine on trout tonight," he said.

CHAPTER 28

That day just before nightfall we continued down through the mountain valley. We were refreshed and in lighter spirits than before, but Chase was quiet. I wondered what he thought of me and my plans.

We reached the ranger station. Indeed, there was a vehicle there, out in a shed next to the main building. But it was a decrepit military jeep so old it looked like it had last been driven during the Korean War. It lay under a heavy tarp and a thick coating of dust.

Chase and Arie pulled back the tarp and raised the dust into a dense, choking cloud. They opened the hood. The ancient hinges made a pained squawking noise. Dust motes wafted and turned in the bars of sunlight that fell in through a south-facing window. Arie turned on his flashlight and they checked out the engine.

"She looks like she's intact," said Arie with a cautious shrug. He pulled on some cables and rubber hoses. "Electric looks good. Belts look all right. It all just looks really old."

"Well," said Chase, "hop in and see if she'll turn over."

Arie got behind the wheel and pressed the push-button starter.

The thing roared to life.

But only for about three seconds. Then the engine chugged to a stop. Arie tried again, and the engine turned over once. And then it did nothing.

"Battery, probably," Arie said.

Chase nodded with a look of deep disappointment.

"Been sitting here for who knows how long," Arie added.

"Let's eat some dinner, get some rest," suggested Chase. "See what we can do about it in the morning."

There wasn't much of anything useful in the ranger station itself, but there was a large fireplace made of stones, and there were actual beds—sort of. They were ancient bunk beds made of angle-iron and springy, metal fabric. Some were equipped with musty old plastic-clad mattresses. I didn't complain a bit. Anything was better than sleeping in the dirt again.

Everything was very dusty, but Arie and I found a broom and some desiccated towels, and so we did some housecleaning while Chase went off to try his fly rod on the nearby stream. He came back after dark with several trout as long as his forearm. He'd also collected a few armfuls of firewood.

"Let's eat!" he cried.

Built into the big rockwork fireplace there was an iron grill that swung in over the andirons. Arie made a fire and Chase dressed the fish with some salt from Steele's supplies. We ate a huge dinner of roasted trout fillets and dried fruit.

There was no furniture in the place except one wooden chair so rickety that none of us dared sit on it. Instead we dragged the mattresses from the beds onto the floor and sat around the fire to eat. It was only fish and salt, but it was surprisingly delicious. I ate till I thought I might burst. My body seemed physically grateful for the infusion of fat and protein. I could almost feel my tissue repairing and restoring itself.

Still, when Chase offered me a third helping, I said, "I couldn't eat another bite. But I do think I'll brew up some tea."

"I'll take some more fish," said Arie.

"Eat up," said Chase, serving him more of the pink, flaky flesh.

After dinner, we lay on the mattresses by the fireplace, staring sleepily into the flames.

"So, you can get that jeep running?" I asked Arie.

"I think there's a good chance, yeah," he said. "We can push-start it. We can try, anyway. First thing in the morning, we'll give it a go."

"Let's just hope it's got some gas in it," said Chase. "And that all the other parts hold together."

Arie nodded and looked intently into the fireplace.

Chase stood up like he'd all at once remembered some important thing. Then he moved around the room as if he'd set down his wallet or keys and wanted to find them. He lit a candle and held it up while he studied the floor. He pressed on the floorboards with his toes. Now and then he turned on his flashlight and shined it on the floorboards. He banged the heel his fist on the wall.

"What are you doing?" I asked.

"I just remembered. I once heard a rumor about this place," he said. "Guy I knew in the camp told me something. That guy Brett. No—Burt. Remember? The tall guy with the really thick glasses that were basically just all tape and wire?"

Arie said, "Oh yeah. Brett. He was nice."

"Yeah, he told me a secret about this place. I'd almost forgot."

"What is it?" I said.

"Well, hang on and let me look around," he answered, still searching. He banged the wall again. Then he rapped it with his knuckles. "Did he say it was the wall or floor?" he muttered. He stomped on the floorboards, searched the floor with his flashlight again. This went on for fifteen minutes.

"What is it, Chase?" I said. "Either tell us what you're looking for or come back to the fire."

He snapped his fingers. "The fireplace!" he said.

He came to the hearth and ran his hands along the stonework. After a few more minutes he said, "Bingo!" and removed one of the large stones from its place in the mortar.

This he set aside and then he reached into the void it left. He felt around inside.

"What's in there?" said Arie excitedly, getting to his feet.

Chase grinned and produced a long-necked bottle made of dark glass.

"Oh my gosh, is that wine? Real wine?"

Chase flashed us a broad grin.

We got our tin camp cups out without saying much.

"Ah, hell," said Chase, his shoulders slumping. "We don't have a corkscrew."

"Yeah, we do," said Arie. He pulled out Steele's Swiss army knife and flipped open the corkscrew.

"That doesn't mean you can have any," I said. "You're too young."

"Ah, c'mon!" protested Arie.

"A sip," I said.

We laughed. Arie passed Chase the knife and Chase opened the bottle and held the cork to his nose. He passed it to me. It had a dark, fruity aroma, like cherries or blackberries, but smoky, too. Chase examined the bottle as he let the wine breathe.

"*Gianni Paoletti Cabernet Sauvignon*," he read, sounding out each word as he turned the label into the fire's flickering light. "I'm not sure this pairs well with fish and dried prunes. But, holy smokes, it's from nineteen ninety-nine!"

I gasped a little. To think we would drink something so old, and that it might still be delicious not just decades later but after an entire changing of the world. I suddenly grew very thoughtful. Here was an expression of civility and culture that I couldn't recall, created long before the world I knew, back in the back before. Chase and I were just kids then, and Arie hadn't even been born. And yet here it was, hiding in these mountains, waiting for us, a firm reminder that our past was real, that it existed, that it could be found.

And that's when the answers to Chase's questions came to me. Why keep going back? Why the risks? Because this dusty cabin or a late-summer mountain valley did not have to be the end of the world. Why keep tangling with the Agency and flirt with having my few memories yanked again? Because we had the ability to start over. It was possible. With the secrets the Agency held, we could remember, and with those memories we could tear the Agency down and re-boot the world and start again. We could have the lives we truly deserved. The mountains and the camps we built and the earthy lifestyle we lived were often beautiful and fulfilling in their way. But that wasn't our objective. We wanted to live free, safe, and happy. And obtaining that was worth almost anything.

"That should be long enough, I think," said Chase. He poured for each of us.

Before we drank, Arie held up his cup. "Aren't we supposed to drink to something?" he asked.

We chuckled and then we were quiet for a moment, thinking.

"To remembering," I said.

Chase and Arie smiled and nodded.

"To remembering," said Arie.

"To remembering," said Chase.

Our cups clinked in the firelight, and we drank.

If I'd been a connoisseur of wine in the back before, I didn't remember much about it now. I didn't know or remember how to talk about how the wine tasted, but that meant it was, necessarily, the best wine I'd ever remembered. It was rich, complicated, and satisfying.

Arie, on the other hand, wrinkled his nose at the taste.

"Did it taste better in 1999?" he asked, sticking out his tongue and setting his cup aside.

Chase and I laughed.

The fire popped and cracked and collapsed into orange glowing embers. Arie wrapped himself in a blanket and fell asleep.

Chase lay next to me and I leaned into him. He put his arm around me and pulled me close. I felt warm, and the warmth felt hopeful.

"Chase," I said, turning my face to his, "I don't want to live in the end of the world. I want to live in the beginning of it."

He thought about this for what seemed like a long time, but I knew he understood, and I think he felt the same way.

After a while he picked up his cup and said, "I'll drink to that."

CHAPTER 29

We slept late. For the first time I could remember, I slept past dawn. It was just too irresistible. I justified it by telling myself I was recharging, healing, recouping my strength for what was to come.

It was warm in the cabin; I was lying on something that was almost exactly like a bed, and I felt safe. So the sun came up, and I opened one eye to see its rays coming in through the windows, but I turned over and kept sleeping. I didn't wake again until I absolutely had to get up to relieve myself.

Chase and Arie had the same idea. I heard them rise, go outside to pee, then return to their beds. I got up and built a small fire, but in the name of conserving my reserve of tea, I did without my morning cup. Instead, I sipped hot water to drive off the chill and then ate some of the dried fruit. Arie and Chase soon joined me, and we dressed and made our way to the shed.

"Let's check it out as best we can, first," said Arie. "Check the plugs and fluids and everything."

"There's a tool chest right over there," said Chase.

"Yeah, we'll check out what we can. I'm not what you'd call a mechanic. I mean, squeeze, bang, blow—that's about the extent of my expertise."

"Same here," said Chase with a shrug.

"If it seems like there's a chance that it'll run," Arie went on, "we'll push it out onto the road. Then we'll pack up all our stuff and get it rolling and then pop the clutch and hopefully be on our way."

"What if it won't run?" I asked.

Arie tilted his head and shrugged. "Guess we keep walking."

"I've got a back-up plan," said Chase, biting his upper lip.

We looked at him. "What is it?" I asked.

"Let's check her out and then try getting her started, first," said Chase.

The guys fetched the tools and lifted the squeaky hood again. I packed our gear into the backseat and then watched them, trying to learn something. I hated to be the girl who didn't know anything about cars, but not much of it made sense to me. I could build a fire with only flint and steel. I knew my way around a gun. But there just weren't that many chances to work with cars, and so it was a bit of a mystery to me.

For an hour, the guys moved around the jeep, disassembling and opening up various covers and cowlings and plates. They peered into hoses and banged on various parts with a wrench.

"This gas gauge is obviously wrong," said Arie, tapping the little circle of glass on the instrument panel. "It says it's full, but the tank is obviously not. And the gas might not be any good."

"Yeah," said Chase. "But it's got at least some gas in it. We'll just have to see how far it takes us."

They took off the distributor cap. They removed the spark plugs. They yanked on the fan belt. I had a fuzzy sense of what these parts were and what they did, but I wouldn't know if they were in working order or not.

Arie got underneath the jeep and looked around.

"Looks good," he said, though it was almost a question.

Finally, they put everything back together, slammed the hood, and shrugged at each other.

"I can't see anything that's obviously busted or missing," said Arie, clapping the dust off his hands. "It really should run."

"You probably know more than me," said Chase, "but I think you're right. Let's give it a go."

"Mom," said Arie, "I think you should be in the driver's seat."

"Yeah, you're good with a manual transmission, Al," said Chase with a smile. "Trust me, I know."

"I just put it in first and then pop the clutch?"

"Wait 'til we've got you going fast," said Arie. "Like a slow run."

"Slow run," I repeated. "Then let the clutch pop out?"

"Yep."

They pushed me down the logging incline. But the road was uneven, and the jeep had practically no suspension. It was like driving on square wheels. I bounced around in the seat, barely able to hang onto the wheel. I pushed in the clutch. The jeep bounced wildly. I somehow grabbed the stick shift, but I couldn't find first gear. The jeep was going faster, now. The guys were barely pushing it at all.

"Now! Now!" they cried.

I tried to say "I can't find first!" but I was bucking and bouncing in the seat so furiously it just came out as gibberish.

"Pop it! Pop it!" shouted Arie.

The jeep reached a steeper incline and gained speed. I fiddled with the shifter, groping to find the pathway into the gear. The guys gave the jeep one last big shove and then let go, but they ran alongside panting. The jeep gradually pulled ahead of them as they shouted for me to pop the clutch. I finally found what I thought was first and slammed it into gear. Then I released the clutch, and the jeep slowed suddenly, as if it had hit a wall of gelatin. It threw me forward in the seat and crushed me against the steering wheel.

But it started.

The engine turned over a few times and then started.

It sputtered and chugged alarmingly, and a big plume of blue smoke billowed from the exhaust, but the engine was running.

Arie and Chase jumped onto the jeep and gave it some gas. The engine coughed like some old jalopy. The guys hooted and cheered, and I put it in second, and we wound down the logging road.

And then the engine stopped, and we sputtered to a halt.

No one said anything for a few seconds.

"What happened?" asked Chase.

"Just stopped," I replied.

"Damn," said Chase.

"It's fuel," said Arie.

"Think so?"

"Yeah. Just kind of a gut feeling, but it sounds like it's out of gas. Maybe it's the fuel filter, or the pump, or maybe the gas in the tank is just too dirty or jellied up."

Chase nodded. "We could siphon up some gas from the tank and pour it right down the carb."

"Yeah, that's what I was thinking."

They tried that idea. And some others. They took a few more things apart. We tried pop-starting it again. And with every try, they got the motor to start up briefly, but it always died again.

"It's something simple," said Arie. "Something just barely above my pay grade."

"It's the fuel pump," said Chase. "Like you said. Or the filter."

"Well," said Arie, wiping the grimy sweat from his brow with his shirtsleeve, "it's getting late. Too late to be monkeying around with this heap."

"What's your back-up plan, Chay?" I asked.

Chase nodded, capitulating.

"Okay, look," he began. "This logging road goes pretty steep downhill, right? Why don't we just coast this bucket of bolts as far as we can?"

I hadn't thought of that.

"Just ride it down the hill like a giant go-cart," Chase went on.

Arie and I nodded at each other.

"This logging road connects with a highway," he said, "way down the mountain. Probably a good eight, ten miles. And I'm not sure, but it's gotta be downhill most of the way. So, we stick it in neutral and coast."

Arie and I nodded. "Then what?"

"Then," Chase continued, "we go west on the highway 'til we find the cut-off that leads to our old camp."

"Why go there?" Arie asked.

"Because the way I figure it, ole Steele has a vehicle somewhere around there."

"Yeah, that's what I was thinking, too," I offered.

"He had to have some way to haul us off, right?" added Chase.

"Yeah."

"So, I'd be willing to bet he's alive. He's a tough little turkey, but I think he's like the old grizz—he's resting somewhere up there in the mountains until he recovers from his beat-down. So, we roll downhill in the jeep, hit the highway, head west, and search the area for Steele's ride. Considering how he was outfitted, I bet it's a pretty nice set of wheels."

"Then we better get going," I said, "while we still have some daylight."

CHAPTER 30

The plan wasn't a terrible one. We coasted down the rocky and bumpy logging road for several miles. Sometimes the road was very steep, and I rode the brake pedal so we wouldn't careen out of control. Other times the grade was rather gentle and we would almost run out of momentum before reaching the next steep part. But we jostled along, and it was a beautiful day, and we made progress. The guys were doing most of the hard work—I was enjoying myself.

Then, inevitably, we hit a longer level stretch of road and the guys hopped out and pushed the jeep along until the road inclined and we were off again. But as we came down out of the mountains, there were fewer and fewer long downhills, and there were even several slight uphill pitches. Now I was getting out to push, too, staying by the driver's seat and pushing with one hand on the fender and the other on the steering wheel.

"This isn't fun anymore," I complained.

"Yeah, it's less and less productive," said Chase as we began rolling to a stop. "We might have to ditch this old bucket soon."

After a short downhill pitch, the road leveled out again, and the jeep slowed. We jumped out quickly and pushed, trying to keep it going. Arie and Chase were both panting hard by this time, and they looked tired. Sweat darkened their shirts. We leaned into the task and the jeep rolled along.

"How far do you figure we've come?" I asked.

"I don't know," panted Chase. "Maybe six miles, I guess. At least five."

"Wrong," I said. I was breathing hard, too. "You're not far off, though."

"How do you know that?" he said.

"She's been watching the odometer," said Arie.

"Yep," I said smugly.

"Why didn't I think of that?" gasped Chase. "Okay. How far have we come, then?"

I grinned. "Guess."

"Ten miles," said Arie.

"Way off."

"Nine?" guessed Chase.

"Eight."

"Ah, well, that's not so bad," said Chase. "The road can't be much farther."

"No," I said.

"Let's push to the next downhill, ride it as far as it goes, then leave this old heap behind."

I was about to agree with him, but we had come to a section of the logging road that passed through a narrow place with hillsides close on either side, and in the gap ahead, four men stood pointing hunting rifles in our direction. The weapons looked old and rusty.

"Ya'll can stop right there," one of them shouted.

Arie stopped pushing the jeep, but Chase, at the rear of the jeep, had evidently not heard the man and was still pushing. Arie walked along and watched the men. I jumped into the driver seat and pressed lightly on the brake.

"Chase," I said in a low voice. "Stop."

Being at the back of the jeep with the sound of the wheels on the gravelly dirty road, Chase apparently didn't hear me, either, and when I pressed on the brake, he strained hard to keep the jeep rolling, both hands on the spare tire bolted to the back of the jeep. In fact, he pushed harder as the jeep stopped. He put his whole weight into it, grunting and straining with his head down between his shoulders. The men in front of us were now just fifty feet ahead, and they brought their rifles to their shoulders to aim down the barrels.

"Hey, what'd we run into up there?" croaked Chase, still vigorously pushing against the motionless jeep. "Rock? Log?"

"Chase!" I turned and shouted at him.

His head popped up from behind the spare tire. "Oh," he said when he saw the armed party. His chest was heaving and his face was smudged with grime. "Hey, fellas," he said with an arch grin.

"Get away from my truck," said one of the men. He was tall and gangling, with long hair that hung lank about his bearded face. His voice was rough and baritone.

"What, this hunk 'a junk?" Chase sneered, still breathing hard. "Doesn't even run."

"I know that," the man answered. "I'm planning to fix it up."

Arie and Chase scoffed in unison.

"It's a hundred years old," said Arie.

"Never you mind. Just shut up, put your hands in the air, and tell me who you are."

"Well," I asked, "do you want us to shut up or tell you who we are?"

The gangling man opened his mouth, but he said nothing, his mouth working, waiting in vain for the retort to arrive. Instead, another of the men, this one short and squat like a fire hydrant, stepped forward and shouted, "Just shut up and get offa that jeep! And getcher hands up!" This one's voice was rather high and squeaky.

We held up our hands and moved away from the jeep.

"Who are you guys?" said Chase. "You're not Agency, and we're obviously not, either. I'm thinking we're on the same team, here."

The short squat fellow held his rifle on us while a third man searched us. They took Chase's pistol and Buck knife from him. They took Steele's pistol from Arie, and they piled our packs and other belongings on the ground alongside the trail, arranged like some tiny yard sale.

"If we was on the same side, you wouldn't be stealing my truck," said the tall one, poking our things with the muzzle of his decrepit rifle.

Arie rolled his eyes and said, "You know, it's a jeep. Not a truck."

"We didn't know it was yours," said Chase, bemused. "And, frankly, I'm still not convinced it is. It was sitting up there on the hill ten miles away under two inches of dust. Doesn't belong to anyone. Might as well say you own that tree over there. Or the ground."

The tall man stormed over to Chase and poked him with the barrel of his rifle. And again his mouth gaped open to retort, but before he could speak, Chase snatched the rifle by its barrel, wrenched it away from the man, and tossed it easily aside, where it clattered into the dust of the road. Two of the other men hastily pointed their rifles at Chase's head. Then the lot of them fell into shouting and shoving and threatening.

Arie got into the middle of it, too, and I suppose I could have easily picked up the thrown-aside rifle, but instead I placed my index fingers between my lips and did the loudest horse-whistle I could manage. They paused their shoving and grabbing for a moment to swivel their heads in my direction.

"Listen," I hollered. "Everything's cool. We're with Ruby. You know, Ruby?"

They stared blankly.

"Central camp?" I continued. "It was raided by Agency thugs, in case you haven't heard. We've been on the trail ever since. We really are on the same team. I'm Alison. Okay? That's Chase. Ever heard of us? Chase has probably even been to your camp. Right, Chase?"

Chase nodded. "Yeah, most likely."

"Well, tell them—aren't they part of our collective? Haven't you met these guys?"

"Maybe," Chase breathed.

My face reddened as I considered that maybe these were Agency soldiers. If that was so, I'd just given them some useful intel and an invitation to ask for more.

But they didn't look or act like Agency troops. Not at all. No uniforms, no military weapons, and no discipline. And it wasn't as though every Agency goon or trooper I'd ever met was a super-genius or tactical prodigy, but these guys were just dimwits.

I wondered if we should try to make a run for it. Grab the gun, fire a few warning shots, then high-tail it to the trees. After several camp attacks and fending off wandering raiders, all three of us were good at both fight and flight. We'd catch them off-guard. I glanced at Chase, knowing he was thinking the same thing, or that he would catch my meaning.

He caught my glance, but he shook his head—nearly imperceptibly, but sternly. "Bad idea," he was saying. Arie sent the same message with only the look on his face.

"We ain't never heard of you," said the tall one, trudging over and lifting his rifle from the dust.

The others stepped back and trained their rifles on us again.

"Okay, well, do you know Mac?" said Chase. "He still runs your camp, I assume."

Their faces darkened, and there was a jittery nervousness in the way they glanced at each other.

"Mac's dead," said the short one after a quiet interval.

Chase shot me a look. He said nothing, but I knew what he meant: "Not now. Not good."

CHAPTER 31

They herded us with their absurd hunting rifles into their camp, a hike of two or three hours. As we stopped to drink from the stream, Arie and Chase and I tried to coordinate a whispered plan, but the dimwits shushed us, and we were quiet until we reached their camp. If it bore any resemblance to the camps we established with Ruby, it was only in the strictest sense. It was a camp. It had tents and firepits and a few crappy chairs, but it was untidy, squalid. The tents leaned and drooped, unkempt and ragged, and there were piles of debris and food leavings here and there, over which swarms of flies and ants held sway. And instead of manicured trails running efficiently from place to place, the vegetation of this camp had been generally trampled flat, and in the bare soil there were puddles of brackish, standing water.

The people we saw wore a sullen, miserable aspect, and they regarded us with a suspicion that bordered on open hatred. Most of them were armed, too. This was unusual—in Ruby's camp only those assigned to guard duty or patrols carried weapons in the camp. It was a safety thing. Here everyone seemed to have a gun, though most were in poor condition. One had a rusty pistol jammed into the waistband of her pants. Another had a battered .22 rifle slung across his back with a length of frayed twine.

Our armed escort stopped us outside a sort of shack-tent pieced together with lengths of cord and frowzy tarps and tent parts. The tall man ducked inside and there was a testy exchange of words. Soon the tall man came back out, accompanied by another man, plump and pale with heavy-lidded eyes and large, wet lips.

"Who are you?" the man asked.

Chase spoke up. "Is Mac around? He can vouch for us."

"Mac?" the man said disdainfully.

"Yeah," said Chase. "Mac."

The plumpish man stepped over to Chase and struck him across the face. For a moment I felt bad for what Chase would do to him in retaliation, but Chase absorbed the blow as if a child had playfully slapped him.

"I'll let that one go," said Chase. "But don't do it again."

The man lifted his chin haughtily, but reading his body language I knew he'd take Chase's advice to heart.

The guy with the lips and the other camp men moved a short distance away and quarreled with each other, occasionally looking in our direction and gesturing. After a few minutes, the tall man who'd captured us left the group and approached us.

"Come over here," he said tersely, motioning with his rifle. "Sit down."

Lips and the rest of them walked off toward a cluster of tents. We found a place on the ground that wasn't too muddy and leaned against an old fallen tree. The tall guy sat on a log nearby, ostensibly to keep watch over us, but he was soon pre-occupied, using a twig to absently scrape the mud from the treads of his boots.

"Chase, I don't understand," I said, my voice low. "What's going on?"

"Yeah, aren't these guys aligned with us?" asked Arie. "Aligned with Ruby and the other camps? I thought we were all on friendly terms."

"Hey," said our guard. "No talking. Shut up."

"Or what?" said Chase. "You'll shoot us?"

The man waved a dismissive hand and went back to scraping the mud from the creases of his boots.

"I don't know these guys," said Chase quietly. "I mean I think I recognize a few of them, but I haven't been here since spring. Back then a fellow named Mac was running things, and—" he paused, sighed, scratched his beard.

"And what?"

"And I guess my opinion was Mac wasn't exactly what you'd call executive material," said Chase. "I got the feeling he didn't have a firm grip on the reins, if you take my meaning."

"Think these clowns got rid of him?" asked Arie.

"Yeah, that's exactly what I think," replied Chase. "And whoever took over apparently doesn't seem to know or care about Ruby or anything else. I mean look at this place. No organization, no discipline."

The tall guy flicked the muddy twig away, stood up, and stormed over to us. He pointed the rifle at us.

"I said no talking," he barked.

"Go sit down," said Chase, glaring up at the man. "I took that piece of junk away from you once. So unless you mean to pull the trigger, you better put it away or I'll take it again and club you over the head with it."

The man took what looked like an involuntary half-step backward.

"Because that's all it really is, right? A club? It's not loaded, is it?" scoffed Chase. "Remington .207? Where would you even get any? The gun's empty, isn't it?"

The man's eyes widened with sudden horror. He didn't have to say more.

Chase rolled his eyes and let out an exasperated sigh. "Listen, pal," he said to the tall guy, "what is going on around here? Who's in charge?"

The man's eyes blazed for a moment with anger, and his jaw muscles pulsed. But then he blinked a few times, looked around as if to check for eavesdroppers, and his face went slack. He looked around again and came closer.

"Everything's gone to hell," he whispered, crouching beside us. "Mac's gone. There was a fight. Big one. 'Bout a month ago."

"So who's in charge now? The pudgy little squirt?"

"You mean Hickman. No, he ain't in charge. I mean he was at first. But now I guess we got a new leader. They're off talking to him now about what to do about you."

"In other words," said Chase, "the camp's falling apart."

The man nodded reluctantly, his expression forlorn. "There's never any food. No one will work. People keep fighting. People keep leavin'."

Chase sighed and shook his head.

I smiled and extended my hand. "I'm Alison. This is Arie. Chase you've already met."

The man looked at my hand for a moment as if he might have forgotten what the gesture meant. Then he reached out tentatively, took my hand in his, and shook it.

"I'm Chester," he said with a faint smile.

"Nice to meet you," I said, "such as it is."

Chester nodded wearily.

"I've met you," said Chase, his tone conciliatory now. "Right? When I was here in the spring?"

Chester again hesitated but then said, "Yeah. I 'member you. I met Ruby once, too."

"Then what's the problem? Why are we being treated this way?"

"I couldn't vouch for you. Too dangerous. Hickman thinks you want to take over."

"Well, I don't, but you'd think he'd want me to," said Chase with a chuckle. He looked around the camp. "Hell, a ten-year-old could do a better job."

"Like I said, we got some new guy running things. He seems more, what's the word? Competent?"

Chase shrugged. "I don't see how things can get much worse."

Just then something caught Chester's eye, and he sprang to his feet. "They're coming back," he said.

We turned to see. Hickman was tromping in our direction, flanked by a few men with rifles. They came within a few steps of us and then stopped.

"So," said Hickman. "You're with the Agency."

"Yessir," quipped Arie before either Chase or I could answer. He threw up his hands in a cartoonish surrender. "Ya got us. Fair and square. I'm the Agency president. He's my vice-president, and that lady there is commander of the Agency submarine fleet."

"We're not with the Agency," Chase sighed.

"No?" said Hickman. "Prove it."

"How do you suggest we do that?" I said. "You want to see our IDs?"

Hickman's moist lips parted in a sneer. "Come with me," he said.

His men pointed their rifles at us. I wondered how many rounds of ammo they had between them—if any at all.

"Chester," barked Hickman. "You can go."

Chester's gaze wandered from Hickman to us and back again.

"I said you can go," growled Hickman.

Chester wandered off, looking back at us a few times as he went.

"Get up, Agency goons," Hickman shouted at us.

We got slowly to our feet and followed the pudgy little figure. His armed men stayed behind us, their rifles leveled at our backs. When we came to the edge of the camp, Hickman looked back as if to confirm we hadn't been followed. Then he waved us on and we continued into the woods.

"Hey, uh, Hick?" said one of the men behind us. "I thought we were s'posed to bring them back to—"

"Quiet," snapped Hickman. "Shut your stupid mouth."

"Where are you taking us?" I said.

"I'll ask the questions," said Hickman.

We kept walking. I caught Chase's glance. Now it was him who had the scheming look in his eyes. They hadn't even bothered to tie our hands.

Hickman stopped the group in a small clearing.

"Sit down here," said Hickman.

We sat. The men stood about twenty-five feet away, gripping their rifles and shifting their weight from foot to foot. Hickman stood behind them.

"Let's make a move," I hissed at Chase.

Arie shook his head.

Chase scoffed. "They're not gonna kill us."

"Kill them," ordered Hickman loudly. "They're spies from the Agency," he declared. "Kill them. Now."

Two of them raised their rifles and aimed at us. The other went on looking perplexed.

We were on our feet in an instant.

"Shoot them!" hollered Hickman frantically.

"You can't shoot us!" said Chase. "We're on the same side!"

One man was squinting down the barrel of his rifle, his finger on the trigger. I'd decided to sprint into the woods, and I was almost positive Arie and Chase would be close on my heels or three paces ahead of me, but before we made any move, a gunshot rang out. I flinched and dropped instinctively into a crouch, but the only thing that happened was that the gunman yelped and dropped to the ground like a giant sack of potatoes. Almost before he'd hit the ground, there was another shot. We dropped to our bellies. A third shot rang out.

I poked my head up and saw both of the men who'd pointed their rifles at us, along with Hickman, lying on the ground, squirming in the dirt. The third man flung his weapon into the grass and raised his arms. My ears were still ringing with the concussion of the gunshots. Hickman was yowling and writhing, clutching at a bloody wound on his arm.

Chester appeared from the shadows at the clearing's edge. He stepped into the clearing diffidently, gripping his rifle and keeping his eyes on Hickman. So he had ammunition in his gun after all?

Then I saw another figure emerge from the trees, a smoking revolver in his hand. He was bandaged, and he limped, but I recognized him instantly. We all did.

It was Colonel Steele.

CHAPTER 32

As evening came on, we sat around a richly blazing firepit. Arie and Chase and I sat on a crude bench constructed of big logs stacked and stabilized on rocks. It must have been quite old—the seat and back were worn smooth with use and it was surprisingly comfortable. We'd put our coats on and cupped mugs of tea in our gloved hands.

Steele sat across the fire from us on an ancient aluminum lawn chair. Chester was there, too. It was he who'd fetched Steele when it became clear that Hickman meant to execute us.

Chester hung a cast-iron pot from a cross-member over the fire and made a thin stew from rabbits he'd captured using snares and deadfalls.

"Know what they really go for? As bait, I mean? In the traps?"

We said nothing but nodded for him to tell us. I for one really wanted to know.

He grinned. "Carrots. Can you believe that? You figure rabbits only eat carrots in old cartoons and books, like it's just a joke, but they really love carrots. They're easy to grow; I got some growing up there on the hill and some closer in here by camp, but I don't know how I'll catch rabbits when I run out."

Soon the stew was bubbling in the pot. I sipped my tea as the evening's chill crept in around us.

"He broke my arm right away," Steele was saying, "swatted me like a damn housefly. Gave me some pretty good lacerations."

He indicated his various bandages.

"And he must have stepped on me at some point and cracked a couple of my ribs. I don't remember everything clearly. I think I had a concussion, too, from when you clubbed me." He pointed at Chase.

Chased winced, shrugged.

"He bit me on the ankle," Steele added, lifting his foot, which was wrapped with what looked like strips of an old beach towel. "That one still hurts."

We shook our heads with equal parts sympathy and amazement.

"But you got away," said Chase with an expression more worshipful than he probably intended.

"I put a couple slugs into him," said Steele with a nod. "When he first came at us. I got two shots off and then he hit me hard, and the pistol and I parted ways. At first I thought I'd missed because the bear wasn't acting injured at all, but later I figured I'd hit him in the liver or guts and he was probably bleeding internally. Anyway, I guess I managed to keep out of his reach until he realized I might not be worth the effort."

"You made it over here in good time," I said.

"Yes. Infection was my biggest concern," Steele went on. "That kept me moving. I knew there was a camp around here somewhere. I suppose I could've walked back to the road, but I came here first to see if I could get my hands on some antibiotics."

"We won't be joining you," Chase said.

"No," said Steele with a grim smile, "I'd given up on that course of events the moment the bear appeared."

"What do you mean?" I asked.

Steele gazed at the fire for a few moments. "I wouldn't try to re-capture you even if I were in perfect health and had the means to subdue you. I thought about what we talked

181

about while we were on the trail together," he said. "About payments and purposes. And I agree that I was in the wrong line of work. I think I'll pursue a new one."

"So, you're taking over this place?" asked Chase.

"No," Steele answered with a curt chuckle. "They just needed a little guidance," he continued. "They had a couple idiots in charge, taking advantage of them. They're all pretty desperate. Not a lot of leadership or expertise among them. I've heard them say things have gotten so bad that people have left here with the intention of returning to the Agency."

"That's awful," I said.

"They get three squares and a bed with the Agency," said Steele with a shrug.

"So, you're going back to your family," I said.

He nodded. "When I'm fit to travel, yes. I'll help these people as much as I can. Help them decide what they want to do. When I'm healed up, I'll go."

We ate the stew and talked more as it grew dark.

"What will you three do now?" asked Steele.

"We've got some plans," I said.

"What kind of plans?"

"We'll just keep those private," said Chase.

"I understand," Steele returned.

"Actually," I said, "I have a couple questions for you."

"About the back before?"

"No, about why you came after us."

Steele pressed his lips into a tight line. "Okay," he said after thinking awhile. "Ask me."

"Do you know the name Bellington?"

"Yes," he said with a nod.

"He sent you?"

"No. You already know Rachel sent me, but I was directed to consult Bellington about you and your camp and other things that might help me apprehend you."

"Did he ever say anything about a treatment or medicine that restores memories of people who've been wiped?"

"As a matter of fact," said Steele, nodding again but looking a little surprised at the question.

"So there is an antidote?"

"As far as I know, yes."

Arie and Chase and I exchanged astonished looks.

"Do you know where it is? How it works? Where to find it?" I would have peppered him with more questions along those lines, but he held up a hand.

"No, no," he said with a smile. "He didn't say anything about any of that. I only know that Bellington told you about it to entice you into letting him go."

My face reddened. "He told you he tricked me?"

Steele tilted his head thoughtfully. "No," he said, shaking his head, "he didn't say that. He never said explicitly that he'd told you a lie or the truth."

"What's that mean?" I asked.

"It means it was probably a lie," said Arie.

Steele was shaking his head. "No. That's not what I'm saying. What he said to me was, 'I told her about the treatment we have to restore memories'. Those were his words, as close as I can recall. You see? If he was telling me about a falsehood he'd told you, he almost certainly would have put it a different way. He'd have said, 'I told her we had a treatment,' or 'I made up a story about a treatment.' Instead, he said, 'I told her about the treatment.' That makes me think he was telling me that he told you about something that really exists. See the difference?"

"Yeah," I said. "Yeah, that makes perfect sense."

Chase had been listening intently. Now he spoke up. "You're telling us the truth," said Chase. It sounded like not so much a question as something he needed to tell himself, aloud.

"We're no longer rivals or adversaries, Chase," said Steele with his usual cool frankness. "At this point I have no reason or interest in telling you anything but the truth about what I know."

The air seemed charged with new potential, a new purpose. I'd had the feeling that the antidote was real. Now I knew.

"Colonel," I said after a few moments of quiet, "can you help us?"

"If you mean will I join you in going to some Agency installation to steal the treatment, then no. I wish you well, but I'm going home, and to paraphrase Chief Joseph, I hope to fight no more forever. Now, if there's something I can do for you before that, here, while I'm convalescing, then yes, I'd be open to discussing it."

We sat thinking for a minute. "Well, we need a vehicle," I said. "We coasted down here on an old jeep, but we need a vehicle that runs. We need to get to the Agency borders."

He grinned broadly, paused, and then let out a deep, hearty laugh. It was the first time any of us had heard him do so. He seemed genuinely amused. We looked at each other bemused until he composed himself again.

"Alison," said Steele, "as you know, I'm a highly skilled tactical operative."

"Yeah," laughed Chase, "it's been several days since you reminded us of that."

Steele smiled sheepishly at the wisecrack, then said, "Well, you'll all be interested to know that there's probably only one area in which my skills are more excellent."

"Fixing cars?" I asked hopefully.

He grinned and slowly shook his head. "No," he said, "Fixing jeeps."

CHAPTER 33

We couldn't get Steele down from the camp to the jeep nor the jeep up to Steele. Not right away. Steele could walk only short distances before he risked tearing the crude sutures he'd stitched into himself to keep his wounds closed. The lacerations on his feet looked especially gruesome, and I saw no signs of infection, but even standing up for more than an hour left him exhausted and in pain. So, we stayed in the camp for a week while he healed. We rested and took turns teaching the people who remained in the camp how to make a living in the woods. I taught them how to gather and preserve wild forage. Chase taught them how to capture fish and grouse and even muskrats and beaver.

Steele stayed in his tent, sipping protein stock made of boiled rabbit and bird bones. In the afternoons, Chase caught fish with his fly rod and brought fish to Steele four or five at a time.

"It's protein I need," said Steele. "I'll eat as many fish as you can catch."

There were almost no books in the camp, but I somehow got my hands on a big paperback romance novel about a duchess whose illicit lover was secretly the pirate who'd murdered her beloved father in a bloody raid on the high seas. The duchess didn't know this, however, because although she had been aboard the ship and indeed at her father's side the night of the fatal raid, she had of course gotten a nasty case of amnesia during the melee when a free-swinging yardarm conked her over the head. The duchess turned out to be the only survivor of the attack and would have perished herself had she not fallen quite conveniently into a passing lifeboat, and had she not been rescued by the very same father-slaying pirate captain, with whom she immediately fell in love.

I rolled my eyes and muttered, "Oh, puh-leeze."

The front and back covers were missing, and the book was stained and swollen with water damage and difficult to read. I almost tossed it aside, but soon the duchess began remembering things about the night her father was killed, seeing flashes of the pirate captain's face, and I was almost ashamed at how engrossed with the story I eventually became—until I realized that the final chapter was missing.

After a week, I think I started going a little crazy. I was having dreams of getting all my memories back. I was dreaming about remembering. I dreamed that I was Chase's wife in the back before. I dreamed that Arie was our son and that we'd resisted the rule of the Agency together but had eventually been captured and mind-wiped. I dreamed that Chase was secretly an Agency operative. I dreamed that I was the Agency operative and that once I got my memories back, I would turn on Arie and Chase. Even when I'd just doze off in the sun after eating in the afternoon, I'd dream of various lurid versions of my past. That wasn't so bad at first, but then I started to dream that my dreams of remembering were actually my mind's way of remembering my real past. I distrusted my own thoughts. I walked around in a sleepy fog of anxiety.

After ten days, I burst into Steele's tent.

"Alison?" he said, blinking awake and hiking himself up on an elbow. "Everything all right?"

"Colonel, I'm sorry to bother you, but I gotta know when you think you might be well enough to hike down the hill and get that jeep running. I've got to get back there. To the Agency. I've got to know if there's an antidote and, if there is one, I've got to have it. I'm losing my mind. I'll walk all the way if I have to, but if there's any way you could give me an estimate, well, yeah. Please. Did I say I'm sorry for bothering you?"

He blinked slowly, a look of fatherly understanding on his face. "You're not bothering me," he said. Then he lifted his foot off the bed and flexed his ankle. He thought for a few moments more and said, "Plan to set out first thing tomorrow morning."

"Tomorrow? Really?"

He stuck out his bottom lip and gave me a firm nod of his head. "I'll be ready."

CHAPTER 34

Steele worked on the jeep for almost a week. Every hour was agony to me. The jeep needed various parts, tools, and fresh fuel and oil. Runners were sent off to other settlements to find what was needed. Steele enlisted Arie and Chase and others to hold things, fetch things, hand him things. At first he returned to camp in the evening and by candlelight he disassembled virtually every mechanical item there was to be found—lanterns, rifles, an old gasoline generator. He spent hours hammering and plying and filing away at bits of the cannibalized iron. Then he ordered a tent and cot be brought down to the jeep and worked there practically around the clock. Chase and Arie and I likewise got tents and bedrolls and slept at the jeep.

Steele would start the jeep, turn it off, work on something, then start it again, but it seemed to be always just shy of being truly fixed.

After the fifth day, I despaired. Steele never seemed discouraged, but I knew in my heart that we'd be walking back to the Agency. How long would that take? Weeks? Where would we get provisions? Water? We'd have to live rough and arrive at our objective totally spent and probably half-sick with exhaustion—assuming we made it at all. I cried myself to sleep.

But when I got up before dawn the next morning, Steele was already lying across the fender of the jeep beneath the hood, working by lantern flame. He was so short that his legs dangled off the ground, and when he needed to reach deeper into the guts of the jeep, his feet flailed in the air.

When he heard me approach, he straightened up, slid down off the fender, and gave me a friendly wave.

"There's hot water on the embers over there," he said. "Have some tea." And then he ducked back under the hood.

"Dare I ask?" I said.

He chuckled. "There's never any harm in asking."

"Okay. How's it going?"

"I'm getting close," he said flatly, and without looking up. "You'll be driving away tonight, tomorrow morning at the latest."

For an instant I could not draw a breath to reply. Something about the tone of Steele's voice told me this was not just optimism nor even informed speculation. He was stating a fact, like always. I made us both some tea.

"You're gonna need to find more fuel," he conceded, his head still down in the engine compartment. "And I'd recommend you keep her under about 50 miles per hour, but this old heap wouldn't be fun to drive any faster, anyway."

It wasn't easy to say goodbye to Steele. I felt a keen sense of loss as we packed up the jeep. The things we could accomplish with Steele on our side, the things we could learn from each other—it was painful to think of the unrealized potential.

"He'd be an incredible asset," said Chase that night as we turned in.

"The guy knows, like, everything," said Arie.

I sighed and shrugged. "He's got his own plans."

As we pulled away the next morning, Steele raised his hand in farewell, kept it raised for a few seconds, and then turned back to Chester and his other men as though he were immediately ready to move on to the next item of business.

CHAPTER 35

It took three days to reach the outskirts of the Zones. Bellington had explained that there were a few places we were likely to find the Agency's memory antidote, but I was familiar only with the dispensary near the housing block where I'd lived with Gary, so we focused our planning on that location. We discussed various approaches as we drove, scrapped a dozen plans and formed a dozen more. We planned as we drove, raising our voices over the jeep's clattering engine. Sometimes Arie disagreed with my ideas, sometimes Chase did, and often they both did. There were arguments. We drew diagrams in the dust on the hood during rest breaks, and we bickered long into the night before we fell asleep on the ground around our small fires.

As we passed through the final mountain pass that lay between us and our fate, we adopted a plan that Chase and Arie accepted with no small skepticism. I thought it might work, but even to me it seemed too simple, too direct. We agreed that we'd need to be flexible, and we formulated alternate plans B through F, but even though I knew I was flying mostly by the seat of my pants, I just wanted to get there. I just wanted to see if it might be true.

A prickly dread stole over me when, as we crested a low rise along a back road in the foothills, I saw the dark spot of an Agency troop carrier cruising along a highway down in the valley. Beyond that lay the sprawling Zones gray and grimy looking. I felt a heavy but familiar knot forming in my gut.

When night fell, we were creeping along the outer protective fencing of the Agency infirmary. We were all familiar with how easy it was to move in and out of Zone obstructions—they simply didn't have the personnel to patrol the entire rambling perimeter effectively, but getting into the infirmary was a different matter, a piece of the plan I thought would either go very smoothly or disastrously. During my time with Gary, the infirmary sometimes seemed to be heavily guarded, but there were other times when there was hardly anyone there at all.

"Here's where I find out if I'm a genius or a damned fool," I said in a hoarse whisper.

Chase and Arie didn't agree out loud, but even just their body language told me they were thinking the same thing.

"So, if I understand correctly," said Chase, "the first step was us cutting this fence, then you go up to a side-door in a secure Agency facility and try Gary's old access code on the keypad to a building that he wasn't authorized to enter."

"Yeah," I said. "That's the plan."

"And you think the door is just going to—open. Just like that. It won't set off some alert? And what if Gary's code doesn't work at all? And what if this is all just a trap anyhow?"

"We've been over this," I sighed. "If he thought I was gonna be captured or killed in a raid he'd order, he'd have no reason to lie."

Chase squeezed his lips together and shook his head slowly.

"Chase, you weren't there," I said. "I really think Davey was being honest with me."

"Davey," spat Chase.

Arie laughed quietly.

I rolled my eyes. "Look, guys, I may not remember the overwhelming majority of my own birthdays, or what I used to do for a living, but I know that I have become very adept at detecting deception. Besides, what do you want to do? Change the plan now? Here?"

"She's right, Chase," said Arie. "This is the plan. Let's do this. I've been wanting to take them down for so long I can practically taste it."

"I should have said something earlier. You're okay with this, kid?"

"If her gut feeling is all we've got to go on, I guess I trust it," said Arie. "Yeah. I'm okay with it."

"I think it's wishful thinking," said Chase.

"You're outvoted, hon," I said. "This is happening, with or without you."

Chase blinked slowly and made a small nod. "We'll cover you from here," he said. "If anything goes wrong, you know what to do."

Chase drew his pistol and Arie produced a pair of bolt cutters. He clipped a gash into the heavy chain-link and then pulled on the fencing until there was a void for me. We'd returned Steele's pistol, but he'd given me a snub-nose revolver that fit perfectly into my pocket. I checked to see that it was ready and then slipped through the torn fencing. As I set off across the expanse of brown dead lawn between the fence and the door, I looked back and saw Chase gazing at me from his place in the gloom.

I thought the first time I'd kissed Chase was shortly after we left Lotus burning, crumbling, but I found out later that wasn't true. I'd asked Chase about it once, and he smiled slyly, but then shook his head. He said it didn't matter. It was in the past. But it mattered to me. How could anyone be okay with special moments like that just being erased? Even bad times had their own special place in our hearts, and forgetting them, letting them drift away like autumn leaves on the current of a stream simply wasn't an option for me. I had no doubt that we'd make many new memories, but what about the past? Whenever I had ever said anything like this to Ruby, she would call me to attention.

"Stay in the present, Al," she'd bark. "The grass ain't never greener."

But I rankled at her admonishments. Remembering Arie as a little boy? A baby? I'd risk almost anything for that. And what if Chase was there, too? What price was too great? If I could feel such excitement and joy over just the idea of it, how much grander would it actually be to experience it? The best part was, it wouldn't just be for me. We'd share it with everyone. We'd get to find out who Ruby really was. Chase. Woolly. And everyone else. I was just as excited for them as I was for me. What greater way to show my appreciation and gratitude to the people who meant the most to me than to give them their memories back? To give them their lives.

I ran through the half-light toward the door and the keypad that just might unlock many lifetimes of memory. It was only fifty yards. When I'd cut the distance to forty yards, I felt a thrill of victory. When only twenty yards remained, I knew the plan would work.

When I was just ten yards away, the door opened and two people stepped out.

I dove onto my belly and held still. Surely they would see me.

It was a man and a woman. They looked around suspiciously. How could they have detected my approach? The man seemed to look directly at me, but his gaze passed over me, and he made no sign that he'd seen me.

Then the man and woman turned to one another and embraced, sharing a long kiss.

Agency goons in love, I thought.

They stood just outside the door and kissed for what seemed like an hour. I was starting to shiver on the cold ground. They talked quietly, laughed, and then kissed more. Then the man looked around again, and again I thought he looked directly at me.

They walked away together.

I let out the long breath I'd been holding, but I waited there on the ground for what I guessed was another ten minutes before I finally started to get to my feet. When I did

I felt a presence coming up behind me. It was Chase, and Arie was behind him.

"I couldn't wait back there for something like that to happen again," he whispered. Then he kissed me on the cheek. "Let's do this then."

We crouched down and scurried over the remaining lawn to the door. Chase and Arie had their guns drawn. Chase nodded at the keypad, signaling me to enter the code.

"It's not going to work," Chase said under his breath. "It's just too easy. That door is not going to open."

8-2-3-5-Enter

And just like that the door clicked unlocked. I pushed the door handle, and we were in.

CHAPTER 36

The interior was a long hallway with many old metal doors painted with blue paint. Again I felt the prickly dread of returning to this terrible place. But my purpose drove me ahead. The ceiling was dropped-in with ugly tiles and the lighting was that especially grim yellow-gray fluorescent. They buzzed and flickered and a couple moths that came in with us bounced against the lights.

Chase stopped us just inside the door, as if expecting a rush of guards. But after a full minute, nothing had happened. No one had appeared. No alarms had sounded. The only sound was that of the lights and the bumping moths.

So far, it was just as Bellington said it would be.

We walked down the hallway quietly.

There were camera pods here and there, but Bellington had told me they were poorly monitored at night, and sometimes they weren't working at all.

I counted the doors. One. Two. Three. Four. Then fifth on the left. Another keypad.

It wasn't a struggle to remember the numbers. I memorized them practically the moment they passed Bellington's lips, like they were engraved on my brain. But still, I'd repeated them to him several times to be sure I knew them and later I wrote them down. The paper was rolled up in my pocket. I didn't need to look at it, but my fingers shook as I pressed the buttons. Not from fear. It was pure exhilaration.

0-5-2-1-Enter.

Again the door unlocked, and we moved into a darkened room.

"I don't like this," said Chase. "It's too easy."

Arie turned on a flashlight and shone it around the room.

"Look, there's a camera in here, too," he said.

It was indeed a lab or depository of some sort. There were an industrial sink and marble workbenches. There were shelves and cabinets of medical supplies and bottles of powders and pills.

Bellington said the cabinets would be locked, but the key was under the sink, hanging from a nail up underneath out of sight. I knelt by the sink, opened the doors underneath it, and groped around inside.

I found the key.

Chase got a look of panic when I held it up to Arie's light. His composure seemed to deteriorate a little more after each small success.

I unlocked the cabinet and opened it. Bellington had told me what to look for. A small, gray plastic case that looked like a first-aid kit.

"It's here," I said. "Just like he told me it would be."

"I think we should abort," growled Chase. "This is a trap."

"I agree," said Arie. "Something doesn't feel right."

But it was all just as Bellington had said. I set the case on the workbench and opened it. Hypodermic syringes. Small vials. As Bellington had said, the liquid in the vials had a slightly amber tint.

"Al," said Chase, looking out the small window in the door. "We leave. Now."

"But it's here, Chase. It's all right here."

"Then bring it with you, but let's go. Now."

"Chase, think about it. If this was a trap, they'd already have us. They never dreamed we'd make it here, never dreamed we'd make it this far. If they did, they'd already be lined up outside this door with twenty armed thugs. It's not a trap!"

Chase's face was red. He breathed a frustrated sigh. Arie looked cagey, the whites of his eyes flashing. They came to my side.

I picked up a syringe, and then I picked up a vial.

CHAPTER 37

"You're not using that here," said Chase. "No way. I insist, Al. What if it knocks you out for three days? Like the wiping serum? What if it is a wiping serum? There's just numbers and codes on these vials. It could be anything."

"He's right," said Arie, placing a hand on my arm. "We should get out of here."

I returned the vial and syringe to the gray medical case. We left the lab room and headed down the hall toward the door. I held the case tightly in my hands.

But as we hurried down the hall and toward the exterior door, we saw the bobbing beams of flashlights, headlamps. People were approaching. We stopped and watched, frozen and silent. Then we heard their voices, a lot of them. The flashlight beams grew brighter. They were getting closer.

"Follow me," growled Chase.

We turned around and ran further into the building.

As we sprinted down the dark halls, we heard them enter. A door thrown open, banging, echoing. There were barked commands and more slamming doors. They were quartering the building, searching each room, moving in. Shouts of "move up!" and "clear!" clamored sharply down the hallways to us, even though I thought we were getting farther away. We turned one corner and then another, running almost blindly through the lightless hallways. We came to an open foyer and a row of glass doors that led outside.

"There!" hissed Chase. "Come on!"

We ran toward the door, Arie out front, then Chase, and then me. Chase glanced back to see if I was falling behind. I gave him my "keep-going-I'm-fine" look.

But then we both almost blundered into Arie, who'd stopped short of the exterior doors. In another instant we saw why—three more armed men stood outside the doors in the light of the lamps outside. They hadn't seen us—it was brighter outside than inside, and the men only stood there looking bored. We backed slowly away from the doors and were just turning to run again when one of the men outside must have caught sight of our movement. He pointed. The others looked. They all rushed toward the doors.

We practically flew down a new corridor. The men from outside would enter slowly, I thought, their weapons ready. Chase was trying doorknobs as we fled. They seemed to all be locked.

"In here!" he said, at last finding an unlocked door. "Maybe we can find a window! C'mon!"

We hustled inside. It looked like a small classroom. No windows, but there was another door.

"You two, go through there," Chase whispered, pointing at the other door. "Find a window. Bust it out."

"But—"

"Now!" said Chase.

"What about you?"

He was already shoving a huge steel desk over to the door. We heard more shouting from the corridor. They hadn't located us yet, but they were close.

"I'm right behind you. I'll block this door and follow you. Go! Hurry!"

Arie tried the door. It opened.

"Let's go," said Arie.

I looked at Chase and our gazes locked. Arie looked at me and then Chase. We knew it was the end, but there wasn't time to process it. I'm sure I was afraid, terrified, infuriated, but I didn't feel it. And so we had this moment, a last look shared between the three of us to somehow say the things we had no time to say out loud. In that moment, we had to say everything about the way we felt about each other—all three of us. We loved each other. That is how it felt to me.

I learned something. I learned that when death literally arrives at your door, you look at the people who have traveled with you, the people you've invited into your life, who have become your family, and the thing you are thinking is not what you will lose, but the reality of all that you have.

So much, I thought. I have so much.

"Arie!" snapped Chase in an urgent whisper. He was pulling a huge bookcase over to join the desk. "Get her out of here!"

Arie nodded, and we went through the door.

I had often thought of how Chase and I would grow old together. Even without our memories, and in the midst of the Agency chaos, I thought of being by his side for the rest of my days. Because that's what you do with the people in your life. You see them day after day, and you assume they will always be there. And when I thought of death, I thought of it coming at the end of my life, after we'd escaped Agency tyranny, after I'd done all I'd wanted to do. When I reached that stage, I'd be ready to go, eager for my next adventure, whatever that might be.

I never pictured it would end this way. There was no final embrace. No kiss. No tender words. Arie pulled my arm, trying to lead me. There were no windows here, either. Only another anonymous door. I wasn't ready. I hadn't said goodbye.

If I'd been able to, I'd have said three things to Chase. First, I'd have told him I was sorry. Sorry that my impatience and eagerness had led us here. I had no long-term memories, of course, but I had a feeling, a deep-seated hunch, that this was not the first time I'd been here before. Not this place, not this exact situation, but something like it. I wanted to tell

200

Chase that I was sorry for not listening to him, for dragging us down into another disaster.

And I would have told him thank you. Thank you for being a light in my life. Thank you for every moment we spent together. The times when we sat in the grass and ate wild strawberries. The times when we walked trails in the sunset. And for the times when we were fleeing and in danger. The good times and the bad.

And finally, I would have tried, but probably failed, to tell Chase just how much I loved him. Not just to say "I love you," but to explain it to him.

Maybe it was because I was stunned or because everything happened so fast, but I didn't even think to say the words until Arie and I were engulfed by the darkness of the next room. I shouted, "I love you, Chase!"

But it was too late. The door was shut. And if he heard me, I didn't know.

CHAPTER 38

"Stay down," Arie told me. "Stay low." It was another classroom, almost identical to the last one. There were no windows here, but no other door, either.

We heard muffled shouting and the sound of someone pounding on the door where Chase was. Soon they'd break through and capture us all.

What was the point of it all? We couldn't escape. Chase might buy us some time, but there was nowhere to go from here.

Rachel most likely wanted us all dead. Would her soldiers kill us, or would they take us back to Rachel first?

It didn't matter. I pictured Chase with his gun drawn, coolly waiting for them to storm the room. Would he put up a fight? I thought maybe he'd surrender and maybe try to divert the troopers' attention from us.

He'd put up a fight, I decided. He wouldn't make it easy for them.

There came a great crash and then the back-and-forth blasts of exchanged gunshots. Guns firing indoors never sounded right to me. It was incredibly loud, but the sound was somehow too brief, unreal.

I crouched with Arie and covered my ears and waited. They had killed Chase and would now kill Arie and me. I squeezed my eyes together as tears ran down my cheeks.

And then all at once it was quiet.

Arie and I exchanged a short glance, knowing what the silence must mean. Chase would not have surrendered, but, could he have slipped their noose? Could he have gotten away and made a run for it? I didn't want to think about any other possibility.

"They're securing the room, now," whispered Arie. "Checking it out. Then they'll come in here."

"Arie," I said.

"Don't say anything," said Arie. "It's okay."

"I'm sorry," I said.

He shook his head. "You don't need to say anything."

We heard their voices outside.

Arie trained his gun on the door.

I opened the gray plastic case in my lap. I took out one of the vials. It seemed to glow in the dim light.

"What are you doing?" snapped Arie.

I looked at him and shrugged. "What does it matter now?"

I plunged the needle into the vial and pulled back on the stopper, filling the barrel.

What was the right dose? I didn't know, couldn't know. But I didn't care. I tapped at hollow of my elbow, looking for a blood vessel.

"Alison," said Arie, "don't do it!"

I squinted in the darkness and stabbed the needle into my vein. A rush of icy electricity flowed up into my shoulder and on through my chest.

They were at the door now. I heard their boots scuffling on the smooth floor outside, heard their voices. They were setting up to rush in. Then the door flew open. I saw their rifles, black and sinister, and their armor and goggles. They looked like nightmare beasts. They shouted and pointed their weapons. I think Arie threw down his gun and put his hands up. I think they wrestled him to the floor.

I was only partly paying attention. Because I saw Chase. Seated as I was, I saw between and beyond the legs of the troopers. Chase lay on the floor, a smear of shiny darkness spreading around him, and the troopers left dark, wet footprints. More troopers crowded in around me. I leaned and tilted to keep my eye on Chase. Someone was dragging him away by his feet. He was limp and lifeless.

I heard a trooper say, "We've got two in custody," and the finality of that shot through me like a bullet. I surrendered to the cold sensation that now seemed to be ripping through me like radiation. My thoughts began to disconnect, to wobble independently. The Agency troopers shouted, but the noise of it receded. Arie shouted back—but I heard him as I would through thick layers of cotton. My vision blurred, blackened.

I shut my eyes tight and images flashed through my mind, chaotic, busy, impossible to interpret. There were faces, houses, places, each followed by the painful sting of a hot, white flash, as though I were being beaten on the head, or receiving electrical shocks directly to my brain.

I saw Arie's face. Flash. A teacup. Flash. Chase's face. A Ferris wheel. Flash. Faces, colors, doors, sounds. Flash. Flash. Flash. I knew they were memories, my memories, and they were all there. I saw everything, but it was too fast, too loud, too large. My mind sizzled. Agency troopers grabbed my arms and were hauling me out of the room but I was only vaguely aware of it.

CHAPTER 39

I was in a bare place, a strange place. I won't say I awoke there because my first realization was simply that I was there, in this bare room. It was square with concrete walls and concrete floors. One metal door, shut, presumably locked. No windows. Jittery fluorescent light tubes flickering high overhead in a protective metal basket bolted to the concrete ceiling. I was lying on a metal cot which was also bolted to the concrete. In one corner there was an odd metal fixture that appeared to double as toilet and sink. Bolted to the wall above that was a plastic mirror.

I sat up and was struck by a strong wave of nausea. I dove toward the toilet, almost too late. I vomited several times and when there was nothing left I went on dry heaving.

My head pounded and my eyes felt hot and scaly. The air and floor were cool, for which I was mildly thankful. I lay on the floor and tried to work out where I was, how I had gotten here.

I couldn't.

I'd never been here before. Nothing seemed familiar. And that would be bad enough, but I couldn't remember where I'd been before this. Or where I'd ever been.

The room stank of body odor and urine.

I stood and tried the door. It was locked. So, this is a cell, I thought.

Again I tried to remember where I was, or anywhere I had recently been, and even where I wanted to be. Home?

Where was that? Nothing came to mind. I lay back down on the cot.

I was dressed in a simple gray shirt and pants made of cotton, like you might see at a mental hospital. Or prison. Is that where I was?

Back up, I thought. "Where am I?" might be the wrong question for right now.

"Who am I?" I said.

Alison. That was my name. I knew it, but it took some time to realize that I knew it. I tried to think of something else, anything else, but there was nothing to think of.

So, for now I was Alison.

But who was Alison?

There was the feeling that all the rest was on the tip of my tongue, I just needed something to get it started, to jog it free. There had to be in explanation for why I was here and where I had come from.

I told myself I was probably just very ill, feverish. I'd fallen sick and was in one of those dreadful hospitals in some impoverished, foreign country.

Okay. So. Where?

I should just rest and let my mind relax, I thought, and then it would all come back to me. But my heart slammed around inside me in a panic. My hands shook, moving around almost on their own, as if groping for something I'd dropped or lost. I was missing something I badly needed, something precious.

I began to dry heave again. I went to the sink and turned on the water. It was ice-cold. I cupped it in my hands and splashed it on my face. When I looked up, I saw my reflection in the warped and hazy mirror above the sink.

I didn't recognize it, which is not to say that I didn't know it was me. I knew it was me, but I couldn't recall ever seeing this face before. I couldn't place a time when I'd looked at myself before. So I spent quite a while looking at myself. There was a bandage on my forehead. I lifted it and saw a gash there, only a day or two old. Where had it come from?

I looked at my eyes. They were tired-looking, and they seemed sad to me. My hair was frizzy and unkempt. I needed a bath.

But these thoughts came to me as though I were observing someone else—a separate person—because I knew nothing of this person in the mirror. I didn't know where she came from or what her childhood had been like. Or her adulthood for that matter. Didn't know what things made her happy or what things made her sad. She looked sad now. Why?

"Hello," I said. It was an introduction. And my voice seemed familiar, though, again, I couldn't recall ever having heard it before. I felt immensely curious about this person—who was apparently me, though I felt like I'd somehow stolen someone else's body. As I looked at myself in the mirror, I turned my head side-to-side, touching my face, lips, nose, ears, collar bone.

"Who are you?" I asked the mirror.

When I'd had my fill of looking in the mirror. I went back to the cot and sat on it. The dizziness and nausea were passing, and I suddenly felt quite hungry. I wondered how I'd get food. Would someone bring me some? Why was I locked in? Did anyone know I was here?

I shook my head. Stop being foolish. You're a prisoner.

But am I a prisoner who is fed?

I wasn't particularly thin. I wasn't starving. So they must feed me. Unless I was new here. Was I new? Would I have food or not? Would I ever leave this room? How long was it that people could go without food? I had water. So, I could go quite a while. Somehow I knew that without water, I would die very quickly—a few days, maybe—but I could survive quite a while without food.

Maybe it was because I was alone with no apparent memories, that these questions and thoughts circled in my mind. My brain felt as though it had nowhere to rest, so instead it brewed and agitated over these few questions I had.

My name was Alison. I knew that I knew things. I knew that if there were a book in the room, I'd be able to read it, yet I had no memory of when I learned to read. I could conjure up images of what an apple was or a banana, yet couldn't remember having ever eaten one.

How does this happen? My brain felt as though it were pushing a rock up a mountain and though I had done nothing but sat there, I felt exhausted as though I'd used up all of my physical strength in thought. I faded in and out of something similar to but not exactly the same as sleep. Time passed, but whether it was days or minutes I did not know.

Then I heard footsteps outside my door. I don't know why, but I was keen to work out how many sets of footsteps there were, and who they might belong to. There were two or three sets of footsteps, I concluded. At least one of them must be wearing boots or heavy work shoes, for they clomped dully on the floor outside. The other footsteps were the click-click-click of a heeled shoe. A lady's high-heeled shoe.

Next came soft, muffled voices and the rattle-jangle of keys.

CHAPTER 40

The door swung open and in billowed a breath of fresher air.

A woman stood at the threshold of the door. Attractive, statuesque. She was a professional of some sort. A lawyer, perhaps? She wore a slate-colored pencil skirt, a lovely black blouse, and black, patent-leather heels. She didn't enter.

Three soldiers or policemen stood just behind her. Those were the boots I'd heard. But I'd miscounted them and felt a tinge of disappointment in myself. The soldiers were young looking, baby-faced.

I smiled. Involuntarily, I suppose. "Hi," I said, eager to finally get some answers.

The woman peered into the room. Her expression was almost completely passive, but for a hint of disapproval. A sinister look. She looked directly at me, unblinking. She didn't change her expression or even blink, but I somehow knew that she recognized me. I didn't know who I was, but she did.

I rocked forward to stand, to ask the woman, beg if needed, to explain why I was here. But before I got a word out, she nodded to the soldiers, stepped backward into the hallway outside, and I heard the click-click-click of her heels retreating down the concrete floor of the hallway.

The soldiers entered, their faces angry, already flushing red. Not so boyish now. They raised their fists, and that is when I saw their batons. I crouched down desperately, covering my face and head with my arms. Without a word, they each hit me with the batons. I screamed and scrunched myself into a tighter ball, absorbing strike after strike. After a while they abruptly stopped, for what reason I don't know—whether one gave a signal or they'd been some sort of earlier instruction. Then they swiftly left the room, pulling the door shut behind them. Another rattle of keys, the lock turned over, and then the only sound was my sobbing.

I checked myself, and bruises were already showing on my arms and my side where they'd hit me.

"What did I do?" I asked the room, sobbing, and then lay still until I fell asleep again.

Maybe an hour or two had passed when I heard the booted feet of the soldiers returning. I immediately shrank into a corner, balling into a fetal position, trying to expose the least of me as possible. The door opened, and I saw an arm clad in the same black uniform. A tray of food was placed on the floor and the door slammed shut again.

It wasn't much. Some runny lukewarm soup and a few stale crackers. But I was hungry and didn't know when I'd get to eat again, and so I ate it eagerly.

And that is how it was for a long time.

The soldiers came in periodically and hit me with the batons and kick me, for no apparent reason. Or they came to bring food. But they never spoke with me. Never seemed to even regard me as human. Sometimes I would plead with them for information. Where was I? Why was I being punished? Why couldn't I remember anything?

But they never answered. I felt certain I was being punished for something, yet I couldn't remember what, and that seemed wholly unfair. I didn't know how long I'd be kept there and speculated that the most likely answer was forever.

A despondency grew in me to the point that when the guards brought food or came to beat me, I couldn't even muster a response. I didn't get out of bed. All I knew of life and living was misery.

It occurred to me that I had not even one happy memory.

In the early days of that captivity, I tried creating an imaginary life for myself outside the concrete walls. But it was very difficult. The thing I tried to imagine the most often was being outside—out of this prison, yes, but more than that, actually outside where there was sunshine and flowers and trees and grass.

I always started with one tree. I'd look in the hazy plastic mirror by the sink. I looked at myself and then tried to imagine a tree next to me. If I managed that, then I'd try to add another, and another. Try to add grass and dirt. Some days I did better than others. But always, the vision in my mind was fleeting. Difficult to hold on to.

And when the despondency grew too great, the imaginary life required too much effort to conjure. For all I knew, me and my entire life were the full sum of misery. I'd never known happiness, and I never would.

So when the soldiers came to hit me. I'd lie there unmoving, until a baton would connect with my stomach or the side of my face, and I'd react reflexively. But my lack of reaction seemed to take some pleasure out of it for the soldiers, so it seemed to become half-hearted for them, the same way one might mop the floor only because they'd been told to and not really caring if the floor was cleaned.

I stopped eating. The tray would be brought and then picked up again.

I didn't care. Not about the food. Not about my imprisonment. Not about feeling pain. Nothing. I only wished to fade away. To disintegrate, to somehow cease to be. I could no longer be hurt because I was numb to everything.

I don't know whether I would have starved to death or if the soldiers would have intervened before that happened, but one day, there was a change. Two soldiers came to beat me, but they simply couldn't anymore. Instead, they swatted the wall next to my cot a few times. *Clack, clack. Clack-clack! Clack.* It was as if they thought that even though they could no longer stomach the idea of beating me, they must do something or be punished themselves. So they hammered on the wall several times and abruptly left the room.

When the heavy tread of their boots was gone, I heard something else. There was a banging or rapping on the wall, seemingly where the soldiers had struck the wall with their batons, and something more—it was in the same pattern or cadence of the batons.

Clack, clack. Clack-clack! Clack.

I stared at the wall, and the sound repeated. It shook me from my stupor. Goosebumps formed on my arms. I fetched the metal dinner tray, not caring that the food on it spilled on to the floor. I hit the wall with the tray twice. *Tap, tap. Tap-tap! Tap.*

I waited.

After a few seconds I heard it. *Tap, tap. Tap-tap! Tap.*

I tapped again, this time in a different pattern. *Shave-and-a-haircut…two-bits.*

The tapping from the other side came back the same way.

I reached out and touched the wall. And I pictured that there, on the other side, was another person, who understood what I was going through.

From that point on, my wall-mate and I would share taps throughout the day. I'd tried shouting to see if he or she could hear me, but I never heard a response and that always seemed to trigger the guards barging in with their batons. Soon we established that the pipes worked even better. There was a short length of exposed drain pipe at the sink and I could rap on this just with one knuckle and be heard. We exchanged our tapped-out messages every day, all throughout every day. I began to imagine trees in the mirror again. And a river. And warm rocks to sit on and take in the sunlight.

I wish we knew Morse code so that we could have conversations, but the noise itself was enough for me to imagine what the other person was saying. A tap first thing each day meant, "Good morning." At meal times was,

"Mush again?" After the guards left my room, "Are you okay?"

I felt like this other prisoner was my guardian angel. I began eating again. I started exercising. I would sing and talk to myself and whenever I was feeling sad or lonely, I'd rap on the pipe and wait for the response and then smile and nod. We were the same, the two of us. Strangers, but friends.

And while this crude form of communication had made the conditions somewhat bearable, it was still a miserable existence.

Nobody had told me why I was there or even who I was. Nobody had told me anything. Besides what I could do to keep myself clean with the water from the sink, I stayed in the same dirty clothing. I used the crude commode, but it was never cleaned, and the cloying smell of sewage hung in the room. Having known no other way, however, these conditions seemed normal to me, and I had to work hard with my mind to imagine anything different or better.

I named my wall-mate Winn. And besides the tapping, I'd converse with Winn through the wall. Which is to say I spoke in the direction of the wall and imagined how Winn might respond.

I had settled into a routine, complete with even a social life of sorts now that I communicated with Winn. And maybe life would have been okay, maybe I could have lived forever that way.

Then, one day, Winn didn't tap back.

CHAPTER 41

Usually it was Winn who sent the first greeting, the *shave-and-a-haircut...two-bits* knock we'd used after our first contact. But a lot of time had passed without hearing from Winn. I tried the morning knock, waited for the reply.

Silence.

Maybe Winn was still sleeping.

So I waited a bit and then tried again.

No response.

I tried not to think about it, but I became obsessed and moved to continuously knocking on the wall every few seconds.

I'd put my ear on the pipe itself, straining to hear even the slightest tapping response, but there was nothing.

Had the guards discovered what we were doing? Had they moved Winn to punish me?

I began crying. "Winn, Winn," I moaned.

I knew then that it was only the knowledge that someone else was there, that at least one other person on earth would offer me kindness—I knew that it was the only thing keeping me sane, keeping me alive. If Winn was gone—I didn't know how I could cope.

Terrible thoughts filled my mind. I wondered if Winn were dead. Still in the room, body decaying and rotting away.

Was Winn sick? Barely hanging on, desperately in need of medical care? Could Winn hear my knocking but was unable to even lift a hand to knock on the drainpipe?

When food came, I got off the bed and banged the tray against the door, hit it with all my strength, bending the tray in my hand and leaving dents in the metal door.

Soon guards came to the door, opened it, looked in with surprised but disapproving faces.

I knew they would beat me but I cried, "Where's Winn? You need to check on Winn." In my panic, I'd forgotten that the prisoner's name wasn't Winn and that was only the name I'd given them. But my desperation left no room for logic.

The guards didn't have batons though. One of them held an electroshock weapon, and as soon as I saw it, I yelped, and went to run away, but it was too late. Tiny barbs shot into my filthy clothing, and hair-like wires sent a burning, convulsing shock through my body. And then the guards left, leaving me on the ground, trembling, gasping. When they left, there wasn't any more pain, but I was filled with dread and unease, hoping to never experience something like that again.

I wouldn't act up anymore. Wouldn't make any more noise. But I kept my face pressed against the pipe and cried for Winn.

CHAPTER 42

At some point I must have fallen asleep, or perhaps I slipped into the awake but dazed and incoherent state that I sometimes languished in for days. Without stimulus, without a break in routine, one can fall into a sort of waking catatonia, neither aware nor unaware, letting time unreel like a ball of kite string. I don't know how much time passed, but when I came to my senses, I heard a noise outside.

Footsteps.

There were lots of footsteps, more than I could count, more than I'd ever heard, out in the hallway. There was shouting out there, too, and the lights in my room flickered.

Then there was a tremendous explosion. I heard it, and it was deafening, but I felt it, too, and the vibration shook my insides. Then came what I took to be gunfire. Rapid runs of machinegun fire and the pop-pop-pop of smaller weapons. More shouting. What could it mean? I huddled on the floor. I could only assume this had something to do with the disappearance of Winn's signaling, but how? Outside my door there was a commotion of footsteps and voices and then a short but powerful boom, and the door was dished in and deformed and suddenly hung limp on its mangled hinges. The door swung open and a cloud of acrid smoke billowed into the room.

From this cloud a woman appeared, but she did not wear a pencil skirt or stylish shoes. She was not tall nor was she young. She was old, stout, and draped in a long coat. She was not a soldier or police officer. She wore spectacles that were small and scratched, and her hair was short and wild.

She entered with a slight limp, and she supported herself with a cane. There were others with her, and these also were not dressed like any others I'd seen. No uniforms, no machineguns or armor.

"Here she is," said the woman over her shoulder. "We found Alison."

More shouting echoed through the hallway and I heard my name repeated. I heard distant gunfire and explosions. The woman looked at me. I huddled on the floor in the corner where the sink pipe was.

"Hi, there," she said.

I was too afraid to answer. It was the first time I could ever remember that anyone had actually said anything to me.

"Do you know me? Ya don't know me, do ya?"

I shook my head.

"I'm Ruby," she said with an unmistakable heaviness. "Let's get you the hell outta here." She stuck her fingers into her lips and blew a loud horse-whistle.

Two people came into the room and helped me to my feet. They gingerly guided me into the hallway. My senses blazed. I wanted to go somewhere, anywhere, away from here. But I stopped.

"I can't go with you," I said, "without my friend."

I looked to the place where I assumed there would be another door, but it had been wrenched loose, like mine. Coming out of the door were two people carrying between them a thin, bedraggled figure. His face was wet and clammy and gray and overgrown with a filthy beard.

Winn. Had to be.

I stumbled toward the door with the man and woman still supporting me.

"We gotta hurry," someone said. "They'll be back with reinforcements soon."

Ahead of us were a few more people, assisting a young man who was wearing similar clothing to me. He was limping, leaning heavily on a man beside him.

217

Outside the enormous concrete fortress, an armored truck sat idling. There was a door in the back of the vehicle, and I waited while they helped several other people inside. They looked like me and were dressed like me. Desperate-looking, shattered. Then they lifted me and placed me inside. There were two benches that faced each other. A few people seated on the benches were bleeding. Others were smeared with soot, their eyes darting around, impatient.

One of them smiled at me, a big man with a fringe of beard around his round face. He smiled and nodded and patted my shoulder with his beefy hand.

I could smell blood and gunpowder and the sewer stench of myself and the other prisoners. Still, I thought, this must be what heaven was like. The hardships and sorrow are over and now you can rest. It's hard to describe exactly how that felt. It was joy, overwhelming joy. I felt it in my whole body, so much that my heart actually physically hurt. Tears streamed down my face. Sitting next to me was a young man, shocking thin and pale looking, dressed like me, filthy like me. He was crying, too.

"Thank you," he said to the big man. "Thank you so much."

And I likewise turned to each of them. "Thank you. Thank you." The tears ran down my face. The others smiled back, nodding.

Then they were helping Ruby into the truck.

She looked solemnly at me. "This ain't over yet," she said.

The bearded man they'd taken from the cell next to mine, the man I assumed was Winn, was lying on his back, wrapped in a blanket. I looked down into his face. He'd saved me, and now he lay here looking like death. He was pallid and slick with sweat.

"He's got an infection," said Ruby to no one in particular. "Looks bad. Looks real bad."

CHAPTER 43

I worried for the man, my so-called wall-mate, the man I'd called Winn. Ruby said his name was Chase. He was obviously someone close to her because she doted over him and fussed about him even as she barked orders at the others. Before loading him in, they'd cut off his shirt to reveal two oozing black wounds that smelled terrible.

Ruby had produced a small bottle of clear liquid—probably moonshine—and had poured it over the wounds. Then she scrubbed his torso with a clean cloth. The man was unconscious, and even with the vehicle's bouncing and the whine of the diesel engine and the caustic liquid poured over his festering injuries, he didn't stir in the slightest. I wrung my hands.

Another of the rescued prisoners, a young man they called Arie, likewise seemed completely consumed with the welfare of Chase—he wore deep creases in his forehead as he stared at the man on the cot in the center of us all. I assumed they knew one another.

Through his knocks on the wall, Chase had rescued me. It had kept me physically alive. Perhaps the young man didn't know him either but had been similarly rescued. Had Arie been on the other side of his wall?

We drove for a long time. I wanted to know what was going on, ask fifty different questions, but I was exhausted. Someone pressed two small red pills into my hand and gave me a bottle of water. "Take these," she said. "It'll help you relax." Someone else had thrown a blanket around my shoulders, and after the initial clamor, the transport vehicle got quiet and pleasingly warm. My eyes grew heavy. They shut once, and I opened them again. They shut again.

To my embarrassment, when I opened them again, I wasn't in the truck anymore.

I hadn't just fallen asleep. The drugs reduced me to something beyond sleep, because I didn't wake when the truck stopped nor when someone evidently moved me from there to a bed. When my eyes fluttered open, I found myself in a green nylon tent. The sun shone on the fabric, giving it a warm, comforting glow. I was lying on the most comfortable bed and pillow I could ever imagine, and I was wrapped in a frowzy flannel sleeping bag.

At last, I thought. A pleasant memory.

Sitting next to the camp cot there was a bottle and a small burlap sack. In the bottle was cool water with a sweet mineral flavor. In the sack were two small apples. I drank and ate voraciously.

I arose, drank the rest of the water, and unzipped the tent. Nearby in a big camp chair was the large bearded fellow who'd given me had told me that I'd be all right that night in the transport vehicle. Had that been just last night? He rocked himself up out of the chair when he saw me.

"Good morning," he said cheerfully. "We were thinking you were a regular sleeping beauty."

"How long have I—"

He looked upward, squinting, calculating. "Almost thirty-six hours," he said with a chuckle.

I gasped.

"Don't worry about it. Francesca gave you some sleeping pills. Plus, after what you've been through, you needed the rest."

I nodded, as I looked around at what appeared to be a city of the nylon tents. And trees—a dense forest of the most beautiful trees.

"I'm Woolly," said the man extending his giant paw. I extended mine, and we shook hands, mine dwarfed in his.

"Alison," I said.

He smiled. "I know who you are."

"You do?"

"Afraid so," he said, smiling again. "But don't worry. We'll explain everything. We thought you might want to get cleaned up, so down the path a'ways we have a tub with hot water waiting for you." He handed me a bundle. "Here's a towel and some clean clothes."

"Thank you," I said, looking down at the clothes. "Woolly?" I asked looking back at him. "You know who I am? You knew me before all this?"

He nodded frankly.

"Were we—were we friends?"

He blushed deeply. "Yeah. Good friends," he said.

I smiled. "What was I like?" I felt like a shell of a person. Who we are, what we're like, so much of that is based on our experiences. On our memories. I had none. Not many, anyway.

Woolly rubbed his scruff of a beard. "That's hard to answer. You were nice—are nice, I mean. Always took the time to talk to me. Hard-worker. Didn't mind being on dish-duty or helping haul rocks, things like that, even if you couldn't lift much. But, uhm." He paused, glanced down. "You're different from most the folks here."

"How so?"

Woolly shrugged. "I don't know. You seem to think the impossible is possible. You take action."

I looked at the ground. "I caused a lot of trouble, didn't I?"

"Hey," he said. "No risk, no reward. Anyway, go take your bath, and then come get some food and we'll talk. It's barley stew tonight."

The tub sat in a copse of trees on a hill that overlooked a ravine. A small fire burned there with buckets of water and a kettle to boil it. There were coarse rags for washing and few hunks of what looked like homemade soap. I lowered myself into the tub.

It was a cloudy day. Banks of gray damp clouds moved across the face of the sun, and the valley glowed and shadowed by turns. It was glorious. I scrubbed myself, soaked myself, ran the soap through my hair. My feet and fingers were completely pruned when I finally got out to dry.

As directed, I joined Woolly and some others, including Arie, around a campfire. My hair was still damp, but I was clean and warm and the fresh clothes were soft and comfortable. I was given a crock of hot soup. It was simple but very filling, better than anything I could remember ever eating.

Noticeably absent were Ruby and Chase.

But that's where Woolly recounted everything he knew—about the pandemic that almost wiped out civilization, the serum that erased our memories, how I'd joined Ruby's small gang, and on and on. Arie laughed to hear about his leadership in Lotus. I was surprised to learn that Chase and I had been lovers. All that Woolly told us—it didn't seem real. It felt like campfire stories. And finally, Woolly explained how we'd gone looking for an antidote and ended up back in the Agency's hands and how Ruby found out and put together a rescue team. They'd lost one man in the effort, the news of which caused all of us to grow solemn and to stare into the fire.

Then Woolly asked us what it'd been like in the prison cells. Arie and I had similar stories—of mind-collapsing tedium and desperation and hunger and abuse. And of the tapping on the wall to communicate. So Chase had been Arie's wall-mate, too.

"And Chase," I asked. "How is he?"

"Doing better," said Woolly. "Ruby won't let him get any worse. I think he'd be scared to even try. Color is returning. Antibiotics seem to be working."

"Good," I said, nodding. I didn't want to say it, but I wanted desperately to see him. In part because I was curious about this man with whom I apparently had a past relationship, but also because I felt enormous gratitude to him. He'd been my beacon of hope in those dark cell days, and I needed somehow to let him know.

"So Ruby, is she still mad at me?" I asked. "For—well, everything."

Woolly and the others were silent, exchanging glances with each other.

"Yeah," Woolly said, almost apologetically. "She's still mad."

"But she'll be okay with me, right? I mean she rescued me."

"There's no way Ruby would've let you suffer in the Agency prison, Al. Despite everything, she cares an awful lot about you. She always has."

I bit my lip. "I can't imagine what I was thinking when I let that prisoner go."

"No one else can, either, Al," he said.

CHAPTER 44

The next morning, I joined the others by the campfire and was brought a cup of what everyone referred to as "mountain tea." There were also eggs, a little fish, and some coarse, grainy bread. It was all so delicious. I looked around for Woolly, then I heard someone say he'd be along later.

Arie was there, too, eating his breakfast. We'd been told that we were mother and son, but there was an awkward unfamiliarity between us. Arie nodded toward me by way of greeting, but said nothing.

Behind me I heard a harsh voice. "Lookie who's up and feeling better."

I turned to see Ruby and Chase coming down the trail to the meal area. Ruby was limping and using her cane. Chase had a blanket draped over his shoulders. He walked slowly and carefully.

The other campers gave a cheer. Chase waved back, though he looked perplexed at the recognition. Camp chairs by the fire were pulled out and Ruby and Chase were helped into them.

"Well, well, well," said Ruby. Her voice had an edge to it, a chiding quality. "Lookit all three of youse here, together again. Good. Cuz I wanted ta give us some instructions, so listen up."

She took a deep breath, looking slowly at Chase, then Arie, then me. We sat still. I could almost feel her gaze on me, like it was something physical that pushed against me.

"Ya'll look like crap," she pronounced.

We smiled nervously.

"Especially compared to whatcha looked like just a couple months ago, which since ya can't remember I'll tell ya was just fine. Ya'll were doin' just fine. And so that tells me you had it hard in that there prison. So—" here she slapped her leg "—you three are gonna take some time to rest and heal up, ya hear? I don't want you worrying about chores or cooking or pullin' your weight, at least not yet. You focus on building your strength and recovering."

"Ruby, I—" I began, wanting to talk to her about the incident that had started all of this, the incident I couldn't remember but somehow still felt poignantly responsible for.

She raised her hand up to stop me. "I don't wanna hear it. Just do as I say and stay outta my way. Capeesh?"

We nodded.

"Good," said Ruby. She slapped her knee again. "Well, I'll leave you to it. I got things to do." She rose unsteadily, using her cane as a lever to pry herself from the chair. Then she hobbled away, leaving the three of us alone together.

"How are you feeling?" I asked Chase.

"There's room for improvement," he said, wincing as he shifted in his chair toward me. "But it beats yesterday."

A man named Andre brought Chase a plate of breakfast and mountain tea. Chase balanced the plate on his knee and took a sip of the drink. He sighed. And I understood what his sigh meant. It is soothing to the soul to be in a safe place with something warm to drink. It was soul care. A new memory, still only the first of a very few we even had.

"Do you know who we are?" asked Arie.

Chase nodded. "I got the basic story. We were co-conspirators and, later, after some, um, trouble, we were prison neighbors. Right?"

We nodded.

"So," Chase went on. "We're friends." And then he gestured toward me with his mug, "And, um, apparently, something more." He smiled awkwardly.

I blushed deeply and cleared my throat. "Yes, that's what they told me."

"Leave me out of this," said Arie with evident sarcasm, waving his hand dismissively.

Chase smiled faintly and said, "I'm sorry, I don't remember you."

"I don't remember you either," I said.

"Right, but what I mean to say is that I'm sorry that I don't remember you. You seem like someone I would want to remember."

Was he—flirting?

It all seemed so strange. Like we were play-acting roles. Like we'd just been given parts in an acting class and were told now to play our parts.

Alison, you'll be playing the role of mother and girlfriend. Chase, you're the boyfriend. Arie, the son. And, action!

"You don't have to act like that," I said. "We can just start over."

"Act like what?" Chase asked.

My cheeks got warmer.

"Act like—you know—like you're interested. Or something."

My eyes darted to Arie. He was listening intently while trying to pretend not to be listening intently.

Chase chuckled. "Sorry, I'll try to ignore you from now on."

"That's not what I meant," I stammered. "What I meant was—"

"These two at it already?" it was Woolly. He'd sidled up and was standing behind Arie.

"Apparently, yeah," said Arie.

Woolly shook his head, but then pulled some notebooks out of a bag. "I saved these when we had to leave the last camp. I knew you'd want them." He passed a couple to each of us. "They're diaries that Alison and Arie kept. It details a lot of the stuff you've forgotten. It'll help you refresh your memories."

Woolly kept one of the notebooks. It was red with a skull erased into it. "This one I'm going to keep hold of," he said. "It was a project that Arie and I were working on, and well after you, uh, went away, I kept working on it on my own. It's not quite ready, but I'll give it to you when it's done."

Woolly went away then, leaving the three of us relaxing by the fire, reading the journals. When there was something particularly interesting, we read it aloud to share with the others.

"Alison, listen to this," said Chase. He read from the journal: "There are several new people I've met who I'm working with. I've been working a lot with a man named Chase since he apparently doesn't know how to drive a manual vehicle. He is cocky and stubborn. I hope I won't have to work with him long."

My mouth dropped open. "Oh, I didn't actually write that, did I?"

Chase laughed, and I honestly wasn't sure if he was making it up or not.

Later, Arie looked up from one of the notebooks and said, "Here are some entries from after this Agency group took me away and told you I was dead. Jeeze. That's just evil."

"What do I say about it?" I asked, without immediately realizing what an odd question that was to ask.

"You say that you miss me. You seem pretty broken up. It's really touching. I mean, I can't say it feels like me that this forgotten you is talking about, but the person who wrote this—they really cared, obviously."

"I get what you mean," I said, holding up the pages of the journal I was reading. "It's one thing to read about it, but it's different living the experiences. It's crazy to be reading about things that happened to me. I mean, it's insightful, I guess, but it doesn't bring the memories back. I wish it did."

A few weeks passed. Chase, Arie, and I spent a lot of time together. Maybe it was because we had all experienced the Agency prison together, or had been rescued together, or maybe it was because the journals told us that we were close. Whatever the reason, we felt bonded together in a way that was different even from how we felt about the people who'd rescued us and helped us out of that horrible place. It was almost like that experience had made a dark mark upon our hearts, a sensitive area that only other people who had gone through the experience could understand. The three of us acted passively in our actions, reserved, as though any loud noise or actions could trigger an Agency soldier to step out of the woods and beat us with a baton. Woolly said we were traumatized and that it would take a while to get past it.

"If you feel like your memories are upsetting you, just try to focus on the present," said Woolly. "Try to notice the things around you—what you see, smell, hear. If you find you can't stop thinking about something bad that happened to you, tell yourself, 'I'm having a thought about something unpleasant.' That will put some distance between you and the experience."

We nodded. It made sense.

"Where did you come up with all this?" asked Arie.

"I didn't," said Woolly. "I read it in books."

"My dreams are always about the prison," I said.

Woolly nodded. "I'm sorry. That must be difficult. But I'm not surprised. You guys don't have many memories, so it's easy for you to get stuck in the few that you have. Focus on today, now. Stay with us here."

Eventually, it felt like things were getting better, like it was easier to breathe.

I'd cry sometimes, for no clear reason. I'd just be sitting there doing something else, and a wave of fear or sorrow would wash over me, and I wouldn't be able to hold back the tears.

"I'm so sorry," I'd always say to the people around me. "I don't know what's wrong."

The other people would always nod and pat my hand reassuringly, but I felt so embarrassed. There was something wrong that I couldn't quite put my finger on. Or sometimes someone would move past me or go to hand me something and I would flinch and my hands would start shaking.

These were the internal scars left by the Agency.

Still, it felt manageable. It felt like I had it under control. Until one day, Woolly came to me. He had a strange look on his face and there was a heavy gloom between us.

"Woolly, what's the matter?" I asked.

I was reclined in a chair, reading a book.

"Hey, Al," he said, his voice heavy and low. "You know I am your friend, right? I'll always be your friend."

"Okay," I said. "Why are you saying this?"

He kicked at a rock on the ground. It was about the size of a grapefruit and was embedded in the dirt. He kept kicking at it until it dislodged.

"Ruby wants to see you," said Woolly. He said it without looking at me. My stomach fell.

Woolly walked me over to her tent in silence. Whatever it was, it was serious. I wondered if someone had died.

When we reached the tent, Woolly said, "You have to go in alone, Al. I'll see you later."

I stepped inside. It took a moment for my eyes to adjust to the dimmer light inside, but once they did, I saw Ruby sitting in a chair. There was another chair set up across from it.

"Have a seat, Alison," she said.

I did, keeping my eyes on her while I sat. She looked sad, or maybe just tired, or maybe it was both.

Even though I hadn't seen her much outside of the night I was rescued, she somehow seemed older than I had remembered her.

I liked Ruby. A lot. She rescued us. She had risked her life and her team for me.

She opened her mouth to speak, but then paused, before letting out a deep sigh.

"This is a lot harder for me than it is for you, you know," she said.

"What do you mean?" I asked. "What is going on? Have I done something wrong?"

She exhaled with a kind of laugh, and then said, "That's kind of an interesting question, innit?"

"Whatever it is, just tell me."

Ruby nodded and took her glasses off and wiped them with the tail of her shirt.

"What I mean is you're like a daughter to me. I care about you, which makes what I'm about to do really difficult. But you barely know me. From your perspective, we are essentially strangers."

"That's not true, Ruby. I feel very close to you."

She sighed again.

"Alison, I'm moving the camp. After the Agency stormed our last site, we lost fifteen people. They were taken or killed. More were injured and the amount of supplies and resources we lost were substantial. We can't risk another loss like that. It'd devastate us."

I nodded. "No, of course not."

"This time I'm going to move the camp far away from the Agency. Too far for them to give a rat's ass about us."

I wasn't sure what she was getting at. "That's sounds like a great plan. Whatever I can do to help, I'll be glad—"

"Al, you're not invited. Not this time."

Her words fell on me like a tree. "I'm—not invited?"

"Al, I know you don't remember, but I do and the other people do, too, and the fact of the matter is that you let us down. We're at the point where we can't be taking anymore risks. It's not your fault and I'm not saying you're a bad person, but frankly, you're a liability for us. And I can't in good conscience bring you along. Not after what's happened."

I could only look at her, my mouth open.

"Al, I wouldn't want anything bad to happen to you. Never. That's why we rescued you from that prison. But now it's time for us to go our separate ways. We'll set you up with whatever supplies you need and we'll take you where you want to go. Within reason, a'course. If you want to go find folks to stay with in the Zones, we'll do that. If you want to meet up with another group in the mountains, you can't wander too far around here without bumping into one of 'em. And if you want to just be on your own, that's fine too. You just can't be with us."

I felt like I couldn't breathe. My heart beat rapidly. "But Ruby—"

"No 'buts' Alison. It's already been decided."

She looked away from me, and I heard her sniff. I wondered if she were crying.

"I wish you the best, Al. I really do. Woolly will help you gather up the things you need and then he'll take you wherever you want."

She stood up to go.

"Wait," I said. "What about Arie? He's my son."

Ruby paused at the door without looking back at me. "He's just about grown," she said. "I don't own him. He can do what he wants. If he wants to go with you, he can decide that for himself."

CHAPTER 45

Arie didn't want to come with me.

"I feel bad," he said. "But it's just—I don't really know you. Not that I know anyone anymore, but I feel like my chances are better here with the group. I hope you understand."

I understood. We were strangers, connected only by the finest of threads. Yet, when I'd read about him in both his journals and my own, and when I'd learned he was my son, something had changed. I'd already had an affinity for Arie before the journals, as we were spirited from the prison in the troop carrier. I'd attributed it to our shared experiences, but once I learned about our relationship, I wondered if it was more than that. If maybe the heart remembered, even when the mind forgot.

I wanted the chance to build a relationship. I wanted to be there to make sure he was okay. But he hadn't picked me. Logically, it made complete sense.

Still, Arie's choice stung more than expected, and I had to clench my jaw to avoid letting my disappointment show on my face. And after that, I didn't want to stick around any longer than necessary. Every time someone asked how I was doing or why I was packing things up, my eyes welled with tears. I was so ashamed. I just wanted to gather my things and go.

That's what I was doing when Chase appeared. He poked his head into the tent where I'd been staying, the tent I'd almost gotten ready to call home.

"You going somewhere?" he asked.

I glanced briefly at him, then returned to packing a large backpack that Woolly had given me.

"I can't stay here," I said tersely, flatly. "I, uh, I'm gonna, just, you know, go." I couldn't say more, couldn't talk about it.

"Oh," he said. Then he was quiet, his head still poked into my tent. After a long moment he said. "Okay."

I said nothing in reply.

"So," he said, "just to be clear, you're leaving the camp?"

I didn't turn in his direction. Just nodded.

"And you're leaving now?"

"It's as good a time as any." Now my voice had a bite to it. An anger that I couldn't keep back. I suppose I knew on some level that if I let in even a little vulnerability, I would fall apart and bawl my eyes out.

"Do you need help?" Chase asked.

"Woolly's helping me," I said.

"Is it all right if I come in?" he said. His voice betrayed his confusion.

I kept packing.

"Al?" he said. "Can I come in?"

I nodded, again without looking at him. He stepped inside. I stole a glance at him. His brows were knitted and he was blinking rapidly. He removed his ball cap and scratched his head.

"Where will you go? Kinda risky to wander around on your own, you know."

I stopped shoving things into the rucksack. Where would I go?

"Doesn't matter," I said. "I need some alone time."

He nodded. "Well, good luck then." He went out.

As he walked away, I went to the tent door and called his name. He turned around, took a few steps toward me.

"I just wanted to say I'm sorry. For, I guess, you know, everything. The things they told us about. For tricking you and involving you in my stuff that got us captured."

"You remember doing that?"

"No," I said, "but it sounds like me."

"I don't think you need to go apologizing for things neither one of us remembers," said Chase.

"The others remember."

"So apologize to them. Besides, they don't know how we got captured and neither do you. You're making a lot of assumptions."

I started crying and looked at my hands. "I've messed up," I said. "I'm messed up."

Chase was quiet for a moment. He looked at his shoes. "Well, who hasn't? Who isn't?"

"Not like this," I said. "People died. And everything's ruined. And I can't be here anymore." I rubbed my eyes.

"Do you think you meant for people to get hurt?" he asked.

I shrugged.

"No, answer me," he said. "The woman who didn't want to hit a goon with a bat—you're saying that woman wanted people to get hurt? To die?"

"I don't remember."

"Look, things might have gone south, but I don't believe for one second you intended for that to be the outcome. You may have been negligent. You're paying for that. You may have made a terrible choice. You're paying for that. But you didn't shoot anyone and I know you didn't want that to happen. In fact, I'm willing to bet what you were going for was the exact opposite. You wanted to help. I'll bet you anything. Bet me right now. Name your stakes."

He stepped up to me and put his hand out to shake on it. I smiled a little, then shook my head.

"No bet, huh? I thought so. Al, you're not the one who put us in this horrible situation. The pandemic, the Agency, this life on the run, living in the forest. There's evil at work here, some kind of incomprehensible evil machine, and we're just being ground up in the gears. So. Yeah. Don't apologize to me. From where I stand, you were just trying to help people. You just weren't very good at it."

I chuckled then. And sniffed and wiped my eyes.

"Chin up, huh?" he said.

I nodded glumly and watched him go. Again, he was there just when I needed him, first tapping on a pipe, now making a bet with me that maybe I wasn't the most terrible person in the world. It didn't surprise me to know what they said about Chase and me—it was more than just his rugged looks and his easy confidence. Turns out he was a decent person, too. Even now I wanted to go to him. But losing him was a price I had to pay for my mistakes.

CHAPTER 46

Woolly wasn't melancholy as we bounced along the old logging roads. Now and then he turned his head to me, as though he might say something. But after an hour of driving, we had said little. Then the road narrowed and became very rough.

"I'm taking you to a spot I know," he said. "It was a candidate site for our own campsite, but we thought it might be too small. It'll be perfect for just one person. There's a spring nearby, lots of deadfall for firewood, good cover and concealment. Plus, it's just a beautiful area. You'll see what I mean." He gave me a searching glance.

I nodded.

"If you decide you want to join one of the other camps," he added, "there are at least a couple that are close to here. You should be able to find them, no problem. Then again, if you want to keep your solitude, you can do that, too."

I nodded again.

Woolly had asked me the night before where I wanted him to take me. I'd told him I didn't care. One place was as good as another. I felt like maybe I was in shock. Like my mind wasn't ready to comprehend the fact that I was being removed from my place of safety and thrust into the world all on my own. I was being abandoned by the only people who, to my knowledge, had ever treated me with decency. And so there was some anger, resentment, because although I'd been told what I'd done and why I deserved this sentence, I didn't remember it. I was the whipping boy for someone else's crime, and even though the someone else was an earlier version of myself, it felt unfair.

We bounced on down the road.

"So," said Woolly, "what do you think you're going to do?"

"What do you care?" I said. Woolly didn't deserve that, but as my banishment drew closer, the hurt became more than I could handle.

"Don't be that way, Al. I didn't want you to leave."

"And you didn't try to stop it, either?"

"How do you know what I did? I gave my opinion, I cast my vote. It wasn't up to just me."

I stared straight ahead.

"Who put Ruby in charge, anyway?" I asked. "Why's she so important?"

"Alison, I was hoping that you and I could have a nice drive, spend some time together as friends. Make a good memory. And maybe if you told me your plans, I could come back and visit you sometime."

"My exile. What a fond memory it will be."

"Al."

"I'll probably be dead within a week."

Woolly stopped the truck. The tires hissed in the dirt and gravel.

"Alison, please stop. I'm going to miss you. I am. We can mope and whine about what's happened. Or we can move forward. What's it going to be?"

I clenched my jaw and folded my arms.

"Fine," said Woolly. "I'll just drop you off."

He continued driving without saying more. I expected him to be angry or disappointed, but he was nonplussed. He grabbed an old battered CD player from under the seat which he plugged into the radio and began playing folk music. And he kept driving, calmly, contentedly, easing the old pickup over the rough road with a gentle ease.

This made me even angrier. I wanted a reaction. I wanted to have the fight I didn't have with Ruby. I wanted to yell at someone.

"I'd volunteer to drive anywhere just so I could listen to music," said Woolly as though he were speaking to himself.

He drummed his finger on the steering wheel and whistled to the tune.

I sighed. Then I sighed again, more loudly. I shifted around in my seat testily.

Woolly didn't seem to notice.

"Just let me out here," I said.

"We're not there yet, Al," said Woolly. "The spot I have in mind is much better, safer."

"I don't care," I said.

The sun was setting and the sky was turning purple and pink.

"Alison, do you ever consider that you're so anxious pursuing the future that you're missing out on the present?"

"It wasn't the future I was after," I told Woolly. "From what I've been told, I was chasing the past."

Woolly shrugged. "Same diff," he said. "I'm just saying instead of worrying about the future or the past, can you just be in the moment?"

"How very zen of you," I scoffed.

"I mean it. Here, close your eyes and listen to the music for a minute."

"I'm not going to—"

"I'm not asking," Woolly said in the sternest voice I'd ever heard from him. He turned up the volume. "Stop your fussing for just a moment and listen to this music."

To placate him, I took a deep breath and closed my eyes.

There was the sound of a harmonica, the lilting words of the singer talking about being without a home and nowhere to go. I had to laugh. I opened my eyes and saw Woolly nodding along with the beat. His eyes were half shut and he wore a smile on his face. The song played. It was sad, but it seemed to carry away some of my sadness.

When the song ended, Woolly asked me, "Do you feel better?"

I nodded.

"Yeah. You can't beat Bob Dylan."

After a while, he pulled off the road and drove overland and up onto a hilltop that was mostly barren of trees. He turned off the engine and shifted in his seat to face me.

"You're a rolling stone, Al." He opened his door. "The campsite is just inside that line of trees," he said, pointing.

"Woolly?"

"Yeah?"

"Could we keep listening?"

"You bet," he said. "But I've only got the one CD."

"That's okay."

We listened all the way through disc one of The Essential Bob Dylan before we were done unpacking the truck, and after that, we listened again as the sun set and the headlights shone into the forest. We listened to the songs so many times that I learned the words. Woolly played the air guitar and I fashioned a microphone out of a water bottle. We listened and we sang and laughed as if we didn't have a care in the world. It was the best moment of my life.

And then when wound down, late into the night, with sleep weighing heavy on both of us, Woolly said we should just sleep in the truck that night. I had already propped my backpack against the window and was blinking sleepily.

"Woolly," I said through a yawn.

"Hm?"

"You think I'll be okay out here by myself?"

He waited a beat before answering. "I think you will, Alison."

"And will you—" I stopped, my head nodding, unable to complete the question.

"Will I what?" he asked.

"Will you come visit me? Check on me?"

"Alison, old pal, you couldn't keep me away."

239

CHAPTER 47

In the morning, Woolly helped me with the provisions and equipment Ruby had supplied me with. It looked like there was plenty to get me through winter. Woolly helped me site my new camp and erect my heavy canvas tent. It came complete with a tiny wood-burning stove made from a rusted-out propane tank.

"Why don't I help you set up a nice big firepit," he said when the tent was standing taut. He wiped the sweat from his face. "Let's go find some rocks."

I followed him into the trees and we stooped and bent among the brush, looking for rocks that would stack and fit together. We piled them up a few at a time.

"You'll do great here, don'tcha think?" he said as we wandered, searching the ground.

"Yeah. Sure. This little camp is starting to take shape," I said. "I think a little me-time will do me good. I got some books, a couple blank notebooks. Yeah. I'll be okay."

I was trying to be brave. Woolly had been so patient; the least I could do was let him believe I wasn't afraid or depressed. And I suppose I'd made my peace with my exile, but it would be a long winter. Very long.

"Well, if you change your mind, just follow the river downstream," said Woolly, picking up a big flat rock that would become the warming fender of my firepit. "Follow it for two or three days and you'll find the Martinez camp."

"Thanks," I replied. We walked back to the campsite. "I feel like I'll stay away from the communities for a while. You know, stay out of trouble."

Woolly dropped his armload of stones and hitched up his sagging shorts. "That'll be the day," he said.

We built the firepit. It took a couple hours. It was large and sturdy. We banked soil and stones along the far side to reflect heat toward my tent, and we set flag stones around it in a kind of patio. Then Woolly built up the sides and installed a stout cross-member of green aspen to hang a kettle or cook pot.

Then we ate some lunch—canned chili from the supplies Ruby sent, warmed up in the can over a fire we made in the new pit. I thought Woolly would leave then, but he insisted on helping me drag a big gray fallen tree over to make a bench by the fire.

"Can't have a firepit without a place to sit now, can ya?"

"I've got a chair," I said.

"Well, this'll be for when I come to visit."

He busied himself with the bench, fitting it with rocks and smaller logs to make it sturdy.

"It's gettin' late, Woolly."

He stood and squinted at the sun. "Mm. Guess you're right."

"Thank you, though," I said. I didn't want him to go, but the longer he stayed, the worse it would be when he finally went. "It's a beautiful camp."

"Yeah," he said, looking around admiring the place, nodding, wiping the sweat from his face. "It ain't bad, is it? So, you'll be okay here?"

"I think I'll be very comfortable."

"Okay then. Guess I'll get going," he said with a sad smile. But then he held up a finger. "But there's one more thing. Hang on."

He went back to the truck and from under the driver's seat he removed some kind of bundle tied together with coarse string. He grinned widely as he returned. It was the notebooks.

"These are yours," he said as he handed the bundled-up journals and notebooks to me. "Well, technically, they're yours and Arie's, but you're the one who saved them."

I'd already read everything in the journals, but there wasn't a better gift that Woolly could have given me.

"Thank you, Woolly. I mean it. That's really nice."

"There's one in here you haven't read," said Woolly, tapping the notebook at the top of the bundle. It was the red notebook with the skull. "I've been working on this a long time. There were errors and inconsistencies that made it rather difficult. But it's finally finished."

"Doesn't this belong to Arie?" I asked.

"He told me he wanted you to have them."

My heart twinged a little at this.

"What's in it? What's it say?"

He raised one eyebrow and lifted his shoulders in an exaggerated shrug. "I would never encourage you to read something that might lead you to do anything rash or risky, Al. You know that. So, I'm not saying, 'Hurry and read it,' but I will say this: the whole reason we even know each other is because you were trying to figure out what this notebook said."

I ran my finger over the symbol, the outline of a skull with a clockface. Staring up from the battered notebook, the symbol was sinister, haunting.

"It's all there," said Woolly. "An interesting read for sure. It might give you some answers I know you want. And, well, if you don't find that interesting, there's also a copy of *The Great Gatsby* there that you can add to your winter reading list. Pardon all the weird marks and notes."

"Thanks, Woolly," I said, "for this and for everything."

He gave me a goodbye hug, lifting me off my feet as though I were just a doll. He promised to come and visit once the snow fell.

"If you move out of the area," said Woolly, "or if something goes wrong, leave a note. Stick it under a rock in the fireplace."

"Okay."

"Take care, Al. Be careful." His eyes were brimming, but he turned away and got into the truck.

I waved goodbye as he drove away in the slanting rays of the afternoon sun. I watched until he was out of sight and stayed until I could no longer hear the motor of the truck.

Then, all at once, a solemn loneliness settled around me like heavy banks of snow piling up in a November storm.

CHAPTER 48

I had food. I didn't have a lot, but I was sure I had enough. They had supplied me with several cases of canned goods that, if they weren't exactly delicious, they were at least palatable. I also had some cornmeal, beans, oil, salt, and a few other staples that would feed me comfortably throughout the winter.

And tea. I had resupplied my reserve of tea, begging and trading for any little extra I could get.

I had sturdy, warm clothing and shelter, a fine hunting knife, an ax, a rusty but serviceable bow-saw, and fire-making tools. Someone had gifted me a crude fishing rod and Chase had taught me a little about catching fish from the creeks and rivers so common in those mountains. A nice, older lady had given me a "winging stick," a kind of smooth wooden weapon meant to throw at grouse, like a boomerang that wasn't designed to come back. Woolly and the others had shown me how to set snares for rabbits and squirrels.

If I rationed my food and supplemented it with wild forage, I could probably hold out all the way to summer.

Happily, I had a few books to read, and notebooks of blank paper to write on. And there were the notebooks, the ones that Woolly had given me. I could read and re-read them all winter, read and re-read about my former self.

And I had work. There were many chores to do each day. Collecting water, gathering firewood, cooking food, improving my camp, and preparing for the hard winter to come.

I felt the weight of my solitude, and although I'd been showing a brave face to Woolly when I told him I needed some me-time, I hadn't been completely disingenuous. In the prison I'd learned to be alone with myself, an ability that I found valuable. And I considered searching out the other camp, maybe just for a visit, but I decided it really would be best to give myself some time. I felt like a screw-up, a failure, someone who just made things worse for others.

For their sake, I would stay away.

And so I set out to keep busy, take care of business, and be content. I chopped wood, stacking up a supply against the cold. I set snares for rabbits, thinking I might make myself a rabbit-fur comforter. I didn't catch any rabbits, but my luck was better with the fish. At first I could catch one or two per day, but later I caught more, and it didn't take as long. In any way possible, I tried to live off the land.

At night, I fell into bed with not an ounce of remaining energy, and I slept soundly.

Each day seemed to get colder. I sealed up and secured my tent until it was as warm as I thought it could be. I piled up firewood and even experimented with dried fish.

On some nights, however, sleep wouldn't come despite my exhaustion. The few crickets that were still chirping reminded me of the klaxon that wailed out the night Ruby's team had rescued me and Chase and Arie. That reminded me that someone had been shot and killed that night. And that reminded me of what they told me about before—how I'd put Ruby's entire camp in danger, and how people had died in the raid that followed.

Chase had told me that I was a cog in an evil machine that I couldn't control. He said that I couldn't take so much responsibility. It had weighed on my conscience, but I had listened to and very much appreciated what Chase had said. It had helped me to push it out of my mind.

But now, all alone in a quiet, secluded place, I could not stop my mind from opening up the box and sorting the pieces of these events as though they were shipments I'd received. I examined every item in every package.

I wasn't told who had died. I purposely did not ask. I wouldn't have remembered them anyway, but at the time, I thought it would be easier to not know.

Now, I wanted to know. Not just their names, I wanted to know everything about them. What they looked like. Who they loved. What their dreams were. I felt it was part of the burden I needed to carry.

As the days wore on and light snowstorms blew through my little valley, an ache began to form inside me. I wanted to make things right, or at least better, but I knew I never could. How can you bring back something that's gone? You can't. I knew. I sniffed. My nose was already runny from the colder air. And sometimes, as I reflected on the people whose deaths I was responsible for, hot tears ran down my cold cheeks.

Almost a foot of snow fell, and it stayed. My camp was ready—I had firewood, a little dried fish, and I was even able to trap a few rabbits and wing some grouse. I'd barely put a dent in the supplies Ruby had given me.

But my mind was constantly whirling. How could I fix what I'd done? And always the answer was that, without the benefit of a time machine, I couldn't. I lay in bed, not sleeping. With snow on the ground it was utterly quiet outside while my thoughts clamored inside my head. In some ways I welcomed the hurt and the anguish. I deserved the pain and accepted it. But there was nothing I could do with it. That was the problem. I could not trade places with those who had suffered, and I couldn't otherwise reverse their suffering.

One morning, I went to the spring and hauled a three-day supply of water through the cold. Then I hiked a mile to the nearest creek and caught fish, chopped firewood even though I didn't really need any, and set new rabbit snares in a wide circuit around the forest. I returned to camp in the dark, lit the coals in my little stove until the tent was hot, ate a big dinner of canned food, and lay down on my cot. Sleep came, finally, but before dawn the next morning I was visited by terrible dreams, ghostly images of dead people, those who I knew I was responsible for. They gathered around my tent, their fingers stretched out and pointing at me. Men and women, young and old. They came into my tent and pointed their fingers at me.

"You," they said, one by one.

"You."

"You."

I woke abruptly, covered with sweat. The stove had gone cold. I lay back down and pulled my blankets up around my ears, but sleep did not come back. I lay on the cot with my eyes closed, but I was awake with my thoughts. When the sun rose, I knew I should get up. I needed to light the stove so that my water didn't freeze. I needed to eat. I needed to check my tent lines and stakes to make sure they were secure against future snowfall.

But I was numb—the guilt had finally caught up to me. And so I didn't get up. I just stared at the side of my tent, watching the sunlight move across it. I got up at some point to pee, but then I went right back to bed. I didn't have the energy for anything. Eventually, I even quit thinking about anything. I'd shut down.

It was in the afternoon that I heard the vehicle. I don't know if it was that same day or if another day or more had passed. I was in a mental fog.

The vehicle was obviously a truck with low gearing, something that could climb the logging road. At first it was far away, at the bottom of the hill, grumbling up the steep grade and through the slippery snow. It was at least something for my mind to focus on. I listened but didn't move from my cot.

Was it an Agency detachment, rounding up stragglers from the summer's raids? Was it Woolly, coming to check on me? I'd left him with the impression that I'd be fine, and he'd be disappointed to find me this way.

The truck neared. I could picture it at the clearing where the road stopped. Through the clear, cold air, I heard the engine stop. Then there was the thunking of doors. I may have heard a voice. Then the vehicle started again and slowly receded.

Silence again. I didn't respond. I didn't care.

But soon I heard a new sound. Boots crunching on snow, approaching. They came closer. First, they were at the edge of the woods, then they came down the trail to my camp, and to the front of my tent. I stayed quiet, not because of fear but because I simply didn't care what happened next. Friend or assassin—what difference would it make? Someone fiddled and fumbled with the front flap of my tent. The outer fly was opened and there came the heavy metallic buzz of the heavy brass zipper being drawn open.

It was Chase.

CHAPTER 49

"Hey, Al," said Chase.

It surprised me so much that for a moment I didn't respond. I blinked my eyes and tried to puzzle out if he were really there and, if so, why.

"Al? You okay?

"Yeah," I finally said.

"Can I come in?" he asked.

"Yeah," I said again.

I felt that I'd reached some new low, some rock-bottom. At least in the prison I was looking for ways to survive. Now I was lying in bed wondering how long it'd be before the winter took me. And I'm sure I looked low. My heart broke at the sight of Chase.

He stood in the tent, taking in the scene. My red and swollen crying eyes, my matted hair.

"You sure you're all right?" he asked.

"What are you doing here?" I said.

He didn't have a ready answer. I wondered if Ruby had sent him. Or Woolly. Someone had brought him here. I wondered if they'd changed their minds; if they would let me back in. Was he bringing a message from them?

"Can I sit down?" he asked.

I didn't move, but I nodded, and he perched himself awkwardly on the edge of the cot. He was sitting on one of my feet, but he didn't seem to notice.

"Did Ruby send you?" I asked.

"Uh, no," said Chase. "In fact, she kind of ordered me not to come here."

"What are you doing here?" I asked again.

He pursed his lips and scratched his beard, as though he'd been asking himself the same question.

"They're leaving," said Chase. "Ruby's group. They're packing up heading east."

I nodded. "Ruby told me," I said.

"Yeah. Well, I don't feel like I belong with them," said Chase.

"You don't?"

"No," he said. "I don't know them. They don't know me. Or, I should say, they know some older version of me, someone I don't know." Chase was quiet then. I still didn't understand why he was here, so I asked him a third time.

"So—what are you doing here?"

He looked at me—right into my eyes. It felt as though he really knew me, didn't just recognize me, didn't just consider me an acquaintance, but actually knew me. But that wasn't possible. His memories had been wiped the same as mine and we'd barely spent any time together at the camp. There was an unspoken intensity in his looks that gave me goosebumps.

"I—can't really explain it," he said. "When Woolly got back, I asked him where you were and I just felt like I needed to be with you."

"What for?"

He looked away then. "I don't know. I mean maybe I do, but I don't."

His responses irked me. There was something else I wanted him to say. Something else I was longing to hear, but he hadn't said it.

"I don't need your help," I said sharply.

"Of course not," he said. "Your camp looks incredible. The tent facing south. Got your little stove in here. Looks like you have enough firewood for a year. And that firepit outside, I mean. Wow."

"Woolly helped a lot."

"Still. It's really great."

"So?"

"So, I guess what I mean is, I think maybe I need your help."

"With what?"

"I don't know. Just a feeling I have that I should stick by you. That with you is where I need to be. Sounds stupid, doesn't it?" He squinted his eyes at me. "Alison, have you been crying?"

"You're just now noticing?"

"What's wrong?"

I stared at the floor of my tent. "I killed them."

"Who?"

"The people from camp, when I let Ruby's prisoner go, and the man who died when they were rescuing us."

"You didn't kill them," said Chase. "It wasn't your fault."

"Don't tell me that. My actions led to their deaths," I said. "It was my fault. I know it. Ruby knows it. You know it. Their lives are over."

"So, what are you going to do about it?"

"I should turn myself over to the Agency," I said. "I don't deserve to be happy."

"That's the stupidest thing I've ever heard. Do you not remember what it was like there? Seems like a mighty big waste—these people sacrificing their lives for you to just throw yours away. You don't deserve that."

"Well, what can I do? How can I make it better?"

Chase put his hand on my shoulder. "Did you ever consider that we aren't always supposed to make things better? That maybe that's part the experience of life?"

"No! I did this, Chase! I did it. I can't just move on," I cried, raising my voice. "I can't just say it was an accident or that it doesn't matter. I can't forget it!"

"Then don't," Chase said. "Remember them; don't forget them."

"But I don't remember," I said.

251

"Good point. Listen, Al, you've been put in prison, you've been banished. If you ask me, you've paid the price. If you really think there is something you can do, then figure it out and use that to move forward." He pulled me up and into his arms. I collapsed into the hollow of his shoulder and cried.

"When will it stop hurting?" I sobbed.

"I don't think something like this will stop hurting," he said. "You just gotta make room for it."

Chase held me for a long time, until I stopped crying, and then he made us some tea on the rusty little stove. The tent got warm, and we sipped the tea, and I started feeling better. We went out to my firepit and lit a big fire. We sat side by side on the log bench Woolly had built.

"You really have an impressive stockpile of firewood," he said. "You certainly have not been lying in bed this whole time."

I showed him my hands and the big gray callouses that had formed on my palms. Chase took my hand and kneaded the muscles between his fingers. His hands were rough, too, but warm and gentle as well.

We laid on more wood and the flames rose up brightly, pushing back the descending gloom of late afternoon.

"I brought some food with me," he said, nodding at the giant backpack he'd set outside the tent. "But you're doing fine. You're curing fish?" He gestured at my drying rack.

I nodded.

"How's it taste?"

I shrugged.

He walked over and plucked one of the pale fillets from a bundle. He had a bite and nodded approvingly before rejoining me on the bench.

"Have more. I've got plenty. Canned food, too."

He sipped his tea with a thoughtful look on his face. "So, you'd really consider going to the Agency and having your memories wiped to forget alla that?"

I nodded uncertainly.

252

He looked at me sadly, and with pity.

"Forgetting doesn't change the past. It doesn't erase it from happening. It wouldn't change anything except you wouldn't know it." He sipped again. "Wouldn't you rather know?"

"It just hurts so much," I said, and my chin quivered as I spoke. "Out here, where it's so quiet, and there's no one to talk with, I just think about it all the time."

"Like I said, you've paid your price. Or you're paying it. That's the cost of life. When we make mistakes, we have to feel them, own them. That's what makes us human."

His words were reaching me somehow. That maybe my punishment, my real punishment, would be to remember— to know that I'd cost lives—but maybe it could be a blessing too. It certainly made me acutely aware of the value of life.

"Besides," said Chase with a wink and a wry grin. "Who knows what other mistakes we've made?" He reached over and clinked his mug against mine.

I smiled for the first time in a long time. Then I remembered what they often said in the camp.

"Well," I said, "maybe someday we'll remember."

CHAPTER 50

Among the provisions Chase had brought with him there was tea. Real tea. Not the stale and doubtful leaf shreds in metal tins we'd hijacked from the Agency's always-disappointing food rations. This was from the back before, in a brightly colored (though battered and worn) box. It was probably stale, too, but it was so flavorful and different I either couldn't tell or didn't care. I rationed it carefully.

Chase had not brought enough food with him to support even himself alone for the winter, but he had a rifle for hunting game and a wrist rocket to shoot smaller prey. He said if he hadn't found me or if I didn't want him to stay, he'd plan to stay on the move, hunting and camping and moving southward to warmer climes.

But I wanted him to stay and he moved in. We settled into the harsher routine of winter living, working together, sharing chores, sharing our warmth. It was good. We read to each other and laughed and sat together staring at the fire.

Still, the thought of the people who'd had lost their lives—sixteen of them to be exact—was never far from my mind. When Chase made me laugh or when the sky turned crimson as the sun went down, I thought of those people and how they would not laugh anymore or mark the beauty of a sunset. I got accustomed to carrying them with me—whoever they were—but it got easier, especially with Chase around.

I discovered that when two people live together with no one else around—they develop a very strong bond. In the few weeks since Chase had joined me, we had grown so close. He'd come back from a full day of fishing or hunting, and just the sight of him would make me warm and happy, and I couldn't help myself from smiling.

We knew, of course, that we had been a couple before. And so to us it seemed that we were fated to be together. It also seemed to us that we'd somehow been given our relationship all over again—it was something that had been taken and returned. It was new and fun and a sort of daily delight to learn each other's ways, to adapt to each other. Even when we quarreled, there was a chemistry, an intensity.

"I don't remember anything from before," Chase said one night as he pulled me closer on the bench by the fire, "but right now it kinda feels like we've always been together."

"Mm," I said, leaning into him.

What I liked the most is that our love seemed more powerful than anything. Stronger than anything. The pandemic couldn't kill it. The Agency could erase it. Ruby couldn't banish it. Winter couldn't freeze it.

And as I emerged from the cold cage of guilt that I'd built there in the woods, I realized there was another, sweeter ache I carried with me. At first I didn't want to mention it to Chase. I didn't want him to think I was just one big collection of complaints and hurts and wants. But as my love for Chase grew and grew, there was something missing. Someone.

Arie.

At first I just read and re-read his journals. I'd rest from our chores and find a sunny spot where it might get warm. I'd daydream about fixing bikes with him and collecting chicken eggs. I read scenes where we dodged Agency goons and searched old abandoned neighborhoods. It was strange—imagining being the person in those journals, even though I really was that person.

Soon I began talking about Arie a lot with Chase.

"How'd he seem when you left?" I asked.

"He seemed okay," said Chase. "He was excited for the adventure, the exodus. That kid craves adventure."

"Mm. Did he seem like he missed me at all?"

"Oh, he interrogated Woolly for a couple days after he got back from setting you up out here—how you handled it, where he'd brought you, asked about the camp."

"What else?"

"He was sorry you couldn't come along," said Chase.

"He said that, or you're just guessing?"

"He said it. Said it to me, to Woolly."

"So, he did miss me."

"I mean, we all did. But yeah, he missed you. He not only said so, but I could tell, too."

It also felt strange to pine for Arie because he was as much a stranger to me as anyone else I'd met since coming out of the prison, including Chase. And Arie had decided for himself not to join me. I didn't hesitate when it came time to accept his decision, but I was his mother. And I clung to that role, and although it felt like a chair I was saving for someone else, I was glad I was Arie's mother.

What I didn't do was read the coded notebook Woolly had given me along with the journals. I had grown afraid of what the strange red notebook might contain. Judging from what Woolly had said, the information in the red notebook had led me to do the things I'd done to get myself exiled in the first place. Woolly had been provocative when he pointed out the red notebook. He'd made a playful, teasing effort to tempt me into reading it, but that'd had the opposite effect. I took the white skull symbol as a warning, as a caution. I'd put the red notebook on the bottom of the pile and I had never even opened it.

And so it was a surprise when I found Chase reading it one day when I returned from checking my rabbit snares. He was boiling grouse bones for stew stock, and he sat near the fire studying a page of the strange text.

"What are you doing?" I said, dropping my captured rabbits into the snow and feeling slightly panicked. "Why are you reading that?"

"You've never read it?" Chase asked.

"No," I said, "and I don't want to."

"Why not?" He furrowed his brow.

"Because it's nothing but trouble."

"Al," Chase said, shutting the notebook, "I think we need to talk."

CHAPTER 51

I'm not sure I would have gotten out of bed ever again if Chase hadn't appeared, and I know I wouldn't have read Arie's coded notebook if Chase hadn't read it first.

"What's in it?" I had asked him. "What is it about this mysterious notebook?"

"Well, it's information, Al. It's a story."

"Are you being purposely vague?"

"I guess I am," Chase replied.

"Why? Why can't you just tell me what's in it?"

"Let me ask you a question before I answer," said Chase. "Why haven't you read it? You've been here all this time without reading it—why?"

"I'm not sure," I said. And I meant it. Why hadn't I read it? "I guess I thought reading it might be kind of, you know, dangerous. I thought it might nudge me into my old reckless and headstrong ways, which apparently has gotten me into more trouble than I can remember."

"Fair enough," Chase said thoughtfully. "So, would you like me to tell you what the notebook's about?"

"Well, was there anything in it you found useful?" I asked, eying the notebook as though it might be a viper.

"Yes," he said. "In fact, calling it useful would be putting it mildly."

I folded my arms. Then unfolded them. I sat on the log bench. I stood up. Then I paced for a few moments. Then I sat down again and folded my arms. Chase sat watching me. I stood up again.

"Al, hold still for a sec."

258

I stood still.

"I think you should read this." Chase held out the notebook.

I took it.

I read it until the light failed, and then I did something I hadn't done before: I lit a light. I had a few tallow candles from Ruby's camp, along with a small bottle of kerosene and a lamp with a rough cotton wick, but I hadn't used either until then. I'd been reserving them, knowing the days in winter would get shorter and darker and I'd need them then. As Chase lay dozing on the cot, I lit a candle and sat in my camp chair with a kettle of tea.

I read about Arie and the man who'd been attacked and left for dead, Eudrich. I read about the Agency's attempts to restore memories. I read about various experiments they conducted and their failed attempts, and then about somewhat successful attempts. The language in the journal was often technical with scientific words difficult for me to follow or understand.

A lot of it had information we'd already been told—from Ruby or Woolly—and most of it was fairly dry and boring, not like the journals Arie and I had written, which I found completely engrossing and fascinating.

At one point I almost gave up reading the rest, as though it were a dull pulp novel or tedious history book. But then the story moved from medical experiments and chemical formulas and on to Eudrich's theories about memories that were more esoteric and philosophical.

Arie had learned that a group of about six people who'd been captured and arrested on some charge of thievery or subversion. This had happened in the Zone where Arie and I had once lived together, where we wrote our journals. The six people were imprisoned, of course, and they were, in Eudrich's words, "closely examined." Arie understood this to mean that they were questioned under duress. Tortured. And in the course of these close examinations, it was discovered that they had all of their memories. All of them.

They remembered everything that had ever happened to them—before the serum, before the pandemic, and on back to their childhoods. The Agency records were consulted and re-consulted—these people had escaped from the Zones, after all, and should not have remembered anything but the past year of their lives. Even Agency personnel had lost their memories of the back before. And yet, the six remembered everything.

How had they gotten their memories back, Eudrich wanted to know, even after being dosed again and again?

They wouldn't say at first. Eudrich said the examinations were "intensified," which Arie took to mean life-threatening torture. And finally, they revealed their secret.

There was a man, said the six, who had a way to restore memories. This man, a recluse who they referred to as "the Guide." did not use medicine. The encoded text was infuriatingly incomplete in this section of the notebook, and there were notes in the margins from Woolly explaining that transcription errors in the code had likely made these parts of the notebook untranslatable. And so there were several passages that were not decoded, and some had only fragments of decoded text, such as "when you make your secret journey," and "walking with oneself" over some kind of "higher path."

And there was this cryptic line: "Memory is not a matter of thinking of something that happened in the past. It is a matter of discovering oneself. To recall, you must discover."

After studying with the Guide, after taking this so-called secret journey, the six had regained all of their memories, and the first thing they wanted to do was to return to the Zones to collect the friends and family members they now recalled with perfect clarity. But this was their downfall, because of course those they came back to rescue did not know them and did not trust them.

Tragically, they'd probably been reported by one of their own family members or friends, and this is what had led to their initial capture by the Agency.

The candle was burning low now, and it was very late, but I read furiously, my breath shallow. The Agency pressed the same question that I now had: Where was the Guide? Where could he be found?

The six refused to say. They would not give up their guide. The closest they ever got to a real answer was from one of the six, a man who was apparently quite old. Just before he died while being "examined," he told the Agency the guide lived "deep in the forest, on the mountain of the bear." The remaining five were also killed while imprisoned—Arie assumed they, too, were tortured to death.

At this I gasped, and something inside me awakened. I didn't take time to think about it, didn't even really acknowledge it at that moment, but on some level I knew it was the drive I'd had before, the urge to make things right, the urge that had led me to trouble again and again. I read on.

A search was made for this "mountain of the bear," but nothing came of it. Sure, there were several mountains with "bear" or "grizzly" in their map names. They searched anywhere there was a road, town, river, or even trail that had anything to do with Bears.

The Guide was never found.

Instead, Arie postulated, this was how certain individuals within the Agency's medical core, such as Eudrich and Bellington, were first alerted to the possibility of total memory restoration. Hypnosis? Exposure to familiar stimulus? Drugs? The information squeezed out the six under "intense examination" generated several hypothetical lines of research and testing began for ways to restore memories.

I read these pages furiously, my heart beating hard and an excitement growing within me.

"Chase," I called, kicking the cot.

Chase mumbled and rolled over. He hiked himself up on one elbow and squinted against the candle light.

"You read this? About the Guide? About the man in the mountains?"

"Mm-hmm," he said, rubbing his eyes.

"Well?"

"Well, I thought you'd find it very interesting," he said. "That's why I suggested that you read it."

"Yes, but do you think there is really a man living in the mountains who can restore memories?"

"Yeah."

"Do you think he really lives in the mountains? Like these mountains where we are?"

"Yeah, I do."

My body, my whole soul, felt energized. As if this whole time I'd been sleeping and only now had awaken.

"Well, how could we ever find him?" I said, feigning my skepticism. "I mean, it says here that they sent out search parties all over the place. They searched every bear place they could find, and they came up empty."

Chase shrugged and said, "I think I know where he is."

"What? Where?"

He stood, stretched, and then went to his backpack. "Al, I've forgotten everything about my past. Who I was, where I came from, what I did before—it's all gone. But there's a few things I know about me. One thing: I like maps. I'm fascinated by maps. I like looking at 'em, I find it easy to read them, and once I see something on a map, I remember it."

"Okay. That's nice. So?"

He drew a folded map from a pocket in the pack, sat on the cot, and unfolded it on his lap.

"I, uhm, 'borrowed' some maps from Woolly and Ruby's stash," he said. "They're old. They'll never miss 'em."

I wanted him to hurry and show me whatever it was he wanted to show me, but I didn't want to interrupt. He must have read this on my face.

"I'm getting to the point he said," holding up a finger. "As soon as I read that this Guide fella lived on the 'mountain of the bear,' I knew where it was. I knew I'd seen it before on a map. A map of this area."

He unfolded his map. It was deeply creased and worn. Some of it was only faintly legible. Chase picked up the candle, held it near, and pointed to a spot on the map. To me, maps were confusing conglomerations of lines and contours and colors. I didn't have a good mind for scales or grids or terrain. I was more into landmarks, more of a "turn-left-at-the-big-crooked-pine-tree" sort of navigator, and I had to really try hard to find my way by maps. But I looked at the place on the map where Chase pointed. I could tell it was a mountain within a larger region of mountainous country. The whole space was covered with snaking contour lines stacked closely and precisely together, a two-dimensional representation of very three-dimensional ground. Chase tapped the map.

"This says Caspian Peak," I said. "What's it got to do with a bear?"

"Look closer," said Chase, holding the candle closer. "Look at the lines."

I looked. A few drops of tallow dripped from the candle onto the map. With my eyes, I followed the contours, blinking, squinting. Chase's finger guided my gaze. Then I began to see what he meant.

"The bear," said Chase in a whisper.

I saw it. Goosebumps formed on my arms and neck. Caspian Peak was shaped uncannily like a bear. Its valleys and draws and ridges outlined the body, legs, and head of a galloping bear.

It was the Mountain of the Bear.

CHAPTER 52

We left the next day. There wasn't any question of whether we should go. We didn't even really discuss it. Instead, we immediately went to sleep and in the morning there was tea and a little breakfast and we loaded our packs. I wrote a note for Woolly and tucked it under a broad, flat rock on the firepit.

By midday we were on the trail.

The Mountain of the Bear was a mere twenty-five miles away. I had to believe that there had to be a time in my life when I thought at the very least that twenty-five miles through a rugged wilderness was a long way to hike. In a past life, I may even have thought it was impossible to make such a journey, especially with the cold weather and snow. But on that day, I knew it would take only three days—two days if the weather was good. It would be a cold trip, to be sure. And there was a very good chance that we'd encounter a storm or two. If it got bad enough, we'd have to hunker down and wait it out, but we wouldn't stop altogether. We were going to the Mountain of the Bear.

We hiked with determined quickness for about two hours without saying much of anything. If there was any talking, it was about the trail.

"I think the trail turns back south up ahead, but it'll be hard to see under this snow, so keep your eyes open."

"Okay, will do."

As we stopped for a breather and filled our water bottles at a stream crossing, I finally asked the question I knew we both were turning over in our minds.

"What are the chances?" I asked between gulps of water.

"Chances of what?" replied Chase.

"You know what I mean," I said. "What are the chances?"

"That he'll be there? That we'll find him?"

I nodded, gulped my water.

"Well," said Chase, "that's a question within a question within a question, isn't it?" He drank a mouthful of water and then wiped his beard with the back of his gloved hand. "First, is this really the Mountain of the Bear? Second, if it is, is the Guide still there or has he moved or died or been captured? And third, if this is the right mountain, and if he's still here, can we locate him? I mean even narrowing the search area to the mountain that has the vague shape of the bear itself, we're still dealing with something like ten square miles. That's an almost impossible area for two people to search. And what if he wasn't really at the Mountain of the Bear, but that was just a landmark? What if he's somewhere in the twenty square miles surrounding that particular mountain?"

I shrugged.

"So, I guess it's three questions wrapped up in a fourth," said Chase, looking off toward the mountain.

"Then why are we doing this?" I said, again, faking a tone of skepticism to keep my own hopes at a manageable level.

"Doesn't hurt to try," said Chase turning back to me with a sarcastic grin. He clunked his water bottle against mine in a chilly, trail side toast, and we were off again.

We encountered a storm. Big flakes of early winter snow pounded the area, left another foot of snow. We trudged through it. We kept walking until it was almost too dark to see, and then even I was ready to stop. With the snow on the trails it was difficult enough to find our way. They were slippery, too. It was a miracle we didn't fall and break our necks in the daylight; we couldn't continue in the dark.

We found a level spot in the woods, tramped down a flat spot in the snow, and built the small tent Chase had brought with him. We took off our boots but left our snow clothes on and wiggled into our sleeping bags. Chase threw a mylar-coated emergency blanket over us to trap our heat, and then we lay on our sides, close together in the small tent.

"There's another question to answer here, ya know," said Chase. He lay behind me, one arm around my middle. "One that's arguably bigger and more important than finding the Guide."

"What's that?" I asked.

"Do you want to remember?"

I would have thought that was an easy question. In fact I almost blurted, "Of course I do!" Who wouldn't want to remember? But I didn't say that. Because it honestly was a question I hadn't answered yet. A question I hadn't truly asked yet.

I knew why Chase has raised the question. He raised it because we were okay, he and I. We were happy. We had been together before, and we had either found one another again or had been thrust together, depending how you viewed it. But we were together, and we were happy. We stayed busy, we helped one another, and at the end of the day we collapsed into one another's arms and slept peacefully. And it sometimes felt like we could go on that way for a very long time.

So, what did I need from the past? What could knowing about my past do for me now?

It was easy to think our memories would be nothing but happy times and delight, but I knew better now. A person can't live through a pandemic without witnessing suffering or without feeling pain. I knew there was loss back there in the back before.

There may or may not be happy memories, but there would undoubtedly be sorrow and pain and suffering. I wasn't sure I wanted to remember. Knowing that I'd been responsible for the deaths of others was already a heavy

266

burden that affected me daily. What if there was more? What if I'd made even bigger mistakes?

Chase waited in the darkness as I considered these things.

I turned to him. "I'm not sure," I finally said.

"I know," he said. "It's okay. I'll be with you whatever you decide. My choice is to stay with you."

Over the next two days of hiking, what I couldn't discount was the excitement that I felt every time I thought about finding the Guide. I may have been theoretically or psychologically or intellectually unsure about the prospect of remembering everything, but my heart was all in. My mind pulled on the reins; my feelings cracked the whip.

I wondered sometimes if subconsciously we still knew everything, still made decisions based on our previous experiences. I may have believed that to be true, but which direction was my subconscious leading me? My heart pounded, and I felt full of life when I thought about getting my memories back. But it was always followed by a queasiness in my stomach, a feeling of dread and regret.

But in the end, I knew what I had to do.

"I've decided," I told Chase.

"Great," said Chase. "But this means we'll have to hurry. The later it gets the harder it will be to find Arie."

I scoffed in disbelief.

"That's what you meant, right? That you want to re-unite with Arie? Convince him to stay with us?"

"I didn't realize I was that easy to read."

Chase exhaled. "You're his mom, Al. Despite what you do or don't remember or whatever the relationship has been lately, it's obvious. I don't think that's something they've been able to erase out of you. Or maybe it's because I'm almost as good at reading people as I am at reading maps. But I agree with your plan. We find the Guide, then we find Arie."

I nodded. "He's free to make his own choices, but if we find the Guide, and if he can do what the notebook says he can do, I think it's imperative that I let Arie know. Is that selfish?"

"No. How could it be selfish?"

I couldn't put it into words exactly, so I just shrugged. There was one thing I wanted desperately, and that was for Arie to remember me.

"Like I said, though, we have to hurry. Ruby's got her plans to head east. I figured she was gonna need at least two months to get ready for that, which doesn't give us much time. We'll have to hustle."

CHAPTER 53

After the first day of our hike to find the Guide, Chase went back to warning me not to get my hopes up, even though I could tell he himself wasn't taking this advice.

"I mean, look at this terrain," he said as we trudged through the snow. "With the weather holding us back, and so much area to search, I don't want to say it's hopeless, Al, but I sure as hell ain't hopeful."

We were relying on fragments of rumors and hearsay, Chase reminded me, and we had re-assembled those fragments in the most optimistic way possible.

"I'm telling you right now, it could take weeks to find this guy, and we don't have weeks. So keep your expectations low," said Chase. "Very low."

And I'd already adopted that outlook on my own— trying to convince myself that nothing would come of this— but I was only saying it to protect myself, and alongside my innermost thoughts, I couldn't stop those hopes from rising secretly up, the way a helium balloon keeps floating up when batted down.

But all of the hedging and expectation management turned out to be for nothing. We didn't so much find the Guide as he led us to himself. It appeared he wanted to be found.

It started with the sound of chimes. There were wind chimes hanging from high in the trees. First just one, and then one every mile or so, and then more. Some were made of delicate metallic slivers that rang and jangled ethereally with the slightest motion. Others were made of wood that made hollow, clonking notes. Some of the chimes were like those you'd find on a back porch; others were just tied-together collections of metal and glass that made discordant clankings.

After a while we saw strands of yarn and ribbon tied around branches, hanging down over the trail, and tied like fencing between tree trunks to guide searchers. Some of these trail markings looked to have been there for years.

Chase and I said almost nothing, but we exchanged amazed glances as we felt ourselves getting closer and closer to the Guide.

And then we found the camp.

It was a small oval-shaped glade in the trees. Not a clearing, exactly, but a place where the trees were larger and the forest floor was more open, with no undergrowth. It was an oval about three hundred feet long and maybe two hundred feet wide. At the center of this camp there stood a massive tee-pee, its outer skin made of canvas and animal hide. Long, slender pine trunks held it up, converging high in the canopy. The tapered ends mingled with the branches. There were more wind chimes here, creating an unending, atonal musical chord.

The tee-pee dwarfed several other tents, which had been erected in a rough circle around it. They were of various kinds—canvas, vinyl, and makeshift lean-to's constructed from blue tarps. Some of them had been there long enough that they were anchored to the ground by grass and accumulated pine-needle duff.

The snow cover was only just a dusting here beneath the massive pine trees. Chase and I trudged toward the tee-pee with our heavy packs and our breath smoking in the cold.

Outside the tee-pee there was a large, ornate rug. On the rug there was a man seated cross-legged.

The Guide.

He was dressed in simple, coarse clothing—a loose woolen tunic and roomy, natural-cotton pants. He wore no shoes. His long, silvery hair was pulled back into a ponytail.

His arms were outstretched so that his upturned hands rested on his knees, fingers touching thumbs. His head was slightly bowed and his eyes were shut.

Chase and I stopped about twenty feet from the man, waiting for him to notice us, but he sat completely still.

I set my backpack on the ground. The vinyl fabrics swished and zipped and the backpack thudded into the snow, disrupted the tinkling chimes and the generally serene setting. Then Chase took off his backpack in a similar noisy fashion. We exchanged a look. The man still had not looked up, had not done anything to acknowledge that two strangers were now standing in front of him.

"Should we say something?" I whispered to Chase.

"No," Chase whispered back. "Let him finish."

The man let out a rough sigh. "I can hear you," he said.

He opened his eyes and stood up.

"Sorry," I said. "We didn't mean to interrupt."

He smiled accommodatingly, but didn't answer us. Instead, he rolled up his rug and headed for the tee-pee.

I approached him, my mouth suddenly dry and my breath ragged in my windpipe.

"Hey, uh, hi," I said. "I'm Alison, and that's Chase. We've been looking for you."

He stopped walking and turned to me. "Looking for me? Who do you think I am?"

"Well, uh, what I meant was—"

"You said you were looking for me, right?" he said. "You must know who I am, then."

"No," I stammered. "Not exactly. It's just—we heard there was a man here who knew how to restore lost memories."

"Interesting," he said.

"Well, can you?" asked Chase.

"Can I what?"

"Can you help restore lost memories?" said Chase, with an impatient buzz in his voice.

"You've lost your memories?" said the man with a bemused smile. "Where? How? Did you leave them at the bus station? Did they fall out of your backpacks?"

Chase and I traded a perplexed glance. It was like talking to the Cheshire Cat. I couldn't tell if he was annoyed with us, or if he was only joking, or if he was being completely serious. Chase was about to answer—angrily, I suspected—so I stopped him by placing my hand on his forearm.

"I'm sorry," I cut in, smiling. "We're being impolite. We haven't even met you, and we don't know your name."

"Peter," he said.

"Peter," I said, "it's a pleasure. My name is—"

"Alison, yes," said Peter, "I heard you. And that is Chase. Hello. Nice to meet you both. Nice day, don't you think?"

"Oh!" I said. "Yes. Well, it's rather cold. But yes, lovely, I suppose."

Peter nodded, surveyed the sky that shone through the trees. He stood barefoot in the snow with no apparent discomfort.

"Al!" grumbled Chase.

I shushed him. "So, Peter. Is it true? Can you restore our memories?"

"Restore your memories?" he said, furrowing his brow. He seemed bemused. "No. I can't do that." He turned and ducked through a canvas flap into the tee-pee.

Chase picked up his pack again. "I don't think that's the Guide," said Chase.

I put my hand on Chase's arm. "Hold on," I said. "Look at this place. If this guy isn't the Guide, then there is no Guide. We've come so far. We can't just leave. Maybe he's not the Guide. Maybe he tells us where the Guide is. The guide that leads us to the Guide?"

"I really feel like we need to talk to him. Let's give him a day or two."

Chase shrugged and then let out a sigh.

We picked up our packs and approached the tee-pee.

"Uhm, Peter?"

"Yes, come in," he said.

We pushed aside the canvas door and went in. The interior of the tee-pee wasn't what I figured it would be. It was roomy and tidy, with a clean floor of tarpaulins and animal furs. On one side was a bed. On the other side there stood a small table. There was a fire in the center of the floor, and it was comfortably warm inside, but it wasn't at all smoky. A little smoke came from the coals of the fire, but it was drawn up through a vent at the top of the tee-pee, which also let in plenty of light. Peter sat near the fire, a small book in his hands.

"Take off your boots, please," said Peter politely, "and then join me. I was going to do a little reading, but I enjoy company, too."

We took off our boots and sat at the fire across from Peter.

"Peter," I said, "we don't want to keep disrupting your routine, so we won't stay long, but, may we camp here for a while?"

"I don't see why not," he said. "There is good water nearby. I don't have much food, but if you help with chores, I'll share what I can."

"Thank you," I said.

Chase sat stony-faced next to me, watching Peter as if conducting an assessment.

"Can I offer you something to drink?" asked Peter. "The tea should be ready by now. It's quite lovely."

"Oh, you read my mind," I said. "I would love some tea. Thank you. We'll just have a cup, and then we'll go see about our tent and such."

"How about you, Chase?" said Peter, getting to his feet. "It'll warm you right up."

"No thanks," mumbled Chase.

"Suit yourself."

Peter stooped at the fire and lifted an iron teapot. He moved somewhat slowly but smoothly and deliberately, without wasted effort. A plume of steam rose from the spout of the pot. Peter took the pot to the table and from it he poured two cups of the tea. I stood and met him halfway across the floor of the tee-pee. He handed a cup to me, smiled, and bowed slightly to me.

"Thank you," I said.

"You're most welcome."

The tea was in a China teacup with matching saucer. Both showed signs of wear but were of very find quality, decorated by intricate and beautiful vines and flowers. I put my nose to the vapor that rose from the tea.

It smelled awful. It smelled like mud.

I sat down and, setting the saucer aside, cradled the little China cup in my hands, letting the warmth radiate up into my wrists and arms.

"So, Peter," I said, blowing uncertainly on the tea. "How long have you been here?"

"Here?" he said, sipping from his own cup, "like what exactly do you mean?"

I chuckled. "Well," I said, "I guess I mean how long have you been camping here? Here in the mountains. In this area."

"Oooh," he said, elongating the word as though he'd thought I meant something completely different. "Here. You mean like here." He gestured broadly at the tee-pee.

Chase scoffed quietly.

"Yes," I said.

"You know," said Peter, "that reminds me. I went to the river one night this past autumn. It was in the evening, not too long after it got dark. Night of the full moon. Harvest moon. I went down to the river, and there's a place there where I like to sit. It's where the river makes a bend, and there's a rock there that's good for sitting. I go there a lot. I went there to watch the full moon come up. So I sat there, and the moon came up, and I had this, like, thought."

Peter took a sip of his tea. Then he set the cup down and gazed at the fire as if maybe he had only just then realized it was there. There was a small pile of firewood nearby, and he took a few sticks and laid it on the coals.

I sat waiting for him to continue, but a minute went by, and then another. I looked at Chase. He rolled his eyes and shrugged. I looked back at Peter. He was staring at the rekindled fire now as though it were an old friend of his who was getting ready to leave him on a long journey.

"So—you had a thought?" I prompted.

"Hm?" Peter returned his gaze to me. "Oh, right! I did have a thought. At the river on the night of the harvest moon. It was a thought about here. And there. And being somewhere."

"I'd love to hear it," I said.

"Okay," said Peter. He looked up at the vent at the top of the tee-pee. "Let me see if I can explain it." He pursed his lips in concentration.

I took a little sip of the tea—and nearly spit it right back out again. It was bitter, like brackish water, but it tasted like soil, like rotten mud. No amount of honey or sugar could have improved it. I couldn't imagine that this was how Peter meant it to taste. I held it in my mouth, trying to swallow it, but my throat reflexively constricted at the bitterness. I looked over at Peter. He was still contemplating the roof of the tee-pee, so I doubled over, pretended to cough, and spit the tea onto the canvas floor.

"All right," said Peter. "I've got it."

I sat up again.

"How wide is the universe?" asked Peter, holding his arms out questioningly.

"I have no idea," I answered.

"No, of course not," said Peter. "No one does, I suppose. It might be, like, infinity. It might be only approaching infinity. But if we just pick like an arbitrary distance, for the sake of argument, it'd have to be, like, big, right? Like a hundred-billion light-years? Right?"

"Sure," I said, trying not to sound patronizing. "Works for me."

275

"Okay. Good. Now, if the universe is a hundred-billion light-years across, then smaller distances mean essentially nothing, right? Like, say, two-hundred thousand miles is nothing in comparison, right? Doesn't even count."

I thought about this. "Yeah. Sure."

"Okay. Good," he said, holding up his palms. "Now, follow me down this rabbit hole. Two-hundred thousand miles is how far away the moon is from Earth. That's the distance between me sitting on that rock and the moon itself. But, within the greater universe, which we have decided for our purposes is a hundred-billion miles wide, I am basically at the moon. Aren't I? Like if you go to the store and you're outside in the parking lot, you'd still say, 'I'm at the store,' even though you're not, like, at the aisle where the breakfast cereal is, right? So, on a cosmic scale, I'm practically as close to the moon as I am to you or the continent of Africa. See? So, my thought was, what is the point of saying I'm here or there or anywhere? Because what if the universe in reality is so massive that even a hundred-billion light-years is a minuscule distance in comparison? Then what?"

He waited, as if I might give an answer. All I could do was blink a few times.

"I'm a point in space, Alison," he said, putting a hand on his chest. "That's all I can really say for sure. How long have I been here?" He shrugged. "This whole time, I guess."

Chase said, "Huh."

I looked at Chase, and instead of another eye-roll, he wore a thoughtful half-grin.

Then I looked back across the fire at Peter, and said, "Huh."

Peter smiled back at us.

CHAPTER 54

It went on that way for days. We'd ask Peter a question and he would answer with a rambling riddle that rarely answered the question but nevertheless made a certain kind of sense. And not just existential or philosophical questions, but practical questions.

Chase asked: "Hey, Peter, you think the fishing's any good down below that big waterfall?"

Peter answered: "A wise man once said that the charm of catching fish is that it's elusive but attainable. It's an endless series of occasions for hope."

Chase replied: "So, yes?"

I followed Peter around his camp, helped him with various tasks. Even now that there was snow on the ground, Peter was still harvesting tree bark, pine needles, and the roots of certain herbs and plants. These he dried over his fire in the tee-pee. He made a very strong liquor from juniper berries and wild grain. On the far end of the camp, Peter had built a sort of wigwam, a dome of stout, arched branches. This was covered with sod and formed a hump in the forest floor the size of a small car. On one side there was a small opening, covered by a door of densely woven willow shoots. Inside this mound it was completely dark, and the floor was covered with a fragrant black compost that was always slightly warm and steamy. A garden of mushrooms grew there—boletes, morels, and others I'd never seen. He lovingly tended the little fungi farm, harvesting only a few each day.

As I assisted Peter with these bucolic chores, I questioned him gently and obliquely about memories, about the Agency, about his life in the mountains. He didn't exactly ignore these questions, but he'd never answer them straightforwardly. Sometimes he'd only smile at my questions, sometimes he'd just give me one of his existential answers.

"I don't know anything about this Agency you're always talking about," said Peter, "but you sure seem to hate them."

"I want to be free of the Agency," I said.

"Ahhh," he replied, holding up a finger, "well, you remember what Buddha said about hatred and freedom, don't you?"

"No," I answered.

"Oh," said Peter. "I don't either. I was hoping you did. It's a really good quote. Something about chains and hatred. Oh, that's it—hate is the ultimate chain, the ultimate enslavement."

One day we were hiking a trail along the river where a swampy area of slow water had formed. Peter brought along an old rusty machete and a five-gallon bucket.

"I'll show you how to harvest cattail roots," Peter said. "They're delicious in the fall, but you gotta get 'em before the water freezes over."

I nodded and followed him, much less interested in cattail roots than in something, anything, he could tell us about his possible role as the Guide. He sat on the trail and shucked his boots and socks, and then rolled up his trouser legs to wade into the frigid, slow-moving water.

"How do you feel about memories, Peter?" I asked him. "Do you think memories are important?"

Peter pulled up one stalk and then another. "Well, Alison, life is just a series of moments, right? Like one moment followed by another, followed by another after that. Right?"

"Yeah."

"But you can only actually, like, live in one moment at a time, right? The same way I can pull up only one of these roots at a time. Once I pull up this root, I can't pull it up again, and I can only pull up the next root after I've finished with this one. I pull up the roots one at a time."

"Okay."

"Okay," he continued, "so, do you agree that you can only really live in one moment at a time, the present moment?"

"Yeah."

"Well then, try doing that."

When he'd collected a few armfuls of the cattails, he hacked away the stalks with the machete and tossed the starchy, potato-like roots ("rhizomes," he called them) into the bucket. I said I'd carry the bucket and Peter thanked me and put his socks and boots back on. We were walking back toward camp when Peter paused and gazed with a pleased expression at a large aspen tree that grew at the side of the trail. It was nearly as big around as me. I stopped behind him with the bucket full of muddy roots.

Peter stood there for a long moment, staring at the tree trunk and smiling. Then he patted the tree, nodded, and went on. I stepped up to the aspen tree and examined it. The white bark shone in the mid-morning sunshine, contrasting with its own coarse, black markings. There didn't seem to be anything special about the tree, and I was almost ready to interpret the incident as part of Peter's love for just about everything around us—trees, rocks, birds, small twigs, dirt— when I noticed something.

In the convolutions of the white and black aspen bark, there was the shape of a heart, a valentine heart. At first I figured it was just a large, heart-shaped knot, a happenstance of how the tree bark had formed, but then I saw that within the heart there were letters, words. They were only barely legible, but they spelled out:

PETER
+
MARY

It looked as if the folds and ridges of bark had grown the letters, but my mouth fell slowly opened and I blinked in amazement as I realized the more astonishing truth: Peter had carved the heart and the names into the smooth white bark long, long ago, and the bark had healed around the carving until the scar looked like it had grown there naturally.

But how long ago must his have been? More than a decade. Maybe more than two.

I hurried down the trail. "Peter!" I cried.

He slowed on the trail and turned his head to smile at me.

"How long have you been here?" I asked, gesturing vaguely back at the tree.

Peter laughed, waggled a finger at me, and said, "You've asked me that before."

Chase and I doubled our efforts, questioning Peter to see what he knew—if anything. We asked him directly and indirectly. We pleaded with him sincerely, and we acted utterly unconcerned. But it didn't seem to matter. I thought Peter might be toying with us. Or maybe he didn't take us seriously. Or maybe it was that he didn't know how seriously we took him.

"Why are you here?" I asked Peter forcefully. "Why here? Why you, here with all these tents, where other people have obviously come and gone? What is your role?"

"You say you were looking for me," said Peter. He said it slowly, as though explaining something to a small child. "Seems like you should know the answers to all these questions."

After a week, the riddles, the non-sequiturs, the evasiveness—they began to weigh on me.

"Come down to the river," Peter said one day. "Sit with me. It's warming up. It's peaceful. I'll bring some tea."

"I don't want tea, Peter," I said, without hiding my mounting bitterness. "I want answers."

He looked at me with an impassive expression. He wasn't surprised or amused or hurt or moved in any way at my annoyance, my unconcealed resentment.

"Suit yourself," he said with a wan smile. Then he filled a dented-up old thermos with the disgusting dirt-flavored tea and disappeared down the path to the bend in the river, the place where the sitting rock was.

I knew he'd sit down there for hours, sitting on the rock, his eyes mere slits, neither asleep nor awake. And if I followed him and pressed him with more questions, he wouldn't say a word in answer.

That night Chase and I lay in our tent.

"I had so much hope coming here, Chase."

"I know, Al. Me, too."

"We had a good thing going back in our little camp," I complained. "Tea by the fire. Our little cabin tent. Snuggling down in bed with a few coals in the stove."

"The fishing was way better there, too."

"Chase, I'm freezing."

He drew me close, placed his stomach against mine. I pressed into him and wrapped my legs around one of his.

"What should we do?" I asked.

"Not much we can do," said Chase. "The guy is a sphinx. An enigma."

"Isn't there some way we could force him to tell us something?" I asked.

"What—you mean like break his legs?"

I sighed. "No. We can't do that. Maybe we can find something to barter with. Figure out what it is he wants or needs."

And so in the morning, we offered him things. Everything we had with us and more. Vehicles. Food. Supplies. Weapons. Labor. Anything. Everything.

Peter held his arms apart and gestured expansively to the trees around us. "Take care of the earth, and the earth takes care of you." He turned in a circle. "The answers you're looking for are all right here."

"He's crazy," Chase said to me when we lay down again in our tent that night. "We can't crack this nut."

I cried a little. "This has all been a big waste of time."

"I'm sorry, Al," said Chase softly. "I really hoped it would work out."

"It's not your fault," I said. "It was a dead end."

When we awoke, we packed our things and took down our tent. It was much like the day we set out for the mountain of the bear. We didn't have to speak or make a decision. We simply began packing.

When we were ready to leave, we went to Peter's tee-pee. We announced ourselves and Peter invited us in.

He was just laying on a brew of his tea. Always the tea, I thought, shaking my head.

"Hey, pal," said Chase, "just wanted to let you know we're gonna get outta your hair. We're moving on."

Peter looked up. "Already?"

"Yeah," said Chase. "We've got other places to be."

"But did you find what you were looking for?" Peter asked.

"No," said Chase. "We didn't find anything."

"That's too bad," he said. "That's a bummer. I don't suppose you'd like a cup?" He gestured at his teapot. "One for the road? No?"

Chase sighed heavily but said nothing. He only scrubbed his face roughly with his hand. He was getting to his feet when it hit me. The tea. I grabbed the sleeve of Chase's coat and made him stay still.

"Peter," I asked, "what's in this tea of yours?"

He shrugged. "Just the mushrooms. I dry them, grind them into a powder. There's nothing else in it. Want some? I kinda thought maybe you weren't like a big fan, Alison."

I thought about everything. The tents in a circle that looked as though they'd grown there. The ancient marking on the aspen. The mushroom garden.

282

"Peter," I continued, "people have been coming here to visit you for a long time, haven't they?"

He nodded as though this were common knowledge. He readied three of his teacups on the low table.

"People looking for answers," I added.

Peter nodded again with a small, peaceful smile on his lips. Chase's brow was rumpled and he looked from me to Peter and back, like he was following a tennis match.

The tea. The camp. Peter was the Guide, yes; but not just for people who'd had their memories scrubbed by the Agency. Peter didn't know anything about the Agency.

"It was you and Mary at first, wasn't it?" I asked. "And you were young then. Decades ago. People came here looking for answers. All kinds of answers. All kinds of people."

Peter smiled wistfully. "Yeah. It was me and Mary at first."

"She's down at the bend in the river," I said.

He nodded again, and the smile on his face was more to comfort me than himself. When the tea was brewed, Peter brought us the cups. They had been very fine antiques when Peter packed them here into these woods as a young man. They were still beautiful, finely detailed and slightly translucent. But they bore the marks of wear—small cracks and chips, and even a scorch mark or two.

"Thank you, Peter," I said.

Chase took his cup from Peter but regarded me with a quizzical look.

"Drink it," I said.

CHAPTER 55

The tea was beyond awful-tasting. It made me think of the black mud where Peter pulled up the cattail roots. It was earthy and musty, and I gagged as I coughed and swallowed it in small sips. But I choked it all down, and so did Chase.

"What happens now?" I asked Peter.

He blinked at me serenely and held up a finger. Suddenly, I knew what his answer would be. I mouthed the words as he said them: "That's an interesting question, Alison."

"Peter," said Chase, "you're one of a kind."

"I'm glad you two stayed," said Peter, "if only for a cup of tea."

Peter told us the story of the first day he'd climbed to the peak of the mountain of the bear. He said something about seeing the whole land stretching out before him. There was something he figured out when that happened, but soon I began to lose the thread of his story. I was staring at the fire, at the coals, and I was all at once intensely interested in the way they throbbed and flashed under the slightest movement of air. Then I noticed a floaty feeling, a feeling of well-being. And underneath all of this there emerged something even more profound. It was a sensation of complete mental openness, and a sense that I had stepped onto the very precipice of a massive discovery.

I looked at my hands. I looked at the woodgrain on the poles that held up the tee-pee. I looked at Chase's thoughtful, scruffy face. We sat in the tent for several hours, staring at the fire, asking each other questions of the most wildly theoretical nature. Most of that conversation is hazy to me now, but this much I do remember: I was in the moment. I was living each moment as it arrived, and this felt so right.

At some point I must have drifted off, into sleep or some other state I'm not sure, but I knew it was evening when I was next aware of my surroundings, because the vent at the top of Peter's tee-pee was dark. I saw the stars burning brightly in the sliver of sky. Chase was next to me, sitting up, drinking from his water bottle. When I stirred he looked over to me. He smiled and offered me the bottle. I sat up and drank.

I didn't have any more memories than I did before, but I felt as though I did have something new. I couldn't say what it was, but there was something new inside me.

Peter was boiling a starchy cattail root stew on his fire, and soon he ladled it into small pots and we ate. When the stew was gone, Peter made more of the tea.

"Is this how we get our memories back?" I asked Peter as I accepted a fresh cup of the bitter, brown liquid. "We know that others came here and got their memories back."

Peter shook his head. "I told you guys. I don't know anything about memories. And this tea can't, like, give you anything. The answers you're looking for can't come from a pot of tea or a pot of gold or a pot of anything else."

I thought: Then why drink it?

Peter, as if reading my thoughts, said, "The tea isn't the answer. The tea is a way, a path, to the answer. The tea is, like, a guide. But you have to answer your own questions, Alison. Ultimately, the most important answers are for us to say."

As the effects of the tea came on again, I figured out what was new inside me. It wasn't that I had acquired something new—it was that I had let go of something old. My anxiety, impatience, and restlessness seemed to have vanished, melted away like a thick coating of ice. We talked more. Peter told us about his life in the camp, about the people who'd come and gone from here. And we asked questions of Peter, many of the same questions we'd asked him already, but instead of being confused and annoyed by Peter's evasive, obtuse answers, I pondered them deeply. Sometimes they made sense to me, sometimes they left me thirsting for knowledge. I drifted away again, completely at peace for what I now know was the first time in many years.

As I faded into a waking dream, I saw Chase's face far above me. He grinned and said, "See you on the other side."

CHAPTER 56

Somewhere a calliope played a marching tune.

I saw a galaxy of winking lights.

There were flashes of colors—red, purple, gold, green.

I saw human skulls on spikes lining a dark hallway with many doors.

I saw a Ferris wheel circling, the wheel spinning faster and faster, like a bicycle tire, like a fan.

There was the sound of laughter, someone singing a lullaby, the sound of someone crying.

The ground rose and fell around me. I felt dizzy. I closed my eyes.

I saw faces. Hundreds of faces. People talking, eating, reading, sleeping. They passed before me like visions. I ran after them. But they swirled around me like the Ferris wheel.

It was chaos and motion. Everything loud. Everything bright. Everything dazzling and explosive and alive.

I waved my hand in front of my face and a trail of hands followed the movement, as if I were watching in slow motion.

Thousands of birds dived and climbed, their flocks forming vast shapes in the sky that formed, stretched, and reformed.

There was an explosion in the distance. There was another explosion, this one so close I could say that I was in it.

The ground fell away from me and I fell. I floated, weightlessly. I could let myself go here—let myself be washed over by the colors and the sounds to be eased into a reverie of peacefulness. It would be easy to float through this place to drift where the whims of my mind wanted to carry me, but I remembered Peter saying that my questions were mine to answer.

So I tried to focus, tried to resolve the fuzzy colors and haziness around me into images. I swam in the space, making long strokes with my arms, until I reached firm ground. I concentrated on finding my memories and as I did rows of doors appeared in front of me. I ran to them, opening them, but behind each one was only darkness.

This isn't working, I thought. There's nothing here.

But the secret was here. I knew it. I just needed to keep searching.

I opened another door and found myself in a bedroom. There was shag carpeting and a twin bed. I felt an impression that what I was looking for was here in the room. Had I been here before? Was this a room I knew? I began searching the room. I pulled the drawers out of a dresser. Emptied a shelf of books and knick-knacks. Threw out the clothes in a closet. Pulled off the bedding from the bed. I even pulled up the carpet. But I'd done this before, been here before. The strongest sense of deja vu, like I was reliving some part of my life.

What was it I was looking for?

I sat on the bed to think and felt a strange lump under me. I remembered this. I remembered.

I ran my hand down the side of the mattress—and yes, just like I remembered—a slit cut right next to the edge of the mattress. Barely noticeable. I reached in and pulled out a red notebook.

My heart pounded and my hands shook.

I opened the notebook and a brilliant white light shone out, so bright I couldn't see. So bright I shut my eyes. So bright that I could feel it burning into my soul.

CHAPTER 57

I opened my eyes knowing beforehand that I'd see a bright light. It had shone onto my eyelids as I came out of a sort of dream state, and I knew I was bathed in a warm, bright light. I opened my eyes slowly. The tee-pee was aglow. The rising sun beamed directly onto the western side of the tee-pee and the cream-colored canvas caught the light and glowed so brightly I thought it might burn the canvas away.

My memories had returned.

I didn't have to think about it. I didn't have to concentrate. I just remembered. Everything. Indeed, some part of my mind had already accepted all of this and was roving merrily through my entire catalog of remembrances—memories recent and those very distant. A million moments flashed in my mind so rapidly that they seemed almost simultaneous.

When my conscious mind caught up and realized what had happened and what was happening, I gasped so deeply it was as though I'd had the wind knocked out of me, and it took several frantic moments to breathe properly again. After that it was still a bit overwhelming but in a pleasant, bountiful way.

I wept for a while with gratitude, because of course I remembered the periods when I could remember only back to the prior Agency treatment. And I wept for a while for myself in those dark times, but soon I was laughing and nearly delirious.

I remembered my father, and his kindly face and glasses. I remembered my mother, plump and pretty and always busy, always smiling. I had an older brother who loved motorcycles and a younger sister who was a soccer champion in college. I remembered growing up in a suburb where kids rode their bikes everywhere, and we played night-games in the streets all summer. I remembered going to college and backpacking in South America and working in a big city and getting married and giving birth and holding Arie for the first time—the feeling of fascination and immediate and overwhelming love. I was transfixed by his inquisitive eyes. There were days at the park and first-days of school. There were lazy moments when Arie and I sat close together, doing nothing but just being together, even breathing in and out at the same rate. There was stress, too, so busy with a young kid to take care of and there were hard times that slowly got better and there were joyous days.

I remembered it all.

And I remembered Christopher. Chris. Chris, my husband, my love, Christopher. The memory of him and the loss of him was most wrenching of all. I had loved him with all my heart, still loved him. I remembered holding his hand as he died from the virus, holding his hand so tight, trying to keep him here with me, willing him to stay, praying for a miracle. Praying to please not take the light of my life from me.

Chris.

He was the husband who showed up to my first obstetrician appointment with flowers, who blinked away tears when we first heard Arie's heartbeat. All of his life Chris had been so full of health and vigor. He was handsome and charming, and I'd fallen in love with him so quickly and overwhelmingly that it hardly seemed real.

And then I lost him, and when he died, it created an ache in me that never went away—I knew that now. I'd always ached for him in some way, even if I couldn't remember him, just as I ached for Arie when I couldn't remember him.

So many memories. Memories of the back before and after the first of the Agency's treatments. All the horror and all the exhilaration. I remembered sweet little Gracie, the girl Arie coaxed with apples in our back yard. I remembered the wise and beautiful Brigitta. I remembered the defiant and reckless Lotus kids. My very happiest and my very saddest moments had filled up all the once-empty places in my mind, accessible at the speed of thought, and I cherished them all, with all of my heart. They were the most precious thing I could ever think of.

I stood up. I was alone in the tent. The fire had burned low. I crossed the tee-pee and pushed the canvas aside and went out into the light.

Chase stood outside the tee-pee facing the sun. He was shading his eyes with one hand. He turned to me as I approached.

"Hey," I said. "I remember you."

Chase smiled broadly and broke into an episode of laughter that consumed him until he was wheezing and bending over. I went to him and he took me in his arms. Then he turned me to face the blazing sunshine.

"Look at this," said Chase, gesturing to the east. "I never noticed before but Peter built his tee-pee so that the door faces this open place in the trees and the valley out there so that the sun would shine right through here. It's set up perfectly."

It was an astonishing view. The sun rose between two far-off mountain slopes, and a complex series of overlapping mountain ridges. The sunshine filled the valley with light that radiated like a super-nova. It must have taken Peter weeks to find a site like this, and he awoke to it every single morning. No wonder he was always so calm, I thought.

"It's gorgeous."

Chase had tears in his eyes, too, and I knew why. I'd wondered so often if I knew Chase before all of this. Sometimes I'd been sure I had. Now I recalled that I'd never met him before that day in Ruby's amusement park lair.

291

But as I watched him there by the tee-pee, facing the sun, his fogging breath golden-white in the morning sun, I knew that I loved him. With the full record of our many interactions—interrupted here and there by the Agency's hideous treatments—and with the full recollection of my entire life, I knew I loved Chase with a heart-stopping, calamitous love. As much as I loved Christopher, and I loved him full-heartedly, I loved Chase, too.

Chase turned to me and smiled. There was something in his expression, something in his eyes that told me he was full of new realizations and recollections, too. All the memories of his life were back, and he knew now that we'd met only after our memories had been wiped. Had he lost a love, too? Surely he must have, but I knew he loved me.

That's when I learned that there is no limit to our capacity to love. It's endless and infinite. It can grow and grow and never run out.

"I want to tell you everything I remember," I said.

"I want to hear."

"I want to know everything you remember," I said.

"I want to tell you."

We got our boots and went down to the river bend where there was a big dry rock to sit on, and we began to talk. We talked and talked. We laughed and cried. We embraced and smiled. We kept talking all day, and it wasn't enough time to say everything, but that was okay, because we'd have a lifetime together—to share old memories and to make new ones.

CHAPTER 58

In the afternoon we wandered back from the river bend to find a little food. Neither of us had seen Peter—it seemed that he'd left us on our own, knowing that he'd only be a distraction, even if we were very excited to tell him what had happened to us.

The sun had crossed through the sky above the camp and was sinking down behind the tee-pee, and we saw a plume of smoke rising from the vent. The air was cool and still, and we could smell the aroma of stewed meat and perhaps some kind of bread.

"I'm in here," said Peter, his voice slightly muffled inside the tent. "Supper'll be ready in like ten."

We went into the tee-pee and it was warm and inviting. Peter had made a tremendous cauldron of rabbit stew and he'd made a kind of flat bread of wild grain flour. On the fender of the fireplace there was also some kind of dark pudding of berries and seeds.

"What's all this?" I asked.

"A celebration," said Peter. "You found what you were looking for, didn't you? Or, I guess I should say you found out that what you thought was lost really wasn't?"

I smiled and nodded.

"You too, Chase?" asked Peter, smiling.

"Yeah," said Chase. "Me, too."

"Well then," said Peter, "take a seat. Alison, maybe you could check that bread—make sure it's not scorched. Chase, you could fill up these cups—there's a bota bag of currant wine there on that hook."

"Sure, Peter," we said, and he kept us busy as he put a few finishing touches on the meal.

When everything was ready, we ate slowly, savoring each bite and sip and morsel. It was all very rich and delicious, but as good as the food was, something else happened that overshadowed even the berry pudding.

We reminisced.

The rabbit stew reminded Chase of the squirrel stew his grandpa made when Chase was a kid in the South.

"He'd shoot these stringy little squirrels out in the woods," said Chase, his eyes intense and gleaming with the wine, "like six or seven of them, and he'd skin 'em and dress them out, and my grandma would quarter them—just like a chicken, and she'd add all her spices and carrots, and this stew would just simmer in a huge iron pot for hours and hours, until it was thick enough to eat a whole bowl of it with a fork!"

That sent Peter into a story about how he worked as a prep chef in a restaurant in Oregon when he was in college, and his specialty was a Texas chili with mango.

"It was like this really crazy flavor combination," he said. "The bite of the chili peppers and the smooth sweetness of the mango. Ahh, I'd eat half of it just tasting it in the kitchen."

"Oh, that sounds heavenly," I said, and then I launched into a story of a trip I took to Peru. "On every street there were vendors selling these things called antichucos," I told them. "It was strips of grilled beef on a stick with a potato stuck on the end of the stick. And they gave you this aji sauce—it was so hot my eyes would cross, but I couldn't stop eating them."

They laughed, and I laughed, and the stories continued until all that remained was the wine in the bota. When we finished that off, we were quiet again, and we watched the fire reduce itself to a bed of embers that pulsed red and violet.

Peter smiled at us from his place across the fire. "You guys are two of my favorites," he said. "I've really enjoyed our time together. I've learned a lot." He was still slightly cryptic—surely the only thing he could have learned was that we were annoyingly impatient and persistent—but I felt that we were finally in the company of the real Peter, the one he kept secret, the one he saved for special occasions.

"We should probably leave in the morning," said Chase.

Peter nodded serenely. "I know."

I said, "A few days ago I couldn't wait to leave. Now I want to stay."

"No, you need to keep moving," said Peter. "We all have different, like, purposes, you know? I don't mean like one person's a doctor and another person drives a taxi. I painted houses for years and years. That's not what I mean. I mean your actual gosh dang purpose. I didn't know what mine was at first, but now I know. It's to be here in the mountains. That's mine. Yours? Yours is to go. Find your son and friends do whatever comes after that. That's yours."

I had told Peter about Arie and Ruby and the others, but I never thought he was listening.

"Yeah," I said. "You're right."

"Hey. Guess what?" said Peter suddenly. He clapped his hands once, making a bright, cheerful sound, almost like a chime. "I've got something for you. A going-away present."

Chase and I watched him rise and wobble, a bit tipsy, to the wall of the tee-pee where from a peg there hung a satchel the size of a hefty paperback novel.

"I know don't like the taste," said Peter, "but I thought maybe some of the people you'll be meeting might like to try it."

I put my nose to the satchel. "The tea?"

He nodded. "Doesn't take much. Maybe like a teaspoon. But don't be stingy. I know it tastes like soup made from dead bugs and dirt clods, but, well, I guess you know."

"But there must be almost a pound of it here," I protested. "How long did it take to grow this much? We can't take this much." I tried to hand it back to him.

Peter scoffed. "I'm not liable to run out," said Peter. "Not anytime soon. Trust me. I can afford it."

"And this will—?" I trailed off, unsure of what I was asking, precisely. "This will do for others what it did for Chase and me?"

"Like I told you," said Peter. "I'm not sure what you were struggling with. Memories, I guess. There was another group with the same issue who came through a while ago. Will it help? I don't know. But it can't hurt."

"How can we thank you, Peter?" said Chase.

Peter scoffed again and shook his head.

"No, really, Peter," I said. "You don't understand. You saved our lives. We're different people now."

"You're always a different person," said Peter sternly. "I'm not the person you first met here in this very tee-pee, and you're not the person who walked in all cold and scared. One moment at a time, Alison. We discussed this. You can never step into the same river twice. Chase? Help me out. This is basic stuff."

"Yeah," said Chase with a smile. "He's right, Al."

"No, Peter," I said, raising my voice. "We owe you our lives."

"Why? You visited me. We talked. We shared. You learned some things. I learned some things. Now it's time for you to go. You thank me and I thank you. There's nothing owed."

"You gave us a present," I said. "We want to give you one."

Peter stuck out his lower lip. "Hmm. Well, when you put it that way." He put a finger to his chin and thought.

Chase and I waited.

"Two things, I guess, would make me very happy."

"Anything."

"Help your people find their answers. To be honest, I don't think the tea is, like, necessary. I think it's all about knowing yourself, questioning yourself, believing yourself. But the tea is like helpful. I'll be here if you need more, and if I'm not here, well, this stuff just grows right up out of the ground around here. You'll figure it out. But take what I packaged up for you and help your people. Show them the Guide."

I wanted to do something for Peter, or give something to Peter, but it was obvious he wasn't having it. "Okay," I said. "Done. What's the other thing?"

"Well," he said. "You were looking for memories, right? Something like that?"

"Yes. So, what's the second thing?"

"Remember me."

CHAPTER 59

It seemed we reached Ruby's camp just in time. As we came from the mountain of the bear, we hit the main trail and began to make the climb to Ruby's camp, where we met a line of hikers carrying supplies, presumably down to the road, where they'd be loaded onto vehicles.

They smiled and greeted us as we passed them by, but it wasn't long before we were intercepted by guards.

"What are you guys doing here?" asked a guard named Richard. He was armed, but he didn't take his pistol from its holster, and the guard he was with left his rifle slung on his shoulder.

"I guess we're back," said Chase.

Richard sighed and put his hands on his hips. "Well, I'm sorry to have to do this, but we have strict orders to take you into custody on sight."

The lookout guards recognized us, and we recognized them.

"That's fine," Chase said holding his hands out so they could be cuffed.

"I'm not gonna cuff you," said Richard. "Long as you promise not to do anything stupid."

"Oh, man," said Chase. "If I had a buck for every time I made that promise."

"I think you should cuff us," I said. "I don't want you to be in trouble with Ruby."

"I appreciate that," said Richard. He and the other guard each produced a pair of handcuffs. They offered to carry our packs, but we told them we could manage as long as they cuffed our wrists in front of us.

"So, Ruby's still here?" I asked. "You'll take us straight to her?"

"Those are my orders," said Richard.

"Good," I said. "We need to talk to her." I was telling the truth, but I could hardly contain my excitement to see Woolly again, and especially Arie.

Richard and the other guard marched us into the camp. Very few tents were left standing, and there was gear and provisions stacked up here and there awaiting transport. We went to Ruby's tent. The tchotchkes and fetishes and wood carvings had been packed up, and most of the maps had been unpinned from the back wall, but the warm scent of Ruby's mountain tea remained. A torrent of memories came to my mind—not just of being in this camp, but going back to my first meeting with Ruby, when Arie and I were attacked by the dogs. I thought about her hideout under the haunted house ride at Thrill Harbor, and Ruby visiting me, basically uninvited, at the house where Arie and I lived in Zone 1891. We take for granted the places that are home for us—not necessarily just the places we live, but the places where our souls are comfortable.

And there, sitting in a camp at her pine-plank desk, was Ruby herself. She sat with her bad leg stretched out in front of her, tilting her head and angling her spectacles and reading that day's notes and messages with a testy grimace on her face. Surely she'd heard of our coming from someone who'd run out in advance, but she would not raise her eyes to us. She let us stand there.

Standing behind her were Arie and Woolly. Arie was apparently a lieutenant now, and this was the new leadership team. They looked at us nervously as we entered. Arie shifted his weight from one foot to the other and back again. Woolly greeted us with his eyes only, then pretended to study something interesting on the canvas ceiling of the tent.

I couldn't help myself; I broke into a broad grin. I remembered all the times I'd been reunited with these people, my friends, my family. There'd been times I thought I'd never see any of them again, and times I'd seen them again but didn't remember them. There was the time we all helped Woolly after he took the serum. And I thought especially of re-uniting with Arie, meeting him so many times for the first time. This time it was different. This time I was not meeting Arie as a stranger who merely hoped for some connection. This time I remembered him. I remembered everything about him from the first moment I'd felt him stir inside me. I knew him. I knew him as a mother knew and loved her child.

"Ruby, it's us," Chase said, leveling his full power to charm directly at her.

But still Ruby kept her eyes on the page of notes she was reading. She read it to the end and didn't look up then either. She made a few notes herself with the stub of a pencil, set the pencil and notes aside, drew in a breath and let it out, and only then did she raise her head to see us.

Chase and I smiled weakly.

Ruby's face was impassive, almost sad. Definitely weary, but then again, she usually was these days. The last time I'd seen her was when she had banished me, and I imagined the last time she'd seen Chase was when he'd told her he was leaving to be with me. I thought she was probably trying to project a certain imperious dissatisfaction, but I detected a guarded uneasiness.

"Take them cuffs off 'em," she said, exasperated. "Then you two go back on watch."

Richard unlocked and retrieved the cuffs, and then they left. Ruby struggled out of her chair and stood, but then waited for the sound of their footsteps to recede. When she was sure they'd gone away, she shouted, "What in tarnation d'ya think yer doin' here? I haven't changed my mind about nothin'."

That wiped the smiles from our faces, anyway. Ruby hurried on.

"You're still ban—er—restricted from this here camp," she said sharply, pointing at me, "an' you walked out on us," she added, pointing at Chase.

"We know," I said. "We're not here to stay."

Ruby frowned at us, her mouth open, searching for words but not finding them. She sat in the chair again.

"Well, then git, both a ya'," she said.

"Ruby," said Woolly quietly.

"What?" she said, turning in her seat to address Woolly. "Whaddya want me to do? Throw 'em a damn party?"

"Just listen to what they have to say," he said, with his quiet boldness. "Judging from the looks on their faces, this is gonna be pretty interesting."

"Ah, hell," said Ruby. "Fine. What is it? Why ya messin' around these parts?"

Chase took a step forward. "Ruby, remember back when it was just me and you?"

Ruby knitted her brows, tilted her head.

"Back then," Chase continued, "there was no sneaking into Agency buildings or planning raids. We were just two people who hated the Agency goons and were sick of the rations. Remember? And you came up with this system to trade and barter and make life a little easier. And you brought me in on it because I'd gotten that old Honda to run."

Ruby's eyes grew wide.

"Remember what you said to me?" Chase asked. "You said, 'Nothing will change for the better if nobody tries to make a difference.' Remember saying that?"

"And remember at the safe-house?" I added. "When you taught me how to shoot a gun? In fact, the first time I'd ever touched a gun, ever, in my entire life, was that day those goons were after you, and you gave me your pistol out in the neighborhoods. I hid in an old church until you got back."

Ruby's gaze zipped from me to Chase. Her mouth gaped and her eyes got big.

"How?" she whispered, elongating the word into an amazed sigh.

Behind her, Woolly stood with his arms folded but eyes narrowed, trying to decide what to make of all this. Arie was still and quiet, but listening intently.

"You went back to the Agency?" Ruby marveled, rocking in her seat to stand again. "You got it? You got the cure? It's real?"

"No, not the Agency," said Chase. "We don't need them."

"But your memories are back? All of 'em? How far back?"

"To the beginning," I said. "Everything. The virus was real. The Agency serum was real. Whether or not the memory wipe part was necessary, we don't know. But, Ruby—" my voice caught in my throat "—I have my life back. You can, too. All of us."

She regarded us with open suspicion. Woolly and Arie seemed wary, too.

Ruby slowly shook her head and said, "Listen, you two, I ain't gonna open up this whole camp to getting their hopes up fer nothin'. You're gonna hafta explain to me how this all happened. You're gonna hafta prove it. Take them packs off and sit your asses down. Woolly, take the kid and quick and get us some food and coffee and we'll get to the bottom 'a this. Don't leave nothin' out."

CHAPTER 60

I shouldn't have been surprised at Ruby's suspicious reception of the story we presented. Ruby's doubt, her mistrust of us—I guess she had to approach our claims that way, for her own benefit and protection, and on behalf of the others in the camp. In fact, if I had brought the information to Ruby all by myself, I think she would have simply laughed in my face and sent me away again. But even with Chase to confirm it all, we had remarkable difficulty convincing her. We told the story at least three times. She cross-examined us again and again, asking for more detail, trying to trip us up, making sure my version of events agreed with Chase's.

In the end, it was our actual memories that made the case. There were certain moments Chase and I had shared privately with Ruby that we could not know unless we had really lived them.

When Ruby had absorbed it all, finally accepted that Peter's strange tea was our way forward, she sat in her chair for a long time. On her face she had a sort of shattered expression. I think I knew how she felt—a certain disbelief, a heavy sense of finality.

"Listen," she said, her chin and lips quivering as though she were about to break down sobbing, "you all gotta give me a few minutes to myself here. I need a minute to just kinda think about—" and then she lost it.

Her stout frame shook heavily with great heaving sobs, and tears practically squirted from her eyes. She pressed the bridge of her nose between her forefinger and thumb. Her cheeks and neck were wet in no time. We stood up to go, but we crowded each other awkwardly to get out of the tent.

"I'm sorry, everyone," said Ruby between her moans and sobbing, "I just can't hardly believe we've finally made it."

Woolly put one of his large hands on her shoulder as we went out.

There was another meeting after that. We crowded back into Ruby's tent and discussed at length how to test the tea, how to distribute it, and what to do after that. We decided that a test-subject or two would be best to confirm that the concoction that Peter had given us would work the same way it had in Peter's camp. Arie and Woolly instantly volunteered.

"No," said Ruby. "Not you two. If I was ta' lose you two I think I'd about die."

"You're not going to lose them," said Chase. "It's a mild hallucinogenic."

"It's a mushroom!" cried Ruby. "Mosta them things is poisonous!"

"You mean toxic," said Woolly.

"Same difference!"

"Ruby," said Woolly, "this seems very safe. I'm still dubious about how or if it will work, but Alison and Chase are standing here, perfectly healthy and with their memories. Arie and I will be more useful for managing this project after we've gone through the process and after we have our memories back. Who knows what we'll remember?"

But Ruby would not relent. She scolded, shouted, waved her arms.

After what seemed like hours of bickering, Ruby agreed to let either Arie or Woolly serve as the test subject, and a coin-flip would decide the matter.

Ruby produced a coin—an ancient quarter from the back before. It was rubbed almost smooth, it's markings distinguishable but only just.

"It was in my pocket the day I first woke up in the Agency infirmary. Don't know where it come from, but I kept it ever since."

Chase took it from Ruby's palm.

"Call it in the air, kid."

He placed the coin on his thumbnail. There was a soft ping! as he flipped it. It arced into the air, rotating, a blur.

"Heads," shouted Arie.

Oh, please let it be heads, I thought.

We all stepped back to let it bounce on the floor of Ruby's tent. It came to rest and we leaned in squinting to see.

Tails.

Woolly said, "Yes," quietly, through clenched teeth.

Arie's expression fell. I winced internally, too.

Ruby sighed. Her eyes welled with tears. She said, "All right, then. Go an' try it."

"What do I do?" said Woolly turning to me.

"We should set you up in a tent by yourself," I said, "Where you can be comfortable and relaxed for a day or two. There's still time tonight for your first cup, and then I guess we'll see what happens."

"My tent is still standing," said Woolly.

"Then let's go," I said.

Ruby's face was a mask of fear. She tried hiding it with her grim impassive "boss" face, but it wasn't working.

"You'll be all right, Wool?" she asked pitifully.

"Yeah," said Woolly. "I will, Ruby."

We went out of Ruby's tent and were crossing camp in the cold darkness when Woolly said, "Wait."

"What is it?" Chase asked.

"I think it'd be better if Arie went first. I think it'll sit better with Ruby. And she really would be lost if something bad happened to me."

We returned to Ruby's tent. She and Arie were sitting there in silence, their faces stony. But when they saw Woolly, it was almost as though they knew what had been decided. Arie sat up straight and Ruby's face brightened.

"I think you should do the honors, pal," said Woolly to Arie.

Arie stood up and smiled. "Really? You sure?"

"Yeah. You got more to remember," said Woolly, tilting his head in my direction.

We took Arie to his own tent. He was packed up for the move, too, like the others, but his tent was still standing, serving as a storage place for the important and sensitive supplies that awaited transport to the vehicles. Arie made up his bed and shed his winter clothes until he was wearing only long underwear and socks. I stoked the small stove until the tent was nice and warm. Then I brewed the tea according to Peter's instructions.

"Are you ready for this?" I asked.

Arie nodded. "I'm just trying to remember this moment right now," he said. "What it feels like to not know your past." He looked at me. "It really works?"

I smiled. "It did for us."

He nodded and took the tea from me.

I walked toward the tent door, then paused and said, "See you on the other side."

He was staring into the mug as I walked out.

Chase and I slept in the command tent that night, but I kept waking up and getting out of the bed and looking out the front door of the heavy canvas tent to see if there was any sign of change in Arie's tent.

"Al," croaked Chase in a groggy whisper around midnight. "Come back to bed. You're letting the heat out."

I wanted to be the first one to talk to Arie when he emerged. I peered across the darkened camp, but the night was too dark to clearly see Arie's tent. The candle inside was out now; probably it had guttered and gone out by itself.

"Al!" hissed Chase.

"Okay, okay."

I checked maybe five times throughout the night. Once I even considered getting my boots on and going over there to investigate, but Chase convinced me not to.

I may have fallen into a light sleep for a couple hours, but as soon as the sky lightened with the dawn, I was up and dressed and had had two cups of tea before I heard anyone else stirring. I put on my coat and boots and wrapped a scarf around my face, and then I took a chair and went out to the central fireplace, where I could sit and watch for Arie.

But he didn't come out. The others awoke and joined me, but there were no sounds or signs of movement in the tent.

"I'm going to go check on him," I said as the sun rose over the mountain ridge.

"Can ya do that? Is it safe?" asked Ruby.

"There really weren't any procedures," explained Chase.

Arie's tent was only thirty or so yards away. I got up from my chair and faced the tent. The others watched me. Pine knots popped and cracked in the firepit.

"Go ahead, Al," said Ruby.

"Yeah, Al," said Woolly. "Go check on him."

As I strode down the trail to Arie's, he emerged. He'd slipped his boots on but was still in his long underwear. Around his shoulders he'd draped a sleeping bag. He had a contented smile on his face. His breath smoked in the cold.

"Arie," I said quietly. I felt almost unable to breathe out.

"Morning," he said.

"Good morning," I replied. "How—how are you feeling?"

"Well," he said uncertainly. "I feel refreshed. I feel good. I slept really good. Had a wild dream. It was good, though. Yeah. I feel good."

"Do you—?" I began the question, but I couldn't finish it.

Arie looked at the ground, and then at me. "Do I remember anything? Anything new?"

"Yes," I said, exhaling in a sort of laugh.

But Arie frowned. "No," he said. "I don't."

CHAPTER 61

Chase and I had taken two cups of the tea before our memories returned, so we didn't panic right away. But after two days and four cups of tea, brewed at various strengths ranging from "just a sprinkle" to "this is totally disgusting," Arie's memories had not returned.

"Maybe there was some additional ingredient that this friend of yours used," suggested Woolly. We were seated around the fire on the third night. Woolly had made a soup of roots and grain, but I ate little.

"No," I insisted. "Why would he send us off with some different version of the tea?"

"Why wouldn't it work the same for Arie as it did for you?" Woolly countered.

"I don't know," I groaned. "I don't know."

Chase stood by the fire, arms crossed tightly across his chest. He stared intently into the fire.

"Chase?" I pleaded, "any ideas?"

"Maybe we got lucky," he said. "Maybe it works on some people and not others, and we just got lucky."

The lack of memory restoration was only part of the problem. Arie said he felt disoriented after so many doses of the mushroom's compounds.

"I can't do that again," said Arie, as he came down from the effects of the tea. "At first it was amazing. I had all these wild thoughts about ideas and concepts. Like I had a dream about how to make a longbow and arrows. What trees to use and how to contour the wood and laminate it and how to make a string from sinew and cotton twine. And I really

309

think it'd work. In real life. I want to try it. And I had these ideas about myself, about understanding who I am and what I'm like. But now—now I just feel like I'm in a permanent fog. I spent an hour just now trying to zip up my coat and put on my gloves. I couldn't decide which order to do it in, so I kept starting over."

As Arie's mother, it pained me to hear all of this. How could I keep subjecting him to this? The anguish must have shown on my face.

"What's the matter?" he asked. "Don't cry. I'll be all right. I'm sure I will. It's just—that stuff is powerful."

"I'm sorry," I said.

Arie sighed and said, "I'll drink some more if I have to, I guess. I volunteered to be the test subject. So, I'll do it."

"No," I said. "The test is over. No more tea."

"Was it something I did wrong?"

"No," I said. "You need to rest now and just feel better. Ruby needs you. The camp needs you."

"Okay," he said.

I helped him back to his tent. He sat on the bed. I hoped he would sleep it off and feel better soon, but I didn't know.

"I know you don't remember me as your mom," I told him, "but it's painful for me to see you in any kind of discomfort or trouble."

He blinked sleepily at me. His eyes wandered, trying to focus.

"You know, there was this one time," I said, noisily sniffing back my tears, "back in the back before. You were seven, and you had walking pneumonia. You missed school for a week, and our doctor was thinking about hospitalizing you. It was serious. We were worried. Kids can die of pneumonia, you know. So, your grandma came to stay with us; your dad took days and days off work. On day ten, I think it was, the doctor said that if you weren't any better by morning, we had to bring you in. So I put you in bed and you were so miserable and uncomfortable. All I could do was sit by your bed and watch. You tossed and turned and moaned and groaned."

Arie narrowed his eyes and listened. Sitting on the edge of his cot, he leaned forward.

"So, I was changing the cloth on your little forehead. I had a damp washcloth to try and keep you cool, and as I lifted it up, I could tell that your fever had jumped up again. You were burning up. It was one-oh-five! We called the ER and they contacted our doctor. By the time they called back the fever was up to a hundred and eight—very dangerous. It was a twenty-five-minute drive to the ER from where we lived, so the doctor said to put you in the tub and splash you with cool water until an ambulance could come get you."

Arie swallowed, as though very concerned for his past self.

"Your dad and I put you in the tub and filled it with a few inches of tepid water, which of course to you probably felt like ice. You bawled and bawled and squirmed and kicked and your eyes were so glassy and sad. We almost quit, almost just wrapped you up in a towel and waited for the ambulance, but we stayed with it while you howled and shivered, and within about twenty minutes, your temp was down to one-oh-two, and you settled down and fell asleep right there in our arms, right there in the tub."

"Then what?" said Arie, his eyes blazing.

"Well, we put your pajamas back on you, and your coat, which wasn't easy because you were as limp as a rag, and the ambulance came. We checked you in and you stayed overnight, and the whole ordeal cost a fortune, but the fever had broken. They let you come home the next afternoon. Two days later you were back in school."

"Wow."

"Anyway, that's what all this reminds me of," I said. "Making you miserable by trying to help you. I'm sorry it didn't work. You should rest now."

"Okay," said Arie. "But tell me something. I'm not sure where I am. I mean, I know where this is." He gestured indefinitely at the tent around him. "I'm just not sure if I'm here. Am I here? Are you here? Where are we?"

This broke my heart to hear. My heart had been broken by this damn world so many times, and just when I thought I'd found a way to be whole, once and for all, it went and crushed me again. I put my hand on Arie's shoulder and gave it a squeeze.

"A really wise man explained something to me," I said. "He said this universe of ours is so big, just so unbelievably vast, that worrying where you are really doesn't make much sense. It's so big that it doesn't matter if I'm here in your tent, or just outside the door, or clear across the world. Relatively speaking, we're both here, and we're together. I'll always be with you, no matter where we are, Arie."

A look of dawning realization fell across Arie's face, probably a lot like it had when Peter had explained his epiphany to me that day in his tee-pee. Arie pressed his lips together and nodded slowly.

"You really should go to sleep," I said.

"All right," he said, slipping his legs into his bedding.

"I'll talk to you tomorrow," I said. And then I left him.

CHAPTER 62

"Al, I want you to know I don't blame you," said Ruby the next morning at the firepit. "I still believe it happened to you an' Chase, and a'course I can't say why it didn't happen for the kid, but I want you to know I know you come here thinkin' this would work."

I didn't know whether to take her words as a comfort or a condemnation, so I said nothing. Woolly and Ruby and Chase and a few other members of the upper leadership talked through the morning about what to do next. Woolly was hesitant about taking the tea now—with Arie incapacitated it wasn't wise for someone with so much institutional memory to be incapacitated for even a few days. Word had gotten about that Chase and I were back in camp and that we had our memories, but this information had metastasized into a rumor that the medicine that we brought had caused Arie to lose all of his memories. To further unsettle matters, a long-range patrol had checked in the night before and reported spotting vehicles eight or ten miles off. And of course the entire camp was halfway packed and halfway not. Ruby's camp members were tripling up to sleep in the remaining tents, living off cold rations and growing confused and nervous.

"I'm sorry, everyone," said Ruby, "but we gotta finish loading the vehicles and get started. This just ain't the time to try this out. We're scattered all over hell, Arie's been asleep for goin' on sixteen hours, I got reports of vehicles sighted on the plains, and it keeps gettin' colder every day. Maybe in a month, when we're settled in a new place and

313

back on our feet, we can talk about givin' this mushroom tea to a new test subject."

I nodded indifferently.

"Well," said Ruby, eying me cautiously, "let's get back to work, then. Woolly, you're gonna have to take over Arie's task list. Either that or go wake him up and see if he can work. Meet me in the command tent when you figure out which way it's gonna go."

Woolly slapped his knees and stood up. "I'll go see how he's doing."

"I'll do it," I said.

Woolly nodded and headed in the direction of the command tent.

Again, I arose and started down the trail that led from the firepit to where Arie's tent stood, dark and still.

Again, Arie swept aside his tent fly and stood in the snow in boots and long underwear with a sleeping bag wrapped around his shoulders.

"Morning, Arie," I said.

He took a step and let the sleeping bag drop. "Mom!" he yelled, scooping me into an enormous bear hug and squeezing me so tight, I thought he'd never let go.

CHAPTER 63

I knew Arie was my son, but hearing that word, "Mom," addressed to me, "Mom," melted me. But it restored me, too. My heart, cracked and fractured as it was, seemed to pull itself together. No matter how many times love gets knocked down, it will always get back up.

Arie kept his arms around me, and I gave him a little squeeze.

"You drank another cup," I said.

"I did," he said. "After what you said, I figured I needed a little more cold water splashed on me. And I think it worked. Finally. I remember that night. When I had the fever. I wanted that stupid Winnie the Pooh Bear in the tub with me."

I laughed and squeezed him tighter. "Yeah," I said. "That's right."

"I don't remember the ambulance," he said.

"You slept right through it."

"Hey," he said, pulling back so that he could look into my face.

"Yeah?"

"Thanks for being my mom. I love you."

"I love you, too, Son."

There's more to the moment, but it was more of the same. Tears, laughing, embracing. But we couldn't stand there forever in the cold. Besides, no one had to be told what had finally happened in Arie's brain, and they gathered around us, smiling, spilling tears of their own. And so Arie and I wiped our faces, promised for a long session of catching up and trading memories, and went to find Ruby and Woolly. Once Ruby saw that the treatment had worked on Arie, she reconvened her leadership by the firepit and proceeded to tell us that she and Woolly had already drawn up a plan to administer the treatment to the rest of the camp—in stages, but as rapidly as possible.

"We give the tea to ten people," said Woolly. "The people who successfully regain their memories will then be employed to help others. Like a game of Follow the Judge. Anyone who gets their memories will become a member of the tea team, until we treat everyone. We've got everything lined up. Who goes first, who helps who, everything. And we need to start right away."

"Are we sure we don't want to wait until after the move?" said Chase. "I mean, I know I'd want to try the treatment as soon as possible, but, the added delays, the weather, the long-range patrol reports—"

Even though I could hardly wait for every single person to take the tea, I couldn't help agree with him.

"Chase," sighed Ruby, "I think you're right. It's risky, probably a dumb thing to do, but, this may be the only chance we have to do this. Who knows what's gonna happen when we move? Who knows what the Agency is up to? If you two have brought us a way to remember everything, seems like giving everyone a shot at that is the ethical thing to do. You said you can get more, right?"

Chase and I nodded.

"Then I think we should give out what you've brought, give everyone a chance at remembering the whole sh'bang, and then move the camp."

We all traded looks, nodding tentatively.

"Sides," said Ruby, "there's another possibility here."

"What's that?" I asked.

"Tell 'em, Wool."

"I had a thought," said Woolly. "What we're dealing with here is a psychedelic, which were used in the back before to treat all kinds of conditions. Depression, anxiety,

316

addiction. What if this treatment doesn't just reverse the amnesia that the Agency serum induced? What if it makes it harder, or even impossible, to scrub us in the future?"

An excited murmur made its way around the fire.

"This stuff may give us partial or total immunity to whatever the Agency has been using on us," he concluded.

"I have some thoughts, too," I said, raising my hand. "Something about the tea."

"Go ahead, Al," said Ruby.

"I think the reason the tea worked on Chase and me so quickly is that our minds had been prepared," I said. "We spent more than a week with Peter in a very secluded and low-stress environment. A very thoughtful environment. There were lots of discussions, talking, thinking. We knew what we wanted—our memories—and the tea simply opened the door for us to reconnect with them. Peter told us that the tea was not a medicine, not a cure. It's not even really a treatment, not technically. Peter said it's a guide, and that the effects were a journey—you find what you want to find. I think that everyone who gets the tea should spend a day thinking, meditating if possible. They should talk to someone close to them, talk about what they know, what they remember, what they'd like to remember. And they should only take the tea in the clearest and most relaxed state of mind. This might add time to each individual's experience, but I have a hunch it will actually speed things up."

Over the next four days, everyone in Ruby's camp gained back at least some of their memories. It wasn't easy for some of them—remembering the terror that they had lived through required them to live through it again. And the tea didn't work on everyone the same way. Some of the younger people didn't remember the back before, and a few people reported large gaps in their memories. Woolly had a theory that those people had perhaps forgotten events before the Agency memory scrubbing treatments began. Maybe, he reasoned, they'd seen or experienced things that their subconscious minds had involuntarily blotted out.

Overall, it was a happy time of tears and reminiscence. Many in the camp, like Arie and I, recognized the family members they'd been assigned, deepening their bonds. There were several people who'd known each other as friends in the back before. Everywhere in the disordered camp there were knots of excited chatter—people reuniting, sharing their stories, sharing their memories.

After a week, when nearly everyone had recovered and the moving plan was underway again, I asked Ruby: "What about you, Rube? When are you going to do it?"

Ruby looked down at the ground. "I want to make sure there's enough of the tea for everyone else, first," she said.

"There's plenty left over," I said. "More than half."

"Good," said Ruby. "We oughta keep a reserve, then. I can wait."

Later that day, I followed Chase and Arie's fresh prints in the snow to a ravine about three miles from camp where there was a good-sized stream. They'd brought along Chase's hunting rifle in case they spotted some game, but they were catching fish after fish from the stream. It was cold but sunny. The air was crisp and clear, and the sky was a startling blue with a few lazy puffs of cloud passing by in the high-altitude winds. I perched on a tree-stump and watched, telling them about how Ruby was for some reason still waiting to take the tea.

"I don't know how she can wait," I said. "It'd kill me."

Chase chuckled. "Well, you aren't her. You're a lot more impatient."

"Rude," I said.

"I'm sure she's as anxious as anybody," said Chase. "If she's insisting on being the last one in the camp to take the leap, maybe you could help keep her mind off of it. Keep her company. You two could use some bonding time."

"That's not a bad idea, actually," I said. "You guys all right here? I'm gonna head back."

"You came all this way to say that, and then leave?" asked Arie.

"I guess," I said. "I've got a lot of energy right now. I think I really just wanted the walk."

"Well, if you're heading back, maybe take my backpack with you? And maybe that rifle? With the fishing hitting this way, we're gonna have a bunch of big fish to bring home. That'll be less for us to carry."

"Okay," I said. "Sure you don't wanna hang on to the rifle?"

"I find I catch more with the fly rod."

"I mean if you see a deer, smart-ass. Or a bear? You do remember being attacked by one of those?"

Just then Chase hooked a fish and began playing it to the bank, but it was a large fish and it put up a tremendous fight.

"Have I told you how much I love fishing this stream?" he said to Arie.

"You may have mentioned it," replied Arie.

When Chase got the fish close to his net, it darted away and swam upstream, taking line from the reel. Chase let the fish run, and it went downstream, making leaps from the water as it went. Chase and Arie hooted and laughed. This went on for several minutes, until the fish finally began to tire.

"Sorry, fella," muttered Chase. "There's no escape."

Chase brought the fish to his net at last. It was fat and healthy-looking, flashing in the sunshine. Chase added it to the stringer of other fish, and then looked back at me and smiled.

"Nah," said Chase. "Take the rifle back to camp, if you wouldn't mind."

"Hey, Mom," said Arie. "Maybe have Ruby show you how to shoot it. Seeing you with a gun in your hands will definitely take her mind off her other troubles." He turned and winked at me.

I laughed and picked up the backpack, and then I slipped the rifle harness over my shoulder. "All right, you mighty fishermen. I'll see you back at camp. Happy fishing."

Chase gave me a quick hug and a kiss. "Love you, sweetie."

"Hey, Mom?" said Arie, "Keep the safety on 'till you're ready to fire."

"Thanks, kiddo."

The walk back to the camp was long and cold, but if I walked fast, I felt warm. I was content and relaxed, too. I had so much now. Chase—a man I loved and wanted to spend my future with, Arie, my smart and handsome son, and myself—my own memories. Ruby had said I could come with them to the new city they would build, far away from the Agency and their control. I guess I'd regained not only my memories but Ruby's confidence as well. As I walked along the snowy path, I smiled. It was as though the cold sunshine was beaming through me, renewing everything. After all these years of struggle and sorrow and violence, we were ready to put it all behind us.

But as I approached the camp, an uneasy sensation stole over me. My muscles tensed, and my mind clouded. I stopped and stood still. Had I heard some sound of warning beneath the crunch of the snow and the swishing zing of my snow-pants and coat? I remembered how the bear had broke through the brush on the hilltop that day with Colonel Steele, and had moved with such astonishing speed and power. Had I heard danger at the edge of my hearing? A buzzing sound, like angry hornets? The popping sound of distant gunfire? My anxiety began to spiral upward. I looked behind me. I stared down the trail ahead. After standing still and listening for several solid minutes, I broke off the trail, climbed a small hill, and headed toward the camp through the dense woods on a southern-facing hillside. The unbroken snow made for very slow going, and it was difficult to find the way. I had to backtrack once, but after a lengthy meander through a spruce thicket, I pushed through and the camp came in to view below me.

And indeed something was terribly wrong.

320

I was still far away, several hundred yards, and there were thick trees masking my view, but there in the middle of the camp was a crowd of people. It was too big a gathering to be some kind of meeting or part of the exodus process. It had to be everyone in camp. And then some.

I dropped to my belly and crawled forward from tree to tree to get closer.

The Agency had arrived. The temperature of my blood seemed to drop twenty degrees.

Not a bloody attack like last time. I may have heard sporadic gunfire back on the trail, but there had been none since and there was none now. They had evidently learned from last time and launched some kind of rapid, coordinated enclosing attack through the snow and taken everyone by surprise. They had rounded up all of our campers and herded them to the middle of the camp. These Agency thugs were like none I'd ever seen. Their uniforms looked new and warm and they were all white and gray. They wore cowls that covered everything but their eyes, which made them seem more lethal, like assassins. Their weapons were likewise new and deadly looking, wrapped in strips of white cloth or tape for camouflage. My eyes swept over the snowy camp, and I saw the sleek, gray forms of small vehicles at the margins of the camp. Snow machines. I had heard the buzzing of deadly wasps. That's how they'd done it. A smaller force had probably infiltrated early that morning, maybe a sniper or two to take out our outer guards. After an initial attack, the rest had come in on the snow machines. There'd been no warning this time, and it would have been harder for Ruby's people to melt into the woods—the snow made it almost impossible to run, and the tracks would be easy to follow.

A few of the soldiers were frisking the campers and moving them to a second area, where they were kneeling in ranks and files. I also saw red patches in the snow, and a few casualties lying there wounded or dead. I wondered if the plan was to shoot everyone there and then. I took a chance

321

and slid forward through the snow to the treeline for a better vantage.

Rachel.

Decked out in a typically smart-looking black-and-white camouflaged snow suit with a fur-lined hood was Rachel. In her hand was a pistol, and the pistol was pointed at Ruby, who sat in the snow slouching in utter defeat.

I could hear their voices now but couldn't make out any words. Then I did hear a few rounds of gunfire, very far away, muffled by the snow, I suppose. They were probably sweeping the outer areas and the vehicle parking lot, collecting stragglers, or perhaps simply executing them.

I felt the old pang of guilt, the self-excoriation. If it hadn't been for Chase and I bringing the tea and slowing things down, Ruby and her people would have been long gone, headed out on their exodus to a new location beyond the Agency's reach.

But they had not seen me, and Chase and Arie were not only far away but even more paranoid than I was. If I could get back to them, we could maybe make a run for it. Chase and Arie always kept a few supplies with them these days. Chase and Arie both had sidearms, and I had the rifle. Maybe it could be like last time. We could run away and be safe with the three things I wanted, the three things I needed: Arie, Chase, and our memories.

I worried that I would hate myself for the choice I was going to make. Worried that Chase and Arie wouldn't forgive me. But the choice was clear to me. Peter said that he was in the mountains because that was what he was meant to do. It was his purpose. He had his, and this was mine.

CHAPTER 64

There were three or four guards clustered where various trails led into the camp, but there was no one between Rachel and me. I ducked behind a large tree and unshouldered the rifle. Arie was right to tease me—I'd only fired Chase's hunting rifle a few times, and I could barely remember how to work it. Guns simply were not my strong suit, and now I regretted not learning more. With my back to the tree I examined the weapon. I pulled back the bolt and established that the rifle was, in fact, loaded. Good. I made sure the safety was on so that I wouldn't fumble and fire accidentally. Then I put the stock to my shoulder and squinted into the scope.

I couldn't see a thing.

But it didn't matter. I wouldn't have to use the rifle. I only had to look like I could. And so I stood up, my back still to the tree and took a few deep breaths. Then I turned and passed through the treeline and onto the open ground above the camp.

"Rachel, drop the gun!" I shouted. My voice carried down the slope and into the camp where the other prisoners cowered at gunpoint. I walked forward through the snow with the rifle aimed at Rachel.

Everyone turned in my direction. The soldiers spun and wheeled, shouting orders. They trained their weapons on me, but Rachel shouted, "Hold your fire!"

"Drop the gun, Rachel," I repeated.

"Alison," Rachel greeted me as I approached. Her voice was calm, warm.

"Drop it!" I shouted.

"All right," she said, her voice clear and beautiful in the cold air. "All right. Don't get testy." She laid her pistol gingerly on a nearby tree stump, as though she didn't want to spoil its looks by getting snow on it. Then she stood up and stepped back. She held up a hand to keep her soldiers at bay, and then smiled broadly at me. "You know, I've been looking all over for you. You've been busy since we last got together. Come on over. It's time we talked."

I moved slowly through the snow to maintain at least the illusion that I was really aiming the rifle, that I was ready to gun Rachel down. The soldiers kept their weapons on me, pivoting as I came into camp. When I was only fifty feet from Rachel, I paused.

"Tell me why I shouldn't kill you right now," I said.

"My soldiers will gun you down, for one thing," she replied, as though she were concerned with my wellbeing.

"Tell them to put down their weapons!"

"Do not put down your weapons!" She raised her voice, but again she was completely calm—almost relaxed.

"Tell them, Rachel. I swear I'll shoot."

"So, it's true what I've heard? You remember me? And everything else?"

I took several steps forward, pointed the rifle directly her chest. "Do it!"

"Alison, stop," said Rachel with a playful, dismissive wave of her hand. "You're not going to kill me. I wouldn't be surprised if you didn't even know how to shoot that thing."

"What do you want, you parasite?" I spat, my jaw clenched. "Why can't you leave us alone?"

"I want what you have," replied Rachel, her tone suddenly icy. "And I want it now. You have a serum or treatment that cures the amnesia."

"I don't know what you're talking about," I said, knowing it was the flimsiest of bluffs. Rachel and her soldiers had the entire morning to round up, disarm, detain, and question Ruby, Woolly, and others. She knew everything, obviously.

"Don't, Alison. Don't play games. Give me what I want, and I'll think about not killing you and all of your friends. Don't give it to me and I'll find it myself and then kill all of you. Oh, including them." She pointed behind me.

I didn't want to look, but I knew what I'd see if I did. I glanced in the direction she pointed, but when I saw Arie and Chase coming down the trail with their hands on their heads, followed by three more of the winter-clad soldiers, I couldn't look away. I heard a soft crunch of snow underfoot and the zinging sound of Rachel's snowsuit. I looked back down the muzzle of the rifle in time to see her crossing the final couple yards between us. She was quick as a cat.

I pulled the trigger.

Nothing happened.

Rachel took the rifle by the barrel, swept it powerfully from my hands, and struck me on the side of the head with the stock. Down I went into the snow like a sack of dropped potatoes. I didn't black out, but I was half-blinded with the pain. Chase and Arie called out to me, but I lay crumpled in the snow whimpering.

"You left the safety on, Alison," said Rachel. She pulled back the bolt and ejected the round. Then with a deft motion she pressed some kind of release and yanked the bolt free of the barrel. "I knew you didn't know how to fire it," Rachel sneered, tossing the disassembled weapon into a snowbank.

Soon we were all assembled—Ruby, Woolly, Chase, Arie, and me. We sat in the snow with hands and feet zip-tied, guarded by two soldiers in white. The rest of the campers had been herded into a sort of pen a short way off, surrounded by the rest of Rachel's snow soldiers. The gash Rachel left on my head with the rifle stock had bled copiously for a while but had subsided in the cold. I looked at the others. Each of us had a bloody nose or swollen eye or busted lip. Chase had a cut on the bridge of his nose and a trickle of blood coming from his ear. At least we hadn't gone down without fighting back, I thought.

"Just give it to them," Chase was saying. "She's either going to wipe us or kill us, same diff. Just give her what she wants, Al. Maybe she'll remember that she used to be a human being."

"Agreed," said Woolly. "Let's just get this over with."

Arie and Ruby nodded.

They were right. We'd stood up to the Agency and Rachel too many times and lost. I directed them to my backpack. One of the soldiers retrieved it from my tent and it was emptied out into the snow at Rachel's feet.

"The leather satchel," I said.

"This?" said Rachel? "This is the treatment?"

"Yeah," I said. "It's a tea."

Rachel opened the mouth of the satchel and held it to her nose. Then she grimaced and turned her face away. "Smells like a dead bird."

"Tastes like one, too," quipped Chase. "But it works. Now. You'll let us go?"

"I said I'd think about it," she replied, gazing at Chase down her nose, which had gotten red from the cold but somehow made her look even more imperiously beautiful. "

"How do I know this is really it?" said Rachel, her brow knitted. "How do I know it'll work?"

"Ask anyone here. We've all taken it. We all remember."

Rachel held a conference with her ranking soldiers a short distance from us. The sun was going down, and we all shivered with cold. We couldn't hear what Rachel said to her soldiers, but some of them questioned eight or ten of Ruby's rank-and-file campers, and within an hour, Rachel seemed satisfied that the tea was what we'd used to get our memories back.

"So, you drink the tea; you get your memories back," asked Rachel, eying the satchel with evident skepticism. "Just like that?"

"For some people it takes more than one dose, more than one day," I said. "For some people it takes several days and repeated doses."

"I'm inclined to let you all go," said Rachel. "A nasty generous streak I have, maybe. Is that all I need to know? Tell me everything and I'll let you go."

I traded glances with the others, who in a wordless consultation gave me to know I should explain more.

"There's a certain mindset that seems important to the process," I said.

"What's that supposed to mean?" said Rachel wearily.

"The tea works best when you're in a certain mindset," I added. "Relaxed, meditative, open-minded, focused on what you want. It's not a medicine. It's more like a catalyst."

"Seriously? Mindset? Catalyst? What kind of hippie tomfoolery is this, Alison?"

"It works, Rachel," said Chase. "You win. It works. Now let us go."

Rachel crouched down in front of us as we sat shivering in the snow. When she was eye-to-eye with us, examined us. I stared back at her.

"I believe you," she said. Then she stood. "Sergeant," she said, her voice gruff.

One of the two soldiers guarding us turned to Rachel. The sergeant was a tall woman and thickly built, but with the easy and lethal grace of the natural warrior. She pulled down her face mask. Her eyes were large and thoughtful. "Ma'am?" she said.

"Get your team over here." Then Rachel pointed to me and Ruby and the others. "Get your team over here and execute them."

Over the profane chorus of our protests, the sergeant frowned at Rachel and said, "Say again, ma'am? You want them executed? Shot?"

Rachel reached up and grabbed the sergeant by the front of her snowsuit, then pulled the sergeant's face down to her own. "Yes, Sergeant, that is what I want. Shoot them,"

Rachel growled. "The rest we'll take back for processing. But these I want dead."

As we continued to holler and struggle against the zip-ties that held us, the sergeant hesitated, glanced at us, her large eyes blinking. But then she whistled loudly and yelled, "Second squad! To me!"

Six soldiers broke from their places guarding the campers and hustled through the snow to join the sergeant.

"These prisoners are to be executed," she said, her voice loud but with a halting, hollow quality.

Now protests erupted from the rest of the campers. Many of them stood up and moved toward us.

"If any of them interfere," Rachel commanded, her voice shrill now, piercing the air and carrying in the icy air, "shoot them, too."

I couldn't see the prisoners behind us, but there was shouting and the sounds of rough treatment. One of the soldiers fired a warning shot into the air.

"Sergeant, now!" raged Rachel pointing at us again.

The soldiers looked at their sergeant uncertainly. The sergeant chopped a line into the snow with her boot heel. "Stand on this, uhm, line," she said. "Stand here. Ready your—weapons. Fire on my command."

The soldiers leveled their weapons at us. I stared into the tiny round blackness of six machinegun muzzles. I turned to look at the Sergeant, waiting for her to say give the signal that would end my life. My heart beat hard. But when I looked at her, I had a sudden recollection.

"Sonja?" I said. The Sergeant looked at me, her eyes wide.

I chuckled a little. "Sonja! I know you! You were a preschool teacher. You taught my son, Arie. There was a song you always sang: Good Morning Sun."

She took a step back, keeping her eyes on me, but there was a softening in her presence.

"Fire!" shouted Rachel. "Shoot them now!"

The soldiers shifted, but the sergeant held up her hand. "Wait," she commanded.

There was movement behind me. Something jostled me. I chanced a look over my shoulder. It was Woolly. Although he was bound hand and foot, he was struggling to rise. He had gotten to his knees, and then with a surprising deftness, he rocked onto the balls of his feet and stood upright.

The soldiers' weapons remained trained on us.

"Cal!" shouted Woolly at the soldiers. He tottered a little but remained standing.

One of them lowered his weapon just slightly.

"Calvin Peter Roberts," Woolly shouted, louder. His voice boomed across the snow.

"It's me, Woolly. We used to play Halo in your mom's basement. You drank Mt. Dew by the gallon. You planned to join the army." Woolly paused a moment. "Looks like you kinda did."

"Fire!" hollered Rachel.

We couldn't see the man's face because of his mask, but his eyes twitched with confusion, conflict.

Another cry rang out behind us. "Tamara Rodriguez! Don't shoot! It's Richard! Your brother-in-law! I married your sister, Valerie!"

And then others.

"Oscar!"

"Franklin Pavithran!"

"Hey, it's me, Oscar! We were roomies at Nevada State!"

"I know you! You lived down the block from me!"

I rolled onto my knees, wheeled around. The soldiers were stepping back, lowering their weapons. One of them unharnessed his machinegun, hurled it to the ground, and staggered back, tripping and falling into the snow.

"Fire!" Rachel was shrieking. "Fire on them now!"

"Don't do it," Chase said hastily to the line of soldiers. "Ignore her! Join us. We'll help you remember."

The sergeant looked at me, her thoughtful eyes searching, questioning.

329

"It's true," I told her, nodding. "You can all remember."

Rachel grabbed the sergeant roughly again, but the big sergeant brushed her aside with an almost thoughtless sweep of her arm, and Rachel flew sprawling in the snow like an elegant doll.

"Stand down," said the sergeant to her squad, holding up a hand. The soldiers obeyed.

I looked around again, amazed. An old lady had her arms around one of Rachel's soldiers, who accepted the embrace with a mixture of delight and total shock. Soldiers were shaking hands with prisoners. I heard laughter.

Rachel shrieked unintelligibly at the sergeant, but the sergeant lifted her weapon and let fly a cautionary burst of gunfire into the cold, darkening air.

"No ma'am," said the sergeant. "No more. We're done."

Like a cat, Rachel sprang to the tree stump where she'd laid her pistol. The sergeant lunged toward the stump but Rachel was there first, and the pistol was in her hand. She fired. The round caught the sergeant in the chest and she fell lifeless into the snow.

The rest of the squad turned their machine guns on Rachel and opened fire. It was all over in one very short, very loud moment.

CHAPTER 65

That night, we built the largest bonfire I'd ever been a witness to. A few dead trees were felled, their trunks were sectioned into logs four feet long, and these were tented like the campfire of a giant. Once the fire was blazing, we had to move back almost twenty feet to avoid being singed, but it nevertheless took me another hour to feel warm again after sitting so long in the snow.

Some of the soldiers joined Ruby's camp on the spot, eager to get away from the Agency and its atrocities, but also very interested in the hallucinogenic tea that was purported to restore memories. However, most of them had families and a few of them felt the need to stay loyal to the Agency. No one made them stay, and they left peacefully.

Sonja, former preschool teacher and former sergeant of Rachel's strike team, recovered. She'd been wearing a ballistic vest and suffered some nasty bruising, but she cavalierly laughed this off. Arie could not have been more amazed to meet up with her. He said he had hazy, fond remembrances of her, and he followed her around the camp offering his help.

They buried Rachel where she'd been killed. I was grateful to the soldiers who handled her body with such deference and respect, because as they laid her to rest, I felt my hatred for her melt away, leaving me feeling lighter and more free even than I'd felt before.

The bonfire burned through the night. The last reserves of anything resembling wine or spirits were produced and there was laughter and singing.

Some of us were still snuggled together under heaped-up blankets as the sun came up. We'd talked all through the night, moving our chairs and seats progressively closer to the bonfire as it burned lower and collapsed. It still gave off a great deal of heat as the night's final chill clutched at us, but as the sky turned rosy with the dawn, coffee pots and pans of water appeared on the periphery of the coals and soon we had warm cups to drink from.

Sonja threw off the blanket she was huddling beneath. She stood and went to the fire and held out her hands to warm them.

"I take it none of you have been to an Agency facility in a while."

"We broke into one not long ago," said Chase, hiking up his shoulders flippantly, "but we weren't exactly treated as guests."

"I remember," said Sonja. "I was part of the fast-response unit that night, though I wasn't on the team that apprehended you."

"Why'd you bring it up, though?" asked Ruby.

"The Agency is—struggling, changing, shrinking. It's caving in on itself. Defections practically every day. Zones are being evacuated and collapsed as more and more people escape. And you saw what happened here yesterday. I volunteered for this detail half-expecting something like this to happen."

"So, what are you saying?" I asked.

"Well," said Sonja, "I'm not sure." She winced and pressed her hand to her bruised ribs. "I guess I'm saying that there's not as much for you all to be concerned about anymore. Rachel was really the last of what we called 'the big-game hunters,' the last of those in the Agency who are interested in rounding up folks like you, maintaining order at all costs. Most of the higher-ups are just desperately trying to carve out a decent existence for themselves and any family they have left."

Ruby nodded slowly and stared at the coals of the bonfire. "That actually makes me kinda said," she muttered.

"You think it might be time for a new strategy, Rube?" Chase asked.

"I dunno," she said softly. "We been dreamin' about this moment so long, when we could finally break free and move far away, it's almost like I want to go through with it just because we always said we would."

We nodded and murmured our assent.

"But I also been thinkin' about what Al and Arie always said. That it ain't right to leave all them people in the Zones when we know how to help 'em. And now we got this magic tea. Think about it. We sneak this here tea in. Not just to them in the Zones, but the goons, too. The soldiers, the management, everybody. Can ya imagine?"

"It'd be one hell of a party," said Woolly.

We all chuckled.

"We'd need more tea," I said.

"At first, yeah," said Woolly. "But maybe Peter could teach us how to cultivate it, too."

"So there's no more exodus?" I asked. "No new settlement?"

"Maybe not," said Ruby. "Or maybe the exodus goes back where we come from. Maybe it's time we went home and started rebuilding."

"And what about you?" Chase asked Ruby. "How are you feeling?"

She rubbed her knee. "Well. I feel pretty good, now that I think about it. Thanks for askin'. But maybe it's time I take some a' that tea and think about retirement. I got my whole leadership team back. And maybe a couple new helpers."

Ruby nodded in Sonja's direction. Sonja nodded back.

Ruby had been our leader for so long, it was hard to think of her not bossing us around.

"Let's not kid ourselves," said Woolly to Ruby. "You're not gonna retire just like that."

"I never said I was, ya big galoot," Ruby barked, "but maybe it's time someone else drove the bus for a while."

When every other person in the group professed to having their memories restored, Ruby finally drank the tea herself. Arie and I assisted her, making her comfortable in her tent, but she was so worried about what she would remember, it felt rather like a solemn, almost funerary ceremony.

"What if I'm awful person," she protested as we prepared the tea. "What if I don't like who I used t'be?" It took half the day to get her settled and calm.

Early in the morning two days later she burst joyously from her tent.

"Hey y'all," she hollered, "come hear about me. I was a grandma! I am a grandma!" She hurried to the main firepit. A crowd of us gathered around her and heard the story of her life. There was a renewed sense of youth about her. I realized she didn't have her walking stick. Her face glowed as she told about her children. "Six of them! Can ya imagine?" said Ruby, "Four boys and two girls."

"No wonder you're so good at running camp and keeping us all alive," said Woolly. "You have experience with children."

Ruby chuckled. She missed them, of course, and cried for them, wondering mournfully where they might have ended up, but gone from her eyes was the abject weariness I had seen before. Her eyes sparkled with new life and a new happiness.

"I'll track 'em all down," she resolved, "track all 'em kiddies down and add them to the rest of my family here," said Ruby with a wide grin. And I had no doubt she would do just that.

Later that afternoon, I found a peaceful hillside to watch the sun go down again.

Arie found me and sat next to me.

"I remember," he said. "The Ferris wheel. The Sky Dreamer. You and dad and me."

334

I nodded.

"I miss him," Arie said.

"I do, too. But I missed him before, before I remembered. It's better to know."

Arie nodded. Then he scooped up a handful of snow and threw it down the hill. It struck a tree trunk with a loud pop.

"Mom?" he said.

"Yeah?"

"I love you."

I grabbed his hand. "I love you, too."

Arie looked embarrassed. "Okay, well, this has gotten a bit mushy. I think I'll have a game of chess with Woolly."

Just then I saw someone else coming up the hill.

"You don't have to go," I said.

Arie smirked. "I know. But I'm gonna anyway. Someone wants to talk to you."

It was Chase approaching, coming up the snowy hillside. His beard and hair had been trimmed, and as he got closer, I saw that he was wearing a vest, suit coat, and a tie. Where did he get those?

Arie walked down the hill and as he passed by Chase, they shook hands.

"Good luck, man," said Arie.

Chase took a deep breath and nodded. Arie continued in the direction of the camp. Chase came closer, one hand behind his back.

"Look at you," I said, standing up. "Handsome."

Chase grinned sheepishly.

"I've come to ask you something."

"No," I said. "Me first."

He looked puzzled.

I took his hand in mine.

"Chase, I love you. No matter how hard I've tried not to or how hard they've tried to erase you from me, I love you. And I feel like we are meant to be together. I want to spend my life with you. I want the rest of my memories to include you. Will you marry me?"

Chase laughed. He brought his arm forward to reveal a golden ring. "I thought you'd never ask."

A week later, just before our rag-tag convoy got underway westward, Ruby married us beneath a tall spruce tree as it snowed. The flakes were like shimmering particles of glitter falling around us in celebration.

Today I sometimes marvel at how old I've grown to be. I never thought I would be this old, but I never knew I could be this happy, either. It amazes me that Chase and I lived this long, and that he's still by my side. We have grandchildren and great-grandchildren. The world is better now than it was when I first met Chase and Woolly and Ruby. And it's getting better. We have made a million memories since those days. Wonderful, precious memories that we never will forget.

MORE BY AMANDA LUZZADER...

CREEP FACTOR
by Amanda Luzzader
and Chadd VanZanten

http://www.amazon.com/dp/B07J3X1CM5

It's the feeling that something isn't quite right. The glance of a stranger that lingers too long. A coworker who appears out of nowhere. Creep Factor is thirteen deeply creepy short horror stories that explore the awkward, unnerving, and the terrifying. From backstabbing roommates to vicious pets, from murderous spirits to soul-wracking nightmares, Creep Factor covers the savagely weird to the merely

MIDDLE-GRADE ADVENTURE...

Check out Amanda's new middle-grade adventure.

Coming late 2020.

To be notified of new releases, sign up for Amanda's newsletter on her website:

www.amandaluzzader.com

About the Author

Amanda Luzzader writes upmarket science fiction, horror, and middle-grade books. She is a self-described 'fraidy cat. Things she will run away from include (but are not limited to): mice, snakes, spiders, bits of string and litter that resemble spiders, most members of the insect kingdom, and (most especially) bats. Bats are the worst. But Amanda is first and primarily a mother to two energetic and intelligent sons, and this role inspires and informs her writing, which frequently involves mothers and women as main characters. As Amanda likes to say, "Moms are people, too."

Amanda has worked as a technical writer and a professional editor and is currently employed as a grant writer for a Utah nonprofit organization. She was named Writer of the Year for 2019 by the League of Utah Writers.

CPSIA information can be obtained
at www.ICGtesting.com
Printed in the USA
LVHW092159150320
650134LV00001B/62